PRAISE FOR *THE MURDER OF ALBERT EINSTEIN*

"A fine mystery . . . the twists and turns toward the end lift it out of the realm of the standard thriller and keep it interesting to the last page."

　　　　　　　　　　　　　　　　　—*Boston Globe*

"One of the central themes in the novel is power and its use. . . . But Gitlin's suspense drama goes beyond that to explore the power of information and the manipulation of the media."

　　　　　　　　　　　　—*Los Angeles Times Book Review*

"Todd Gitlin has brought his strengths in media, social, and cultural studies to the game of telling a mystery-thriller story that deals suspensefully with momentous, darkly complex social and political questions."

　　　　　　　　　　　　　　　—*Chicago Sun-Times*

"Amusing, suspenseful . . . I hope he'll write lots of novels."

　　　　　　　　　　　　　　　　—Diane Johnson

BY TODD GITLIN

Uptown: Poor Whites in Chicago
(co-author)
Busy Being Born
*The Whole World Is Watching: Mass Media in the
Making and Unmaking of the New Left*
Inside Prime Time
Watching Television (editor)
The Sixties: Years of Hope, Days of Rage

The Murder of
ALBERT EINSTEIN

Todd Gitlin

BANTAM BOOKS

NEW YORK   TORONTO   LONDON   SYDNEY   AUCKLAND

THE MURDER OF ALBERT EINSTEIN
A Bantam Book / published by arrangement with Farrar, Straus
and Giroux

PUBLISHING HISTORY
Farrar, Straus and Giroux edition published 1992
Bantam trade paperback edition / March 1994

Book design by Glen Edelstein

Library of Congress Cataloging-in-Publication Data

Gitlin, Todd.
The murder of Albert Einstein / Todd Gitlin.
p.   cm.
ISBN 0-553-37366-8
1. Women journalists — United States — Fiction. 2. Einstein, Albert,
1879–1955 — Fiction. I. Title.
[PS3557.I82M87   1994]
813'.54 — dc20   93-35519
                                                                      CIP

Published simultaneously in the United States and Canada

Bantam Books are published by Bantam Books, a division of Bantam
Doubleday Dell Publishing Group, Inc. Its trademark, consisting of the
words "Bantam Books" and the portrayal of a rooster, is Registered in
U.S. Patent and Trademark Office and in other countries. Marca
Registrada. Bantam Books, 1540 Broadway, New York, New York
10036.

PRINTED IN THE UNITED STATES OF AMERICA

CWO   0 9 8 7 6 5 4 3 2 1

To Ruth Rosen, for everything,
and to Tom Engelhardt

PART ONE

*Political passions, once they have been fanned
into flame, exact their victims.*

THE LAST WORDS WRITTEN BY ALBERT EINSTEIN

MONDAY, OCTOBER 22

I T BEGAN, AS DOES MOST OF MY LIFE, WITH A MESSAGE ON AN answering machine.

The air was crisp, I wasn't. I had just staggered off the redeye from California—a weekend in paradise squandered on assignment. The day before flying off to the land where minds stand still, I had broken up with Blond Bart, that deceptively bland dreamboat with stethoscope. My surrogate for love. There had been no more reason for breaking it off than for getting it on. I could do better with electronics—headphones for distraction, word processor for wit, editing room for forgetfulness, vibrator for pleasure. Electronic aliens have already landed.

I should trust my tropisms, like a houseplant in the light or a journalist in the dark. Instincts, if you like. Once in a while, between impulses and maelstroms, I reason. Too late, usually, to do myself any good.

It began, then, late in the second millennium, two stories above a synagogue in the Village. I liked hearing the ancient murmurs drift up the stairwell, bringing back memories of the devotional upbringing I never had. But this was Monday morning.

There were flowers on my doormat, a portable garden's worth covered with plastic, weeping condensation. Too bright. Nobody ever called him cheap.

His voice was first on the machine. I took in phrases: "It's me . . . flowers in hand . . . the concert . . . miss you, kid . . ." I punched fast-forward. An electronic hum lingered. So long, Bartleby Bland, you unguent WASP, I gave up masochism for Yom Kippur. I fast-forwarded again.

The next voice started with a throat-clearing. "If this is the number of Margo Ross . . ." My friend Elaine's husband had recorded my announcement in his bass growl. *We're not in just now, please leave a message.* Bare bones, no names. My sonic stand-in sounded as if he would rip out an obscene caller's tongue for breathing hard.

"Who would have thought," the incoming voice went on in a rounded baritone, surer now, "that we would someday be counting our contacts in decades. I'm delighted to see how well the world's treating you—if this *is* you. How nicely you fill the screen."

His aura came swimming up to me. Astonishing to think of him still among us. He belonged to the past—not just mine, everyone's. And yet this was a voice I'd been longing to hear, I suddenly felt, for years.

"I'm sure you're unimaginably busy, but I need to see you in the flesh. Urgently. Overused word, but if it sounds melodramatic, I mean it to. This is Harry Kramer." There never was anything casual about Harry Kramer. "There's a story in this for both of us. Call. Anytime. But not later than today. I'll be grateful." He left a number. The electronic stamp singsonged: *Sunday, 4:58 p.m.*

I hit the replay button. The same voice offered the same words with the same suggestion of gifts yet to be given, the same alluring mixture of authority and bemusement and generosity. Holy Jesus, Billy Neill and Harry Kramer in the same weekend. What was this, golden oldies?

Barely 7 a.m. and the illustrious past was spilling all over me. I had spent the weekend on the Monterey Peninsula shooting the onetime rock-'n'-roll guru Billy Neill. Of course, I can recite the lyrics to "Only a One-Eyed Clown" like the next ex-freak, but Billy Neill hadn't been my bright idea for twenty minutes of network television. But then, my bright ideas for go-get-'em investigative reporting were being sent straight to the toilet. I had thought a celebrity profile might keep me in good graces for a while. So, for my sins, I had crossed the country and delivered on my part of the bargain: twelve hours ago, Billy Neill had stared meaningfully out over the Pacific and, on camera, declared that, to protest against this post-post-Gorbachev phase of the nuclear arms race, he was changing his name to Billy Null. Who cared? Then again, who cared who cared as long as I lurched home with the requisite number of sound bites, soul-stares, strolls on a beach where the surf obligingly crashed.

I had dragged myself back overnight because my boss, Burke Gilman, wanted *In Depth* to rush the piece for the

week after next, time it to the release of Billy's latest come-
back record. Burke must have struck a deal with Billy's
P.R. man—we get an exclusive in exchange for the rush.
On the 747 from sea to shining sea I took a Harmonium
capsule, scribbled an outline of the script, and got two and
a half hours of churning semi-sleep.

Billy Neill, Billy Null, I was getting too old for this kind
of shit. But Harry Kramer, that was another story.

Now I stared into my mug of coffee and tried to think
about Harry Kramer's emergency, but couldn't focus. My
apartment glared at me: What have you done for me lately?
In odd moments I've furnished this place where I more or
less live with antiques—some certified, some unpremedi-
tated. My Pinocchio bank-turned-lamp, my imitation-Lich-
tenstein Nancy and Sluggo print on the wall (Nancy is
saying: "The trouble with you is that you understand me all
too well"), thirty-two-inch stereo TV with Dolby Ultra,
state-of-the-art VCR—halfhearted yuppie with kitsch accents, that's my aesthetic. Issues of *Vanity Fair, Millennium
Express, Rock & Roll Confidential,* and *Silence: A Magazine of
the Arts* on the coffee table. Am I living or camping here?

I fixed my eyes on the bathroom mirror. Considering the
hour, the trip, and my age, I was as good-looking as I
needed to be. The wrinkles fanning out from my eyes could
pass for experience. Lovers have told me my eyes say: Talk
to me.

But I'm too big. My bones, my ass, too big. My jaw juts
out like a man's. Thank God, my eyes distract the gaze of
men from my skin, which still shows faint pockmarks, reminding me every morning that one-quarter of a century
into adulthood I remain marked forever by adolescence. I

am a woman in her transitional forties but can pass, on a good morning, for a possible forty, only to transmogrify, late at night, to something the werewolf side of forty-five. When I hear *You look great* I also hear the unspoken *for your age.* Having rejected artifice in 1970 and retrieved it in 1978, I wear only the minimum occupational uniform—a smudge of blush, a trace of mascara, lipstick only on air. The severe lines of my penciled-in eyebrows magnify the interrogation effect when I gaze hard.

An O.K. face for a Monday morning. I've seen worse in this mirror. I'm going to see worse yet.

■

I needed to present myself to Burke and get to work on Billy Neill, so I assembled my medium-magnitude-star-at-work outfit—cantaloupe silk blouse, floral scarf adjusted for symmetry and studied casualness, tailored skirt, suede jacket. I stepped into low-heeled boots, picked up a pouch purse and my bag of Billy Neill cassettes, and scrambled out the door. As I left, flattened diamonds of yellow and violet were projecting through beveled glass onto the dark wood wall of the synagogue.

Twenty feet down the sidewalk, in a wooden crate, lives a black man more or less my age. He must have been sleeping late. I walked to the corner of Sixth Avenue in crisp light that promised too much, flagged down a cab, and whizzed uptown through the cute zone—Bread Alone, Chips with Everything, Methusaleh Health & Sports Shoes—past Fourteenth Street, the trucks already unloading flowers and shirts and bolts of cloth and miniature electronics into cramped shops; then into the Forties, where the true Avenue of the Americas kicks in, and I got

off for the thousandth time on the surge, the life-force
crackling between those walls of glass and steel where
the noise of civilization is conglomerated and pumped
back out—Simon & Schuster/Hitachi, Time-Life-Warner,
McGraw/Samsung, General Electric, CBS, Capital Cities/
ABC, until the cab pulled up and let me off in front of the
Con Comm Building. Big Glass. Sir Colin McShane was
known to hate the name, but—or therefore—it had stuck.
Fifty stories of mirror glass—one for each state—reflected
CBS's discreet Black Rock on one side, the pale gray
Gothic stone of St. Anthony's Cathedral on the other.

Set into the black marble wall of the Big Glass lobby,
giant TV monitors inflated the creamy faces of *AM Coast to
Coast.* Overhead, an electronic sign that hadn't been there
Friday, block letters in neon orange oozing across the
lobby: WE TAKE IN THE WORLD. The words pulsed bright blue
and vanished. Images welled up. Dead center, a broadcast-
ing tower radiating concentric circles. The World Trade
Center dissolving to Big Ben to the Eiffel Tower to the
Dome of the Rock to Red Square to the Great Wall of
China to the Sydney Opera House to black. The letters
CON slid out, then sprouted SOLIDATED. Followed by COMM
spawning UNICATIONS. Then: WE . . . TAKE . . . IN . . .
THE . . . WORLD. If Sir Colin didn't exist, he'd have to be
invented.

Marble and Glitz: my title for his biography, the big book
that I should, if I knew what was good for me, have retired
to write. But I wasn't brave or stupid enough to rejoin the
ranks of the freelance. Remind me to live my next life as an
heiress.

"Nobody ever accused Sir Colin of restraint or low ratings," a familiar voice boomed from over my shoulder.

I jumped. "Christ, Burke—"

Burke Gilman leered. His tawny beard was trim, as always. His burgundy leather jacket fell below his thighs. The only thing tall about Burke was his ambition. "Like the fabulous new look?"

"You know me, Burke, I'm crazy for subtlety."

He unbuttoned his coat and inspected me. "Travel agrees with you."

Disconcertingly, I was pleased. I made the right noises. "So tell me something I don't know about Billy."

Burke's voice, which had propelled him from radio announcer to news director, was at its silkiest today, but something was off about him.

The brass doors of the elevator gleamed, having just been polished by a black man in a white uniform. On the smooth way up to 26 I gave Burke a headline version of how beachwalking Billy Neill had changed his name to Billy Null, how he had, on the spot, banged out, for the first time anywhere, a punky version of his old minor hit "Absolute Zero Heart," a staccato rant all about *diamonds turnin' to ashes, everythin's endin' that ought to be fixin' to start, I give you my nothin' o' rainbows this absolute zero* . . . He rhymed *hero* with *zero, news* with *blues,* spat the syllables out like nails he was driving into his own dead heart.

I was still talking as we got off the elevator. The glittering silver *In Depth* logo, in three dimensions, loomed. We walked down the corridor past the show's nine Emmy plaques, four of which I was responsible for, thank you. Good for morale on bad days, which were most days. The plaques weren't dated; a visitor from Neptune might not notice that our good work lay in the mists of yesteryear.

Burke's fingers hovering near my waist steered me past his secretary's work station into his corner office, which was more like walking into a view, a canyon. He punched up his four-monitor rig, muted it, plunged into the far corner of his couch — as if jumping into the canyon — and gestured me to the other corner. I talked, his eyes following me, chilly with surveillance. I left out the part about how Billy tried, on camera, to soul-search me into bed. Burke might insist we *couldn't not run* Billy Neill trying to put the make on his star correspondent-producer, quel coup!

His phone trilled. "Burke," he said evenly into the speaker. I walked to the window, pressed my forehead against the pane, and looked down the vertiginous canyon. Tiny cars, toy streets, ant people. The point of getting this high was to gaze down at the aspirants too far below to see you.

"I looked at the piece again last night," Burke barked. "You've still got all that dead history. Deep snooze. Make it wiggle. Pump up the graphics. Give me the Flextron."

"I've got —" came over the line.

"Can you hold on?" Burke didn't wait for an answer, but punched a button for another call coming in. "Burke," he said. Long pause. "You know what? I don't care if his mother dropped dead in bed with his worst enemy. What's he waiting for?" He winked, whispered aside "Fuckin' spics," punched the first button again, and said, "I know you got graphics, but they died and went to heaven. I want those molecules so high-tech you'd think they're made in Japan. This guy's no putz, he designs brand-new drugs, for Christ's fucking sake. Modifies molecules, and wham bam, they're legal, the suckers shoot up with them, bang, they live the rest of their brain-dead lives in the back wards. I want my mother to look at this piece and say, 'Holy shit.' Get in, get out." Click.

Burke had kept his lust for the hunt, you had to hand him that. An engraved sign on his desk said MINISTRY OF TRUTH. Beside it, a six-inch cube of black glass inscribed 48.2 commemorated *In Depth*'s maximum market share. On the wall, a photo: a smirking young Burke in a pitcher's uniform sandwiched between Chevy Chase and John Belushi, Belushi making rabbit ears behind Burke's head. The assignment blackboard for the coming week, another blackboard stretching three months ahead. A laser-printed sign: IF WE DON'T KNOW IT, IT AIN'T WORTH KNOWING. IF WE DON'T SHOW IT, IT AIN'T WORTH SHOWING. Next to this, a mounted poster, its corners ragged, of Einstein with his white mane and benign, leonine face, riding a bicycle. Beneath it, a bumper sticker: I STOP FOR ROCK 'N' ROLL.

I glanced at Burke and realized what looked wrong. Instead of his usual bow tie, he was wearing a full-length paisley job. In the corner of his maroon sweater were stitched the tiny words HILTON HEAD. Who was looking over *his* shoulder?

"Christ." He smiled his co-conspiratorial smile at me. "I wish everybody in this shop had your eye."

I thanked him perfunctorily and segued back to Billy Neill as the representative figure of his, my, generation. "You'll love the song, Burke. Edit him in and out of flashbacks. He's burned out but he's crisp, if you know what I mean." Perfect for our aging demographics.

Burke's eyes locked on mine, search-and-seizure. Then he poked his right fist in a locker-room way-to-go and said, "Great. Margo Ross meets Billy Neill, the perfect one-on-one. I want it for this Wednesday night."

That meant cutting around the clock, starting an hour ago. Fitful sofa naps, bad dreams, Styrofoam dinners. Crash a serious story, sure, but wrecking my metabolism for Billy Neill was not my idea of a great self-sacrifice in the annals of journalism. I found myself wondering what Harry Kramer would think.

"What about designer drugs?"

"Not to worry. It's evergreen. I want to make sure we get it right." Meaning: Keep it on the shelf. So a dozen more kids would end up with Parkinson's because of what they didn't hear this week on *In Depth*.

I pointed out that rushing Billy Null would mean jumping the release date for his album featuring the reconstituted "Absolute Zero Heart."

"They'd jump it themselves if they could."

Technically correct, but why the hurry? Burke had forfeited the right to be taken at face value. The whole industry was coated with slime, but in my vast experience Burke had the purest instinct for the direct line to power. I had picked up a trick or two from him myself. Welcome to the McShane empire, one long chain of kissy-kiss kneeling communicants leading up to the master.

You're going to owe me, I thought. When I started at *In Depth*, I had a different arithmetic in mind—two for them, one for me. Now it was six or eight for Burke and I was lucky to score a public-service spot for myself. I knew I couldn't trade Billy Null for, say, the long-postponed sweatshops piece. But I would think of something.

"You'll have it, Burke."

"You're a star, star. I'll get you Yolanda." Yolanda was the fastest, slickest editor we had.

Burke wrote on the blackboard, BILLY'S BACK. Son of a bitch had already picked out the slug.

■

My office had no canyon, no view of anything, in fact, except tacked-up picture postcards. GREETINGS FROM PAPUA NEW GUINEA. I was typing script notes when the phone trilled. My secretary wasn't in yet. I picked up without taking my eyes off my notes. "Yes."

"Margo?" An invitation.

"You've got her."

"Harry." His name sounded like a summons, and damn if I didn't feel summoned, a quarter of a century after I thought I'd outgrown that sort of thing. There was traffic honking and rumbling in the background.

"Hey, stranger! Amazing, after all these years . . ."

"I have to see you." An edge came into his voice. This was not the take-charge courtliness I associated with Harry Kramer.

"Harry, lovely to hear from you, but—"

"Listen, I *have* to see you." A little early for a command performance. But there it was.

I hesitated. "I'll call you tonight. I'm on deadline."

"Margo, this may sound . . . excessive . . . but tonight is too late." This was a Harry Kramer without whimsy. But what did I ever know about Harry Kramer anyway?

"I'm in trouble," he said.

I sighed loud enough to feel guilty about it. My watch read 9:32. "How about early lunch? Meet me in front of Big Glass, say eleven-thirty."

"Big Glass."

"Sorry, the Con Comm Building, Sixth Avenue."

"I'm grateful." He didn't sound it. The line went dead.

Harry, whatever the trouble, deserved the best meal my career could buy. Sir Colin, like it or not, was going to pop for Harry Kramer: consultant on the subject of outliving one's moment in history. I clicked for a dial tone and punched up the number for Happening.

■

By the time I got to the street, the Avenue of the Americas was revving up. A messenger, in headband and gloves, snaked against traffic. A car alarm started to wail. No one looked unusually alarmed. A white stretch limousine prowled at the curb, tourists strolled past in the direction of Radio City, and two bored-looking young Senegalese presided over displays of narrow scarves.

I sat on a pink-granite abutment and watched the clouds rip across the still-bright sky, reflecting off Big Glass. We Take in the World. A cathedral of images. The glass panels had been set at microscopically different angles, so that clouds and buildings looked jagged. Next to the downtown corner was a granite block twenty feet square, like a sarcophagus dragged down from the Metropolitan Museum. When Colin McShane had bought out Con Comm, he had torn down the grim old headquarters known, with mandatory affection, as Great Gray. By preserving a slab from the demolished façade, he scored points for innovation and conservation alike. At a stroke, Sir Colin, *arriviste* press lord, took his place among the media gentry.

Harry Kramer taught me to see this way. I am a camcorder.

The early lunchtime crowd thickened. Skirts too short

for some legs, too long for others. Three-piece pinstripes, exchanging Giant, Jet, Met, and Knick talk. Two-piece pinstripes, talking ratings.

I watched for eyes watching for me. A man about the right height and age, wearing a suit and blue shades, a briefcase under his arm, walked toward me, hesitated, produced a smile. I smiled back. Strange, Harry in a suit, but on the other hand, consider myself in Italian calf boots, dressed-for-success . . . Blue shades passed.

I glanced at my watch. Eleven thirty-eight. The car alarm had subsided. I decided to give Harry till a quarter of.

Along the uptown side of the plaza, a couple of white-haired ladies with no Billy Null to worry about and all the time in the world gazed perplexedly at the twin translucent crystals that stood the same height as the granite slab. A fat man holding a green Michelin Guide stared at the roof, where a huge satellite dish was painted a pale lemon yellow. Critical commentaries on the symbolism of the crystals and the dish were reprinted in a brochure available in the lobby: "The satellite dish is to the twenty-first century what the steam engine was to the nineteenth and the dynamo to the twentieth. It expresses the quintessence of our civilization, encapsulating such unity as our fractured planet may find . . ." blah, blah. The architecture critic for *Silence*, however, had dubbed the crystals Pillars of Salt, and the name stuck: "That was all that was left of Colin McShane. He made the mistake of looking back at what he had wrought."

My idea, actually. I had given away the line. That's what happens when you squander two years going out with a critic from *Silence*. Two years of wariness and theft. I suppressed a kind thought about Blond Bart, who looked refreshingly innocuous by comparison.

I felt a hand on my shoulder. The crystalline blue eyes of Harry Kramer were unmistakable, though they were graver and deeper set than I'd remembered and the skin around them was worn. A day's worth of stubble, but no beard. He was wearing a nicely tailored mahogany-colored sport jacket, collar upturned, over a black turtleneck. He had six or eight years on me, but he looked lean and solid. I turned toward him so he could embrace me. He let go too soon. His eyes darted.

"Stay down for a minute," he half whispered. "I'm being followed. I think I lost the guy, but I don't want to find out the hard way." The lunchtime crowd swirled past. He checked them one at a time, like a Secret Service agent.

"Do you greet all the girls this way?"

He cocked his right eyebrow, as I'd seen him do toward many an attentive woman in the old days. He touched my hand. I left it there. His hand was chilly but his grin was electric.

He said, "Only you, Margo."

Heads tilted back, we inspected each other, pretending not to notice all the erosion. His hair had receded an inch or two, and grayed somewhat, and the curls were slacker, more tired, than I remembered them. But there were improvements. He had converted to contact lenses. Interesting—in the old days, I had never known anyone so impressive, and so impressed with himself, yet with so little physical vanity. His chin was forceful, a revelation, making me wonder why he used to hide it behind a beard. Without the beard, he looked, if anything, more intense than ever— fierce one second, self-mocking the next.

"So who's following you?"

"I have a minor idea, but I'm not sure." He twisted around on the stone, half stood to scout the Avenue of the Americas. Then he rose to his full height. He had two or three inches on me, one more thing for which to be grateful. "That's the middle of the story."

"I no longer listen to stories without lunch," I said. He took my elbow as if he had a right to it.

∎

"There's been a murder."

We were seated in white wicker chairs, next to a small potted palm. Harry had the wall seat, facing the door. His jacket wasn't a bad match with the decor. All of Happening was white and tan. The ceiling was low, with no dividers, as befit a place devoted to the circulation of sound and energy. White ceiling fans kept the talk moving. The talk said: I've arrived, I know it, what can you do for me? To be heard, you bellowed decorously, compounding the tumult.

The restaurant was filling up. Customers, I knew, were flicking more than sidelong glances at me, but possibly also at Harry: he didn't look midtown. But all I heard was Harry's voice speaking of murder, all I saw were his eyes, grave again. He had invited me to tell all about my life and times, but I had demurred: "After you. We're wondering why you called this meeting."

"Three people know: the murderer, one other person, and I." He spoke with his old precision. "I think." His eyes appraised the surroundings like a cameraman's, finding focus.

"Why do I have a feeling there's about to be a fourth?"

He forced a small hitch of his lips.

"What I'm going to tell you is going to sound ridiculous,

or worse, like I've gone around the bend. Do me a favor —
even if this sounds like *Twilight Zone,* suspend judgment, all
right?"

I was going to have to wait to find out where Harry had
spent the last quarter century. No ring on his finger, for
what that was worth. "You have till dessert."

"Good enough. Believe me, this is the best story of our
lives. And I mean no disrespect to your, mm, oeuvre. Or
mine." His eyes stopped darting and lounged over to mine.

I rested my chin on my knuckles and opened my eyes
wide. "I don't storm out of restaurants, Harry." I was relieved he didn't seem to get my reference to the time one of
his admirers had left him at the West End Bar holding the
check — something about an abortion she would have preferred to avoid, I'd been told.

A blond waiter glided up, tan trim on his white cuffs, a
cursive *H* on his breast pocket.

"Order something to drink, Harry. On Mr. McShane."

Harry ordered a Kir. I ordered Finnish water, and told
the waiter we needed high-velocity lunch. At a nearby table, a nice-looking man with white hair studied my face.
Hushed talk centered on the question of whether Margo
Ross looked better on air or off. Or did I imagine it?

"Fasten your seat belt, Margo. What do you know about
Einstein's death?"

"Pardon?" I thought I must have misheard.

"Albert Einstein."

It sat there like a small dead animal between us. I waited
for a way out of embarrassment, Harry's or mine, but nothing turned up. "Not a thing, to tell you the truth."

Billy Neill came to my plummeting mind. There's no joy
meeting a genius from the old days and discovering he's a

crank. Was he even then, and if so, what was I? Maybe the less I knew about the last twenty-five years, the better.

"Remember Peter Minasian?"

I rummaged through the garbage dump of memory and came up with a scrap. A hangdog guy who sold advertising at *Eight Million Stories*, the not-so-underground tabloid-looking lit mag where I was working when Harry Kramer walked in one day with his fabulous manuscript and those ice-blue eyes. Peter probably sold more dope than ads, and hung around the office comparing notes on chemical effects.

"You mean the sad guy."

"Bone-sad," Harry said.

"But smart." Remembering now. "He was the guy who dropped out of med school to do acid and search for God—you remember searching for God?"

"He got detoured for a long time before he straightened out. Now he's a lab technician. I run into him now and then. The last few years he's been working in a neuro-science lab, part of the City University."

Our drinks arrived. So did the food waiter, preternaturally perky, rattling off his litany of specials.

"Please simplify life for me," Harry said.

"Crab cakes for the gentleman," I said, "and for me the lobster salad."

Harry, distracted, sipped at his Kir.

"Neuroscience, you were saying," I cued him.

He got back on track. "Right. They study the brain physiology of the extraordinary mind. Which zone of the brain makes which kind of people think and feel which kinds of ways. There's nothing unearthly about the mind, it turns out. Your cells exchange electric pulses, therefore you are. Reason is convoluted because the brain is. Leave aside whether this leads to an adequate understanding of what a piece of work is"—he paused—"woman, or man." He flashed a minuscule grin. "They're dissecting, you might say, the anatomy of brilliance."

"You should make them a bequest."

"Sweet of you. So Peter Minasian calls me up a week ago, out of the blue. He says his lab has a piece of Einstein's brain and they're running tests on it. I say to him what you're thinking right now: Why are you telling me this? He says he needs advice, he respects my judgment, so he tells me." He let the thought drift off. Millennium's end, the clock ticking, I'm on deadline, sitting in Happening while Harry Kramer carries on about somebody I barely remember carrying on about *Einstein's brain,* for Christ's sake.

"Turns out there's something peculiar about Einstein's brain."

"Wait a minute. What's Einstein's brain doing in New York in the first place?"

"Well you might ask. I did, too. Here's the short version: The old man died in Princeton, in '55. An old man's death, age seventy-six. Nothing unexpected. He'd suffered from an aneurysm for years."

I made a mental note to ask about aneurysms while I adjusted my I'm-with-you, keep-talking look.

"There was an autopsy. The pathologist found nothing out of the ordinary. The body went off to be cremated. The ashes were scattered in the Jersey woods; Einstein was modest, he didn't want a grave to attract pilgrims. So far, so good. Meanwhile, the pathologist, Thomas Harvey by name, had saved Einstein's brain. There's a dispute about whether he had permission to do that. Dr. Harvey says yes. The family and Einstein's old friends were not happy. In any case, Dr. Harvey preserved the brain in formaldehyde and kept it. You can understand his point of view. This was the brain that reinvented the world. Shouldn't we know something about it?"

I nodded, wondering when the pace would pick up.

"So Dr. Harvey sectioned the brain—cut it into pieces—and saved it. When he moved back to Wichita, where he came from, he took it along in a cardboard box. Really. Twenty years later, a reporter found him there, the science press got interested, one thing led to another. A Professor Leon Taub at CUNY read an article and asked for pieces of the cerebral cortex. Harvey obliged. Taub wanted to know whether Einstein's gray matter was different from anybody else's." Harry took a long pull on his Kir, draining it.

So I bit like a fool. "And?"

"What do you know? It *was* different. Einstein had an abnormally high number of glial cells—beautiful word, don't you think?—glial cells in two places, left rear and right front." He pointed to spots on his own skull. "That's been known for years."

"Glial cells," I obliged.

"As opposed to neurons. Now, Taub was going to find out whether he had excess glial cells in other sectors, and compare his glial-to-neuron ratio with other brains—musicians, artists, scientists. His theory was that the ratio is why Einstein thought in images. He didn't reason his way to a conclusion, he *saw* it. Pictures came to him. He filled in the logic later."

The waiter deposited lunch. Harry ordered another Kir.

I picked at red-pepper slivers and sleek lobster meat. Harry's crab cakes sat.

"The point is this. Taub did his tests and found the same high glial count all over Einstein's brain. Fine, a nice result. Then he decided he was going to be thorough and see if anything else unusual turned up. He told Peter to run some more tests. A week ago, Peter found methamphetamine."

I stopped picking at my salad, excellent though it was.

"Speed. There was more than enough speed in the brain of Albert Einstein to kill him several times over."

Harry looked expectant, like a big dog planting its claws on a visitor's knees, eager to play. I quietly laid down my fork.

"Of course you think this is crazy," he said with a cock of his eyebrow. "I thought so, too, until Peter showed up with this."

He pushed his plate aside, pulled two folded pages out of his inside jacket pocket, unfolded them in front of him, and pressed the creases flat. The top sheet showed two jagged tracings, one jiggling out from the left margin, the other from the right.

"This is a copy of what they call a strip chart from a high-performance liquid chromatography machine, an HPLC for short, which is what they use to detect chemicals."

"Slow down."

He went through the terms one at a time until I sounded as though I understood. "The peaks measure the presence of the chemical they're testing for. Peter thought maybe he had a malfunctioning machine, so he went to another piece of equipment, which runs the results from the HPLC through a computer and prints out the precise numbers."

Harry peeled off the top sheet and put it to one side. He turned the second sheet, also shiny, so that the columns of numbers faced me. CHROMATOPAC CR601, it said top left. "That's the machine." There were six columns. The first said PKNO. "That's for peak number," Harry said. "This one"—he pointed at the fifth column, headed CONC—"is for the concentration of the chemical." Over the last column, headed NAME, the top line read METH.

"Speed," I said like a dolt.

"Exactly. You see, the peak is way above standard—"

"Spare me the details, but you're sure about this."

Harry had seen a lot of doubt in his time and learned to be patient with it. "Peter Minasian couldn't believe it at first, either. That's what these other run-throughs are— different samples from different parts of the tissue. I suggested he go back and try again." He ran his finger down the page. "Meth concentration 1.1326, 1.1278, 1.1378 . . . Speed, every time."

Jet lag was befuddling me, or the sight of Harry Kramer across the table. I could simulate taking Billy Neill seriously for a weekend. I could get off on a piece about the man who's building the biggest doll's house in the world. But I could not quite bring myself to take seriously the chemical content of Albert Einstein's brain.

"What can I say?" Harry said quietly. "There isn't supposed to be speed in the brain. Einstein's or anyone else's."

Had I been Harry, I would also have taken my time getting to the point. The point was pure upscale pulp. Headline: EINSTEIN MURDERED, alongside RICK NELSON DREAMED OF BUDDY HOLLY NIGHT BEFORE PLANE CRASHED and ELVIS SIGHTED ON MARS. This was getting to be the stuff of *In Depth*. "No, I wouldn't think so."

"Speed doesn't generate spontaneously. It doesn't grow in formaldehyde. But once the stuff is in the tissue, it doesn't break down. It can stay forty years, easy. Are you with me?"

"Why, where do you think I am?"

"Just checking."

"Don't condescend. I'm right behind you."

The waiter arrived with Harry's second Kir. He reached and gulped.

I stared at the printout numbers—solid, imposing, impenetrable.

"So tell me about this lab?"

"Supposed to be state-of-the-art," Harry said. "Flashy research, well funded, possible gene-splicing applications. Taub's a *Who's Who* type, National Academy, big grant swinger."

"Don't take offense, but you have no doubt that this is on the up-and-up?"

His deep chuckle came from way down in his chest. "You know me, Margo, I take nothing for granted. I checked around. Taub is where I'd put my eugenics dollars, if I had any. Anyway, we don't have to take Minasian's word for it, or Taub's reputation, here's the printout. If there's speed in Einstein's brain today, there was speed in his brain when he died."

"This is the point in the movie where I'm supposed to say, *You mean—*"

He looked slightly deflated. "The point is, either Albert Einstein was a speed freak and nobody noticed, or somebody shot speed into Albert Einstein. Or fed it to him. If that sounds crackpot, don't blame me." At last he cut off a small piece of crab cake and swallowed it. "It's not my fault if reality is peculiar."

Took me a skipped beat to get the reference, but when I got it, the frolic in his eyes told me he knew I did. The old Harry, the old office. In 1970, when I went to work as an "editorial assistant," meaning receptionist, typist, gofer, and uncredited advisor, at *Eight Million Stories*, the Che Guevara poster behind the editor's desk said: "It's not my fault if reality is Marxist." Launch my literary career on the slightly wild side, why not? Harry walked in one day, unannounced, bearing his huge, weird, unsolicited novella about big-time bankers and their taste in call girls. Real-estate and casino honchos procuring loans from offshore banks in unconventional ways. Offshore banks linked to onshore banks from Wall Street to Century City. CIA drug money lubricating the deals.

Harry was already highly reputed in my circle as the author of *Fix*, a novel about an intelligence agency which runs drugs out of Vietnam and schemes to assassinate a newly elected liberal President while pinning the plot on a combine of Bolivian neo-Nazis and Sicilians cheated of their ninety-nine-year leases on Cuban casinos . . . and so on. *Fix* was full of syndicates overlapping with combines, mafias, networks, webs thick with payoffs and victims. Critics lapped up his "authentic new voice," blah blah, in reviews, none of which were accompanied by a photograph of the author, the author having refused to unveil his face to a dangerous world. My friends and I read *Fix* as our all-purpose allegory. Smuggling deserters and draft resisters to Canada, we had used the paperback as the basis for our code. 32-2-26 meant turn to p. 32 of *Fix*, go to the second line, twenty-sixth letter. That gave you one letter in your message. We made up short messages.

And then one day there was Harry Kramer, authoritatively thirtyish, in the flesh, standing over my desk, holding a cardboard box full of twenty thousand impeccably typed words about bankers and hookers. It was very far out. It took up a whole issue. People talked about it. *60 Minutes* picked it up. We got sued by a minor player for libel on a small point, got defended pro bono by movement lawyers, and won on a smaller point. Too bad that by the time we won there was no one to celebrate—our backer, a porn king with unrealized literary ambitions and a taste for diversification, got scared, or bored, pulled the plug, and we were all dispersed into crackups and Europe and half-hearted careers.

But for the year plus while the fun lasted, I felt as though, if I paid attention, every week I could double what I understood about how the world works. At first, I wanted to ask Harry how he came to know so much about bankers, or about call girls, though that would have been gauche. Harry just knew. But one night not long after he started hanging around with the staff, I found him at a party uncharacteristically unsurrounded by the most accomplished and/or glamorous women in any given loft, and got up the nerve to ask him how he knew so much about bankers. His twinkle said, Whoever has to ask is hopelessly naïve, but he was too kind to shoo away such an eager and not bad-looking potential protégée. Circulate, he said. Make a lot of friends. And read. Not to believe what you read, but to ask: Who's paying whom to write it, and why now? Most of *Fix*, he said, the CIA drug-running stuff, was true. The same for bankers and hookers. But publishing straight facts would have been foolish. His hooded look said that he knew how to take care of himself. He disapproved of bravado. He thought the movement was reckless, childish, shallow—all these sit-ins, rallies, slogans, symbolic actions, missed the point. Power was vast and intransigent. Power was dead serious.

These were my friends he was knocking for naïveté, so I didn't convince easily. But over the next months he adopted me, more or less. He would stroll in at the end of the afternoon, pass a six-pack of premium beer around the office, sit in the upholstered pew someone had scored for the space next to my desk, and ask me about myself. When I had run out of anything interesting to say, he would hold forth, and then the floor was open for earnest questions. He tutored me on what he called, with a wiggle of both eyebrows, the Prime Movers and Shakers. Say whatever you want about the Ruling Class, he said, the Power Elite, the Fortune 500, the Empire, these were nothing more than the out-of-date and cumbersome constructs of professors who weren't close to the action. Coincidence was another word for insufficient research. Harry read everything—*Fortune, Aviation Week*, Kennedy assassination tracts, congressional hearing transcripts, the North American Committee on Latin America. His eyes gleamed as he talked about secret Italian Fascist lodges, fly-by-night airlines, Nazi cells in Peru. Lesson One was: The world is seamless. Everything is related to everything else. Old boys clinked glasses at the Harvard Club and, on the other side of the world, villages exploded. Lesson Two was: History is crime, and never underestimate the thrill of the game. They do it for money, sure, but the money's a way of keeping score. They also do it for the sheer pleasure of proving that they can get away with murder. Lesson Three was: Think small, it's the little mobile groupuscules who write the plots, make things happen. We played a game: Name any two nouns, find links between them. I'd say something like, Mars Bars and, oh, Marlon Brando. He'd rattle off: Mars Bars . . . sugar . . . U.S. sugar interests in the Dominican Republic . . . Gulf & Western owns megalands in the D.R. . . . G & W owns Paramount Pictures . . . Paramount had a mafia film called *The Godfather* in the works. He drew diagrams on scraps of paper.

Then, with another wiggle of his eyebrows, he was gone. Back to my facts, as he put it. Some nights, I would be hanging out at the West End Bar with my friends and there he would be with some svelte miniskirted type with long hair and a committed look at a dark table for two in back. My friends would be very impressed when Harry waved at me through her perfume, and I would wave back: our complicity. So *this* is what he keeps under his hood, I would think. Then I would turn back to my open-faced friends, thinking: These are boys.

"Nixon and the ozone layer," I said to Harry across the table at Happening.

"Hello?"

I wrote a word in my notebook, tore out the page, passed it across the table. The word was ABPLANALP. One of Nixon's best friends, Robert Abplanalp, was a Basque who had invented the valve for spraying aerosol cans, which produced chlorofluorocarbons, which were eating away the ozone layer all over the globe.

Harry slowly, slowly nodded. "Nice. Great name."

"Thank you. I give up. Who killed Einstein?"

His grin was quick, immoderate, then back under his hood. He leveled his ever-blue eyes on me. "I don't know. That's where you come in."

He had me. Did he know I was fed up with *In Depth*'s moral travelogues, petty black-hat-white-hat sermonettes whose endings I knew from the start? When I was done with Billy Neill, the big fun waiting for me was a piece about the old man who'd spent thirty-six years building the world's biggest doll's house. Fine. But.

"O.K., how did he die? How is he *supposed* to have died?"

He smiled his the-two-of-us-know-better smile, gulped a chunk of crab cake, put down his fork, leaned forward, and lowered his voice. "The official story, as I said, is that Einstein suffered for years from an aneurysm. A big blister, a weak place in his aorta, where it passed through his gut. When it was diagnosed, in '48, it was already the size of a grapefruit, and growing. He knew what it was, his family knew, his close friends knew. He'd suffer attacks, he'd throw up, the pain was horrible, then he'd recover. Sooner or later it was going to burst, but nobody knew when. He kept on working. On April 13, 1955, he was hit by the worst attack yet. Excruciating pain. Clearly, the aneurysm was bleeding. His doctors wanted to operate, but he refused. He said he didn't think he was going to live forever, he wanted to go when *he* wanted to go. Today there's routine surgery, but back then it was questionable. So he stayed home and he waited. On the fourteenth, more pain, he couldn't drink water. On Friday the fifteenth, he agreed to go to the hospital."

"Agreed?"

"Convincing him wasn't easy. He had to be convinced

his secretary couldn't take care of him by herself. Helen
Dukas by name. His stepdaughter, who lived with him,
too, was already at the hospital, sick herself."

"Strange." Now I was scribbling notes. Against my better judgment, I was getting into the spirit. Harry Kramer,
who taught me what homework was, telling me in his
methodical way about Einstein.

"I'll say. Then. Over the weekend he felt better. He was
still in a lot of pain, but his doctor hoped he could stem the
bleeding. So Einstein sent for the papers he'd been working on. He did some work and he had visitors. Just after 1
a.m. on Monday, April 18, he muttered something in German and died. A nurse was there, but she didn't speak
German." Harry wolfed down the rest of his crab cake and
said, "That's the official story."

Official or not, the story was moving at serious speed
inside me.

"And you're saying this cover story that's worked for
forty years is false?"

"Not false, as far as it goes. He had the aneurysm. It did
burst."

"Only now there's this inconvenient speed to deal with."

"That much speed was enough to rupture his aneurysm.
Judging from the amount in these chunks of his brain, way
more than enough. Anyone with minimal medical knowledge could easily have found out that speed would do him
in, then passed it to him in his food or water. Afterward,
why would anyone check for speed, of all things?"

The angel is in the details, and the details were starting
to sing to me. "So, you're saying somebody brought on that
first attack on the, what was it, thirteenth? Or the fatal one
in the hospital?"

"Could be either, could be both. Maybe somebody tried to kill him on the thirteenth, found out he'd failed, then went to the hospital to try again. That's one thing we don't know."

I let the "we" pass.

"Let me see if I follow. The killer"—the word thickened my tongue—"the killer had to know about the aneurysm; otherwise, there'd be no point in giving him speed, right?"

"Right."

"And I take it Einstein didn't broadcast his state of ill health to a waiting world."

"You take it correctly. Usually, doctors came to his house, because he wouldn't go near the hospital."

"So this has to be someone who knew him pretty well."

"You see why this gets interesting." Not to say bizarre. But, I thought to myself, remember bankers and hookers. Kinky enough to be true.

The waiter materialized. "Will there be anything else?"

Harry invited me to go first.

"Double cappuccino for me, thanks."

"Espresso," Harry said, though caffeine wasn't what he required at the moment.

"And the check." The waiter scurried off.

"O.K., this someone who knew him pretty well," I said, "had to have known that Einstein was a dying man. Why go to the trouble of murdering a wonderful man who's virtually on his deathbed? Assuming you wanted to murder him at all."

Harry beamed. There was respect in his eyes, and affection, and pride—I'd apparently picked up a thing or two since his mentor days. "Exactly. Intimates are the usual suspects, right? Now listen to this. I've spent a lot of time at the Forty-second Street Library, went through the Einstein biographies, the *Times* index, the *Reader's Guide,* you name it. On the surface, there are no motives at all. No money to speak of. No insurance. No family intrigue. He lived for years with his stepdaughter and his secretary, both devoted to him. No secret passions, no private hatreds anybody's ever written about." He was composing now, legato. "By all accounts, Einstein was God's prince who'd earned a serene old age. He slept late, read the papers, walked to the Institute for Advanced Study, worked, walked home, played the violin, napped, listened to the radio. He sailed. He was kind to passersby. He helped the neighborhood kids with homework and gave them cookies. He sat in his neighbor's parlor and listened to her play the piano. He was too good for this world." Leave it to Harry to memorize the biography, respect the logic, master the facts. He drained what was left of his Kir.

"So this leaves you . . ."

"Mystified, at first."

"And then?"

"Thinking: Suppose, for the sake of argument, we forget about the usual motives: private gain, personal venom, revenge, and so on. Suppose we remember that people kill for ideas; this is the twentieth century, after all. Then we've got motives coming out our ears. This sweet old guy is a *pacifist,* he's a *socialist,* he's a *Jew,* and it's 1955. Remember, in the thirties, there were Nazi agents trying to kill him."

Nazi agents. Woo-woo.

I looked at my watch. Twenty after twelve and I felt the weasel eyes of Burke Gilman on me.

"Harry, this story is going to have to be continued."

"Two more minutes, O.K.? Thursday I went down to

Princeton Hospital, where Einstein died. I had the name of one of his nurses from a biography—the one who was there when he died but didn't speak German. I presented myself to the personnel office as her long-lost grandnephew and got an address. A nursing home, wouldn't you know it? Sinking feelings. Well. This tiny lady can barely move, but she has every last wit about her. I told her I was writing a new biography. Wait till you see her. Angela Parenti's her name. Pearl earrings, perfect silver waves." With his fingers he made waves in the air.

Burke wouldn't see the point. I still wasn't sure *I* saw the point. Or that I wanted to. But I couldn't help imagining those perfect silver waves on camera. If Billy Neill's no-mushroom-cloud earrings looked good with *In Depth*'s trademark rack focus, why not pearl?

The waiter trotted up with coffee and a tan suede folder with a fair replica of a Toulouse-Lautrec tooled onto it. I dropped my card on top of the folder and started on my cappuccino.

"She's a great talker," Harry went on. "For all I know, she might have been thrilled to talk to anybody ambulatory, but a biographer was too good to be true. *Of course* she remembered when Dr. Einstein died, who wouldn't? She was *honored* to be in his presence, everybody was. She could remember *every detail* as if it were yesterday. Could she remember who visited him in the hospital? *Of course!* She was a *trained* nurse, she knew a fact when she saw it. Lo and behold, she pulls out two yellowing books—a scrapbook full of clippings, and a diary. She licks her fingers and leafs through the diary. Here, she says, Einstein's stepdaughter visited him in his room. Here's his son, a perfect gentleman. Here's his secretary. Here's his friend from

New York—from her description, it sounds like Otto Nathan, an economist, probably Einstein's closest friend, his
executor. And two other friends, professors, she's pretty
sure. At least they sounded like professors. Both with accents."

"Descriptions?"

"Oh, is she *trained*, is Mrs. Parenti! One was short and
chubby, 'pear-shaped,' as she put it, a nice Old World
gentleman. The other had a thin face, with a flat nose,
probably broken once, and a deep voice, 'very impressive.'
And what do you know, this one she thinks she saw a
second time, that night, after visiting hours."

"And do you—"

"I do. The first one matches a friend of Einstein's named
Franz Rosenthal, a mathematician. I checked. Alive and
well in Princeton, it turns out. So I called him up. Said I
was a writer interested in Einstein's death. He gave me an
appointment. Tomorrow. Not a busy man."

"And the guy with the flat nose and the impressively
deep voice?"

"Yet unknown. More material for investigation."

He flexed his eyebrows like Groucho Marx and went for
his espresso. My own cappuccino did not intensify my will
to resist. Once again, my life was being picked up like a
beach ball and thrown. Well, why not? Without quite making a choice, I had at various times in my life gone to *Eight
Million Stories*, married, gone to Europe, ceased being married, come home, gone to *In Depth*. All with a certain light-
ness. You don't exactly say yes, you couldn't exactly defend
the idea to your mother, but the next thing you know,
you're planning the ceremony.

"Well," I said, trying to stave off the inevitable, "these Old World professors don't sound like terrific suspects."

"There's more," he said. "I asked her if she remembered anyone else. As a matter of fact, she remembers a young man hanging around the nursing station. A tall, thin teenager with big ears. She had to shoo him out of the corridor more than once. He wanted to stay overnight in the waiting room. He claimed to be Einstein's 'friend.' She thought he was a little young to be a reporter. She had to call an orderly to make him leave."

The coffee was gone by the time the waiter returned with the suede folder and a credit slip. I wrote in an extra twenty percent courtesy of Sir Colin McShane. I've waited on tables.

I scraped back my chair. I felt giddy, high on sleeplessness, on deadline, on Harry, on caffeine, on this absurd story. *Of course* it was wild. Pure Harry. Was anything better likely to land on my desk this side of the next millennium?

"Harry," I said, "walk me back to my office."

■

"If you feel like taking the printouts," he said, "I have copies." We were standing at the checkstand just inside the front door.

Maybe it implied more of a commitment than I felt like making yet, but I didn't want to insult him, so I tucked the two sheets into my purse while he helped me into my jacket. Outside, the lunchtime crowds were still swarming but the street's enthusiasm had waned. It was colder and darker. People looked guarded. Umbrellas were materializing. I needed one. Stupid to have worn suede. My jogged-out right knee twinged. My boot heels clicked on the sidewalk. My purse was tight under my arm.

Harry put up his collar and loped alongside me, taking long strides, bouncing a little, swinging his arms while keeping his shoulders steady—walking black, I thought. I kept my head down, to avoid autograph hounds. Wherever you looked, there were big shots abusing power or small shots courting it. A stubble-bearded man sitting in front of a topless bar lifted his chin from his chest as Harry went by. The cardboard sign around his neck said: I WILL WORK FOR FOOD. GOD BLESS YOU. Afterthoughts were seeping into my mind, time-released.

A man carrying a sleek attaché case barged toward us. I grabbed Harry's arm and yanked him a step left, out of the way.

"*Watch* it," attaché case said.

Harry stopped, spun around, glared.

"Who would be following you?" I asked.

He shrugged. "You tell me."

We resumed walking. "Who else knows about the speed? Besides Minasian and Taub?"

"Taub doesn't know. Yet. As a favor to me, Peter's holding off telling him."

"So we have a chance to break the story." Feeling foolish again for blurting out the obvious.

"Exactly. Taub is apparently not the easiest guy to work for, or the most generous. Peter doesn't feel like doing him favors."

"So I don't see who else would know you're interested besides Rosenthal and Parenti. And she doesn't get around much."

"And, in fact, Rosenthal didn't seem that interested himself."

"So what makes you think you're being followed?"

"Just some guy in a blue coat walking behind me this morning. I stopped to buy a paper, took it into a coffee shop, and read for, I don't know, half an hour. The blue coat was waiting across the street when I left. I'd swear I saw him again on Sixth Avenue on my way to meet you."

"See anything else?"

"Not really. It was just an impression. I didn't want to get close enough to study him."

I looked over my shoulder and saw no blue coats. We stopped for a DONT WALK sign, in a cloud of unspecifiable meat odor. Cabs lunged through the intersection. A messenger on a bicycle grinned, called out, "Hey, babe!" and I scrambled a step back. Harry held my elbow, delicately. I'm all right, I said, fine. Protectiveness looked good on him. The next second, I thought I saw him wince—some fear working in him, or else he was embarrassed to ask me favors.

It probably wouldn't have helped him to know that I was accustomed to being in this position—to grant favors, but more likely to disappoint my old friends when they popped out of the woodwork with hope in their eyes and facts about child porn in the Philippines, torture in Guatemala, clitoridectomy in Somalia, infant mortality in Harlem, and other atrocities outside my franchise. I disappointed them, pitied them, and hated myself for both feelings. How could they know that a second-magnitude star is a slave of flash-and-trash? Sure, I had a following, medium bucks, minor clout, the privilege of producing my own stuff—whatever I could smuggle into the *In Depth* format, deep as a dime. To them, I amounted to access to the great satellite in the sky where the society tells itself stories. Civilians had no idea what I went through for my privilege, nor could I expect them to pity me. Burke smirking. Terrific, he says, welcome to the wonderful unwatchable world of public television. This piece sounds good for you, like cough syrup. This is a rating the size of my shoe . . .

Dirty secret time: I also got off doing Billy Neill, a doll's house, and the disease of the week. Something I couldn't expect Harry Kramer to understand.

"Look, I'm trying to imagine how to sell geriatric talking heads to an action freak whose idea of a good story is whether there's sex after death. So I have to ask you the dumb questions I'm going to be asked."

"Ask."

"Why not go to the police?" Oh, in the days of *Eight Million Stories*, at the bright dawn of a new nonexistent age, in the light cast by the bonfires of Richard Nixon and John Mitchell and the blaze of Chicago guns tearing apart Fred Hampton's walls, I wouldn't have had to ask.

"Not the reason you think, my dear. Practical reasons. The cops will only drag their feet and fuck up. They've got too many murders lying around with the blood still damp, relatives breathing down their necks, reporters nagging. You know reporters. Why should the cops get worked up about something that happened more than a minute and a half ago?"

Ditto for *In Depth*, I thought. The light changed and the crowd pressed behind me. I felt the pressure of Harry's arm against my shoulder. A comfort in the crowd, a contact. I glanced at him, striding alongside, expectant. I cast about for irresistible arguments. Take an absolute flier, Burke, on the strength of a printout and my say-so. Go ahead, tie up a crew on the crime of the century.

"Don't bet I can sell this," I said, "and even if I can, I doubt Mr. McShane is going to support you in the manner to which you're accustomed."

"I care less about that than about getting the story out."

"You sound like you mean that."

"I have a fellowship called unproduced screenplays." He pursed his lips. "I'm like a farmer paid not to produce. And I have rent control. A couple of weeks at network scale would feed me for longer than you can imagine."

"Too bad you're not a former Secretary of State with a tragic sense of life that comes from once having ruled the world. You'd be on retainer for life. Sir Colin would feature you at all his dinner parties for rehabilitated war criminals."

"So, what is my kind of has-been worth on the not-so-open market with a story that's a historical knockout?"

"Have to find out. For my boss, history started at Woodstock. But I'll try."

He flashed pure delight, a trace of little boy. "Margo. Working with you is going to be a pleasure."

In that late-October chill, I warmed. A world in which Einstein could be murdered was a world in which, who knew, love might exist, or at least animal sex might amount to something more than Blond Bart or the threat of contagious death. For the moment, wouldn't it be a kick to be, at last, the accomplished woman who didn't have to wait in line for Harry Kramer? On the third or fourth hand, would that make me anything more than the current front-runner in a very long line?

And then I wondered what to make of the absence of a ring on his finger.

We'd just laid eyes on each other after two and a half decades, and outlandish thoughts were barging into me like sidewalk traffic.

The sky was wholly leaden now, the air cold. We continued chastely toward Sixth Avenue, where we clustered at a light. Next thing I felt was a shove at my left shoulder, a pressure, and something snapped—not my shoulder, but my purse strap. Urban instincts clicked in. Clutching the purse to my body with my elbow, I swung my right hand and grabbed at whatever, whoever, was grabbing at the purse. I had the impression of blue cloth grappling with me until I yelled, whereupon he let go, and the centrifugal force flung me into Harry. The red leather strap dangled helplessly, but the purse was miraculously intact in my hand. A blue blur moved through the crowd like a ripple through wheat. *I'm fine, Harry.* He took off after the blur, yelling ridiculously, *Stop, thief!*, people melting out of his path, some looking up, bewildered, one or two amused, thinking this was a TV reality show. A young man, misunderstanding, dashed after Harry. I watched Harry's head bob. Then the man in blue disappeared down a subway entrance. Harry was a good ten or fifteen yards behind when I lost sight of them both.

People huddled around me. *Are you all right? Yes, thanks very much. You're so lucky. Yes, I'm so lucky.*

I stood there in tears, feeling like an idiot.

Small buzzes of recognition, *Isn't that . . . ?*

The surgical use of a knife on a purse strap was an Italian technique. *In Depth* had done a piece on the dangers of tourism in Rome and Sicily. Seemed only right, my purse being Florentine.

I leaned on a wobbly trash basket and stared at the severed strap. I had lived in New York all my life and never been mugged, never been purse-snatched. The odds had caught up with me, I noted, on a day when my purse contained a chemical report on Einstein's brain. Deposited there by yours truly in full view of Happening's glass door.

All events are connected, right?

I pulled out a handkerchief and dabbed at my eyes. The crowd edged around me as if I were an accident.

After a while, a short man in a black leather jacket brought Harry up by the arm.

"Great work, officer, but you have the wrong guy," I said.

Harry explained to the cop that the thief had swooped over the turnstile, jumped onto a train, vanished into the bowels of the city. The cop studied Harry's face, then mine.

"Valuables in your purse?" the cop asked.

"The usual. Credit cards, cash."

"You got off lucky," the cop said, studying my face. "Aren't you Margo Ross?"

■

I installed Harry in my office and trotted downstairs to the editing room. Yolanda was running the Billy Neill cassettes. "We have to pass through an ego-death, you know," Billy was saying. Yolanda stopped the tape. "What happened?" I told her about the attempt on my purse, not about its contents. "I'm coming along just fine," she said. "You go take care of yourself." I walked down the hall to the bathroom, my wounded purse under my arm. There I redid my eyes, arranged my face to look resolute, and told myself, Margo Ross, you are furious but you are going to transmute your fury into intelligence. Burke Gilman was going to let me do the Einstein piece or I was going to walk the gangplank. Threaten to walk, anyway. I took the elevator upstairs, rehearsing my pitch.

When I was in high school, not long before my father got sick, he sat me down in his armchair, sat himself down on the footstool, and twinkled at me: Whenever you have to ask anyone for anything, imagine you own the place. But be gracious—let him think he's the one in charge. That was the day I acquired my interview technique—make the guest feel like the host; then, when he's settling in, nail him. As at that cocktail party where I met Dan Slotkin, Burke's predecessor, and chatted him up with Watergate theories punctuated by Nixon suck/fuck jokes and reminiscences of my early seventies life as a failed documentary filmmaker. The first surprise was that Slotkin returned my call the next day; the second was that he found a job for me as an assistant, meaning a gofer, but a high-class gofer pulling down fourteen thousand a year coming up with ideas for an executive lush who pulled down five or six times as much, not counting his daily solid and liquid lunch tabs.

The moment I walked into Burke's office, I saw on his wall, as if for the first time, the poster of Dr. Einstein, gloriously carefree, on his bicycle: his monumental head, his bulging beautiful-sad eyes, his halo of white hair. God's prince, as Harry had said.

"What's the problem?" Burke said, rocking in his padded cream-colored leather throne, tossing a ball of blue modeling clay up and down. To get past his secretary, whose name was Tiffany and who looked it, I'd had to blurt out the word *emergency.*

"I never realized you were an Einstein fan."

"As usual, you underestimate your boss. I *love* Einstein. A very unique individual. Bright! A guy who lived for something. I know you don't think of me as a guy who cares . . ."

"Burke . . ."

". . . But there it is. So what else can I tell you?"

He molded his ball of clay into a rope, doubled it over, squeezed, and stretched it again. I told myself that there was nothing to fear from a man who plays with clay.

He felt me watching. "I know, I know," he boomed, "but clay is safer than sex," and he laughed. In the country of the sound bite, the one-liner is king.

I had to laugh, too. And then I was rolling, pacing, pumping adrenaline, rapping about Einstein's brain, the lab, the speed, the nurse—everything but Harry. Burke stopped working his clay.

When I was done, I pulled the printout from my purse, smoothed it out on his desk, walked him through it.

If I could hook Burke Gilman, whose attention span was shorter than his name, I knew I could shoot this crazy story under the skin of any audience in the world, could tell them what they long to hear, night after night: *There is evil in the world, and lucky you, we're going to let you in on the secret.*

Burke said, "Holy shit." Just that. Burke thinks if you can get a "Holy shit" out of him you can get it out of anybody—thirty million anybodies, in fact, fingertips poised on their remotes.

He took hold of the edge of his desk and rocked his chair. "Now suppose, for the sake of argument, that somebody in Iowa might care about this. Tell me why I should believe you. Aside from the fact that you intimidate the shit out of me and could probably do the same to a witness who's been dead forty years." He started drumming on the desk as if in code.

Reach for the sky. "You should believe me because there are two other people who take this story incredibly seriously. One is my source. The other has gone to the trouble of following my source, and doing this to me." I slapped my purse down on his desk and exhibited the strap.

"Say more."

"This person apparently cares a great deal about what my source knows, which I now know, and which the viewers of *In Depth* could know soon."

"Slow down, go through this again."

I did.

"Who's this fabulous source?"

I told him.

"Not the novelist," he said.

"Yes the novelist. Also journalist, investigator . . ." When you were still watching *Mister Rogers' Neighborhood*.

"Jesus. I mean, *Fix* is a great book, but—" Burke was just old enough to remember the last days of the Harry Kramer cult.

"Well, do you think he just made that stuff up?" I told him the story so far was Harry's accomplishment.

He squinted into the corners of the printouts. "I don't know about you, but I don't see any copyright bug. Let's see what the corporation counsel has to say." He reached for his phone.

"Burke, Kramer comes with the story. He's done the groundwork. He knows who's who, he knows motives.

He's talked to the nurse. He's a consultant or this story is deader than the whales off Staten Island."

Burke stopped drumming on his desk and started twiddling his fingers on his paisley tie. "I don't imagine the guy's ever worked in television."

A decided advantage, but I didn't say that. Instead, I said that no one knew the channels of power, or cover-ups, like Harry Kramer. "I need the help," I threw in. "Remember, I need time to do justice to Billy Neill." What I didn't say was that Yolanda was going to take care of the edit on Billy Neill.

Burke looked at me for about four hours.

"I take it Harry Kramer's a great good friend of yours from your hippie Commie days, which has nothing to do with your unorthodox proposal."

I glared back. "And Con Comm would never be caught hiring McShane's cronies to advise and consent, would it? Madeleine Strong doesn't keep the birthdays of her celebrity chums on her Rolodex, for elaborate floral arrangements, does she?"

"Cute. If this story doesn't pan out, it's you, not me, that gets hung out to dry."

"Lots of stories don't pan out," I said. "So what?"

Behind his straight face, what was he calculating? The odds that, if we did this piece, Tim Craven of the *Times* would address him with sudden respect? Versus the odds on Sir Colin McShane's wrath if he squandered thousands in pirate booty chasing Albert Einstein's killer? Computing pounds of flesh he might exact from me? But Burke Gilman did not acquire his canyon view by being scrutable.

"The Neill piece comes first."

"Trust me, Burke"—demurely.

His eyes dropped to inspect the rise of my breasts. Burke was one of those men who are not repelled by a streak of white in a woman's hair, or by crow's-feet, or even by the effects of too many decades of gravity. All that seemed to matter was the rise and fall, mother's milk, life's fullness. A lot of what passed for men's power was pure dependency. They were as strong and free as goldfish watching flakes of food drift through the fish tank.

I was waiting for Burke's eyes to drift back up from my torso. I knew I had him, he knew he was had. He squashed his ball of blue clay against his desk, and pushed himself up. "Start on it, champ," he said. "Your Mr. Kramer is on for two weeks. After that, week to week. We have his services exclusively. He reports to you. He's not to represent himself as a member of this organization. You're responsible."

"Oui, mon commandant." I saluted smartly.

"And you report to me. Frequently."

I beamed.

"Tell your long-lost friend to come see me about his fee. Shit, I've got meetings all afternoon—tell him, tell him, wait a minute"—he produced a series of squeaks on his electronic diary—"I'll have Tiffany call down to your office. And you're done with Neill when?"

"Wednesday, boss."

"Lovely." He gazed over my shoulder in the direction of the benign, leonine head of Albert Einstein. "In the meantime, nobody else in this building knows a thing, you hear me? Nobody. Not Yolanda, not Tiffany, none of your friendly colleagues, nobody. You're on special assignment. You don't need to know the reasons. You have a need not to know what goes on in this building. Trust me."

I couldn't read the code. Something was up with McShane. Rumors had been circulating around the building like the common cold: he was buying out Cable News, or selling off the film division to the Australians, or what? Starting a new line of products: Deep, the perfume? Or maybe Burke saw my Einstein piece as a move in his own game. This wouldn't be the first time news had to whore around to hold on to airtime.

"Don't tell your shrink either," he said with a wink.

"There is no shrink." Not now. I was on extended leave, there being not enough hours in the week for me to weep my reservoir of stored-up tears all over the ancient leather armchair of Dr. Yes.

"And I don't have to tell you, no police." He squeezed the clay in his hand. "Get out of here before I change my mind."

■

"Congratulations," I said to Harry. "You are a network consultant for at least two weeks at a salary to be announced."

"Terrific." He jounced across my office and delivered a full-body hug. There was an aroma of sweat, left over from his hot pursuit on the street. He pulled away, as if retreating to some cave inside himself, then pleaded an urgent errand. Half an hour later he returned looking triumphant, with a shopping bag from which he extracted a box wrapped in silver paper, tied in thick red ribbon with a bow. Inside was a small handbag, diagonal black-and-red stripes in soft leather, *hommage* to the kind of sack a Depression kid might have run away from home with. And a strap that hadn't been severed. My turn to hug Harry, and this time he didn't retreat.

"The least an employed guy could do," he said.

I left him at my desk—he needed to start setting up interviews—and went back to the editing room, where Yolanda was calmly at work screening footage, numbering sequences, scribbling notes. My idea had been to start with stock footage, the grainier the better: Billy Neill in stubble and tiny round glasses, Billy French-kissing for the cameras on his wedding day, Billy in granny-glass shades stoned on tour, his pet monkey cavorting across the stage, Billy grim-eyed at his child-custody hearing. Then, boom, to Billy today, all in black, double earrings, sitting under his photogenic cypress overlooking the Pacific. Soulful looks, hollow eyes, regrets about drugs, resolute sentences about the end of the world.

"Why don't we start with today," Yolanda said, "establish that Billy's cooled out, you know, then go back to when he was hot, use the stock footage there, whiteouts between the segments, know what I mean? Then, when we come back to the present, we have an idea of what he had to cool out from—and the audience thinks, well, look at that, there's Billy, all laid back. Then we hit them with Billy Null, he's upside your head with the bomb. Then bam, get out." She was right.

The piece would be as perfect as Yolanda's tight black suit. On the strength of Billy Neill demographics—baby boomers soaked in nostalgia, plus their curious children soaked, for some reason, in same—Sir Colin McShane would be able to buy himself the department store that imported that suit from Shanghai. WE TAKE IN THE WORLD.

Embers of heartburn still glowing in my chest.

"Rosenthal's on for nine in the morning," Harry said

with a lilt as I walked back into my office. He was just putting down the phone, which immediately trilled.

"Margo Ross," I said into the receiver.

"Pay attention, Margo."

"Who is this?"

"Listen. This story you're working on." A New York accent—Mahgo, stawry. A hoarse phony whisper straight out of a bad B movie. "Drop it. Forget Einstein or you're brain-dead."

"Come on . . ." I said, motioning frantically to Harry.

"You heard me," the voice went on. "Drop it. I'm not gonna tell you again."

Harry's ear was alongside mine. "Who is this?" I said. Click. "Hello, hello"—knowing it was futile.

My hands were shaking. Harry held them. They were icy, same as when I'd gotten a chain of obscene calls a couple of years back, which had led to my masculine phone message, ditto police protection. This time I wasn't going to call the police, and a new message on the machine wouldn't help.

"Don't worry," I said. "I can control myself." Damned if I was going to fall apart.

I tossed myself onto the sofa. Harry loped across the room and stood looking down at me, wondering how much intimacy to offer.

When the phone trilled again, I jumped a little, let it ring seven, eight, nine, ten times, till it stopped. I said to Harry, "I'm a reporter, I'm supposed to be used to bad guys. You're supposed to tell me not to take this seriously."

He wasn't laughing. "I'm not the one to say that. I dragged you into this."

"Uh-huh, this is all your fault. But, for all we know, my sticking the printouts into my purse in sight of the street isn't connected to blue coat trying to rip off my purse, right? Maybe this is my day for coincidences."

"Sure"—running his hand back over his forehead, his eyes full of something that looked like remorse. I wanted to take this big, decent man home and tuck him under the covers. And then that flicker in his eyes as he ducked into his cave where, I thought, his remorse must live—some deep knowledge that he could never do enough for the world, never go back in time to save Einstein, never protect me, or anyone, one hundred percent. So much responsibility was a lot to be responsible to. I didn't know if I wanted to be under the covers with him.

"And then again," I said, "maybe I'm the Queen of Bulgaria."

He cleared his throat. "Even if you are, awkward as this may sound, I don't think you should be alone tonight."

I needed care, no question about it. I hadn't slept in my own bed in three nights. What I needed most in the world was my own bed.

I walked out the door and told Cyrilly, the secretary I share, to keep a record of all calls and refer nothing, no matter how innocent-sounding, to me without checking first. I reminded her never to give out my home number or address. I told her to tell the switchboard the same, and, on second thought, the personnel office. Then I led Harry clattering one flight down the stairs, with their brass banisters, their pink stone granite walls—all praise to you, Sir Colin!—to the fluorescent corridor of editing rooms. I asked Yolanda to keep a record of any calls. "Everything's cool. You have a good time," Yolanda said, producing dimples. "Thanks," I said, "but it's not about having a good time."

We went down to the basement, through an unmarked door, to the end of a corridor, through a room humming with furnaces. The heavy steel door at the other end led into Rockefeller Plaza. The leaden sky, underlit with reflections of the electrified city, was eking out a drizzle. This was the sort of rain that would cleanse nothing. By the time I thought to take off my jacket and turn the lining outward, it was already ruined. Two women clicked by on stiletto heels. A Japanese businessman with a tiny umbrella was pointing out to another the satellite dish on the roof. I touched Harry's arm and steered him toward Fifty-fourth Street.

Instantly, a cab hurtled by and stopped. I told the driver — René Lavoise, his license said — to head over to Fifth. He was listening to the news: "You give us twenty-two minutes, we give you the world." An urgency theme. A report about an emergency meeting of top Russian officials. René Lavoise punched a button. A low buzz of crowd noise. Precisely as the announcer shouted "Touchdown!" so did René Lavoise. He turned south on Fifth, found a block-long opening in the bus lane, and — the light already turning red — accelerated, pressing us back against the slashed seat cushion, braking hard at the light, with an air of innocence, as if stunned that the signal had just that minute reared up to stop him. A plastic statue of a blond Mary shimmied from his rearview mirror. "Come *on!*" said René Lavoise. If *In Depth* was worth anything, I thought, this guy was a natural for a profile. We should be on our way to

Port-au-Prince to interview his mother. I should be giving René Lavoise his fifteen minutes, showing that the same thing makes him and Sammy run.

A huge white mushroom cloud glassed into a bus-stop shelter. Diagonally across it: WE BLOW THE COMPETITION OUT OF THE WATER. This was the beer ad of the moment. OUTRAGEOUS printed onto the corner in great crude brushstrokes. Pre-graffito'd billboards. Keep command of stray reactions. Stay tuned.

I rested my head against Harry's shoulder, bulky and lovely, and closed my eyes. During the scant minutes it took René Lavoise to slide and swoop to the Village, I almost dozed. In that half haze, I knew that I wanted to sleep more than I wanted to sleep with Harry.

In my apartment, Harry laid his overcoat delicately over the beanbag chair. He scrutinized the six-foot sheet-iron man who hangs on the wall facing my bedroom door. The man gazed back, his carved-out grimace of a mouth caught in mid-yawn. I left him to the living-room couch and a pile of linens, and then, in my own bedroom, next to the ragged foot-high frog of my childhood, under my comforter, I took shelter.

TUESDAY, OCTOBER 23

I SHUDDERED AWAKE, MY CHEST HEAVING. THE SHEETS, yanked loose, were twisted like ropes. The blinds were down, the room almost black, tires swishing down the street. I clutched at the tatters of my dream, but lost them. The alarm clock, set for six-thirty, read six-sixteen.

I staggered out of bed, hauled on my bathrobe and the sheepskin slippers I'd bought myself in California, and lurched into the living room. Harry was still asleep, rolled on his side, with a sweet expression, like an unshaven cherub. His pants, folded just off the fading crease, lay on the floor.

I trudged to the bathroom, rinsed my eyes, inserted my contact lenses. Three white hairs stared at me from the mirror—my ghost, accusing me. I yanked them out at the roots and ferociously combed the rest of my hair. In the tenth grade, a friend and I extracted a few hairs from our heads to put under the microscope. Each minuscule bit of flesh ripped away with the hair looked like the jagged aftermath of a scalping. I did a report comparing the hairs from our two heads, and the teacher wrote back: You have a gift for curiosity that I hope gets noticed around here. Don't let them talk you out of it.

I dabbed perfume at strategic sites and tiptoed across the living room, between the beanbag chairs, into my cubicle of a kitchen. Harry threw his arm across his eyes, grumbled, slumped back into immobility. I put up a pot of water, filled the coffee grinder with beans, and turned it on. When I heard another sound, I swiveled. Harry was blinking at me.

"What time?" he asked. I told him. He shook himself like a wet duck, slogged into the bathroom. I yelled, "Use the new toothbrush in the cabinet." I put out coffee cups and nonfat milk, popped two frozen bagels in the toaster oven. The sound of water gurgling in the bathroom was oddly soothing.

"Here's an embarrassing question," Harry said a few minutes later from the open bathroom door. Morning had turned his voice to bass. Morning timbre, a pleasing attribute of the male race when you wake up and find them swarming all over your nest.

"Who does it embarrass?" Thinking *Whom*, but who cares?

He thought about that. "That's too complicated a question. You don't happen to have any men's shirts—"

I rummaged through my closet and found in a far corner a pale yellow men's business shirt I didn't recognize. The color dated it ten, fifteen years at least. I remembered some spurious and ephemeral comfort, but not the name of the donor. I tossed the shirt to Harry, who snatched it out of the air.

"You must be right," he said with a glint at the breakfast table.

"What?"

"There are no coincidences. Now tell me why you sound so weighed down by your enviable position at one of capitalism's communication hubs."

I complained for fifteen minutes about life in the shallows of *In Depth*, trailing after the whims of Burke Gilman. He listened patiently. At the end, when he reminded me that I now had a splendid opportunity to use my exalted position to expose the assassination of the best man in a terrible century, I felt I'd been a virtual ingrate to gripe.

■

The rain had stopped, but the pavement was still damp. The street lamps produced eerie smudges of brightness, as in a Magritte painting. A jogger in a gray sweatshirt and Spandex pants pounded along the street, looking pained. The man in the crate was not to be seen. Between his slats, slivers of bright blue—a tarp for waterproofing. In an alcove between the crate and the entrance to my building, in fetal position, another man lay asleep—at least I hoped he was asleep. He wore a long khaki overcoat, his shoes lacked laces, his soles were peeling loose from his uppers, the tongues swollen, as if the shoes were starving to death. Why did this man choose this block? Did the man in the crate invite him? Was this a pleasant block from the homeless point of view? Viewer, do not expect to find answers to these questions on *In Depth*.

I deposited a dollar next to the head of the man in the alcove. A toll for living. The day was barely beginning. The light comes up halfhearted. On the other side of the long tunnel to Jersey, the train slides between factories so dilapidated you can't tell whether they've been abandoned or not. The compartment is full of men in commuting suits attending to the *Times* and *The Wall Street Journal.* Harry is slumped in the window seat, scowling.

"Am I mistaken," I ask, "or are you harboring harsh thoughts about the human condition?"

The brooding privileges of men.

"No," he says, taking his own sweet time, "thinking how to put things to Rosenthal."

The train finds its rhythm: *ka-chuck, ka-chuck.*

"Before we meet Rosenthal for this interview I'm theoretically supposed to be conducting," I say, "may I have a hint or two as to why anyone on earth would care to murder Albert Einstein?"

He seems taken aback by my tone. His look says: You really have grown up, I'm impressed. "O.K., there were three things Einstein was working on when he died, two political, one scientific. One." He deploys an index finger. "He had just signed an open letter initiated by Bertrand Russell, calling on the Great Powers to renounce war because the next world war would be thermonuclear. Einstein and Russell had been corresponding about this for months. Einstein proposed that a conference of scientists from East and West should convene to discuss what they could do about the H-bomb. He wrote to Russell on April 11."

"Two days before his attack, right?"

"Exactly. That letter led to regular meetings of American and Russian scientists for the first time since World War II. That was one thing."

"Mighty subversive."

Harry wags his finger half-teasingly. "Don't underestimate 1955. The world's most famous pacifist Jew scientist is setting up a leisurely chat with Commie physicists! You have to appreciate the political mood. The country is in a panic. You can't find a map in a magazine that doesn't show red oozing across the Russian border onto the so-called Free World. The Russians set off their first H-bomb. The Americans proceed to pulverize an island with their own dandy little achievement in modern physics. McCarthy is past his prime, but that's only because McCarthyism can get along without him. Einstein's colleague Oppenheimer has his security clearance lifted. He's been blamed for delaying our H-bomb. Meanwhile, Eisenhower's preparing to rearm the Germans. Einstein's furious about that. Einstein's an old man and he hears the world ticking. His letters are grim. Do you know what his last recorded words are?"

"Can't say that I do."

"On his deathbed, mind you, he tells Otto Nathan that it's reckless to arm the Germans, and that he's worried about the dreadful state of civil liberties in the U.S. So he's not only traumatized, he's mobilized. In his own way, he's a militant. There's no secret about this in 1955."

I'm scribbling notes as I say, "So you're suggesting some right-wing cabal finds out about his letter to Russell and decides to stop him. The CIA, or a secret sub-government, spies in the post office."

A slight smile blows through Harry's features. "Nothing so fancy, necessarily. Einstein's general views about dis-

armament are well known. He's been on the FBI's shit list
for a long time. The killer doesn't have to know about his
correspondence with Russell. I'm just asking you to keep
the possibility in the back of your mind. Just for a minute.
Savor it." The train clunks along, relentlessly. I make notes
for a hypothetical sequence of 1955 stills: *I Love Lucy*, Ike's
smile, a mushroom cloud, *Life* goes to a "take cover" drill.
After each shot, go to black. A monotone rumble for a
sense of dread. Hold the rumble.

"Think about 1955. Millions of people believe that indi-
viduals change the world. A wonderful paradox: Herds of
paranoids think that it took Julius and Ethel Rosenberg to
give the Russians the atomic bomb, it took Alger Hiss and
a few guys in the State Department to lose China. Touch-
ing, really, this faith in the lone individual, and it isn't all
wrong. You don't have to be paranoid to think that Oppenheimer changed history, or Teller with the H-bomb, or
Einstein with $E = mc^2$."

"So you're saying that somebody might be inflamed to
murder by the thought of a Jewish pacifist—"

"Hypothetically."

"—citizen of the world—"

"Possible is all I'm saying. Facts are scarce, so we play
possibilities. Possibility one: Somebody doesn't like the
world's most famous ban-the-bomber. Now. Two." Harry's
second finger goes up. No ring, I can't help but notice
again. "Einstein's also got a hand in the Middle East. Not
bad for an ailing old man, no? The Israelis, mind you, want
him to make a statement on the anniversary of the founding
of the state. They want him to compliment them for their
scientific accomplishments, especially quote the peaceful
use of the atom unquote."

"Atoms for peace. Dividends for mass murder." My old peacenik instincts are gathering. Harry brings this out in me.

"Exactly. But Einstein doesn't get pushed around. He cares about the survival of Israel but, or therefore, he wants Israel to be neutral in the Cold War. He wants equality for the Arabs. He hates nationalism on both sides. He's also worried that Eisenhower, the imperialist—that's his word!—Eisenhower is going to sell out Israel to make Arab friends, meaning oil. He writes to the Israeli consul and says boosterism doesn't interest him, he wants to speak his mind. He wants Israeli officials to come and consult with him. He says that he doesn't want to lose—and again these are his words—'precious time.' Precious time!"

"Sounds like he knows he doesn't have long."

"Doesn't it? So, on April 11, up from Washington comes the ambassador, Abba Eban, and down from New York comes the consul. The three of them talk. The consul comes back on the thirteenth and they talk again. Einstein starts drafting a speech for broadcast. He finishes one page, a preamble. He says—listen to this—" Harry reaches into his jacket pocket, finds nothing, looks puzzled, then reaches into his side pocket, pulls out a sheet of paper, and unfolds it. "He says the Israel–Egypt problem is inseparable from the big problem, which is—it's in German, of course, but in English it reads: 'the division of mankind into two hostile camps: the Communist World and the so-called Free World.' And then: 'Not one statesman in a position of responsibility has dared to pursue the only course that holds out any promise of peace, the course of supranational security, since for a statesman to follow such a course would be tantamount to political suicide. Political passions, once they

have been fanned into flame, exact their victims . . .'
That's where he trails off. The last words he put on paper,
so far as we know."

I take the paper from Harry and read the passage over.
Blunt words. Nothing ornate about Einstein. Death is the
full stop that completes the sentence. I reread the words. I
am developing an intimate feeling about the old man, as if I
were rummaging through his dusty trunk. Across the aisle
and one seat in front of us, a gray-haired man is under-
lining passages in the Bible with a small ruler.

Harry tucks the paper back into his pocket.

"When Einstein gets to the hospital that Friday, he tells
his nurses and his stepdaughter that he simply has to finish
writing this speech. On Saturday, when he feels better, he
sends for his notes, paper, pen, glasses. This draft was at
his bedside when he died."

I stare out the window at the clumps of bare trees hur-
tling toward us, the chill of the Jersey flatlands within me.
"Whatever happened to nineteenth-century dignity?" I
ask. "Imagine a feeling of obligation to finish a piece of
writing on your deathbed . . . A vanished species. Instead of wise men, we have wise guys."

Harry charges on. "So what is Einstein going to tell the
world about the Middle East? Probably three things: one,
that the Israelis are arrogant; two, that the Americans can't
think straight because of the Cold War and Arab oil; three,
everyone wants war. Which the Suez invasion is about to
prove."

"You're subtly intimating that somebody might want to
stop this speech."

"Who wouldn't? Israeli adventurists, Arab apologists,
Cold Warriors. Take your pick. A lot of people besides

Einstein think this speech matters. It was rumored later that there was another page of notes which disappeared from the hospital after he died. The Israeli consulate went to the trouble of planting a so-called reconstruction in the *Times* a few weeks later, claiming it was based on their conversations."

I make a face. "It's a stretch."

"And if I told you that someday a Palestinian with two identical names was going to blow Bobby Kennedy's brains out for supporting Israel?"

"That was later, Harry, when everything came unstuck. Einstein wasn't running for President."

"Speed plus brain equals murder. Material reality. Maybe to get a farfetched effect you need a farfetched cause. Understand, I'm thinking out loud."

The train eases into Newark. A middle-aged black woman wearing a veil and a black pillbox hat stretches overhead for her shopping bag, unsuccessfully. She has round cheeks and looks as though she's been crying. A young black man in a slick black leather jacket lifts the bag down for her; she thanks him effusively, then her face collapses again. Passengers leave, others get on. The sheer profusion of errands and purposes in the world. They go to their funerals and buy their baby clothes, I go to interview an old mathematician.

I lower my voice. "You said there's something else Einstein was working on?"

"Right, the science, but—" He trails off.

"Come on, give. I know a guy in homicide who says that the clues to almost every murder can be found in the victim's last twenty-four hours on this earth. All of them."

"Know your victim. Good. Project number three was his

grand passion in physics. Imagine: For thirty-plus years Einstein had been out on a limb, theoretically speaking, with nobody else to blame, because he'd crawled out there himself. First he helped usher in the quantum theory and now—"

Serves me right for asking. "Slow down, Harry. You could take what I know about physics, fit it into a thimble, and still have room left for Colin McShane's heart."

He squirts a grin at me, like a flashbulb popping. The train slides out of the Newark station. "In the twenties," Harry says slowly, as if picking his way across thin ice, "most physicists became convinced that there were important things that were never going to be known. Like the position of a particle and its velocity at the same time." He touches index finger to sleeve. "Say my fingernail here is a particle. If you know where it is at this precise moment, then you can't know"—jerking his finger across the cloth— "exactly how fast it's going. And vice versa. That's Heisenberg's uncertainty principle—"

At least this is something I've heard of.

"—which means that if you're talking about particles, the only conclusions you can come to are statistical. Like, the odds of this particle being in this spot at this moment are thus-and-such, or, on average you can find so many molecules in this cubic meter. But you can never say definitively whether any particle is just here or somewhere else. Never! It isn't just that your instruments aren't good enough. There's a logical impasse. No instruments can conceivably be good enough. In the very act of measuring, you nudge the particle. So much for progress."

I'd known there was a blockage against progress somewhere in the universe, but hadn't realized where, exactly, it was.

"Are you with me?"

"Enough. Go on."

He ostentatiously slows down further. "Einstein made the point that there were some weird paradoxes as a result."

"Like?"

"Like, is light a particle or a wave? In some respects, a particle—you can nudge one particle loose with another one, the so-called photoelectric effect, Einstein's first big discovery. So if it jumps like a particle and ricochets like a particle, it's a particle, right?"

I'm not going to make a fool of myself.

"But in other ways light behaves like a wave—interference patterns and so on. Niels Bohr said you never deal with reality, only with measurements of reality. When you measure the wave aspect, you lose the particle aspect, and vice versa. This was the so-called complementarity principle. So much for the problem!" Harry wipes his hands in a gesture of dismissal. "As somebody put it, light is a particle on Mondays, Wednesdays, and Fridays, and a wave on Tuesdays, Thursdays, and Saturdays."

"What about Sundays?"

"This was one big fat problem. There were others. But here's the important thing: In the twenties, all the important physicists were won over to quantum mechanics, complementarity, Bohr's interpretation, all that. It explained a lot. But not Dr. Einstein. He refused to believe that God plays dice with the universe—that's how he put it. The idea offended him. He was a rationalist. He believed in the great chain of causation—events cause events, not just on average, not just in a crowd, but one at a time. He was a German, remember, not only a German Jew but a German, and he wanted his universe tidy. So he resolved to spend the rest of his working life on this single project: to rescue the great chain of cause-and-effect by showing how the essential forces in the universe were all hooked up to each other."

"Essential forces?"

Again Harry accelerates. He points into the air, click, click, precise as railroad signals. "Two forces. First, electromagnetism—electricity, radio waves, et cetera. Maxwell had shown that electricity and magnetism were convertible to each other, see, two faces of the same thing, which he called electromagnetism. Second, gravitation. Unfortunately, Einstein didn't take other forces into account. There are short-range forces that operate only within the individual atom—called the strong force and the weak force."

"What's so strong and weak about them?"

He twists his mouth and shrugs. "This passes the limits of my understanding. The key thing is that the old man made a false start on a unified theory, O.K.? If there was going to be any unification—and there are a lot of physicists still looking—it wasn't going to be Einstein who found it. But Einstein was nothing if not unbudgeable. He published his first paper on this project in 1922. He spent the next *thirty-three years*—can you imagine?—thirty-three years fiddling with equations to show that there was basically one field of force, that electromagnetism and gravitation were manifestations of something essential, something deeper."

The pleasure Harry takes in trying to teach me is a pleasure to behold. So is his effort not to condescend. I nod feebly to encourage him. "You mean, like water and ice?" "Mmm, not exactly. Those are two different states of the same molecule . . . Think about, say, more like mass and energy. Part of the relativity theory was that you could start with mass and get energy. That's what it meant to say $E = mc^2$. Now he was staking his reputation to prove that everything was interchangeable. There was going to be one world or Einstein would die trying. If he could only work out the equations, then poof, what quantum theory thought of as chance would be revealed to be an illusion, superficial. Underneath was the real stuff—the field, the God stuff. Technically, he was looking for something called a unified field theory."

"Uh-huh." When you interview experts, look like an apprentice. Big celebrities, you widen your eyes, worshipfully. Small celebrities, banter with them—they like to feel witty. But experts want to feel understood. My eyes widen. I'm doing my best.

"You want me to go on?"

"Absolutely." What kind of a liar do you take me for?

"Well, virtually every physicist in the world thought Einstein was sentimental, or old-fashioned, or dogmatic, or nuts. Sweet old guy rewrote the rules once, but now he'd gone weak in the head looking for God. They said he refused to take account of experimental results. Nobody thought he made sense anymore. Guys like Bohr tried to talk him out of this quirk of his. Which stopped him not in the least. Stubbornness was his middle name." Harry lowers his voice, raises his finger talmudically alongside his nose. "Now I'm getting to the point. Not long before he

died, Einstein told his oldest friend he thought he was close
to that unified field theory. I told you that when he got to
the hospital he sent for the papers he was working on.
There was the Israel speech, of course. There were also
notes on the unified field theory. Calculations."

Experts want to feel understood, producers want to see
pictures. I can't get my mind around a unified field theory,
but a piece of paper in a hospital room is something else.
White or yellow? Lined? Slightly crumpled? Water-
stained? Did Einstein lean on a clipboard, a pad, a magazine, write with a pencil, a ballpoint, or, it being 1955, a
fountain pen? Burke would want a simulation. Over my,
and Einstein's, dead body.

"Doomed from the start." Harry throws up his hands
and deplores Einstein's wasted years. "One of the fattest
red herrings in the history of physics. But you did ask."

The train ticks along past flat fields, bare trees, cramped
marshes of dry grasses. In the bruised light, this is not a
landscape to stop conversation. The conversation has
stopped itself.

I make my way down to the bar car, where I'm alone
with a severely bored bartender. I ask for a plastic cap and
a straw to go with coffee, and buy a $2.50 Space Bar for
Harry because of its name. The coffee tastes like distillation
of Styrofoam. Think about the challenge of producing coffee devoid of the aroma of coffee. Amtrak chemists, whole
armies of specialists . . .

The train rolls through diminutive pine forests. The light
brightens to pale. A heron stands on one leg. At New
Brunswick, everyone who looks displaced, ill at ease, or

tentative gets off. Everyone left appears to be on assignment. Almost entirely men. Three-piece suits, attaché cases, elegant means for transporting documents. Evidently, Princeton is not a place for casual drop-ins. Harry could spend the rest of his days diagramming these people. At the window across the aisle sits a fiftyish man with delicate bones and thick sandy hair, wearing a camel's-hair overcoat thrown open to show a thickly striped purple shirt with blindingly white collar. His long, thin fingers rest on an artfully battered brown briefcase. He is reading Sir John Pope-Hennessey's *Raphael*, a big hardcover, wearing a faint smile that proclaims it might be interesting to look into this. He has an air of never having had to try hard. His fine bones look to be centuries in the manufacture.

I've had enough, thank you, of being impaled on fine bones. Harry you can't call refined. But there's a weight, a gravity that bends my look in his direction. He fills the space around him, and then some, with his intensity. This passion in him to reason out the truth, to find out which bastards are making the world suffer—if he were relieved of this burden, if such a thing were imaginable, would he be free then to bring his energy to a woman? And in that case, would he still be Harry Kramer?

We get off at Princeton Junction, up an embankment to another track, and wait a few minutes for the shuttle to Princeton. The dinky, Harry says it's called—a preppy train, which seems right, a five-minute shuttle on a single track through luxuriant sumac and thick scrub. We pass office buildings whose surfaces are black mirror glass, surfaces that—like Big Glass, like the smooth faces of our fellow passengers—repel all questions.

■

Princeton Station had a village stillness. A small stone
building sedate and unused, like an abandoned ranger station in the wilderness. Bicycles chained to a wood fence.
Newspaper racks reporting that outer worlds exist. Flyers
for a forthcoming performance of Beethoven's Missa
Solemnis, a concert by Leonard Cohen. Another: WHERE
CAN I GET A FUTON IN PRINCETON? which proceeded to answer the question.

A couple of older students waited for the dinky's return
trip: a tall woman wearing a black slicker, hair as black as
her coat, smiling with a distracted intensity; a black man,
steel-rimmed spectacles, attaché case equipped with a combination lock, *The Wall Street Journal.* A kind of hush sur-
rounded them. Whoever we, the passengers, were, *they*
would always be Princeton Class of 1990-something. They
would spend their lives cultivating their air of exemption.

Myself, I was Barnard '70 and had spent much of my life
unimpressed by my own exemption. Dr. Yes had heard
several hundred hours on this subject.

Harry tossed his head and smirked. "The assurance old
money will buy."

"Carriage. Like horses."

"They have no doubt they belong. Place cards are issued
at birth. They're in training to preside. Outsiders don't own
them."

"I've always wanted to be self-possessed," I said.

"What makes you think you haven't succeeded?"

The man carrying *Raphael* brushed past me, excused
himself, and walked briskly toward a parked van marked
INSTITUTE FOR ADVANCED STUDY. I felt for my purse, which
hung reassuringly on my shoulder.

Princeton, a prince's town, where Einstein rested his exiled bones.

■

A blond cab driver in a cardigan and a tie was waiting at the curb, studying the sports section of *USA Today*. Not even a bulletproof plastic divider to shield the driver from lunatic passengers. Harry gave him Franz Rosenthal's address.

All towns, at first glance, look happy. The older, the happier. Princeton's stone positively beamed. From the cab, climbing a small rise, I could see through Gothic arches to green quadrangles, crenellated towers. Privilege has its privileges, but Princeton laid it on thick.

The cabbie was studying my face in the rearview mirror, wondering whether I was or wasn't who he suspected I was. People smile at me in restaurants, even let me cut into line to get to a pay phone—I might, after all, be on assignment. What they see is someone worth looking at. I rub off on them; and they honor me in return, even the wretched ones who barge up to me on the street and insist on telling me their horror stories. Hospitals, landlords. Well, who else are they supposed to petition for redress? My face is my shingle, I'm an advocate, even—for all they know—a judge at the proverbial court of public opinion. The day I went on the air I forfeited the right to be left alone.

The cab stopped at a red light, then turned hard left on a diagonal. There wasn't much traffic on streets or sidewalks. I saw wood frames, lawns, leaves raked into neat piles. Shades of Dick and Jane, the milkman carrying his wire holder of glass bottles onto the porch, bottles clinking. Easy to picture a shoot from a slow-moving car, with an authoritative voiceover: "Princeton, a town where even the squirrels seem well-mannered . . ." Harry pointed at a street sign: "This is where Einstein used to walk. People gawked at him. Somebody ran into a tree once." On the left, across an expanse of closely mown lawn, a lot of instructional-looking pinkish brick crowned by a white, vaguely ecclesiastical tower. PRINCETON THEOLOGICAL SEMINARY chiseled discreetly into a stone wall. On the right, behind more lawn, a long stretch of pale gray stone called Speer Library. The street was almost empty of parked cars. Harry checked his watch: "Would you mind stopping at number 112 for a minute?"

"Einstein's house," the cabbie said over his shoulder.

"The guidebooks must have it starred," I chipped in.

Just past the seminary, the cab glided to the curb. Wide trees hanging over the sidewalk, and, on the side where we stopped, an open meadow. I rolled down the window. Across the street, behind a low hedge and shrubs, a two-story white frame house with black shutters, the black numbers 1-1-2 mounted above a narrow black mailbox, next to a screen door. Gray wooden steps led to a narrow porch with white columns. There was no garage; even the driveway seemed to belong to the neighboring house, which wasn't much different. A small extension thickened the house to the right; that's where the TV antenna was. What was I expecting? A plaque? An admission booth? An illumination?

I imagined Einstein shuffling by, wearing a wool cap.

"Who lives there now?" I asked.

"His stepdaughter died a few years ago." The cabbie shrugged. "Now I don't know." I noticed a padlock on the screen door.

"He said in his will, no museums," Harry said. "For the same reason he said no grave." "You're an expert." The cabbie swiveled back to look. "No, an amateur," Harry said. I patted his hand. Cars passed. A black squirrel skittered across the lawn, scattering leaves. Then everything was still, the sidewalk deserted. The house radiated silence. I wanted to live there. I wanted to live there with my accomplice, my ex-mentor, my all-purpose amateur, and put up preserves and make enough babies to fill up the rooms. I wanted to give birth in my four-poster bed, I wanted to die there. I saw a solid life passing before my eyes—but it was not my life. The mood passed in fourteen seconds.

■

Only the impoverished and the comfortable live on streets without sidewalks. Franz Rosenthal was one of the comfortable. His white clapboard house, set on a small rise, was freshly painted. Gables winked from the third story. Smoke curled from the chimney. On either side of the flagstone path, near the street, stood a sycamore, its blotched bark aged skin, a hemisphere of dead leaves raked together beneath it. Diminutive spruce trees framed the steps. *"Alles in Ordnung,"* Harry said, with a nod at the trees. "Symmetry."

The doorbell activated a deep chime. After a half minute, the door opened slowly, and a short, thick man stood before us. A swirl of yellowish-white hair fringed his skull. There was a large, elliptical age spot over his right eye, but his skin was curiously smooth, except for his neck, a tortoise's. He was dressed to accord his visitors the respect they deserved—suede sport jacket, white shirt, gray-and-

tan striped tie. His thick middle was outthrust, all the more
so because his chest was thin, and he wore his pants high
above his waist—he looked off-balance. Pear-shaped—a
point in favor of Mrs. Parenti's memory.

He squinted through Coke-bottle lenses. With his left
hand, he leaned on a cane. The right he extended first to
Harry, then to me, and he said, "I am Rosenthal, as you
might expect." His grip was surprisingly firm. "Won't you
come in? Please."

He gestured toward a mahogany rack, where we hung
our coats, and waved us into a dark sitting room full of
bulky furniture, heavy like Hapsburg monuments, grouped
around a worn Persian rug. A neat array of logs burning in
the fireplace. A gallery of family photographs lined up at
one end of the mantel, a set of finely featured porcelain
dolls at the other. "Please," Rosenthal said, waving us
toward a deep blue sofa, full of fin-de-siècle curves. The
cushions were flattened from many sittings. The man was
used to *Gemütlichkeit*—convival evenings, *Kaffee mit Schlag*,
brandy, earnest conversation about the world going up in
flames.

Rosenthal eased himself into a matching armchair. Behind him, a grandfather clock, the hands stuck at 8:46.
Camera-ready.

"You will pardon the discomfort of the sofa. Since my
wife passed away, this house is a museum."

"I'm sorry," I said.

"Thank you, so am I." He turned to Harry. "Now, how
may I help you?"

"We appreciate your agreeing to see us," Harry said.
"On such short notice."

"It is I," Rosenthal said, "who should thank you for

coming all this way. I am not exactly overrun with visitors." His accent was mild and pleasant—perhaps Viennese. "I hope you had a pleasant trip. Or a reasonable one, in any case. The Amtrak food is less than magnificent, in my experience. I should explain, by the way, that the light is kept dim in this room deliberately, because of my eyes. I am like a delicate drawing that can be ruined with overexposure. May I make up for your sufferings and offer you coffee?"

"Please, that would be lovely."

As if by some inaudible signal, a thin elderly woman in an apron appeared through a swinging door. "Elise, could you bring some coffee for our guests, and the debilitated version for me? Unless"—he turned toward me—"you would like to join me in my decaffeinated state? I hear no volunteers. Then please bring both, Elise. Thank you."

Elise smiled and withdrew.

"If you are lucky," Rosenthal said, looking at Harry, "you will be spared these infirmities. If you are unlucky, I hope you learn to weather them more gracefully than I have."

"I don't see how you could be outdone in gracefulness," Harry said.

"That is kind of you. You may address me as 'Your Grace.'" Cheer reverberated around the room. Harry had charmed him already. Rosenthal didn't seem to recognize me. I took out my notebook.

"If you don't mind my saying, I am surprised that you are interested in Einstein just now"—he pronounced the name "Einshtein," *echt Deutsch*. "For years there was a veritable Einstein industry. There was the centenary of his birth, there was the twenty-fifth anniversary of his death, the fiftieth since he wrote to Roosevelt proposing the atomic bomb, and so forth. Of course I was only a minor supplier, so to speak, but even then, my phone rang so often I was unable to work. A relic like myself becomes more valuable with age."

"I hope we aren't the usual parasites," Harry said. Grace notes upon grace notes. I should have been focusing on Rosenthal but I kept thinking about Harry's courtliness. How rare to see such care with language. Remembering that this was one of the qualities that had entranced me way back when. So different from the formulaic and almost mandatory crudity of the twenty-one-year-old politicos I'd started hanging out with. Fuckin' this and fuckin' that, up against the wall, that was how boys were boys, trying to teach themselves how to live by pretending they already knew how. But the ease in Harry's voice suggested that he really did already know how.

I smiled, but Rosenthal did not seem to react.

"In any event," Rosenthal said matter-of-factly, "my work is behind me, so there is nothing to interrupt other than my naps."

Elise returned with three china cups, two thermoses of coffee, and a dish of biscotti on an inlaid wood tray. After pouring from one thermos for Harry and me, and from the other for Rosenthal, she poked at the fire and retreated.

Einstein, I thought, sat on this sofa. Molecules in this room passed through Einstein's nostrils.

Harry sipped. "You already knew Einstein in Berlin, I understand."

"Of course." I'd have thought he'd have been pleased to get a knowledgeable question, but he sounded faintly irritated. "I went there to study with him, in 1929, a difficult year to concentrate. I was twenty years old. In Vienna, I had done some minor work on relativity which Einstein found interesting. He obtained for me a stipend from the Kaiser Wilhelm Institute. He had already started work on the unified field theory. I confess I harbored sympathies in that direction myself at that time. So I became his assistant."

"What did that mean?"

Rosenthal peered at Harry, his eyes like fish behind aquarium glass. "I am not sure that I understand your question."

"What were your duties?"

"To listen, to talk, and to compute. Einstein would say, 'Truth comes *"zu zweien"* '—by twos, in company, and by opposition. He needed young people. He would throw out a line of argument and I would think with him and against him."

"You argued with him, then."

"Or if it happened that I had half an idea, he would complete it or argue with me. Of course I also helped him work out computations. Occasionally I would talk back to him. Today there are computers to do the first, although not yet to do the second."

"How did Einstein feel about your talking back?" I asked. Harry scowled. I knew what he was thinking. On television we were always, insufferably, asking people how they felt, not what they thought or, perish the thought, why. I knew the objection, but it was a man's objection.

Rosenthal's eyes twinkled, or his glasses refracted a new angle of light. "How did he feel? I am not a mind reader.

But this was his method. I would think up counterargu-
ments, and he would come back the next day with rebut-
tals. He was pleased enough to invite me to dinner from
time to time. At least I did not spoil his digestion. Although
we did not discuss these theoretical matters in front of the
family, of course."

"And you were committed to the unified field theory—"
Harry began.

"Committed? No, that is too strong. I had not the conviction that Einstein had." Rosenthal weighed his words. "I
thought that it was a promising line of development. My
doubts came later."

"Did Einstein express doubts?" Harry asked.

"Never! Not in my hearing. No, he absolutely detested
the thought of a discontinuous universe. Once he said,
'Particles do not have a mind of their own. It is the other
way around.' He was the one who had a mind of his own."

I couldn't tell whether Rosenthal was admiring or de-
ploring.

"Of course I agreed with him, then. He liked the way I
put it once: 'Anthills are more predictable than ants, but
that does not mean that ants materialize whenever and
wherever they like.' I was talking about atoms, you see."

"Where did you go from Berlin?"

"Well, Hitler was planning his own unification, as you
know." I wrote that down. "In late '32, Einstein left Germany for his health. Berlin was not hospitable to the so-
called Jewish science. But I was a stupid sentimentalist—I
refused to leave Europe. Moreover, I could not expect to
be welcomed with open arms in the United States or England or even Canada. I had a modest talent for theoretical

questions, but Einstein I was not. So I returned to Vienna. There were theoretical questions I wanted to work on. I had also the strange idea to do mathematical work, in particular certain problems of logic."

"Undecidability?" Click, as Harry played a card.

Rosenthal nodded, evidently impressed. "In a way, yes, related. You know about this. So I thought I could be safe from the Nazis in Vienna, the city that succeeded in making the world forget that Hitler was an Austrian. Such is my political genius. My other reason was Gödel." He paused. I made a note to ask Harry who or what that was.

"Well, after a while you did not have to be a genius to see what was coming. I wrote from Vienna to Einstein to ask what employment I might find in America. He was gracious as always. He wrote back that he would welcome my collaboration again. That pleased me."

"You mean, you were still interested in the unified field theory?" Harry asked.

For a fragment of a second, annoyance flickered in Rosenthal's prismatic eyes. "Interested, yes. Committed, absolutely not. But commitment was a luxury under those circumstances. Frankly, I would have been happy to shine Einstein's shoes. He offered me still better. He arranged that I should be his assistant at the Institute. In February of 1938, a month before the Anschluss, I came to Princeton, and as you see I have been cooling my heels here ever since. Gödel waited two years more to come. This was not possible for a Rosenthal."

In short, Rosenthal owed Einstein his life.

"And the unified field theory?"

Rosenthal shifted in his seat. "If you mean, did Einstein

hold me to it, the answer is no. For two or three years, I collaborated with him in the old manner. Then he understood, well, I had other interests."

"Was he disappointed?" Point to Harry: he *was* interested in feelings.

Rosenthal made a face as if this were grotesquely stupid. "Mmm, a little, possibly, but he was not a man to feel ill will. Anyway, he had no trouble finding other assistants, younger people. In any event, we remained good friends. His wife had died, as you know." Rosenthal hauled himself up with the aid of his cane, took two steps forward, picked up the plate, and approached the sofa. "Please have a biscuit."

Since it would have been impolite to refuse, I took a biscuit.

"I'm interested," Harry said, leaning forward, holding his coffee cup on his knee, "in his enemies. Would you say that anyone wished him ill?"

As Rosenthal plumped himself down in his throne, his cane, which he had leaned against the armrest, clattered to the floor. Harry retrieved it for him. The thought of Einstein having enemies seemed to have unnerved the old man. "No one could hate Einstein! He was a kind man, never did I hear a nasty word out of his mouth. Too generous for his peace of mind. Why should anyone hate Einstein? I do not understand why you ask such an outlandish question."

"But might there have been people who didn't know him," Harry continued evenly, "people who hated him for his ideas, what he stood for?"

"I don't—Who do you have in mind?"

Protests too much, I wrote. *Or loyal.*

"This is hypothetical, of course, but I was wondering about militant anti-Communists. Einstein was a pacifist, after all, an—"

"But no one *hated* Einstein," Rosenthal repeated. "Even Teller only thought he was naïve, a little soft about Communism. I thought so myself, to tell the truth."

"Well, surely there were those who envied him, then," Harry went on.

"Envied?"

"He *did* win the Nobel Prize. He *was* world famous."

"Ach, ridiculous. Let me tell you something. There was, frankly, more pity than envy. The press was more a nuisance than anything else—you will pardon me. And the Nobel, relativity, the photoelectric effect, Brownian motion, the *Wunderjahr* of 1905, well, all that was decades earlier. By his last years there were those who thought he had become a living monument to his earlier work—not an enviable position."

Harry had the look of a man who has put out a line only to have it chomped off by a barracuda. "But the Nazis, of course, hated him."

Rosenthal sat back, pleased that anyone nowadays would take Nazis seriously as a threat. "Well, the Nazis, of course, that is another thing, in the Hitler years, yes. Even before the Hitler years. There was a public meeting where he was denounced, you know. In Berlin. Later there was a price on his head. In Belgium, before he came here, the Queen sent him bodyguards."

"And in America?"

"Here? No, there were never any serious threats. Not that I know of. Of course I cannot say that I knew everything."

"What about unserious threats?"

"It has been many years since I have thought about this." Rosenthal paused and scratched his ear, where a patch of reddish hair was sprouting over the lobe. "I remember hearing that when his boat docked in New York the Institute thought that he ought to keep out of sight. Yes. As a result he was spared the speech that the mayor gave in his honor, and the brass band, and a ridiculous parade—for which I am sure he was profoundly grateful. But no one attacked him. He refused to ask for guards."

"And in Princeton?"

Rosenthal answered abruptly. "Unthinkable. You see, anyone could find out where he lived. He walked down Mercer Street over there"—Rosenthal waved vaguely— "every day. He was not exactly an unknown figure. But you are reminding me that in the early days there were anti-Semitic letters. He showed me one or two, full of the crudest things, misspelled. The post office faithfully delivered piles of this garbage to the Institute, hundreds of letters and postcards in gray mail sacks. 'I see you are famous again in the press,' I would tease him. Whenever they printed their silly articles about him, the invective would pour in. You are intelligent people, you should be ashamed to see what has been done by the fools in your profession."

"Tell me about it," I said with what I hoped was my most endearing smile. "Any articles in particular?"

"Oh, periodically, you know, the newspapers decided that Einstein had solved the riddle of the universe. This kind of garbage goes back to relativity. You would not believe the stupidity. As if they were waiting for the great man to deliver the tablets. They wrote as if the unified field theory was a fait accompli. Great symphonies of misunderstanding poured out. *The New York Times* was one of the worst. Then Einstein's mail would start up again. Requests for signatures and the like. As if he was a movie star!"

"When were these articles published?"

"This I do not remember exactly." I made a note to look them up. "I think the last one was not long before he died, perhaps two or three years. At such moments, the lunatics would gather. Mental cases—flying-saucer worshippers, orgone enthusiasts, pseudophilosophers. Pathetic! One was even arrested, lurking around the Institute. The man had escaped from an asylum. Harmless, but he annoyed the secretaries. Einstein laughed it off, as usual."

Harry inched forward. "Did any of these people ever threaten Einstein?"

"Seriously? No. These people were nuisances, not enemies. And, you know, it must be said that the people who wrote to him on these occasions were not all cranks."

"Oh?"

"Yes, he answered the serious ones. If they persisted, he might agree to meet them." Rosenthal trailed off. Was it my melodramatic imagination, trained by too many years at *In Depth*, that he was anxious to slip away from Harry's gaze? "One or two were actually interesting," he went on. "In his last years, Einstein had a weakness for these *Wandervögel*."

Harry let him stare into the fire for several seconds before asking: "What can you tell me about these *Wandervögel*?"

"Misfits of various sorts, self-taught, overeducated—" Rosenthal seemed to make up his mind about something. "There was even one who would visit him, a *Luftmensch*, a would-be philosopher, a poet of sorts—not for me to say how good a poet—" Rosenthal spread his hands. "Einstein took a liking to him. He gave away his time like alms. He did so with the Israelis, he did so with the peace crusaders . . ."

"Tell me about this would-be philosopher."

Rosenthal gestured with an open hand. "An intelligent fellow but undisciplined. Friendly. Very, mmm . . ." He trailed off.

"Yes?" Harry asked after an interval.

"American, I was going to say. Young and unformed. You will not take offense, I hope."

"Not at all. Where did he come from?"

"Greenwich Village, no doubt. A kind of beatnik full of half-baked ideas about the nature of the universe, exotic religions. But clever in an undeveloped way. I believe that he was what today they would call a dropout. Einstein agreed to see him once, and before you knew, he was a regular visitor. I met him at Einstein's house once or twice. Also at the Institute."

"I'm curious," I jumped in. "Why would Einstein put up with this fool?"

"He said he amused him. 'I like the song of this *Wandervögel*,' that is how he put it."

"You thought these discussions were odd?"

"Well, I have to admit, yes, a little unusual. But Einstein said that you could never tell where an idea was going to come from. A clue, he said, isn't responsible for the people who furnish it."

Harry had said Einstein thought in images. Maybe a weirdo was just the one to jolt him into a useful image.

"I'll tell you, Mr. — "

"Kramer."

"I'll tell you the truth about theoretical physics, Mr.

Kramer. The search for order in the universe is deeply unnerving. If you go on with it too long, a hardening of the cranial arteries sets in, leading to metaphysics. The more we know, the less we know, and the better we know how little we know. You have heard this before, perhaps, but that makes it no less true. We play at philosophy as we approach senility. Heisenberg, Schrödinger, Bohm, Oppenheimer, Crick—it happened to all of them. Even my teacher Gödel wrote a paper on time travel, with space twisted up in knots. Inspired by Einstein, in fact. Of course Gödel was particularly—"

"Yes?"

"Well, strange. But never mind. I am not above strange ideas myself . . ." I nodded. My father, never a religious man, studied the Kabbalah during his last illness. You don't believe in this stuff, do you? I asked. Belief has nothing to do with it, he said.

". . . I confess that in my own modest way I, too, enjoy pontificating about the nature of life and the universe." Rosenthal lowered his voice. "This is hard to do with one's maid and the four walls. My children have long since wearied of my tiresome thoughts. Possibly Einstein needed a son as well—for a while, let us be frank, that was my privilege."

Einstein had had two actual sons, Harry had told me: one of them hopelessly schizophrenic in an asylum in Switzerland till the end of his days; the other a professor in California—neither exactly available for metaphysics.

"His stepdaughter lived with him to the end, a kind woman, but not equipped for these matters. In any case, Mr. Gottehrer permits me to pontificate without limit."

"Gottehrer."

"That is his name, yes. I have to admit he is a stimulating visitor—a learned man in his way, well read in several languages—how shall I say, a speculator. He tolerates my silliness. So I tolerate his."

Harry hunched forward on the sofa. "You mean you still see him?"

"As a matter of fact, he visits me, oh, once or twice each year. He was here not so long ago, actually."

Harry thought that over. Then, cheerily: "And did you happen to tell Mr. Gottehrer that you were expecting a visit from an inquiring writer with a special interest in the end of Einstein's life?"

His smile must have reassured Rosenthal, but only partway. I was afraid Harry had just gone over the line.

"This is like an interrogation," Rosenthal said.

"I'll take that as a compliment," I said, "for the thoroughness of our research."

"You know, I do not even know what you people are planning to do with your research. What kind of journalists are you?"

"That's a matter of dispute," I said. "I work for *In Depth.*"

"*In Depth* . . ." Plainly Rosenthal was one of the twelve Americans who would fail to recognize our contribution to national enlightenment.

"The news magazine," I said. "I am a correspondent and a producer. Mr. Kramer is a consultant to the program."

"You mean television," Rosenthal said.

"That's right."

Rosenthal chuckled. "You see, I am a troglodyte, and there is no television in my cave."

"I don't see how you get by," I said, then saw in his befuddlement that he had taken me seriously.

"The question is—" Harry started.

"I remember the question," Rosenthal said. "You want to know whether I mentioned to Mr. Gottehrer that a writer was coming to see me about Einstein's final days. The answer is yes."

"You're sure," Harry said.

"Of course I am sure"—irritated. "But I do not want to leave the impression that your research was our primary topic. In fact, we were discussing superstrings, knotted spaces, and the current fads in unification theory. This is one of Mr. Gottehrer's fascinations, you see. Pseudoscience has its appeals. Naturally, I mentioned that you were coming to see me. I thought he would be interested, since he visited Einstein not long before he died."

I had to dig my feet into the rug to keep from jumping for joy. "How long before?"

"I see I have overimpressed you with my memory. I could not tell you exactly."

"At the hospital, do you mean?"

"Of that I am not sure. At least he called at his home, I think."

"You think."

"I was not Einstein's appointment secretary, you understand. But I seem to remember that he mentioned to me a visit in those last days."

"Do you mean that Einstein mentioned it or Gottehrer?"

"I meant Mr. Gottehrer, but the more you ask, the less I am sure. You could ask him yourself."

"Yes," Harry said, forcing the understatement, "I'd like to do that."

"Before you leave"—Rosenthal, slumping in his chair, seemed to be hoping this would be soon—"I will see if I can find his address for you."

There was an awkward silence. We were overstaying our welcome, and Harry, energy blazing, didn't notice. Get him excited and his courtliness momentarily burned away. I could remember the same gleam in his eye as he would trace out elaborate webs of power—postwar army counter-intelligence, ex-Nazis, Argentine land deals, Bolivian counterinsurgency training, the death of Che—those time-less afternoons at *Eight Million Stories*. To me it was obvious that, for Rosenthal, Harry's instinct for hot pursuit was beginning to lose its charm. But I wasn't going to stop Harry now, I was a sucker for hot pursuit myself.

"I don't want to keep you much longer, Professor Rosenthal. But if I may ask a final question?"

Rosenthal, trapped in hospitality or desperate for company, bowed his head. "As you like."

"Do you happen to know who else visited Einstein at the hospital?"

Rosenthal hesitated. "Again, I was not his nurse. But let me see. There was his stepdaughter, of course. His son. His secretary, Miss Dukas. His friend Professor Nathan, of course. They are no longer among us. And I myself, who remain among us provisionally." Rosenthal clearly relished our embarrassment.

Harry was dogged: "So you went to his hospital room on—"

"The day after he arrived, or the day after that, I am not sure which."

"He went to the hospital on a Friday."

"Then it follows inevitably that I saw him on the Saturday or the Sunday."

"And the time?"

Rosenthal paused. "The afternoon, I think. Of course I do not go to synagogue, or church, so it might have been Sunday morning."

"How was he?"

"He looked terrible. Gray. Obviously in pain."

"But he was lucid?"

"Absolutely. He knew he was dying."

"How do you know?"

"This knowledge he wore on his face."

"What did you talk about?"

"So far as I remember, his usual subjects. He was unhappy about Israel and worried about John Foster Dulles. I listened politely. I had, so to say, differences with him, but I was not about to argue under these circumstances."

"And the unified field theory?"

Rosenthal gazed off into the middle distance. "I . . . I do not recall whether he brought it up. He knew I thought this was futility."

"So you wouldn't have brought it up."

"Absolutely not. Contrary to appearances, I am not a sadist."

"Do you remember anyone else visiting him at the hospital?"

After a pause: "You know, as I left, I ran into Janousek, of all people."

Harry hoisted an eyebrow. "*Gustav* Janousek?"

A.k.a. the Big Bomber way back in anno mirabilis 1968, when I got quote unquote radicalized, for which he had been one good reason. Columbia had belonged to something called the Institute for Defense Analyses, IDA, which had started in the fifties to expedite military research. Columbia lent it cachet and professors, and the IDA made good use of both. In '68, the IDA was one of the flash points that ignited the students, and *Eight Million Stories* did a job on him, which helped. IDA had an even more exclusive military division called Jason, which was particularly devoted to counterinsurgency—only forty scientists in the whole country. At Columbia, Janousek was Jason's leading light. His particular contribution, if I remembered correctly, had been a study of the feasibility of shooting off tactical nuclear weapons in Vietnam—hence the Big Bomber. In return, some extravagant soul or souls had torched his office one night. Over the years, I'd seen his name on various full-page ads rallying weak-kneed politicians to support exotic instruments of fiery demolition —and, most recently, Star Wars. Next to Edward Teller— and on such issues he often *was* next to Teller—he was a peacenik's least favorite physicist.

"Who else?" Rosenthal said.

"I would have assumed that Janousek was not so fond of Einstein. Politically, I mean."

"Politically, personally—sometimes there is not so much difference, you know."

"Janousek," Harry mused. "Hard to believe." He turned the name over and over, toyed with it like a cat with a dead mouse. That, I guess, made me the master, supposed to be pleased. Or possibly the performance was intended for Rosenthal. I tilted my head and tried to look gratified. But Rosenthal's face sagged; he was mined out. The room was too dark, too stuffy. I wanted Harry to stop. We could always come back. Instead, he crouched forward: "And what did Einstein think of Janousek?"

I was beginning to understand something about Harry. He did not let go, and his patience had no mercy. And yet people wanted to give him what he was asking for. If only just to see what would come out of his mouth next.

"Well—a good physicist, of course."

"Right. And."

Rosenthal was recalcitrant, but Harry's silence must have gotten the better of him. "He did not say in so many words. But, approximately, it was not hard to know Einstein's opinion: he thought Janousek weaseled about Oppenheimer during the AEC hearings. That is no secret. Many people thought so."

"I take it Janousek's attitude was unusual."

"Unusual! At the Institute he was unique—our own Teller! You have to remember Oppenheimer was our director at the time. There was a certain presumption in favor of him. It did not matter whether you agreed with him on everything under the sun. For Einstein, of course, there was an additional issue. Whatever your political views, you did not give the government the power to certify loyalty. This was the route back to Nazi Germany. I am not saying that I agreed with him—but this was Einstein's opinion."

"So what would Janousek—" Harry started.

"For all I know," Rosenthal interrupted, "he wanted to inherit his office. I am joking, of course. But you see, Mr. Kramer, I am no mind reader. All I am telling you is, Janousek went to visit. Why don't you ask him yourself what was on his mind? You're certain to hear an entertaining lecture."

Elise reappeared, glanced solicitously in Rosenthal's direction, and conspicuously made no offer of fresh coffee. She stoked the fire and added another log. Rosenthal watched in silence.

"And now I am slowing down like my feeble antique," he finally said, glancing toward the grandfather clock. Those hands hadn't budged in years. I looked at my quartz watch, noiseless, battery-driven. 11:45. We had been there almost three hours. Rosenthal wasn't the only one slowing down.

I hauled myself up before Harry had another chance to open his mouth. "You've been very helpful, Professor Rosenthal. I'm afraid we have to go now."

Harry stood up awkwardly. No vigorous protest from Rosenthal.

"Elise," Rosenthal said, "could you find for Mr. Kramer and Miss . . ."

"Ross," I said sweetly.

". . . Miss Ross the address and the phone number of Mr. Gottehrer?"

Elise slipped out. In the awkwardness, I complimented Rosenthal on the porcelain dolls on his mantel.

"They were my wife's legacy from Vienna," Rosenthal said. "All that her parents took with them." His eyes flashed. "Today, for all I know, the idiot son of a torturer who lives in the apartment where she was born has no idea how his father acquired this excellent property. As you may know, after the war the Austrians paid Jewish survivors the grand sum of ten percent of the value of what they stole—ten percent for the lucky ones! Those lousy Austrians were the first victims of Nazi Germany, you see."

As the great-great-granddaughter of Jews who thought they were Germans and the granddaughter of Jews who thought they were Lithuanians, I'm always moved by refugees. Think about Einstein—ex-German, ex-Swiss, ex-German again; no wonder he wanted to unify the universe. Einstein the prophet saw the century coming in 1905, saw the whole nightmare already vivid in one of those pictures produced by his swarms of glial cells: saw a seamless, placeless universe in which nothing rests, everything is a refugee for all time and in all places.

Fact fatigue was settling in. Rosenthal was hiding something. I missed the bright light and stark shadow of the trivial world that was known to me. I wanted to hard-cut out of here to primary colors, Billy Neill, answers to which I knew the questions.

Elise returned with a small square of graph paper, on which, in an elegant European hand, she had written the name Norman Gottehrer with a Lower East Side address and a phone number. At Rosenthal's request, she went to call us a cab.

Would Rosenthal permit me to interview him for *In Depth*? He would be honored. I said I would call to propose a specific time.

We plucked our coats from the wooden antlers in the vestibule, Rosenthal trailing after us for politeness' sake. Harry turned. "By the way, Professor Rosenthal, did you happen to mention my name to Mr. Gottehrer?"

Rosenthal looked preoccupied. Or perhaps he was getting an early start on his nap. "It's possible. I'm not sure."

I asked what Gottehrer looked like.

"I'm afraid I cannot help you very much," Rosenthal said. "As you can see, my eyes were not made for observation. Mathematics is the study of things that do not exist, which I am better at seeing."

I tugged at Harry's sleeve. "We'll wait outside. You've been very generous with your time."

"But you will freeze!"

"The air will be good."

I was staring at Harry's jacket. "Mr. Gottehrer doesn't wear a blue cloth coat, by any chance?"

Like a startled owl, Rosenthal cocked his head and peered up. "As a matter of fact, he does. How did you know such a thing?"

"Woman's intuition," I said. Or glial cells. By now, I doubted there was a difference.

Outside, the day's light had already overexerted itself and gone weak from the effort. The chill revived me a bit.

At the sound of the door closing, Harry raised his hand, then slapped it palm down toward a place inches in front of me. I was late to hold out my own palm, so we struck glancing blows. On the strength of a wild guess, I was now one of the boys. Play dice with your own mind, anything can happen.

A safe distance along the flagstone path, Harry practically shouted: "Brilliant!"

"Blind luck," I said. "But thank you." His jubilation was infectious. I had no choice but to believe in the whole perverse story. Now it was like marriage or my inadvertent career: damn the reconsideration, think about next steps.

At *In Depth*, the next step should always be obvious. In a profile, like Billy Neill, maybe you jazz the character up with an old friend, a spouse, a rival, try to start up their hearts, coax a surprise out of them, but you'll settle for an inventory of standard poses. In an investigation, you pick one each from columns A, B, C, D: victim, whistle-blower, company rep, expert. The Rolodex does the walking for you.

But the murder of Albert Einstein was already loading up with too many characters for too little plot. I had too many questions all at once. Gottehrer, of course, Gottehrer of the blue coat and obscure speculations—I had a personal reason or two for wanting to get to Gottehrer. Janousek was promising. Mrs. Parenti, the nurse—I wanted to find out which other nurses were on duty in April of 1955. See the hospital, and the Institute for Advanced Study, and go back to Einstein's house, gather inspiration from the scene of the crime. And how was Yolanda coming with Billy Null? Think methodically, Margo. My mind drifted like dust.

"We are embarrassed," I said, "by riches. I vote we start with Gottehrer."

Harry was watching for the cab, although there was no other human being in sight, and on these streets, at this hour, a moving vehicle was an event. Then a tiny, narrow truck whirred down the street, stopped, and a black man got out and delicately loaded garbage bags in back. He stopped at every house on the block. Harry followed the man with his eyes.

"Gottehrer," Harry said, "what a gift of the gods to the godless." His eyes sparkled. "Those *Times* articles on Einstein, we have to find out what they were saying to make him look so interesting to Gottehrer all of a sudden." He was the one thinking methodically, picking his way from thought to thought. "Maybe go back to the nurse, stir up her memory."

"About?"

"Janousek, bingo." He stopped short at the end of the

flagstone path. "A flat nose and a deep voice, that's what she remembers. We're up to two witnesses."

I must have looked as blank as the sky. I needed food, a phone, and a train. Janousek sounded like a long shot.

"Don't you see? The nurse thinks she saw flat-nose come back. If that really was Janousek, here's the last person in the world you'd expect to visit Einstein in the hospital, and he visits him not once but twice."

A yellow cab inched down the street, hunting for house numbers. He spotted us and stopped. The cabbie was middle-aged, wearing a natty brown sport jacket and a tie. Did you get deported from Princeton if you didn't wear a tie? Harry asked him to find us a restaurant near the train station. The cabbie said the best he could do was leave us a few minutes' walk away. We drove back down Mercer Street, passing a row of mansions with classical columns set way back from the road, before returning to the two- and three-story homes, Einstein's zone. The neighborhood was in repose, no one strolling the sidewalks theorizing about the unity of the universe.

The cabbie turned onto Nassau Street, as main a street as there was, shops on the left side, the university on the right, phone booths in the form of little huts with peaked wooden roofs. We passed What You Fancy, Laura Ashley, and The English Shop—it looked as though the British had won the Revolutionary War—and got off at a sign promising Viejo Mexico. We went through a long passage lined with slapped-on stucco and into the restaurant. Disco and mild salsa, both too loud. To the right was a bar area with a single pay phone. A man wearing black steel frames and a herringbone topcoat was on it, talking earnestly about Third World debt. He looked as though a small though detectable part of Third World debt had paid for his wardrobe.

We sat near the phone and ordered chicken enchiladas and coffee.

"What I don't understand," I said, "among several thousand other things, is how Gottehrer managed to follow you."

A slow nod, tick-tock, his little I've-thought-of-this smile. "I know. But the lurkers who don't manage, we never hear of." Harry's old lexicon. He meant the Lee Harvey Oswalds and John Hinckleys who crouch in the margins between the organized cabals, freelancers whose obscure attachments and demented motives set them up to blow apart the rational, predictable conspiracies we call history. Harry did his Groucho, mocking his own taste for the paranoid sublime.

I hadn't realized until Harry popped back into my life how much I missed those afternoons when he taught me the world according to Harry Kramer. The closest I'd come in years was brainstorming about bank scams in the network cafeteria with Dan Slotkin and Elaine Barbanel. But Dan had been fired and gone to a lower-rated place, and Elaine, like me, had been at *In Depth* too long and had too many fascinating personal problems to talk about.

"Lurkers do research," Harry was saying. "Remember, this guy found out what hospital they took Einstein to."

"O.K.," I thought aloud, "Rosenthal told him that you were interested in Einstein's last days, right? I can see him wanting to find out what you know. But how did he find you?"

"I have to admit I left my number with Rosenthal."

Your trail, I wanted to say, pleased that Harry was not

quite all-knowing. Anyone with a contact at the phone
company could turn up an address from a phone number.
Delaney had told me that—the cop who had tracked down
the particular lurker who had been in the habit of calling to
regale me with his plans for various parts of my anatomy. I
seemed to collect such people, I put out some kind of scent.

I was not thrilled at the thought of Gottehrer prowling
the streets wondering what was inside my new purse.

Harry was retelling Mrs. Parenti's story. ". . . A tall,
thin kid with big ears. Always around, as if he had moved
into the waiting room. She remembers calling an orderly to
escort him out."

"Let's try to find the orderly." I made a note. "And the
other nurses."

"Good." As in "Good little girl."

I went to the phone, but the man in the black steel
frames was still talking. Apparently, Third World debt was
still outstanding.

When I came back, Harry looked up from the scribble
on his napkin and said, "You know, let's find Janousek
first."

"He's probably retired," I calculated. "I'll call Burke,
he's got a line into everybody."

"Good. While you're at it—I assume *In Depth* has a
morgue."

"Sort of. We prefer data bases."

"But for older stuff. No clip files?"

"Are you kidding? That's *history*."

"Sorry to be so gauche. I want to find those *Times* pieces
about Einstein."

"I could send an intern to the public library, but we'd
probably do better to dig them up ourselves."

The man at the phone seemed to have lined up his consultancy fee or his next lecture, for when I looked up, he was walking our way, nodding coolly. He sat down at a nearby table.

I went to the phone, called New York City information and asked for Gustav Janousek, J-A-N-O-U-S-E-K. "We're sorry," an electronic voice warbled. "At the request of the customer, the number is not available at this time. Thank you for calling NYNEX."

I called the Columbia physics department and in a slightly less electronic voice was told the same thing. I left a message.

I punched up the Big Glass switchboard and asked for Yolanda. She answered on the first ring.

"Hi, it's your absentee producer and on-air personality."

"Oh yes, I remember you, before you got so redundant," she said lightly.

"Beg pardon?"

"Joke, Margo. This piece edits itself. You already told the story in stand-ups. Piece of cake." Her voice through Con Comm's circuits was so brilliantly clear I automatically moved the receiver away: she sounded as if she were yelling inside my ear. Sir Colin had wired the building with fiber optics. "Suppose I said I'm at the rough-cut stage, would you believe me?"

"You're going to heaven."

"Aren't you sweet? There's only one problem."

"What's that?"

"It's thirty-two minutes long, and change."

"Don't worry, we'll whack it back if we have to. I'll talk to Burke. He's so hot for this piece I think we have slack to play with."

I asked her to transfer me to Burke Gilman's office. I heard some electronic pips, then Tiffany came on and put me right through.

"Talk to me," he boomed.

"We're going great guns."

"Great, great." If something was less than great to Burke, it was worthless.

"Clues coming out of our ears."

"Great."

"And characters."

"Fabulous."

"At this rate, we may have a murderer so fast we'll have to preempt next week's show." That would mean postponing designer drugs another week, I realized after the words were out of my mouth. A few more teenagers dead—hey, big deal!

"Don't joke, or I'll call you on it. How's Billy?"

"We have a rough cut."

"I'm a happy man."

"By the way, Burke, I need a small thing." I gave him a rising inflection to turn the statement into a question. I cringed at my father's voice barking, *If you're telling me and not asking me, young lady, speak in declarative sentences.* But my father never had to make a career collecting favors from men.

"I'm even happier. Shoot."

"I need a phone number for Gustav Janousek. The physicist."

"I *know* who he is. I've met him."

"Oh?"

"Socially, I mean. At a dinner party. At Sir Colin's, actually."

Sir Colin did get around.

"Very interesting man," he said. "Bright, God is he bright. Is that what you wanted to know?"

"He was at the Institute for Advanced Study with Einstein. He was one of the last people to see him before he died. The rest you pay me to find out."

Silence on the other end of the line. Then Burke's voice blaring: "Sir Colin is close to him, you know." I shouldn't have been surprised. McShane collected right-thinking ideologues. If the gossip columns were to be believed despite the fact that he paid for some of them, McShane had memorized selected pithy sayings from the likes of Adam Smith and Churchill, scattering them around boardrooms and dining rooms. He fancied a rags-to-riches motif, swallowing his Midlands syllables, boasting that as a mere stripling he had gone around with John Lennon's mum in Liverpool. But he also believed that when in America you should wave the flag as Americans do—he had Burke insert a red, white, and blue logo into the evening news.

So a friendship with Janousek made sense. Their politics would be congenial. When the network had run an hour-long prime-time special promoting Star Wars, it had featured Janousek along with the longest animation sequence ever commissioned for a news broadcast—or so Sir Colin had bragged in full-page ads the morning before. THIS IS THE WEAPON THAT MADE GORBACHEV CRY UNCLE, read the headline. IS THIS THE TIME TO GIVE IT UP? And now the Star Wars revival was on, full force, no doubt giving Sir Colin and Janousek a great deal to chat about over drinks.

"Are you somewhere I can call you back?" Burke finally said.

"I'm in Princeton. I'll have to call you."

"Give me an hour. I'll do what I can." Click.

I dug in my purse for Elise's slip of paper and punched up Norman Gottehrer's number. No answer, no machine, nothing. Such people ought to be fined. Surveying the restaurant, I half expected to see him at the next booth in his pea coat.

Harry was scribbling again on his napkin. The waiter was refilling our cups of so-so coffee.

"You'll love this," I said. "Janousek and McShane are bosom buddies."

"Perfect." He cocked his head like a big bird getting fed. His joy was a joy to behold. On a second napkin he wrote JANOUSEK and MCSHANE, circled the names, connected the circles. "Shield of Liberty's board of directors." I nodded. Even an *In Depth* reporter knew what that was: the old boys' club for the resurrection of X-ray lasers, Brilliant Pebbles, Bright Rays, and other imagined means for interrupting Russian (formerly Soviet) or Iraqi or Iranian or Korean or who-the-hell-knew-whose nuclear rockets before they vaporized any home folks. During the end-of-the-Cold-War years, lots of the Star Wars equipment had been laughed out of the budget. But the laughing days were over and the Shield of Liberty was back, a political force with clout, quotability, and a thirst for vengeance.

"Terrific," I said. That had been Harry's word once. My own shield breaking down. Interesting. Dangerous. Getting to be a believer again.

I looked down at his first napkin. With a single sinuous line he had drawn a labyrinth as tightly bunched as an intestine, filling space with the maximum number of never-crossing wriggles. Horror vacui, they called it in art history —the terror of emptiness. Harry Kramer's trademark.

The white man had been driven mad staring at the blankness of his existence—this was another old theme of Harry's, through many variations. American settlers blinded by the vast New World to the point where they had to pave it, spray it, sell it. Ahab stabbing away at the whiteness of the whale. It could happen to us. Your mission, Harry would say, if you choose to accept it, is to hack a way through the great blur. Follow the diagram.

He caught me studying his face. Telltale sign of the apprentice, the reporter, or the recovering romantic. "What's so interesting?" he asked. But he had already shut down. Something impenetrable behind his grin. What, or who, was down there in his cave with him? What kind of damage, sadness, woman? I wanted to know, I didn't want to know, I wanted to know later.

"It can wait," I said. Enough coffee. We went out to look for the library.

■

We had to walk a long way around to the entrance, under a Gothic arch. Inside, I asked a young guard for the reference room. "Right over there." He pointed, and asked for identification. Not an *In Depth* viewer, I thought; Burke was right, our demographics were graying. I offered my Con Comm ID card and said that I was a journalist on assignment and needed only a few minutes in the reference room, but the guard, in an I-have-my-instructions voice, insisted that I needed permission from the Access Office. At the exit, another guard was searching day-packs and purses.

Across the lobby, a sign over a door read: THE ACCESS OFFICE. I wasn't getting anywhere—was I supposed to have a bomb in my purse? or to be researching how to build one?—until a young woman who had been staring from a back desk walked up, stuck out her hand, and said, "Miss Ross, I deeply admire you." This resulted in two passes and permission to keep my purse.

Harry took his pass to the reference room to look into Janousek, while I went to the microforms division, straight to the *New York Times* index for 1955, then back year by year to 1945. There were front-page stories on Einstein March 30, 1953, and December 27, 1949. The microfilm rolls were in open stacks. I reeled to the right dates and, dime by dime, copied the stories.

Item 1. Tuesday, December 27, 1949, a two-column headline: "New Einstein Theory Gives a Master Key to Universe." Beneath the headline, a page of typescript, dotted with equations. The byline was William L. Laurence. The lead:

"Albert Einstein, whose theory of relativity provided the formula that revealed the existence of atomic energy and offered mankind new visions of the material universe, has developed, after more than thirty years of arduous labors, a mathematical concept that is expected to lead to new and much deeper insights into the cosmos."

It went on: "The new theory, described by Einstein as a 'generalized theory of gravitation,' attempts to interrelate all known physical phenomena into one all-embracing intellectual concept, thus providing one major master key to all the multiple phenomena and forces in which the material universe manifests itself to man." *All-embracing, master key*: you could see where the headline writer had gotten ideas.

Understand, reader: on normal mornings, I skate through the great gray unsurprising *Times* with barely a pause. But I slowed down here, trying to pick through the clauses with wide 1949 eyes still capable of astonishment.

The jump on page 12—"Einstein Offers Key to the Universe"—went on about relativity, declaring that in 1916, with his general theory, Einstein brought "space, time, matter, energy, gravitation and inertia into one all-embracing intellectual concept." Bertrand Russell and George Bernard Shaw were mustered to testify to the significance of this achievement. "However, there still remained one of the greatest cosmic forces that could not be brought into the unified structure, the all-pervading force of electromagnetism. It is this force that Einstein believes he has at last succeeded in bringing into an all-embracing cosmic concept, known among scientists as a 'Unified Field Theory.' This means that the gravitational field and the electromagnetic field, the two major 'fields' in which the material universe manifests itself, can at last be viewed as being two manifestations of one united cosmic entity."

Unified Field Theory: in caps, no less.

I skipped past some filler to the theme of practical application. Maxwell's discovery that magnetism, electricity, and light were all of a piece led directly to radio and television. Then: "Similarly, the mathematical synthesis by Einstein of space and time led to the unification of matter and energy, a concept that found its most spectacular verification when the atomic bomb exploded over New Mexico and Japan, forty years after the promulgation of the original theory of relativity, and that promises the utilization of the vast storms of the energy within the nuclei of atoms for the benefit of mankind." A thicket that called for a second reading. Einstein's theory was verified by the A-bomb but —pregnant pause—redemption was "promised." "Vast storms of energy . . . benefit of mankind"—quaintly pre–Three Mile Island, pre-Chernobyl. After the pregnant pause, the monster birth.

But William L. Laurence's lyrical afterthought was not what interested me. His point was that ideas had consequences. Laurence was emphatic. I went back a few paragraphs: "Such a comprehensive theory not only provides a profounder understanding of the universe around us; it generally makes possible the prediction of entirely new and unforeseen phenomena."

". . . prediction of entirely new and unforeseen phenomena."

Relativity was to atomic power as unified field theory was to what?

I left the microfilm machine whirring, stretched my back, walked over to *Facts on File* for 1949. There was Cold War all over the place. NATO, the Federal Republic of Germany, and the People's Republic of China all established. The Russians testing their A-bomb. Smith Act trials, purges of Communist professors, loyalty oaths, congressional hearings, Alger Hiss, the sense of a crescendo.

Imagine, then, December 27, 1949. The Russians blockading Berlin. The West airlifting supplies. Apocalypse is just offshore. Generals want to nuke the Russians before they can nuke back. Panic is never more than an inch away. What is the country supposed to do, wait for Stalin to leap? Two days after Christmas and there's no sign of peace on earth. Now, suppose you read in the paper: Einstein has found the key to the universe. It's about time. What is Nature, after all? Some kind of Communist keeping its secrets and stealing ours? With the world so dangerous, you want Nature to come out with its hands up. You want your country to crack the code. You turn to page 12, fold the paper, and read that the last time this Einstein had such a bright idea it "found its most spectacular verification when the atomic bomb exploded over New Mexico and Japan." That took forty years after Einstein set pencil to paper. What are we going to verify this time, and will it take forty years?

If anyone knows, Einstein knows.

Those lunatics who (Rosenthal said) used to gravitate to Einstein—lunatics read the paper, too.

I went to the microfilm machine, back to page 12. In the case of the Unified Field Theory, Einstein was "frank to admit that he has 'not yet found a practical way to confront the results of the theory with experimental evidence.' However, the fact that he regards his formulas as 'highly convincing' indicates his belief that he has at last found the 'key to the cosmos' he has been seeking for more than half of his seventy years, though he, above everyone, realizes that the 'key' must first be tested against the cosmic lock before it can be definitely known whether it 'fits.' "

After "Master Key to Universe," this is a bit of a comedown. If, on December 27, 1949, your mind is open to extreme possibilities, do you read this far? Does the tentative note at the end make an impression?

I went on to item 2. Three-plus years later, March 30, 1953, the *Times* front page features "Einstein Offers New

Theory To Unify Laws of the Cosmos," by the selfsame
William L. Laurence, waxing even more breathlessly bibli-
cal. Under the headline, two lines of mathematical symbols:
"Einstein's latest equations for a United Field Theory."
The lead: "Albert Einstein, named by George Bernard
Shaw as one of the eight 'Universe Builders' in recorded
history, has returned from a three-year sojourn on the
lonely summit of his scientific Sinai with a new set of laws
for the cosmos."

I skimmed: ". . . all-embracing concept, which he has
been seeking with the consecrated devotion of a high priest
of science for more than half of his seventy-four years, a
Unified Field Theory." His earlier concept, Einstein
thought, "left one serious difficulty to be solved. This 'last
step in the theory,' he adds, 'has been fully overcome in the
last few months.' "

Laurence rehashes, lifting whole sentences from 1949.
There are passages about quantum theory, fields versus
particles—phrases I recognize from Harry's crash course.
And a new, if dim, note: intimations of fallibility. A Unified
Field Theory is something "most of present-day physicists
regard as unattainable"—a phrase buried in the middle of a
sentence.

Fittingly, the piece jumps to the religion page, sur-
rounded by PRESENT IS TERMED AN "AGE OF ANXIETY," FEAR
SEEN BESETTING SELF-CENTERED MAN, SPELLMAN LEADS RITUAL
OF PALMS (this is the day after Palm Sunday)—and,
weirdly, an inch of "Einstein Talks to Group." One hundred thirteen members and guests of the Chinese Christian
Fellowship of New York City dropped in on Einstein at
home, whereupon he led them three blocks to a chapel
"where he talked to them about science and religion. Dr.

Einstein's brief talk was the climax of a day of sightseeing by the group."

I asked the girl behind the desk where I could find a phone. She told me downstairs, to the right. "You look a lot like Margo Ross," she said. A lot of people tell me that, I said. I wobbled downstairs. As soon as Tiffany told me Burke was in a meeting, acid started pouring into my stomach.

"I know what 'in a meeting' means, but he's expecting my call. I'd like you to interrupt."

"Margo, he said absolutely no calls." She tried, and failed, to sound firm, and waited for me to back off.

"Well, you'd better tell him I need an answer this minute, or a terrible technical problem is going to come up and keep his shiny new Billy Neill piece off the air."

"I can't—"

"He's going to foam at you if you don't, you hear me?"

"Hold on"—annoyed.

Half a minute went by and Burke came on, booming. "Since when do you threaten?"

"Got your attention. Didn't I."

"At the airport they arrest you for bomb jokes."

"I'm full of remorse. And Janousek's phone number is?"

A hush in the fiber-optic circuit. Then: "I'll be frank with you, Margo. Sir Colin would prefer not to mix his private and public life."

"Oil and water, right?"

"Something like that."

"In his private life," I said, "Citizen McShane would never stoop to wining and dining congressmen—"

"Whoa."

"—whose votes he needed for special dispensation to

buy an American network before he'd properly gone and naturalized himself, right?"

"I don't know that happened."

"I do."

The sound of nothing blew through the circuits. "Company business is none of my business and none of yours."

"You're not curious? I thought we take in the world."

"Very funny. The point is, and I don't know why I'm telling you this, he doesn't want you on Janousek's back."

On Janousek's back, in McShane's pocket—I was always wrongly placed in relation to the anatomy of men. "I told you, I need Janousek, he was one of the last people to see Einstein alive."

"Margo, I'm going to talk to you straight."

For a change.

"Colin McShane knows your background as well as you know his. He knows about you at Columbia and that rag—"

"*Eight Million Stories.*"

"—Always liked the name. McShane knows that Janousek was one of your Great Satans. But to him Janousek is a great man. When everyone was making nice to the Russians, Janousek was saving the West. When all the smart money was hustling tickets to the Gorbachev ball, Janousek was screaming to the top of his lungs that Gorbachev wouldn't last."

Amazing that after all these years I could have been so spectacularly naïve. I had gotten ahead at *In Depth* on brains, breasts, and pizzazz, in ascending order of importance. I had delivered the goods I was paid to deliver. I could go after Cosa Nostra or a corrupt judge or a slimebag plastic surgeon who left women's bodies in ruins. Never

mind that I had learned my stuff with Harry Kramer and
Eight Million Stories, Sir Colin McShane would throw his
dinner parties and accept compliments for my work. But
Sir Colin did not get where he got by displeasing his
friends. One word about Janousek and he reached for his
dossier. My name came up in red.

"Burke, I could care less whether Janousek is a hero or
a villain. I want to ask him questions, that's all. I'm a
reporter, that's what reporters do."

"You don't say. But—"

"You can't stop me, Burke."

I held my breath and counted off five one-thousand,
six one-thousand . . . nine seconds. He dealt his words
with care: "I can tell you what not to do on company
time."

"Do I hear you ordering me not to talk to a key source?"

"I'm taking you off the story."

I said the first thing that came to my mind, which was
nothing.

"Hello?"

"I think something went wrong with this line. I heard
you say—"

"Cut it out. Einstein is stale. Not news."

"Yesterday you didn't think so."

"Yesterday was a long time ago, when I was so generous
I forgot my news judgment."

"Dead history?"

"As a matter of fact."

"Speaking of heroes, I thought Einstein was yours."

"Then I'll just have to keep him for myself, won't I, Ms.
Ross?" Stressing the Ms. *"In Depth* is not a showroom for
my greatest hits, or yours. Tomorrow night I'm going with

designer drugs back to back with Billy Neill. About time we had a Margo Ross double-header."

I let the bribe pass. "And you told McShane I was doing Einstein."

"Con Comm is Mr. McShane's candy store. Do you want me to lie to you and tell you it isn't?"

"You're the one who told *me* to keep Einstein hush-hush, right?" Wondering what would happen if I called Sir Colin's secretary, told her I had misplaced Janousek's number.

"Margo, you there?"

"It's your show, Burke. Just do me one favor, all right? Will you please get me Janousek's number? Ask one of your fellow dinner guests, ask McShane's secretary, find a pretext, I don't care: I need that number. Not for the piece, just for me, on the side. Nobody has to know."

I could see his thin lips thinning. "You know I can't do that."

My stomach was only in flames. Sooner or later fires go out. "You know, Burke, some snags have come up. I'm not sure I can have Billy Neill ready tomorrow night."

One one-thousand, two one-thousand, three— "That is unprofessional."

"Tell me about it."

"Anyway, you're too late. I've talked to Yolanda, whose talents you tout so highly. Billy is close to ready. You're too good, Ms. Ross."

"Let me tell you something, Burke. If I walk, I walk right over to Craven at the *Times*, Whitebook at *Newsweek*, what's-his-name at *Time*, and—" I named a few more writers. Maybe the sheer length of the list would concentrate his mind. "I'm telling this whole story—"

"Calm down, Margo."

"—to these guys until I find one who says this is a story he can't refuse. Albert Einstein was murdered and Sir Colin McShane won't let his ace correspondent interview his crony. Hmm, mighty—"

"Margo."

"—interesting. At last report Sir Colin McShane didn't own all the competition. Long live competition."

"Stop it, you're getting—"

"You can never tell, Burke, what a hysterical woman's going to do. I'll tell you something else, we're getting out of our depth, maybe it's time for the cops."

"You know you'll never work in this town again."

"Don't throw me in the briar patch! You know what? I'll work in another town or I'll find an honest job for a change. Do I make myself clear?"

Seven one-thousand, eight one-thousand, nine . . .

"I'll do what I can. Call me back in a few minutes." His voice had a bit of its lilt back. I had to hand it to him: Burke was a good loser, the ideal link in any chain of command. The line went dead.

■

"We're out of practice, Harry. Somebody once taught me to diagram the connections on a napkin. Power flows through the grand canal—Janousek to McShane to Gilman to Ross."

We were standing by the phones. I'd dragged Harry downstairs from his reference books to explain that McShane had killed our piece. When I'd started the story the first time, in the reference room, I'd been loud enough to get shushed.

This should have been a hoot, me telling Harry Kramer

he needed the courage of his own analysis. But he did, and we did, and it wasn't funny. He affected a slight I-should-have-anticipated nod, but he looked deflated.

I tried to spark him up. "Don't tell me I caught you out with an innocent heart, Mr. Kramer. You think that even in high places these jerks who run the truth business are supposed to care about truth?"

He went from sulking to glaring at me, then at the marble wall. Neither gave him the satisfaction of being culpable.

"Look, two days ago you had no job at all. So you're no worse off now."

He searched my eyes for more bad news. "I'll do it for a magazine," he said, unconvincingly.

"Sure, and how're you going to get to Janousek? Look, this is hot stuff. Anyone Colin McShane is that desperate to protect knows something that we need to know."

He appraised me. "I'll miss your company on our little" —he hunted for the right word—"adventure."

"You missed my point, Harry. I said: 'Something that *we* need to know.' "

"With all due respect," he said, "they own your labor."

"They don't own every hour in my day, right? Listen to me. I refuse to make a career out of jerking off Colin McShane. If I can't do the murder of Albert Einstein, I'm paying my dues for nothing."

"Margo, think—"

"You think I'm not serious?"

"Take it easy, I'm thanking you—"

"Thanks a lot—"

"—but I still don't see how—"

"Give me a minute, I'll come up with something."

He put his hand on my shoulder, like a blind man feeling a guardrail. "Don't piss your job away for the righteous thrill. I believe in the division of labor. Outsiders need insiders. Look at what you've been able to get on the air."

"I don't believe this! Harry Kramer is lecturing me on moderation! I'll quit when it suits me to quit. Right now it suits me not to quit."

"So." His smile came back and stayed awhile. "What do we do when we find a murderer?"

"My contract says the network has exclusive rights to my face. I can't advertise perfume without their approval. It doesn't say I can't write an article. And if we solve this murder"—the words tasted odd—"when we solve it, Sir Colin may fucking well change his mind and reassign me the piece. Especially if I threaten to blow whistles on him."

Harry glowed. "Co-conspirator." I shouldn't have been surprised when his mouth came toward me to celebrate. He shouldn't have been surprised that I met him halfway, or that I opened my lips. Maybe neither of us was surprised. For a man who spent a lot of time retreating into his cave, he could certainly leap out when he wanted.

■

I punched up Burke's direct line. This time Tiffany passed me through in a flash. Harry hovered near the mouthpiece. I wanted a witness.

"You're a dirty player," Burke said, his voice flat from self-control. He read me Janousek's number. "Remember, you didn't get it from me." He didn't say how he got it. I didn't ask. Exultant Harry made fists and jabbed them in the air: a little one-two punch.

"You're welcome," Burke said. "He may not be so crazy about talking to you." He meant Janousek.

"I'll take my chances."

"And watch out. Blackmailers always pay." I let that pass.

"Margo, one more thing."

"What?"

"I want to know what develops."

"Oh? I thought Einstein's my after-hours hobby now."

"You know me, I'm a curious guy. Stay in touch."

Burke was always working every angle and a half. We take in the world. "Sure, Burke, fine."

"By the way, it would be nice if you honored us with a visit before we run Billy Neill, so we can talk about the chat." The script had a hole in it, one minute thirty, two minutes, whatever, marked CHAT. Broadcast night, the correspondent was always on hand to chat about the piece, to give the impression of having just fetched it, like a good dog.

"Wouldn't miss it for the world. I'm on my way in. Talk to you. And by the way, thanks, Burke."

"Any time."

I hung up. "Prick," I said.

"Nice," said Harry, beaming with mentor's pride.

■

I thought that I needed to know more about Janousek before calling him, so Harry pulled out his sheaf of reference-book photocopies and I took a short course, the essence of which was this:

Gustav Janousek was born Czech and Jewish in 1911 in a town with too many consonants, a town suffering from a bad case of geography, part of the Austro-Hungarian Empire, which was not long for that world. He studied physics in Vienna, then at Cambridge. On the strength of papers he published on quantum theory, he came to the States, a second-tier whiz kid, in '37, with a job at Columbia, and worked on some of the early chain-reaction experiments. He was a One Worlder then, vaguely left-wing, some kind of a pacifist, but scared to death that the Germans would develop the A-bomb first—and then, of course, most of his family vanished by '41 into the inferno. So Leo Szilard talked him into the Manhattan Project with two curious arguments he seems to have believed—first, that the scientists would keep control of the bomb; and second, that the bomb was the way to sneak world government in through the back door. At Los Alamos, Janousek had the reputation of a high-class technician, a wisecracker, and a ladies' man. His claim to fame was something that became known as the Janousek effect, which had to do with the conditions under which the bomb would detonate—the books were hazy on the details, as well as on his subsequent contributions to physics.

His contributions to the military-industrial complex were easier to trace. He opposed dropping the bomb on Japan, went so far, in fact, as to quit Los Alamos after Nagasaki, but not before he had gotten friendly with Teller, who tried to convince him to work on the so-called Super, the H-bomb. Janousek refused, though, and threw himself into the scientists' movement to control the bomb—he held on to his idea of a world government, but this time one armed with a monopoly on atomic weapons. More bad timing. In '48 came the putsch in Czechoslovakia. He had a brother, just out of a Nazi camp, who barely got away as the Stalinists were about to ship him into the Gulag. Now he was terrified that there was going to be One World, all right, but it was going to be the wrong one. Teller helped turn him. When the war ended, Janousek had gone back to Columbia, but in '47 quit to join the Institute for Advanced Study—around the time Oppenheimer became its director —and during the Oppenheimer hearings, as Rosenthal said, he sided with Teller. Naturally, things got tense for him at the Institute—his colleagues, including Einstein, thought it was ridiculous to call Oppenheimer a security risk. In '56, the year after Einstein died, Janousek gave up his Institute chair, went back to Columbia, and took up military research with a vengeance.

He hadn't thawed out from the Cold War since. In the early sixties, he promoted the fifty-megaton superbomb, since the Russians had one already. Getting picketed at Columbia made him a hero on the right-wing banquet circuit. The fire in his office was even better—he'd lost some data, and who cared if it was inconsequential? He was offered think-tank positions but swore to stay at Columbia to spite his enemies and outlast them. He did both. He became a fixture at war colleges, on government committees. Whatever the high-tech hubris, he stood ready, quotable, and hostile to the press. For example, 1990: "Some of our journalists seem to think that our weapons systems are aimed at them personally and not at our enemies. Or possibly that is the same thing."

Janousek would adore the Ross and Kramer show.

On the other hand, there was a streak of the daredevil— along with the martyr—in him. Janousek took pleasure in '68 in coming out on the library steps and calling the antiwar demonstrators storm troopers. He wanted honor in his own time. I thought there was a decent chance he wouldn't be camera shy.

.   .   .

I punched up his number. The phone rang five, six, seven, eight, nine times. I was about to hang up when a sharp voice answered, "Yah."

"May I speak to Professor Janousek, please?"

"You are speaking to him."

"This is Margo Ross. I'm a reporter for *In Depth*."

His voice turned several degrees warmer. "Hello, Miss Ross. I know you, of course. Or rather, I know who you are."

"Well, thank you," I said stupidly. "I'm sorry to bother you at home."

"That is what home is for," he said sharply.

Do not rise to the bait. Let it sink to the bottom. "I'd like to interview you about the Manhattan Project."

"What about it?"

"Um, we're interested in the origins of the nuclear age, the implications, lessons which leading physicists like yourself have learned about the relation between science and policy." The phrases wouldn't bear much scrutiny, but I hoped their sheer number would establish that I was worth talking to.

"I see." Noncommittal, caught between self-protection and vanity. He may have thought the press had typecast him as an ogre, but he still wanted to be interviewed by Margo Ross. "This does not sound like the typical kind of television subject."

"It's a new departure for us. Actually, *In Depth* is trying to win its name back. We're planning a major report and I would very much like to have your point of view." I'd never heard any network advertise a minor report.

"And when do you have this in mind?"

"As soon as possible. To tell you the truth, Dr. Janousek, your insight at this initial stage would be tremendously valuable."

"In other words, you want me to do your research." But there was a laugh crouching under his growl.

"Not at all. But I'd like"—hoping to sound just servile enough—"to talk with you soon, because of the depth of your experience, you know, your thinking."

I imagined him smoothing his thinning hair.

"Well, possibly I could see you next week."

"Actually, I was hoping for something sooner. Any time that suits you."

"During the days I am writing my memoirs, in fact."

"I'd love to—would it be possible to read them?"

"That is not possible, I'm afraid. But perhaps I could see you Thursday night—no, no, I go with my wife to the opera. Tomorrow night I have no plans but the television set. I am an addict of *In Depth*, you see, while my wife goes to the theater with her son."

"Tomorrow is difficult, I'm afraid. I have a story on the air and I have to be in the studio to introduce it."

"Of course. You do it so charmingly."

"Thank you. This is late notice, of course, but by any chance would tonight be possible?"

Harry nodded.

"Tonight," Janousek said. "Would you hold on a moment?" I heard him call out, "Ilse," then something muffled in German—his hand was over the receiver. Then he came back on the line. "Certainly. Tonight. Why not?"

Glee spread across Harry's face.

"Wonderful," I said. We agreed on eight o'clock. He gave me an address on Riverside Drive.

"I'm so glad I reached you," I said. "When the phone didn't answer, I thought—"

"I will tell you my secret," he said smoothly. "I am tired of interrupting myself to answer the phone only to find out some fool invites me to read his magazine or sell me his cruise to Bermuda or contribute to saving the world. This is half the time. You should expose these invaders of privacy. I only answer the phone after it has rung at least eight times."

Why was he telling me this? Didn't he know he sounded like a crank?

"You must have nerves of steel to put up with the ringing."

"Not at all. I have designed a device which keeps my phone bell from making a sound until the seventh ring. Only someone who genuinely wishes to speak to me will wait while the phone is ringing so long. Or they will call back."

"I'm glad I was one of the patient."

"So am I. I am an admirer of yours, you see."

■

The cloud cover was breaking up, a sickly sun was filtering through. Harry, shoulders back, scarf bunched at his neck, seemed taller, more solid. Confidence reverberated between us. Power on: the electric kick of moving the story along, making the interviews run on time. But by the time we got to the train station I felt uneasy again. Janousek, who claimed to know my work, hadn't tried hard enough to stave me off. True, he liked the spotlight, he wanted to bend the story his way. Who didn't want to lay hands on the media? Anyway, what did he have to fear? I hadn't raised a red flag about Einstein. If Janousek had filled Einstein full of speed and then gone blithely on with his life for forty years, he had a remarkable talent for concealing anxiety. Or maybe not so remarkable. Scientists were supposed to be good at ducking for cover behind their equations, as if emotions would rust the apparatus. Men liked partitions. I once interviewed a guy on death row who had raped three little girls, dismembered them, and left the pieces, mixed together, in three trash barrels at Jones Beach. He assured me in a dead voice that God had told him little girls wearing red ribbons had been chosen for sacrifice. Then he looked me up and down from behind vacant eyes.

But what did I know about murderers? They weren't my beat.

The other reason I felt edgy was that Harry had disappeared again into his private gravitational field—or, at any rate, not mine. Arms folded, he was glaring into the middle distance. "You are a rational man," I said. "Would you explain to me then why, apart from publicity, Janousek is so eager to see us?"

"Not us, you. He's supposed to like women."

I'm glad somebody does, I thought as Harry persisted in looking across the platform at someone or something worthy of his attention.

"Turn around very, very casually." He barely moved his mouth.

I turned. At the other end of the platform, a man in a gray topcoat was leaning against a stone wall, reading the *Times* through black steel glasses, looking vaguely familiar.

The man on the phone, Third World debt. Just how small a town was Princeton?

"I'm beginning to believe every fact is meaningful," I said.

"Exactly. You can see why paranoia can become routine, a form of prayer."

On the face of it, this man had no way of knowing we were going to pick Viejo Mexico for lunch. We hadn't planned it ourselves. On the other hand, here he was. Had he followed us to the library, or waited for us at the station?

"Of course," Harry said, "sometimes a cigar is just a cigar. There aren't that many restaurants to choose from. Mr. Third World Debt may have picked Mexican just to get in the mood."

The dinky was pulling into the station. A few other passengers were also waiting—an array of blue shirts and blue suits, but no blue coats. Two students walked by. One said to another, "A 1987 Porsche costs eighteen thou." "What does?" asked the other. "A 1987 used Porsche. It's got something like fourteen thousand miles on it." The train stopped and disgorged more of the professoriat on parade, including a woman in a black turban.

We went to the end of the car and sat facing Princeton Junction. The man with the *Times* went into the other car. Harry patted my hand and told me to relax.

"You were saying that Janousek likes women," I said.

"I don't know about 'likes.' Collects, from what I read."

"You're right, it's not the same thing," I said, thrown back to a memory of Harry tête-à-tête with all those long-legged experienced-looking women at the West End Bar, the parties, the millions of eligibles in the big city. What was I to him then but a wide-eyed, wide-hipped *girl*? And now—I was reduced to wondering what I was to him besides his partner in unraveling the crime of the century.

Harry, however, was back in his element, loping through the facts about Janousek, which he had gleaned from assorted memoirs. At Los Alamos, Janousek was unmarried—one of the few footloose scientist stars. Later, he was said to have been the scourge of secretaries at the Institute for Advanced Study. There was a suggestion of scandal in his Institute colleague Martin Fleischmann's sudden divorce in 1956 and the remarriage of Ilse ex-Fleischmann, renowned beauty, to Janousek—who, at fifty-two, had never before been married. The memoirs of atomic scientists were discreet to the point of vagueness on this matter (and Fleischmann had yet to be heard from), but divorce was apparently uncommon in these circles. Nor was it common for members of the Institute to graze away from their lifelong sinecures. But wild-hearted Janousek was not a man to fear the improbable. Accompanied by Ilse and her ten-year-old son, he relocated to Columbia, while Fleischmann stayed on at the Institute, where he remained in an advanced state of emeritus.

Harry inspected a photocopied page from *Who's Who in American Science.* 1956, a big year in Janousek's life. Einstein dies in 1955, Janousek's life turns over in 1956.

The conductor stuck his neck out the door and barked, "*All* aboard." The dinky inched forward. The door to the next car opened and the man in the black steel glasses walked in, swaying with the train.

"Harry."

"I see him."

When he had pulled even with us, he sat down across the aisle and leaned toward me. "Excuse me, Miss Ross."

"Yes?"

"Please forgive me, I hate to intrude. Actually, I'm not in the habit of accosting celebrities—" How original, I thought. "But I just wanted to say that I'm an admirer of yours." He was wearing a school ring but I couldn't tell which school.

"That's very kind."

"And one other thing, if I may. One of these days I hope you look into arms sales and international banking. Billions in deposits from Lower Manhattan, guaranteed in Washington, end up in Swiss bank accounts via any number of dictatorships. There is a lot of pure swindle. You'd be surprised. Well, *you* wouldn't be surprised."

I let out a smile. "Do I take it that you're in international banking yourself?"

"I consult." He handed me a neatly embossed business card which said he was Thomas McGregor, Vice President, Interbank Data Analysis, with a Park Avenue South address.

"I wasn't sure it was you at the restaurant." The steel ellipses over his eyes glittered. "Well, I won't bother you any further," he said, and retreated to the far end of the car.

At Princeton Junction, Harry and I walked through a tunnel to wait for the northbound train. Thomas McGregor stayed on the southbound side, heading for Trenton, Philadelphia, Washington.

All the way back to New York, I lay still, trying to doze, but my mind kept kicking up loose facts, biographical fragments, strange trajectories. Thomas McGregor streaked through, a freak particle. As Einstein lay dying, Janousek

and Gottehrer were making their pilgrimages to the hospital. As for the means of murder, who in the fifties couldn't
have procured fistfuls of those festive little yellow, pink,
and orange diet pills? Students lived on speed. Surely this
Gottehrer would have had no trouble. A question for my
onetime protector Delaney, if I wanted to ask a cop.

Motives were still obscure. Rotate the glial cells. Suspect
the butler's long-lost cousin.

Consider Franz Rosenthal, for example. A generous
man, you could tell. Einstein was in tremendous pain. Suppose he begged his reliable old friend Franz to put him out
of his misery. Rosenthal was resourceful, he could have
figured out how to kill him quickly, painlessly.

But, then, how could he have been sure the speed would
work? Moreover, if Rosenthal was right, Janousek paid
his second visit to Einstein after Rosenthal left. Suppose
Janousek had found Einstein dead. Why would he have
held his silence all these years? What was he doing in
Einstein's room, anyway?

Or consider the nurse, Parenti. No one would have had
an easier time getting her hands on a common drug.

Or suppose Rosenthal and the nurse agreed to take Einstein out of his misery, and alibied for each other.

Ditto Rosenthal and Janousek — in which case, why was
the former casting suspicion on the latter?

There were orderlies to consider.

Paranoids never rest. I opened my eyes for comfort. At
my right hand sat Harry, my mentor in systematic suspicion, eyes closed. I was in danger of getting whacked out
on conspiracy theory. Connect Lee Harvey Oswald to a
gay New Orleans pilot who wore eyebrows made from an
orange rug — advance to Go. The plotters always doped out

the right motorcade route, ordered the right rifle, knew where to be seen, whom to set up; they thought of everything—except the dogged conspiracy theorist years later, stockpiling facts like Mannlicher-Carcano rifles.

Except that in *Fix* Harry was right. History *is* an unsolved crime. Paranoia is indispensable. We hold this truth to be self-evident, that clandestine squads have been endowed by their creators with inalienable rights and far-out powers. The CIA really did run the opium trade in Southeast Asia. Nixon's gangs broke, entered, stole, assaulted, lied—that was what they got caught at; but nobody ever stopped them from running their private war in Cambodia. Harry's bankers-and-hookers turned out picayune compared to P2, the secret lodge of Italian bankers, generals, and Fascist assassins. Iran-Contra. B.C.C.I. Was it crazies who made history or history that made people crazy?

I closed my eyes. The train found its rhythm. As Harry used to say, *The question is always, Cui bono?* My mantra, my reason, my rhyme—the depth it is my holy mission to go into. All right, who benefited from the murder of Albert Einstein?

Cold Warriors, bomb-makers, right-wingers, anti-Semites. If we're not going to eliminate anyone, add quantum theorists. Professor X, the dice-thrower, out on a limb with a lot of useless theory.

I reasoned like a rat smashing around in a maze.

When I opened my eyes, we were in the darkness that leads into Penn Station. I understood nothing.

∎

Harry decided to walk to the Forty-second Street library to look up old *Eight Million Stories* pieces on Janousek, while I took a cab to Big Glass. There were sixteen message slips waiting for me. Three calls that afternoon from a Mr. Norman Gottehrer. I would know what he was calling about, he would call back. No number. Cyrilly said his voice was low, gravelly. "He goes, 'Is Margo there?' like a breather, you know. Weird." I half expected to see a message from Janousek, canceling, but there was none. Chip McHargue, Billy Neill's press agent, a.k.a. Cash McHype, had stopped by, "just to see how things were going." "You should have seen the ostrich feather in his hat," she said. "He invited me over to see his collection." She didn't know how he had succeeded in getting upstairs. I told her to call downstairs to security and tell them never again, under any circumstances, to allow Chip McHargue inside the building.

I asked her to track down Yolanda, who turned out to be filling in on the morning show. I took the elevator upstairs. The Muzak was playing "Ain't That a Shame" with too many violins.

A.M. occupied an enormous room on the fourteenth floor. Most of the space was divided into cubicles just big enough to turn around in, partitions just tall enough to look over. Decorations were posted: " 'It Was Worse Than Beirut' " (a yellowed *Post* headline); SECOND CLASS (a rubber stamp). Long glass windows, mirrors—the room was known as the Fluorescent Ice Tray.

A producer with teased hair was on the phone with a prospective guest: "So tell me, what's wrong with surrogate mothers? I *know* you've written about this issue, but I need to hear you put it in, you know, your own words." She listened. "O.K., thanks, we'll get back to you this afternoon, will you be at this number?" She hung up, consulted a yellow notepad, punched up another number. "Hi, this is Stephanie Lopez at *A.M. Coast to Coast?*" Her next-door neighbor was gushing about an infant who had just received a heart-lung transplant. A woman in red leaned over and said: "Forget him, he's already done *G.M.A.*" Stephanie Lopez swiveled and said to the noisemakers, "Would it be possible for this caravan to move on?" I crossed the room.

On the far side of the ice tray were the tiny editing rooms, closets with glass doors, the better for the bosses to monitor the hands. By contrast, *In Depth* showed a certain respect for—as they called it on my floor—the craft of reporting: we got larger rooms, opaque doors. Yolanda was cutting a piece about teenagers who dressed up like robots and took over shopping malls for ritual dances at the crack of dawn. Her eyes were red, her eye shadow electric blue. Burke had requisitioned the Billy Neill piece, she said. One cutaway bothered him.

We adjourned to a larger editing room downstairs and screened our about-to-be-celebrated profile about apocalypse, redemption, and popular music. A sleek little thing, the cuts hard and tight. I particularly liked the segue from a gaunt short-haired Billy on the beach, muttering "It's like, I had to find some peace inside myself," to a sweet-faced ponytailed Billy on tour twenty years ago, roaring "If you ain't got peace you're kissin' ashes." We ended on the beach with Billy Null banging out a monotone guitar chord and spitting out syllables in a sort of spastic rant:

The headlines are screamin', they're tellin' the
children the news

While time chews its bone outside the tomb o' the
    hero
I hear in my heart the porcupine wail o' the blues
I give you my nothin' o' rainbows, my absolute zero
    heart.

Yolanda had artfully inserted over-the-shoulder cutaways
as punctuation for Billy's soliloquies: Margo deeply concerned (brow wrinkling, head tilting, chin forward),
Margo perplexed turning to fascinated (querulous eyes
slowly widening), Margo bemused (the corners of my lips
lifting). Acceptable Margo, except in one shot from slightly
below, where my chin doubled. Digitize that face. The
cutaway Burke didn't like took place during the Billy Null
sequence. I looked skeptical and Burke thought I should
look delighted, "open to experience." I asked Yolanda to
lose the chubby shot and keep the skeptical look.

I also asked her to restore Billy's heartfelt sermon
against drugs—in extreme close-up, emphasizing his soulful look, hollow eyes, and ravaged complexion, which
might or might not have something to do with drugs, but
would send the right subliminal message. Making a nice
cross-link to the designer-drugs piece. Burke liked that sort
of thing.

I went back to my office to write a script for a live intro.
Nothing came. My eyes drifted up to the clippings taped to
the wall. On one, a critic from *Time* said that I was "the
aroused conscience of our spaced-out age." It was growing
a bit yellowish, the edges curling. I got up and tried the
couch. I thought about old Ekecrantz's record-breaking
doll's house. Time to send a crew to see how he was coming. The VISUALIZE IMPEACHMENT sticker on the back of

my desk was starting to peel. Time to cover it with something more current. Propose a new slogan to Sir Colin. WE TAKE YOU OUT OF THIS WORLD. Win an employee incentive award.

Life was a perpetual quest for the right slogan. Which gave me a place to start the intro: "In the sixties, a whole generation hungered not only for the music of Billy Neill but for his guidance. They waited on his words. They quoted him in bed." (He probably quoted himself in bed.) "Bob Dylan, Lennon and McCartney, Simon and Garfunkel, Billy Neill, they were the wise men. But today's young people, who buy the records, have other tastes. So Billy's famous now for having been famous once. His last tour was not exactly a success." (He had to break it off in the middle. He was so strung out on coke he couldn't stand up.) "But Billy Neill refuses to lie down and live on the royalties he collects from his faded glories. After his well-publicized tribulations, Billy is not done surprising his fans. As we see in this story, Billy's back." Barf. But it would do for now. I needed an outro, too, but that would have to wait.

I took the elevator upstairs. The Muzak was playing "Blowin' in the Wind." At the entry to Burke's office, Tiffany glared at me. She was wearing a wide cinched belt and a tight sweater that gave her the look of a black-haired Barbie doll. A cloud of boisterous perfume came my way. "Is he expecting you?" she asked, slight stress on the "you," registering my fall from grace—she might as well have been asking if I was there to fix the copy machine.

"I'm the meeting," I said. She picked up the phone and said, "Margo Ross is here to see you." There was an indecipherable squawk at the other end and she said, "Go right in." If her voice had been any more brittle, it would have cracked.

Burke, squeezing his blue clay in his left hand, was watching his four-screen monitor setup: local news, national cable news, *Blind Date*, *Jeopardy*. The colors were neon-bright by contrast with the overcast canyon outside. The sound was up on the local news, a blonde named Wilde whose news director's style was to freeze-frame a news piece in the middle, go for the burst of feeling. Slow-mo e-mo.

Burke muted the sound. "What do you think of her?"

"Who, Vanna White?"

"Yeah, sure, Vanna White."

"Adorable, Burke, but a five-alarm fire would strain her capacities."

"Yeah, right," he said. "So, how are things in the higher reaches of atomic physics?"

"Fine," I said. "Couldn't be better."

"Good, good." He sucked in his lips and bit them together. Then he inspected me from my hair down, as if surveying the paperback rack at the airport. I straightened my back.

"Listen to this," I said, and read him my lead-in for Billy Neill. He gazed at his monitor the whole time.

"Love it," he said when I was done. "I just want you to know I'm ecstatic that we're going with designer drugs. I always wanted this piece to hit people when they'd be open to it. So about the chat, I think you can hammock from Billy Neill to designer drugs in—" His phone trilled. He picked it up. "Yeah, put him on." He punched a button and blared into the speakerphone. "Yeah, yeah. We've done a lot of that 'last elephants' sort of thing. Snooze city. Iowa wants to know about the poachers. When are you leaving for Antigua? Have a terrific time." He hung up and without skipping a beat said, ". . . in a sort of hammock, so here's Billy Neill who's put his life together, here's a constructive way out for today's fucked-up youth, et cetera, et cetera. Then you come back after designer drugs, hone in on the point."

I leveled my eyes at him. "Great idea, Burke. I've been waiting for an idea like that."

"Did I say something funny?"

As I got up, the phone was trilling. "See you tomorrow," Burke said to me. "Break your neck."

"You, too," I said, but Burke, gazing out over his monitors, was already crooning into his speaker, "Talk to me."

By the time I got back to my office, Gottehrer had called again. "I didn't exactly understand his message," Cyrilly said. "It sounded something like, 'Is she still interested in Einstein?' Does that make sense?"

"If he calls again, tell him I'm very eager to talk to him. Underscore very. Did he leave a number?"

"Said he was calling from a pay phone."

"If anyone happens to ask, don't tell him, her, or it, I mean anyone, even that much."

Not that I needed to caution her. Cyrilly was impeccably discreet. She had answered my phone and typed my mail for two years before turning to me with her big eyes, asking, "Is it true that you worked on an underground paper in the sixties?" I had explained that *Eight Million Stories* didn't start until '70, and was on the respectable side of underground, but yes, there was a resemblance. She'd goggled as though she'd just beheld Madonna the Virgin Mary and Madonna the singer strolling through the door arm in arm.

Now Cyrilly looked as though she'd let my pet parrot out the window and didn't know how to tell me. I asked her what was the matter.

"As, um, a matter of fact, Sir Colin's girl called, she wanted to know if any calls had come into the office about um, Albert Einstein, said it was vital to know."

So McShane was also a hunter and I was also a quarry. Hunter and quarry twice over if I counted Gottehrer. I didn't relish the feeling. To feel the eyes of admirers on your skin, this is a woman's joy if she's lucky—whatever anyone may say—but to feel the surveillance up your skirt, so to speak, that was something else. What would McShane do to kill a story?

"Did you—?"

"I said not exactly."

"Did that satisfy her?"

"Not exactly, but I didn't know what else—"

"You did fine. By the way, did Gottehrer ask for my home number?"

"No, he just said he wanted to talk to you."

"Remember, never—"

The edge in my voice cut her. "I'd never do that."

I took the elevator down to the lobby. The flower seller was just beginning to pack up. I bought two dozen roses, took them back upstairs, handed one dozen to Cyrilly and asked her to find Yolanda and give her the others.

"What did I do?" Cyrilly said.

"What does anyone do?"

■

The doorman at Janousek's building on Riverside Drive was ensconced in a glass-enclosed cubicle to the right of the door. When he turned and looked up from his little black-and-white TV, I could see he was a stocky man with a thick mustache that curved down around his mouth. My face interested him, and he was suddenly all business, buzzing Janousek's apartment. Janousek must have told him to send us up. 16B, the doorman said, take the elevator in back. The dimly lit lobby was lined with dark red rugs, thick tapestries on the walls.

The elevator ticked and clattered. Anxiety clawed at me under my breastbone—my old ulcer again. "Don't worry," I said to Harry. "McShane's lust for the numbers is going to save this piece. He'll dump Janousek over the side for a forty share."

A dark half-smile. "Confidence suits you."

On the sixteenth floor, there were two doors. Between them, a green marble-top table, and above it a Klee reproduction, creamy gold. A bemused face, the shape of a bird cage or a bomb, suspended in the air, arms extended, next to a piano with a candelabrum on top. At the bottom, in Klee's spidery scrawl: *"Tanze Du Ungeheüer zu meinem Sanften Lied!"*

" 'Dance, you monster, to my soft song,' " Harry translated. "But spelled wrong. We've come to the right place."

"That makes us the monster?" I wanted to know.

There was a numbered push-button dial over the doorknob to 16B—a burglar-alarm system instead of a key lock. Harry buzzed.

The woman who opened the door had excellent cheekbones in a refined face, silver hair gathered in a bun—everything about her was fine to the point of frailty. She wore a light gray dress with a mild floral pattern and had an earnest, melancholy air, as if she worked at solemnity. She seemed surprised to see two of us. "Please come in, Miss Ross," she said with a trace of an accent. I introduced Harry. Her smile lingered on him.

She led us into a living room with a high ceiling immediately dwarfed by the view. Most of the clouds had cleared, and the moon, almost full, was a huge white stone hanging over the Palisades. In the moon-drenched light, the great silvered expanse of the river poured into the room. Ilse Janousek examined the panorama as if she, too, were seeing it for the first time. The rest of the room was full of soft, comfortable furniture, vases with dried flowers, little tables with thin curved legs—curves everywhere. On the couch lay a needlepoint circle with a half-finished flower design. I couldn't identify the paintings on the walls, but they looked serious—nonrepresentational collisions of spiky shapes, Expressionist swathes of color. The floor was parquet and it creaked.

Just past the living room, she turned right, opened a door, and ushered us into a long, dimly lit room, showing more moon and Palisades behind another wall-sized window. The backlighting was so brilliant that the small man in the corner sitting in a dark armchair, feet up on a leather ottoman, was at first barely visible.

"Yes," said Gustav Janousek, laying a magazine on a side table, "it is wonderful if you like New Jersey. Personally, I have had enough of that state." He stood up and peered at us.

He was a small man, and his thinning white hair, combed straight back, sharpened his face. His nose was flattened, as if it had once been broken—another point to

Angela Parenti. The sharpness of his voice sliced the air—this our phone conversation had prepared me for. What surprised me were his hazel eyes, which were large and unexpectedly warm.

"This is Miss Ross," his wife said, "and Mr.—I'm sorry, what was your name?"

"Kramer, Harry Kramer."

"My associate," I said.

Harry gave Janousek a steady look and said, "I've been looking forward to meeting you for a long time."

"Thank you," Janousek said. "I hope you are not disappointed." Turning to me, he said: "You did not tell me you were bringing your entire organization. Well, as I said before, I am your greatest admirer."

"Then I hope *you* are not disappointed," I said.

Ilse left, shutting the door behind her. Janousek walked briskly to a chair on the far side of his desk and sat down. The chair must have been high, because he dominated the desk and the desk dominated the room, a fortress of heavy polished wood. There was a telephone perched on top of an electronic box, along with three perfectly neat piles of papers, a German stein full of pencils, three framed photographs standing erect, and in the corner a bronze bust of a stern, handsome man I didn't recognize. The wall behind him was hung with plaques and certificates. The bric-a-brac on the shelves included a shiny metallic model of a missile.

Janousek waved me to his armchair. "Please sit there, Miss Ross, so you are not distracted from my lectures." He pointed Harry to a low, rumpled sofa a few feet away. The one certificate I could read on the wall was an honorary degree from the U.S. Air Force Academy. The thick, well-thumbed large-size paperback on his desk was *Will American Power Outlast the Cold War?* From where I sat, I could also see a fireproof safe in the corner.

"So you are interested in the Manhattan Project," he said with a toothy smile. "I suppose you are going to say this was a terrible waste of funds plucked by unfeeling brutes out of the mouths of homeless wretches."

This interview was not going to go smoothly. I pulled my jacket closer. "Not at all, Professor Janousek. We want to explore how the relationship between the scientists and the government during the Manhattan Project carried over into—"

"Exploring is for astronauts," he snapped. "Do not waste my time with euphemisms. I am a scientist. There is no such thing as exploring without a hypothesis. I take it you have a hypothesis." He ran his fingers back through his hair and glowed triumphantly, his eyes darting from Harry to me and back.

Harry was smooth. "We do. That the Manhattan Project was a shock from which science has never recovered. In order to save democracy, scientists enlisted to build the bomb. In the process, they signed a pact with the government. By signing that pact, they lost the initiative. Ever since, they have been torn about the nature of the pact—should they surrender to it, trying to renegotiate the terms once in a while, or should they try to repeal it and take back control of science? Sometimes they do the first, sometimes they do the second."

"A shock, yes." Janousek leaned forward, propping a pencil between his outstretched index fingers. His fingers were surprisingly long, and as thin as the rest of him. "Among the atomic scientists we used to say the question was whether we would be on tap or on top. On tap or on top. A good question." He lowered his eyes for a second, then flicked a look at Harry. "You are not unaware that this question could be applied to strategic defense, which is fighting for its life. The media typically have this all wrong. Strategic defense is not a fantasy of government. It is science. Science!" He rapped the eraser end of the pencil against the desk. "Scientists want to know, censors want to suppress knowledge. Censorship is for Communists, not for free people! It is as simple as that. The Communists always talked about liberation—well, the real question is whether science is to be liberated to defend this country." He fixed me with his bright eyes. I tried to read Harry's expression, but he was impenetrable.

"I know what you are thinking," Janousek said. "You think that I am an old man living in the past, that I do not understand that the Cold War has ended and Communism is finished—as the press kept crooning for years until their favorite, Mr. Gorbachev, fell off his horse. Now these geniuses discover again that the Communist Party did not vanish simply because some of the apparatchiks changed their uniforms! And we have lost precious time!"

I gave an interviewerly nod.

"You people will never learn: the face of the enemy changes, but one thing that does not is the gullibility of America. You think I am extreme."

No more than a caveman thawed out of a time capsule and ranting about dangerous mastodons, I thought.

"Outspoken," Harry said, deadpan.

"Outspoken, very good. But already I am wandering away from the Manhattan Project."

"No, this is fascinating," I said quickly.

The door opened. Ilse walked in carrying, on a silver tray, a delicate bone-white teapot, three small matching cups, and a dish of butter cookies. She slid the tray onto the desk, poured three cups of some perfumed tea, and withdrew, closing the door gingerly behind her.

"Good." Janousek resumed as if nothing had intervened. "I will take you at your word. The genius of the Manhattan Project is that, once the goal of building the atomic bomb was agreed upon, the army left us alone. That is to say, Groves was a fool, but as a general he knew his limits. It took two and a half years from the chain reaction at Chicago to the first atomic explosion. Two and a half years! Not bad." I didn't care what he said, just that he kept talking. I composed my face and scrawled notes.

"If Groves or Oppenheimer had to go back to Washington and testify before committees of ignoramuses for every appropriation, today we would be holding our conversation in German. Or Russian, who knows?" He showed his teeth and waited for his hyperbole to take effect.

Harry concocted a smile of his own. My eyes grazed over the photos on Janousek's desk. In one, Janousek posed stiffly next to a glowering Edward Teller, whose fierce eyebrows judged the photographer from a superior plane. Another, sepia, had Janousek in sunglasses, part of a group on a hill under a huge sky. This had to be Los Alamos, the garden of transgression, where the scientists first knew sin. In the picture on the side table next to the tea tray, Janousek was accepting a handshake from a twinkly Ronald Reagan.

"Of course," Janousek went on, "Groves heard a lot of grumbling from my colleagues, including myself. That is all very well—science thrives on openness and the military thrives on secrets. I myself, with Feynman, once cracked Oppenheimer's safe just to prove that we could do it." His eyes crackled—larcenous eyes, where a rapscallion of a boy still lived. "But Groves did not have to fight for research funds against the opposition of members of his own profession." I raised an eyebrow. "As it is, some of my colleagues think they know more about national security than their elected leaders. It is truly miraculous. We have biophysicists and reporters who think they know more about Brilliant Pebbles than our colleagues in the weapons laboratories. I mean no disrespect, of course. The lesson of the Manhattan Project is that good science is possible if it is, one, funded; two, patriotic; and three, left alone."

Harry stroked his chin from the underside, as if in homage to his lost beard.

"So you see," Janousek said, "if you are looking for an authoritative quotation, you have come to the right place. I am secretly a dialectician, I think all things come in threes, and the third is not what you expect."

So Janousek had been a Communist somewhere along the line. There was the same ham-handed logic.

"I have no doubt that we've come to the right place," I said.

Janousek's grin was fixed, a nice freeze-frame.

"If I may pursue this a moment," Harry said.

"What are you here for if not to pursue me?"

"Indeed. Well, then, what would you say to the charge that you want to have your cake and eat it, too? You want science absolutely subsidized and absolutely free?"

Janousek did not hesitate. "I would say you are playing a word game. If you will forgive me, the business of the government is to produce knowledge. That is what it means to 'provide for the common defense.' This is the Constitution speaking. It does not say, 'Follow the uninformed opinions of demagogues.' If America does not stand for knowledge, we might as well give up. Which is what some people prefer. Don't bother arguing. I will tell you something. There are people who will tell you the Russians cannot make space defenses because their empire has fallen apart, or because they cannot make an elevator work. Moonshine! The reason they cannot make an elevator work is that their engineers are busy making their space defenses work and selling the technology to the highest bidders. I know what little groups can accomplish when they are, one, dedicated; two, secret; and three, smart. The Manhattan Project was dedicated, secret, and smart. True, we had the advantage of Hungarians. Who knows, the Russians had their own Hungarians, too, once upon a time. The Russians are no fools. Ask any Czech and he will tell you that it's the Americans who are the fools. Fifty years into the atomic age, they still think they are protected by oceans."

He was no longer speaking to me or Harry, especially — he might as well have been orating to the Palisades. And yet he claimed my total attention, the way crazy people do on a crowded street. Nothing could convince him he hadn't seen into the nature of things. I wondered how he had insinuated his way into Ilse Fleischmann's bed. Sharp features, sharp tongue — he wasn't my type. There are unformed women who welcome incisive men, but Ilse didn't appear to be one of them.

Outside, the moon was ice-white on the river.

"This is the American disease," Janousek tossed in.

"You certainly have kept your immunity," I said.

"You will notice that I have retained my accent. That is all I wish to retain of the Old World. I know what an accent can do for you in America." If it's not Spanish, I thought. "But even I have been a fool for more of my life than I choose to remember."

"I find that hard to believe," Harry said dryly.

"Oh yes, I understand deeply the blissful state of mind which is pacifism"—he spat out the word. "I spent many years in the faith. It is like smoking—you cut off your lungs to spite your face."

Harry pounced. "When you speak of pacifism, are you referring, for example, to Einstein?"

Janousek clasped his hands and set them in front of him like a grenade. "Einstein was a delightful man. He was cheerful even when he disagreed with you. He was kind to idiots. No one could stay irritated with Einstein."

Harry turned the sentence over. "No one."

"You would have to be a Nazi," Janousek snapped.

"I take it that you worked with Einstein?"

Janousek smiled a humoring smile. "One did not work *with* Einstein, one worked *for* him. Einstein was busy with his apprentices, chasing his wild goose, his so-called unified field theory. In common with the rest of our profession, I did not share his enthusiasm."

"You were friendly with him, though."

"Why not? We were colleagues—if it is not, mmm, grandiose to speak of being the colleague of Einstein. Our offices were on the same floor. We had, you know, cordial relations. From time to time we discussed problems of mutual interest."

"But not the unified field theory," Harry said.

"He knew very well I thought it was nonsense. Even his apprentices had doubts."

"Then I take it that what was of mutual interest to the two of you was the state of the world?"

"Of course. But"—Janousek swiveled toward me—"I fail to see what my conversations with Einstein have to do with the subject of your investigation."

I had a set piece ready. "One thing we're interested in, Professor Janousek, is how the mood of the atomic scientists changed. It seems to me, and I very much want to hear your thinking about this, that Einstein was representative of one attitude, and you became representative of a different one. Television, of course, dwells on the human element. So naturally your relationship is of interest to us."

"I see," Janousek said, scratching his ear. "Yes, well— I'm afraid I have nothing sensational to offer you."

Harry leaned forward. "You said a moment ago that no one could *stay* irritated with Einstein. I take it, then, that there were occasions when you *got* irritated with him."

Janousek gave a perfunctory shrug. "This happens among colleagues. Even if one of them is God." He picked up a pencil and placed it parallel to the edge of his desk. "I will tell you something. At the risk of puncturing an illusion. Einstein ached for the whole world, but when it came to Czechoslovakia, well, Czechoslovakia wasn't very significant for him. Oh, he said the right things, the coup was terrible, et cetera, et cetera, but he could not find room in his heart. Well, it was not his country." Janousek's sincere self-righteousness filled the room. "It was his philosophical temper to think about universals, the peace of mankind, time and space, the unified field theory, and so on. He *could not feel*"—he stabbed the air three times with his pencil—

"what I felt when that man died." Janousek lowered his pencil to the bust on his desk.

I wondered what Einstein would have said in his own defense.

"That is Jan Masaryk," Janousek said.

"Ah."

"You have heard of Jan Masaryk, then."

"Of course, but I didn't know what he looked like," Harry said.

Janousek put down his pencil. "He was my friend before the war. A believer in reason, peace, all the ideals. The soul of enlightenment, if you believe in a soul. He believed we could come to terms with the Communists. I will tell you without pride that I believed it myself. I was, as you may know, a World Federalist—and perhaps you know that I wasn't the only one among the atomic scientists."

"What years are we talking about?"

He pursed his lips. " '46, '47. At this time even Teller, for example, also believed in a world government. This surprises you. Yes, world government—armed with atomic bombs. What was the alternative? We believed that conflict came from ignorance, or misunderstanding, and then the atomic bomb was going to knock heads together. Do you find this hard to believe? You are not old enough. If you live long enough in the twentieth century, you understand the lengths to which people will go when they need to believe in the good will of terrible people. We were traumatized first by Hitler, then by Hiroshima, and desperate to believe that now everyone is going to be cooperative. You are familiar with this kind of nonsense." The look he shot at Harry was distinctly accusatory. But it only grazed him.

"You discussed these things with Einstein?"

"Of course. Many times. Then, in 1948, the Communists took over Czechoslovakia—half the power wasn't enough for them, Stalin wanted it all—and the next thing you knew, Jan Masaryk was dead on the pavement. They claimed he jumped. Who knows? Does it matter? When he hit the ground, my faith, let us call it my faith, also hit the ground. I was lucky—I picked myself up and walked away. My own brother was lucky, too—he walked through the Austrian border an hour before the guards closed it. A whole year the Nazis had him in Mauthausen, and now he was forced to take refuge in Austria! When I looked around, I realized that for years I had been making allowances for Stalin. Not just in what I said, but in what I thought. Poor Stalin, he always had his eyes set on the higher things, but the mean West drove him into a corner. Poor Stalin, England left him out of the Munich deal, so he had to sign a pact with Hitler. Poor Stalin, he had to develop the atomic bomb because the United States developed the atomic bomb. Enough! When Jan Masaryk died, I stopped making up Stalin's alibis. Let him make up his own."

Harry wore a feline smirk, hearing exactly what he had expected from Janousek, but even more lusciously stated. "Surely you don't think that Einstein sympathized with Stalin."

"Of course not! Don't misunderstand me. He said to me once: 'Holy Russia might as well have been invented by the capitalists to discredit socialism forever.' Privately, he was very disturbed by the coup, even alarmed. But he was reluctant to speak out publicly and join in the 'anti-Soviet crusade,' that is what he called it. You must face facts, Mr. Kramer. Einstein was a socialist and he refused to wake up from his dream. He thought in unities, unified fields, you know—One World, the United Nations, so on. When the world proved more horrible than he wished, he simply closed his eyes and plunged on."

I loathed his smugness—loathed him all the more because I could feel myself drawn into his POV.

"What I'd like to know," said Harry, "is whether your differences affected your personal relations."

Janousek squinted. "No, there was no point in arguing with him. I knew he would start humoring me like one of the psychotics who flocked to his door. No, we sidestepped the subject."

"And later, when you started speaking out in favor of developing the hydrogen bomb?"

"I see that you are well prepared," Janousek said sharply.

"We don't want to waste your time."

"I appreciate that. Nor do I want to waste yours. We are all busy people. About the hydrogen bomb, my position was no secret. After the coup d'état in Prague I changed my mind and supported Teller. This got me in trouble with some of my colleagues, though by no means all."

"Rosenthal, for example?" I asked.

Janousek stroked his chin. "Rosenthal—yah, Rosenthal, for example. Einstein said nothing to me, as I recall. Well, of course he did stop circulating to me his peace petitions. A waste of paper—down to his dying days."

Bingo. I put down my notebook. "You mean the Bertrand Russell statement?"

Janousek nodded. "Very good. He did not wish to fight with me. He was a real man of peace, you see." His irony was like squeaking chalk.

There is a particular pleasure in trapping a liar. "I don't understand," I said. "If he was no longer coming to you with his peace petitions, how did you know about Russell's letter?"

"The same way the rest of the world knew, as if anyone cared," he said with a little shrug. "Through the newspapers, after Einstein was dead."

I hated his little triumph, but there he squatted with it.

The light in his eyes died down. He dusted the desk with his hand. When he raised his eyes, he seemed further away. "I wonder, can you understand? For my part, I felt that I had lost the comfort which one gains with comfortable opinions. There were people who said that I had thrown in my lot with Senator McCarthy. Idiotic. McCarthy was a thug. He made it hard to conduct *serious* discussions about the security of this country and the Free World." The phrase clunked out, defunct slang. "I will tell you something that may shock you. Around the Institute for Advanced Study, it took no particular strength of character to oppose the hydrogen bomb. It was I who was the rebel for taking Teller's side. If I would have to suffer for it—well, suffering is in the nature of things. Peace is an illusion of lazy minds. The universe is a carnivore. I no longer think that truth was invented for the happiness of one's friends."

"And Oppenheimer? Was he one of your friends?"

"I would not go so far as to say that the man had friends. Let me put it this way: we respected one another."

"Then he must not have been pleased," Harry said, "when you said he was a security risk."

Janousek chuckled. "No, he was not pleased. But of course this was nothing personal. I sent him a note to say so. I had the audacity to support Teller on a matter of principle, period. Teller was careful to say that in his opinion Oppenheimer was a loyal American. The only issue was whether Oppenheimer could be trusted with secrets."

"Einstein felt otherwise, of course," Harry said.

Janousek grinned. "Yes, he did, along with the rest of the Institute. They had a parochial interest—rally around Oppenheimer. Fleischmann was particularly vigorous on this issue." I expected a leer at this mention of the hapless Fleischmann, father of his stepson, but Janousek was only bemused. "Even von Neumann testified for Oppenheimer, although they disagreed violently on the hydrogen bomb. Well, we all have to live with ourselves."

"So you were considered disloyal?"

"By some, I was. Imagine: Because I was loyal to my country, I said, sincerely, that Oppenheimer was unwise. For this, I was accused of disloyalty. Whether my erstwhile colleagues were loyal to me is a question I leave to you." Again he maneuvered his pencil parallel to the desk edge. "You know, I will tell you something you may not believe, but it is nevertheless true. Oppenheimer himself held no grudge. An odd man. He wrote to me that I was playing my part in the great scheme of things, and that a proper understanding eluded us all. In those years, we saw each other for afternoon tea, but he could not say this to my face, he wrote. There was some mumbo jumbo about Hindu gods. I could perhaps find the note for you if you like."

"Thank you. Perhaps when we come back to film," I said.

He hesitated before saying, "Perhaps, yes."

"So I take it that Oppenheimer did not force you out of the Institute," Harry said.

"Absolutely not. Who says such a thing? I left for strictly personal and professional reasons."

Janousek was a master sidestepper, and we weren't laying a finger on him. Depressing enough that he held his ferocious opinions. Worse, on camera he was going to show up as an admirable ogre—the kind of strong face and pungent voice that win arguments with a quip. He could run away with the piece if I wasn't careful. That is, if the piece was brought back from the land of the dead.

A few times a year I wish I had never given up smoking. I wanted to be in charge of something, like the movement of poisonous gases through my lungs. I waited for Harry to jab through Janousek's defenses.

"You mentioned the nuts who besieged Einstein. I wonder if you remember a man named Gottehrer."

Did I imagine Janousek hesitating? "Gottehrer?"

"A young would-be philosopher Einstein seems to have taken a liking to. Tall and thin, with ears that stuck out," Harry said, cupping his hands to simulate the ears.

Janousek cast his eyes at the ceiling. A thick seam of paint was showing. "Yes, there was a boy with big ears and big ideas. He would come to visit Einstein at the Institute."

"I'm curious whether, in the days before Einstein's final attack, you might have run into him at Einstein's house."

Janousek made a sucking expression, as if his thoughts were sour. "You seem to have left behind the subject of science and policy. This is beginning to sound more like a police investigation."

I stopped breathing. "That's not my intention," Harry said smoothly. "But it is known that Einstein worked on the unified field theory up to the time of his death. I gather that he sent for his notes in the hospital." To me, he sounded sincere, if oblique. I couldn't tell how he played to Janousek.

"Yes—" said Janousek, waiting for Harry to show another card.

"Well—I'm thinking out loud here—the best way for us to get at the relation between science and policy might be to focus on Einstein at the end of his life. We might want to introduce this Gottehrer as a novice who helps us understand Einstein's point of view."

Janousek thought that over. "Television drama, I see. In truth, Mr. Kramer, I did not visit Einstein at home during those years. I would not know who were his guests. All I can tell you is that I saw this Gottehrer at the hospital."

Surely, if Janousek had killed Einstein, he wouldn't have volunteered that he had visited the hospital. Or perhaps he suspected that we already knew—in which case he was better off feeding us facts, hoping we'd fill up.

"You visited Einstein in the hospital?" Harry asked softly.

"Oh yes, the day before he died. In the afternoon." Perhaps he thought that if he slapped the words down quickly, they would sound casual, but he only succeeded in sounding cruel.

"I'm puzzled," I said. "You were just telling us that you and Einstein were not on the best of terms."

"Correct. But there is no better place than a deathbed to improve the terms. He was a dying man. There was not going to be another occasion."

"But you didn't know it was going to be his deathbed," I said.

"Of course I did not *know*," he said, blinking. "But there was a significant chance, that was plain. I happened to call Rosenthal that Saturday to speak to him about a mathematical problem. He told me that Einstein had been taken to the hospital and that his condition was grave. I called the hospital and spoke to Miss Dukas. His secretary, you know. She said that his condition had improved somewhat. I asked whether he could receive visitors. She said she was certain that he would be pleased to see me."

"Even after what you've just told us." Harry was dubious.

"Of course. You see, Einstein was not the kind of man to hold a grudge. He never soured on me. So there was no reason for his secretary to fear that my presence would disturb him. I decided that the worst that could happen would be awkwardness, which I would survive, so I went."

The sharpness was, for the first time, missing from Janousek's voice. "He was terribly pale and spoke very slowly. He said he was happy to see me. I remember his words—in German, of course: 'I have survived long enough to bring you, I see.' I told him I regretted that our differences had stood between us. I said that my stubbornness was to blame. He insisted stubbornly that his own stubbornness was second to none. He also said that in the end the eternity of the equations would matter more than our passing differences. I told him that I had missed his companionship. He said that likewise he had missed mine. I asked him whether he was in pain and he told me that it had been worse. We reminisced. He asked about Ilse. I told him I had heard he had been instrumental in inviting me to the Institute in the first place, and I wanted him to know I was grateful."

"Was that true?"

"I don't know. He did not say yes, he did not say no. Perhaps he was not eager to confess his errors." The wrinkles around Janousek's eyes deepened.

Sorrow collected, like smoke in the room. It was terribly still. When Harry spoke again, his voice was muted: "Did anyone else come into the room while you were there?"

"I believe a nurse came in at one point, and took his temperature. And Miss Dukas came in with some papers, which she left by his bedside."

"Papers?"

"On a clipboard, as I recall, yes. I think so. It has been a long time, you understand."

Still, his memory was remarkably good—too good by half. His facts solidified into a scene in my mind. Einstein's darkened room, the drawn faces, the anxious denial of anxiety. Re-create the deathbed vigil, run a long electronic rumble over it, like the bass organ note that segues into the main body of "Also Sprach Zarathustra"—but then Burke had killed the piece.

"Could you see what he was writing?" I asked.

"Only the top sheet," Janousek said, "full of equations, meticulous. As you would expect, I did not inquire into his work on the field theory. I could not have said anything encouraging."

"And no one else came in?"

"Not as I remember. But this Gottehrer was waiting

outside as I left, with a puppy-dog look. Of course, there are many varieties of grief, are there not, Miss Ross?"

I gave him the nod he wanted.

"Peculiar about this Gottehrer," he went on. "I don't think I've thought about him in all these years. And here he intrudes again."

"Again?"

"Yes. This afternoon he has called my office and left a message. He calls again, and again. And here you are pinning me behind my desk and putting me under your magnifying glass. An interesting coincidence. Suddenly I am so interesting to everyone. If you ask me about him, I wonder if you also ask him about me."

"We've never met the man," Harry said.

"Fortunate for you," Janousek rasped. "Pathetic, these worshippers, they are hungry for metaphysics. Physics is the closest they can get. But perhaps I am cruel. Einstein cast a spell on many people. You know—the Second Coming in a sweatshirt and no socks."

I smiled despite myself. "May I ask what Gottehrer said he wanted this afternoon?"

"He didn't say. Only that he wanted to speak with me urgently."

"Then you go to the university to get messages?" I asked.

"No, in general not. They notify me. They are under strict instructions not to distribute my telephone number."

"Oh?"

"Oh yes. My beliefs have not kept me safe, you see. The local revolutionaries in the cause of peace and tranquillity once tried to set my office on fire. They did not succeed in bringing my work to a standstill, as they no doubt hoped.

They only succeeded in giving me a heart attack. Yes! You look shocked. These young so-called idealists, who preach their doctrine of so-called nonviolence, they have their own ways of intimidating people. Of killing, in fact. It is not only the bloodbath in Vietnam and the holocaust in Cambodia that is on their hands. Their ignorance was too doctrinaire to be untrained. Well, to spite them, I survived. Since then I do not publicly advertise my whereabouts. I am sure you feel the same way, Miss Ross. It is getting so that one takes one's life in one's hands to stand out from the crowd."

My eyes went to the bulky fireproof safe on the floor. Whether or not he connected me to *Eight Million Stories* and its exposé of the Big Bomber, I felt a twinge of guilt. When I looked up, I saw an old man with unregenerate eyes.

"There are a lot of lunatics out there," I said. "Are you aware of anyone having threatened Einstein's life?"

His head jerked dismissively. "The Nazis, of course. After that, I wouldn't know. I'll tell you something. People have said that the postwar years were so"—he dragged out the word—"*repressive*. Oppenheimer lost his security classification, and for his troubles he was condemned to remain director of the Institute for Advanced Study. Such penalties! I will tell you something. Those were peaceful times. Yes! No one was threatened with firebombs for conducting unpopular research. It was only when the so-called peace movement declared war on America that we began to fear for our lives. And we have never ceased to fear for our lives, have we? Some years ago, I had a colleague who was mugged on the street. He refused to turn over his watch to this thug, whose color I am not even going to mention. He was a liberal actually, my colleague—also from Czechoslovakia, I am proud to say. So the representative of the downtrodden masses stabbed him in the heart and took his watch. Where were the demonstrations against this act of terror? Ach, if I could harness my indignation, I could make foreign oil unnecessary and light New York City all by myself."

The window rattled. A wind had come up. Clouds sailed over the moon. I was weary of Janousek and his martyr's logic. The more we knew, the less we knew. All lines of information pointed to Gottehrer, and Gottehrer, like God, was everywhere and inaccessible all at once.

Harry was staring at the Masaryk bust.

"I'm curious to know," I said finally, "whether you arranged to meet Mr. Gottehrer."

"As a matter of fact, Miss Ross, it might amuse you to know that Mr. Gottehrer is going to visit tomorrow evening. I told him he had to arrive early and leave early so that I could watch my favorite television program in peace." He showed his teeth.

"I'd better go and prepare so that it stays your favorite," I said. "But may we come back to ask you some questions on camera?"

The floorboard creaked on the other side of the door. There were two taps.

"Yes!" The door swung open and Ilse Janousek appeared. She stood in the doorway stiffly, seeming not to know what to do with her hands. Finally, in a softened German, she said something like *"Gustav, Entschuldigung, hast du—"*

"Nein, nein, noch nicht," he snapped.

She stared straight at him, as if there were no witnesses.

In her expression I read annoyance, contempt, and stoicism.

"Ein bisschen später, bitte, Ilse." Janousek's voice was milder now. *"Bitte."*

Ilse pierced him with a stare, then nodded curtly and retreated, pulling the door shut after her.

"You must excuse me," Janousek said. "My solicitous wife is as punctual as a clock, though more expensive. Speaking of clocks, I'm afraid I am starting to feel a little fatigued." He didn't look in the slightest fatigued.

I, on the other hand, was afflicted by a pain that was migrating from my rib cage toward my stomach, its actual and original site.

"I know you are otherwise occupied tomorrow night," Janousek said, standing. "Why don't you come back Thursday?"

"We'd love to." I heaved myself up too fast. Lightheaded, I had to lean against the wall.

"Are you all right?" Janousek said.

"A little dizzy," I said. There was a small buzzing pain in my left temple. "Just a headache. I'm fine."

Janousek watched. "I see I have bored you to dizziness with my lectures."

"Not at all, Professor Janousek."

"Of course, if you did not want to hear my lectures, you would not have sought me out."

I smiled politely. "Shall we say about the same time?"

"Eight o'clock, of course. Or earlier, if you like. My wife goes out with her son to this ridiculous six-hour Broadway version of *Crime and Punishment* — no, what am I saying, that is tomorrow night. More circuses for the remaining literate masses. Thursday, come Thursday at eight o'clock.

I insist that you tell me then the in-depth story of *In Depth*."
He grinned at his cleverness.

"If I could avail myself of your bathroom," Harry said.

Janousek directed him down the hall to the right, and
Harry left to attend to his business. Without him, I felt
exposed. Janousek narrowed his eyes and tried to smile. I
tried my father's method of pretending the room was mine,
but Janousek's all-possessing look stopped me. I folded my
arms into a barricade.

He stopped and said, "You know, I have been for a long
time interested in the so-called media. The potent combination of vast resources and vast stupidity. I do not understand how a great power would permit its communication
system to decay into such garbage. If you told me in 1948
that a mind-destroying machine is going to be placed in
every American living room, I would have said this is a
Russian trick. Television is the Trojan machine. I am always telling this to your employer, Sir Colin McShane."

"Oh?" I improvised a weak smile.

"He says I do not understand business. How right he is
—the line between selling and selling out is a thin one. You
know what Lenin said. The bourgeoisie shall sell us the
rope—"

"—with which we shall hang them."

"You are an exceptional woman, you know. I have followed your career. You are clearly an intelligent person
paid to act, mmm, not so intelligent. It is to your credit that
you do not succeed."

"Thank you."

"I hope that someday after our work is done you will
have lunch with me and explain to me how intelligent people succeed in disguising themselves so well."

I thought it wise to convey the impression that he was charming the socks off me—which in fact he was, by sheer force of character if not his grotesque ideology.

"I couldn't possibly refuse such a delightful invitation." So I wrote out my home number on the back of a business card.

Janousek rested his hand on the back of his armchair, and I saw that his nails were bitten to the quick.

Harry came back looking refreshed, alert, more handsome. My turn for the bathroom. Old white hexagon tiles, three or four of them cracked, and a huge, ancient bathtub with claw feet, which had something of Janousek's gargoyle quality. In the mirror, my face was haggard, lumpy. Little lines under my eyes made them look as if a screen door had slammed there. The harsh acoustic version of Billy Neill's "Absolute Zero Heart" came caroming through my mind. I swallowed a Tylenol and two antacid tablets and rinsed my eyes.

As I walked back into the study, Janousek was saying, "In his youth, he unified space and time, you see. And so there is no question: he was spending the rest of his life trying to relive his youth. Silly."

"But noble, don't you think?" Harry said.

"Leave nobility to the savages! This had nothing to do with good science."

The two of them seemed to be hitting it off. I stood there feeling redundant and, worse, suddenly weary of Janousek and his glib pronouncements and all the motions I had been going through to seduce him into the piece. Harry read my mind, or my sagging face, and put out his hand to Janousek, saying, "Well, Professor, this has been edifying. I want to thank you."

"I look forward to seeing you on Thursday," Janousek returned, and led us through the living room. Ilse looked up from her needlepoint and composed a gracious smile — just as happy to see us go as she'd been to see us arrive. She had made progress on her floral design.

■

All the relief I felt to be out of Janousek's sight had fizzled by the time we got to the ground floor. The upper reaches of my stomach were burning. I harbored a monster who was not dancing, I had no soft song. I was spending my best hours catering to men I loathed — McShane, Gilman, Janousek. A solicitous Harry was a vast improvement.

His arm was around my shoulders. "We picked the right enemies."

"Goody."

"Look, Rome wasn't destroyed in a day. We have witnesses galore that Gottehrer was hanging around the hospital. We've established that Janousek knew about the Russell letter. We're swimming in motives and opportunity."

"Whoopee," I said. "You're swimming, I'm drowning. If you ask me, his memory's much too good. Meanwhile, as you may recall, I'm about to be fired. From a meaningless job, but it's *my* meaningless job."

The doorman, a short, lean fellow — evidently the new shift had begun — was standing in an enclave, polishing the brass mailboxes to a high shine. Outside, the moon was a luminescent wrecking ball. We walked a few steps up Riverside Drive, and as we turned toward West End, Harry craned around. We weren't being followed. Too bad: I wanted Norman Gottehrer to stroll picturesquely out of the night and confess. Or Gustav Janousek to say that he had decided to come clean. Instead, a couple my age walked down the sidewalk, the man carrying a baby in a car seat, the woman clutching a car radio, solemn with some kind of achievement. Why didn't I have a solid New York life like that? Because I was busy scrambling in and out of quandaries, that's why. Enough of Einstein, I wanted to move on. Write this down in my Filofax: Wednesday, A.M., CHANGE LIFE. But I didn't say any of this: I wasn't about to decompose in front of Harry. Instead, I asked him what the Janouseks' German had meant.

"She said she was sorry to interrupt and asked whether he had something or other. He said no, not yet."

"Maybe she meant a motive. Figure it out. Einstein signed zillions of peace appeals. Why would anyone care about Bertrand Russell's?"

"I think we're too rational," Harry said. "Suppose a man hates Einstein for years. Then he finds out that Einstein is dying. Could he kill Einstein *because* he's dying—he doesn't want to lose the chance?"

"You think Janousek's that unhinged?"

"Don't you think he's schizoid on the subject of Einstein? All this sentiment, on the one hand. On the other, Einstein a Commie dupe. Look: Einstein once lived in Prague himself; I find it hard to believe that he took the news of the coup in '48 so casually. Janousek's still riddled with envy—jeering at 'God,' he called him in quotes. You know my sister's a biochemist. I learned something from her: scientists are driven by blind, animal envy."

The antacid was starting to cool my insides. The fleshy tip of Harry's nose looked soft and adorable. We reached West End, where I hailed a cab. The driver was a scrawny

black woman in her midthirties with a fey smile. I gave her
my address, leaned back, closed my eyes. Harry began
kneading my shoulder. A couple of blocks down West End,
the cab suddenly slowed—sharply enough that we swayed
forward. I opened my eyes and saw no other car, no pedes-
trian, nothing. "Lucky," the driver crooned. "Mm," I
agreed, and closed my eyes. She accelerated. In the middle
of the next block, she braked again. Still no cars in front of
us, none behind. Gastric flames rekindling. I thought: This
is all I need. She went on jumping from brake to accelera-
tor and back, humming fragments of a show tune I didn't
know. Her name, I noted, was Janette Pilgrim. If I told her
to let us out, that might send her over the edge; she might
speed up and refuse to let us out—it had happened to Dan
Rather. Janette Pilgrim was higher than a kite and braked
for hallucinations. But she also stopped for red lights. I am
encouraged by small virtues.

Not the best time, not the worst. Much preferable to an
exercise in getting-it-over-with. What was it, then?

Clumsy. Sweet. Considerate. He groped his way around
my clothes. Endearing fumbles. At one point, his tongue
froze, as if he were kissing himself. I told him, Relax, and
later he got to tell me, Relax, which made me laugh. Afterward he held his lips to my shoulder as if it were an amulet
and I was good luck. "Something else you're good at, Mr.
Kramer," I said cheerfully, and then regretted it. He was
thicker around the middle than he looked in clothes, a
warm bulk, the familiar fact in my life, Harry Kramer, my
rabbi, shepherding his thoughtfulness through the world.
St. Harry, patron saint of lost causes. He was there with
me for a while. And the rest of the day fell away.

PART TWO

I . . . believe that we would be unfaithful to the tradition of Western civilization if we were to shy away from exploring the limits of human achievement.

EDWARD TELLER

WEDNESDAY, OCTOBER 24

I WOKE UP WITH A LITTLE WAIL THAT SANK LIKE THE SOUND of a train passing through a station. Harry lay asleep on his back, his face surprisingly tender, a comfort to a woman beside herself with fright.

The dream was streaming away from me, dissolving. I closed my eyes and clutched at remnants—a hospital room, flowers, nurses, needlepoint, terror. Was I Einstein or Ilse?

By the time I dragged myself out of bed and threw on a robe, Harry was sitting on the sofa leafing through *Vanity Fair*, looking bemused, whether at me or the magazine I didn't know. The traces of dream in my brain were more vivid than the traces of sex.

It was after eight. I had forgotten to set the clock-radio.

But the thought of arriving late for work filled me with pleasure.

"That was" — Harry said, closing the magazine, searching for words — "very satisfying last night."

I swept the hair out of my face and said, "Like a good interview?" I stood in the middle of the living room not knowing what to do with my arms, so I folded them.

Already moments of truth, the morning after. No makeup, and every word seems to imply a commitment to a whole set of feelings. There were two strangers in my apartment exchanging foolish words.

Time for me to drop into my own cave. "I'm sorry."

"Sorry for what?"

He wore his years well, as certificates of achievement. I walked over to the sofa and pressed the tip of his nose. A button to take me somewhere. I didn't want to dwell on the subject of sex — a sure sign of a "relationship," that dance of death. Was I enlightened, then? Before, Harry is Harry; after, Harry is still Harry, right? I'm a connoisseur of disappointment, I don't even wait for coffee before I start. I've seen the faces of married women. I've seen my own.

He started to smile, stopped, started again. He was sexy, compassionate, taken aback, and, in his own way, disappointed, too. All he said was "Bad night? You were thrashing around."

"Another lousy dream. I was Einstein, I think. Janousek brought me flowers. I broke out in a rash." The way I said it made him laugh. But I didn't feel very funny. The headache of the previous night was gone, but the knot on the back of my neck was sore to the touch. I rotated my shoulder, which helped only a little. When my robe started to come open, I tucked it closed and tied the belt.

Harry put down the magazine and watched. "Come on over here," he said, patting the cushion. I sat down next to him and he worked his fingers into the muscles downslope from my shoulder.

"Too hard," I said.

"Feels like a rock."

"I meant your touch."

"How's this?"

"Better." His fingers were present, his attention absent. Where did he go? Was what I needed a benign drug—once a day, a maintenance dose of Harry Kramer? When he was AWOL, what was I supposed to do with the dangerous fondness I felt?

He blew me a kiss as I went to the kitchen. I poured two glasses of orange juice, ground some coffee, loaded the coffee machine. The light on the answering machine was flashing. From the kitchen I called out, "Are we adults now, Harry?"

"There are no adults. Listen to this." He read from *Vanity Fair:* " 'I wanted to be a rock star, but my father convinced me that women worship doctors.' 'Show the world your Japanese shoes.' Everyone in this magazine talks that way. Is that what adults talk like?"

In the bathroom, after a quick shower, I did the best I could with mascara, eyeliner, pencil, foundation, blush, and added a modest perfume called Everything. For the rest, I would place myself in the hands of makeup professionals and lighting engineers.

When I came back into the kitchen, Harry was standing by the window sipping his coffee. I went to the answering machine, punched playback, and the first voice I heard was Blond Bart's: "All right, if you're boycotting—" I hit the fast-forward button and looked over at Harry, whose eyes were ostentatiously calm. Next, the overly firm voice of my friend-producer Elaine Barbanel, suppressing deep disturbances, wanting to have lunch. My mother wanted to know if I wanted to go with her to the cemetery to pay respects to my father. Cash McHype wanted to know how my piece on Billy Neill was coming along and whether there was any way he could help. How the hell had the bastard gotten my number?

I walked over to Harry. There were a few cloudy streaks in an otherwise pale blue sky. A huge moving truck was parked across the street, featuring the WE BLOW THE COMPETITION OUT OF THE WATER mushroom-cloud ad.

"I'd love a Gauloise," I said.

"I never smoked."

"Harry Kramer, too good for mortals." Funny, I'd remembered everyone smoking in the old days. The collective smoke rising from the collective pyre.

"Only dope." He laid his arm lightly around my waist and said, "Gorgeous day. Why don't we stay home and see how long we can go without talking about sex?"

"I wasn't aware we were talking about sex."

"My ex-wife talked endlessly about sex. The worse the sex, the more the talk. The more intricate the talk, the worse the sex. Then she talked about the great love of her life she had just met. Then we talked about divorce."

I wondered whether the ex-wife had tired of his in-and-out cave routine. Or whether he would ever tire of it himself. Was I up to retraining him?

I backed off, went to the bedroom, and put on a high-necked silk blouse.

"Very nice," he said as I came back into the living room.

How could this man be friendly, appreciative, and noncommittal all at once? I wanted to hold on to him for dear life, I wanted to flee. I wanted to write my Billy Neill script, throw it on Burke's desk, slam every possible door, and walk away from *In Depth*, the murder of Albert Einstein, all of it. Harry, the hell with interrogations, let's blast off into the A tour: Antigua, Aruba, Andorra, the Andes, Azerbaijan, Atlantis. Away.

"I understand about interludes" was what I said. "I also understand that Gottehrer's out there among the eight million and we have to find him. Meanwhile, I have a script to write, and it would be wise for me to show my face at Big Glass and fend off the schemes of Burke Gilman." I started proposing a rain check but bit my tongue.

"You think I'm too casual?"

"I think you think I'm a good fuck. I think you're a good fuck yourself. Can we go to work now solving the murder of you know who?"

"Anything you say. At least this way I get to change clothes. Diplomatic of you not to comment." The truth was, the faint aroma was fine with me. We breathed each other in.

"I could come back after the show," he said, "unless you want to come to Brooklyn. Or . . . by the way, who is it who thinks you're boycotting him?" He pointed at the machine.

"That was Mr. Wrong. Mr. Wrong is not, as we say, happening. He's 'history.'" I made quotation marks with my fingers. "Or should I ask you who you're keeping in Brooklyn?"

"If you're so inclined."

"Well, who is she?"

"Who is who?"

"The one you keep yourself in reserve for. What's she like?"

"Don't be ridiculous."

"Cut it out. I'm not your wide-eyed little apprentice anymore."

"I've noticed." Impressed, maybe regretful. Arms akimbo. Standoff.

"Look, let's save the fencing for when we have more time," I said. "Meet me here after the show?"

"Love to." His smile switched on gloriously, then he ticked off his missions for the day. First, Brooklyn. Second, call Peter Minasian, make sure Professor Taub hadn't discovered yet what was in Einstein's brain. Third, plant himself at Gottehrer's building and wait.

■

The light through the synagogue's stained glass fell beautifully yellow and blue on the carpet downstairs. The man who lived in the crate was just stepping out. I gave him a dollar. He said, Bless you, you take care of yourself. His smile seemed original. I will, I will.

"Have you ever seen a longer memory?" I asked Harry. We were walking east, Harry swiveling to see if we were followed. A jackhammer was tearing up the gutter. We spoke in bursts wedged between the machine's bursts. "Janousek's memory."

"Masaryk."

"Exactly. He's mourning Masaryk, what, fifty years after. What does he care that the Czechs had a revolution in the meantime? The key to this guy is revenge."

"A lethal mind."

"A razor."

"A hammer. A mind that smashes atoms."

The jackhammer tore things apart behind us. Trucks swished past.

"So why," I asked, "would Ilse want to stay married to him? You'd think with those cheekbones she could have done better."

We floated weak theories back and forth, lined with inadequate information. The dependency of women, their attachment to harsh men who wield power. Needlepoint as compensation, sublimated resentment. Marriage as mystery in a secular world.

At Seventh Avenue, the herd paused to gather strength for its next surge. A white-haired man picked at the curb with the tip of his white cane. After the light flashed WALK, he waited a few seconds before crossing. I felt like a blind woman, tapping away at curbstones.

At Sixth Avenue we caught a cab. The cabbie was Polish and his braking was entirely called for. By the time we got to Big Glass, it was almost nine-thirty. On the street, the Senegalese were standing behind their spreads of scarves and kerchiefs, but the plaza was almost empty. As we stood at the edge of the plaza, Harry was saying that he would catch the subway home from Rockefeller Center, meet me at my place after the show. "In your clean clothes," I was saying. Suddenly, out of the corner of my eye, I saw bulk in motion—and my first thought was that this big shape was about to sideswipe me, like a drunk's car running onto a sidewalk. The shape was a skinny man who swerved up to me and said in a small voice, "Margo Ross." Too fast to be a panhandler or an autograph hound. I thought, He's one of the stalkers, I'm now going to die for no reason. Then I thought, I'm going to be served with a subpoena. His scraggly hair, white, streaked with remnants of black, was held back in a stubby ponytail with a rubber band. He stank of desperation. He was wearing a blue sailor's coat that was too loose.

"I want to talk to you," he said. His eyes were anthracite, feverish.

"Listen—" Harry started.

"My name is Norman Gottehrer." *Nawman* was how he pronounced it. Behind the harshness was the whine of a man who was not used to getting what he wanted.

The next thing I knew, Harry had spun around and wheeled himself between Gottehrer and me, his hands shooting out as if to push Gottehrer away. But Gottehrer gave no sign of an impending attack. He put on a somewhat abashed grin and said to Harry: "Hello?"

"Bastard." Harry's cheekbones were working.

"Who are you?"

"Very funny."

"I don't get the joke."

"This is a dumb time to go dumb," I said.

His ears *were* oversize. The grin faded, leaving behind a furtive, puzzled look. I felt as though I were caught in some complicated street hustle I didn't understand and devoutly wished to bypass, thank you very much.

Gottehrer's eyes stopped on mine. "I'm here to talk to *you.*"

"This is Harry Kramer," I said. "Mr. Kramer is a producer on special assignment. We work together. If you want to speak to me, you want to speak to him. Suppose we all go up to my office."

Harry looked inescapable, I looked adamant, Gottehrer couldn't decide whether he was resigned or victorious.

In the lobby, he didn't so much as glance at the WE TAKE IN THE WORLD sign, still new enough to astound me. The neon outlines of the letters were sharper than I remembered. Harry didn't have to be told this wasn't the time to go home to Brooklyn.

I should have bugged my office, like Nixon. Or had a concealed camera. As it was, I had to work too hard to stay sharp, pay attention, keep things moving, so I missed the signals I should have caught. I never saw anything coming.

When a man whose hair is more white than dark wears his hair in a ponytail, he's making a statement. Gottehrer's hair wasn't even long enough for a serious ponytail—which pumped up the statement. You'd expect such a man to be mighty sure of himself. But even at second glance Gottehrer didn't look so sure. His shoulders were hunched. His coat was too long. There was a shiny patch on the left shoulder, where a navy insignia had been ripped away. I wondered whether it had been his.

Cyrilly eyed him dubiously as we walked him past her desk. I scooped up message slips, told her to hold all calls, and led Gottehrer into my office, followed by Harry. I gestured Gottehrer to the side of the couch closest to the wall. Now that I had him, I wasn't about to let him bolt. He sat without taking off his coat. Harry sat at the opposite end of the couch, folding his own coat, depositing it neatly next to him without taking his eyes off Gottehrer. I sat behind my desk. The distance was good for my composure.

"Well," I said. "You wanted to see me. Here I am."

Gottehrer's stare was intense but impersonal. Unlike most visitors to my office, he showed no interest in collecting impressions, traces of glamour, flakes of my aura. He inspected me silently, like a Navaho elder I interviewed once. This old man's name was Kingman and when I asked him a question he stood in front of the camera for two, three minutes, and started his answers when he was good and ready. He was waiting for the right moment.

Gottehrer's moment finally came. "I've been told that you're interested in the, ah, end of Dr. Einstein's life."

"That makes three of us," Harry said. He sounded mild for a bad cop, actually.

"I've been interested for a long time," Gottehrer said. "I'm not here to play games. I'd rather you didn't, either."

"What do you call following me? What do you call threatening her?"

Gottehrer looked down at the floor, gnawed at the underside of his lip, then said with his oddly self-pitying rasp: "I'll tell you. I don't have the faintest idea what you're talking about."

"Why don't we get to the point, Norman," I said. I opened a notebook. "You came to talk. We're here to listen."

Again Gottehrer waited. "I'd rather you didn't take notes. If you don't mind."

Harry opened his mouth to object, but I flicked the notebook shut. I wasn't crazy about his glare. "O.K., no notes."

Gottehrer's eyes danced with the pleasure of having an audience. "I knew Dr. Einstein for a number of years."

He stopped. I threw in: "So I understand."

"I knew him well. I'm not going to waste your time with

false modesty. He took an interest in me. Some people thought much too great an interest. I know what they thought. I was young, I was untrained, I was a dilettante, you know, a poet, an oddball. One-track minds were scandalized that Einstein made time for me. You know how that is." Gottehrer sprayed us with bursts of speech.

"You would visit Einstein at the Institute for Advanced Study, then?"

"Right, right. I know how they looked at me when they saw me with him." He gave a strained little laugh. "They envied me. Snobs. Einstein didn't come to their afternoon kaffeeklatsch, but he wasted himself on this screwball. They all wanted a piece of him. So I was one more proof that he'd lost his marbles."

"Office politics." I smiled him on.

"Yeah, they thought that he was taking up valuable office space. Can you imagine! Of course, Einstein got a big kick out of philistines. He said to me once"—Gottehrer assumed what passed for a German accent—"'People in neckties, dey alvays look for scandal. Dey haff to proof dat deir respectability is in vorking order.'" The grin flashed back. It had nothing to do with me. When it faded, he looked wounded.

Like the good cop I was supposed to be, I cranked up my sympathy. "Would it be going too far to say that Einstein saw a bit of himself in you?"

"You are exactly right. I was, what, nineteen, twenty years old, bright, I had languages, I was a poet—a good poet—I knew Western philosophy, I knew the Upanishads. I was a nobody, but Einstein could see from my first letter that this wasn't because I was an ignoramus."

"You wrote him a letter, then."

"I was drowning in the fifties. I was a poet from Brooklyn! You might as well say a pope from the Bronx."

I laughed a trifle more than I felt like laughing.

"I dropped out of Brooklyn College after two years. A two-year sentence in solitary. Suburban poetry! John Crowe Ransom! Allen Tate! Let me tell you how the universe looks from my barbecue pit. So far as they were concerned, the *Bhagavað Gita* might as well have been jungle music, as they would have called it. Whitman: an embarrassment. Pound: a lunatic Fascist and that's that. Then there were the Stalinists, with their tiny minds, who got stupider as they got persecuted."

"I recall," Harry said dryly. Gottehrer eyed him with a flicker of irritation.

"So I quit, got a job in the MacDougal Bookstore. The hours were good, I had time to write. They had a loft where they let me live. I read around in the history of philosophy, cosmology, a lot of things. I was a monk. Preserve the books, that's all you can do. I read the Hindu epics, Vergil, Lucretius, Olson, Heidegger, and worked on a long poem. Three years on New York as ultimate Being. I thought I was Hart Crane. I could have picked worse." Gottehrer had found his rhythm. He was loping along, in love with his own voice.

"And Einstein?"

"I'm getting there. I read an article about Einstein and unified field theory, and I thought, this is fantastic, just what I'm trying to do in the long poem: unify the field."

I broke in: "Which article was that?"

"The *Times*, '53, something like that. So I wrote him a letter."

I cocked my head, waiting.

"Why not?" Truculent. "I had some ideas. It's a free country, so they say, right?"

"I'm interested. What ideas?"

"Oh, Christ—things, you know, like science is the reinvention of philosophy in our time because it searches for deep structures. Reason is a tribute to God, but the sin of the modern world is the crazy idea that reason itself is God, which is like saying prayer is God. You know, the idiot points at the moon and falls in love with his finger."

I was wondering whether this sort of exercise kept Gottehrer busy on long winter nights. Whether there was a Mrs. Gottehrer on the receiving end. I nodded. "So you mailed this off to Einstein."

"Right. But he didn't answer."

"So you—"

"I waited."

"And?"

"I read relativity theory. Then I wrote him again. This time my idea was that unified field theory was a return to the pre-Socratics. I dropped in a couple of passable sentences about atomic physics. Aha! This was interesting. He wrote back a short note. Not convinced but, mmm, interested, said he hadn't read much of the pre-Socratics and apologized because his education was faulty. He thought he should know more. He also remembered what I had said the first time, about mistaking reason for God. Which amazed me. You can imagine how I felt." I gave him wide eyes and a flight-attendant smile. "I floated! I wrote back and asked if I could visit. A long time went by."

Here I was in producer's heaven without a camera. I could have killed, preferably Burke. Gottehrer's eyes were incandescent. A phone trilled somewhere out in corporate space, but he was oblivious.

"You say a long time—do you mean months?"

"Mmm—weeks or months, I'm not sure."

"And then?"

"He wrote back and proposed a date and a time, 'if this will be convenient.' Einstein asks if this will be convenient for Norm Gottehrer!" His life's moment of triumph glowed in the room.

I thought, Am I supposed to believe that this man, sitting here reliving his single moment of glory, killed his idol?

Harry said, "Quite a coup for a, what, twenty-one-year-old?"

"Right, right," Gottehrer rasped. "Or, twenty, yeah."

"So you went to see him."

"Oh, did I go to see him! I got off the train and there was a van waiting to take me to the Institute. Einstein was very gracious, but weary, weary—" Gottehrer's voice sank. He shook his shoulders downward, thump, thump, to illustrate.

"And?"

"And? What do you think? We talked, I don't know, an hour or two . . ." He trailed off, whether into reverie or reluctance was hard to tell.

"What about?"

"The pre-Socratics. Their reputation for irrationality disturbed him, but the essential thing that interested him was their idea of permanent flux. Heraclitus. He saw relativity there. That was the beginning. He asked me if I would like to take a walk. A very slow walk, as it turned out. From the Institute all the way to his house. He talked about the UFT."

"UFT—"

"Sorry, unified field theory as an extension of relativity. The idea of a single all-embracing cosmos—the convergence of all the traditions—romantics, Buddhists, the most advanced physics . . ."

Gottehrer hypnotized himself with his phrases. His sentences swarmed all over the room. He'd fallen in love with Einstein and never fallen out. I could see why Einstein hadn't ushered him to the door, enough is enough, goodbye. The intensity must have overcome him.

"You know"—Gottehrer interrupted his trance—"you haven't told me why you're so interested in Einstein. I mean, you're television. I don't see the point."

"Some of us have the idea that television has educational responsibilities," Harry said pompously. "I would think that as his—I'm not sure what the right word is—collaborator?—you'd be pleased that we care."

"I was his—friend." Gottehrer played with his earlobe.

"Tell me," I said, "did he discuss the work he was doing?"

"Sure, in layman's terms."

"How often?" Harry came barging in. I worried that he was forgetting that his bad cop was an act. He was falling in love with the role.

Gottehrer was cagey. "Every few months, maybe three or four times a year. I'm no physicist. You realize that. But I'm good at following contours, getting rough images. He said I understood the first principles of unification better than his colleagues. He said there is an art to asking the right question."

"This is not exactly a secret," Harry said.

Gottehrer ignored him. "You know, the standard line is

that once upon a time Einstein had two or three great ideas and then he blundered around the rest of his life in a blind alley. This is absolute garbage. The Establishment made a monument out of him to avoid coming to terms with his deepest ideas. They'd gesture at the monument whenever they wanted to get their hands on government appropriations. $E = mc^2$ shows there's a payoff to theoretical physics, et cetera. So this fossilized Einstein was useful to them — but as a living physicist, nah, he was an embarrassment."

I heard that: As a *living* physicist.

Gottehrer went on. "But *he* knew he wasn't dead yet. You know, one time he threw up his hands and said, 'There's no fool like an overeducated fool.'"

"Who was he talking about?" I asked.

"Could have been a lot of people"—vaguely. "The point is that he was under way. That was a term he liked: *'unterwegs.'* His work was in progress"—he threw up his index finger—"one work, one journey, all of a piece. You know what Einstein means?"

"One stone, now that I think about it," Harry said.

"One stone. Roundness. Unity. Look, relativity was, what, one arc in a whole long curve, you know, a curve of discovery. A crucial arc, absolutely, but incomprehensible if you cut it out of the whole curve." Gottehrer made a long curve in the air with a series of flourishes. "Newton, Kepler, Maxwell, these guys moved the curve along, arc by arc, each move was always the next move *in the same curve.*"

"Yes." Without committing myself.

"Einstein was a methodical man. Relativity's done, so he moves to the next arc. The UFT." Gottehrer's hand swooped through the air again. "If it takes thirty years, so what? That's science, see, which is *sequence.*"

"Einstein said this?" Harry asked.

"Not in so many words, but that's exactly what he meant. Real teachers have their own ways of pointing out the path. In his way, he was saying that philosophy was the easy part, because philosophers flit around. Aristotle hopped off Plato's shoulders, see, and went out on his own. But science was continuous and steady, more human, right? One arc after the other, all evolving toward a unified field theory."

I nodded mindlessly. Harry had bad-cop business to do. He stood up, ambled to my desk, perched on its edge, folded his arms. I couldn't see his expression, of course. But I could see Gottehrer's: a tremor.

"So tell me, if it was all leading to a unified field theory, did Einstein get there before he died?" There was an edge in his voice, an amateur's strain. A proper cop like Delaney would have brought this scene off with the aplomb it deserved.

Gottehrer's grin showed a lot of crooked off-white teeth. "That's not for me to say. Physics isn't my language. But you want to know the truth? What he said to me, on the last day of his life, he said, 'I am very close to the unification.' "

There it was. Harry opened his mouth to pounce, but I didn't want Gottehrer to realize what had come out of his mouth. So I shook my head quickly and slightly No. Harry saw and frowned, but held his tongue.

"When did he say that?"

"I told you, his last day."

"But exactly when?"

"Do you check your watch during visitors' hours? Sometime in the afternoon, when I visited him."

"And just what did he say?"

"He said, 'I hope I do not come to my end before my life's work does. Still, I am not frightened. *"Ich hab" keine Angst.'* "

The words cleared a space around them. I've never believed in dybbuks but I swear I could hear Einstein speaking from beyond the grave.

"What didn't frighten him?"

"Death, what else? Death didn't frighten him." He had the self-satisfied look of a man who enjoys his secrets. "Or he might have meant the pain."

"But the doctors had told him there wouldn't be much pain."

Gottehrer flung glances around the room. "You know, it's possible that what he said was: 'They do not frighten me.' Words to that effect."

I wish I could have seen Harry's face. " 'They do not frighten me,' " he repeated.

Gottehrer didn't appreciate the echo. "Possibly. It's been a long time."

"I understand. Tell me, who might 'they' have been?"

"I don't know."

"Did he give any names?"

"No. I'd remember a name." He suddenly looked his age —no, more than his sixty or so years; he looked like a bony relic ready to shatter. "I really don't remember. You know, you're making it sound much too melodramatic." He laughed, a grinding sound like a gear failing to fall into place. "There was nothing melodramatic about Einstein."

The phone trilled, I jumped. I grabbed the receiver and said, "What, Burke?" Only one person could have bulled his way past Cyrilly.

He boomed into my ear, "Just checking to see how you're coming."

"Fabulous, Burke. The words are leaping onto the page."

"You make me a happy man. When do I see scripts?"

"Two o'clock at the outside."

He barked: "How long have you worked here? We have to time this stuff." If I went long, even by seconds, a commercial might have to be bumped at a cost to the network of very big bucks.

"Burke, don't worry, all right? It's almost there. I'll time the run-throughs on audio."

"Call me as soon as you're ready, O.K.?"

"You'll be the first to know."

"By the way," he said, skipping a beat, "Janousek loved you."

"What?"

"Absolutely loved the way you open your eyes. He can tell you're fair. So I just want you to know I'm reconsidering your favorite piece."

I should have known Janousek would be on the phone checking us out with McShane before we'd hit the lobby. "What does reconsidering mean?"

"Just what it sounds like. Stay tuned."

"Burke, I wouldn't mind owing you."

"I'll remember that." Click.

When I hung up, Harry and Gottehrer were scrutinizing each other—snake charmer and snake.

"Sorry," I said with a professional smile. My mind was racing. I had to get this guy in front of a camera. Harry had heard "reconsidering," he could figure out the rest.

"You were saying"—Harry was cool—"about whom

Einstein wasn't afraid of." That *whom*, that breathed *wh*, that prep-school decorum of Harry's.

After a pause: "If I had to guess, he probably meant the quantum guys spinning out multiple dimensions. Drunken spiders, one web after another. Now it's superstrings. They're up to twenty dimensions now, can you believe it? Intellectually a disaster."

"Look, I can see why they annoyed him. But why would they *frighten* him?"

Gottehrer opened his mouth, stopped himself, then said: "Good question." He waited for me to intervene, but I didn't. He stared into his lap but his lap didn't answer. Finally he resumed: "It might have been right-wing fanatics he was scared of."

"Fanatics?" I said. The word had a certain glow.

"You know, the maniacs who thought the Russians were coming." He forced a bony grin.

"Do you have any particular fanatics in mind?" Harry asked Gottehrer.

Gottehrer's eyes darted around. He was searching for a scrap of memory, or some kind of plan. I had the feeling, not for the first time, that the physical creature called Norman Gottehrer was on the verge of flying apart from a surplus of jagged energy.

Harry pressed. "Anyone in particular?"

"Well, you know, Janousek, that type."

"What type is that?"

Gottehrer made his grinding laugh.

There were two sharp raps on my door, and Elaine Barbanel stuck her head in. "Oh, you're busy. I'll come back later."

"Thanks, Elaine." She withdrew. I'd have to have a word with Cyrilly.

"Sorry again," I said. "We're not big on privacy around here."

Harry glared at Gottehrer. "You mentioned that there were people who thought Einstein was taking up valuable office space. Would that have included Janousek?"

"I heard Einstein joke about it, yeah. But I wouldn't make too much of that. He had a sense of humor."

"What was the joke?"

"I don't remember."

Harry had ice and insinuation in his eyes. "I understand that you ran into Janousek at the hospital when Einstein was dying."

Gottehrer tried a smile. The experiment failed. "You've talked to Janousek?"

"As a matter of fact, we have. Do you remember seeing him there?"

"Why ask me? You seem to know the answer already."

"We want *your* story," I said.

"Yeah, I was waiting to go into Einstein's room when I saw Janousek leave."

"You were surprised?" Harry pushed.

"Absolutely amazed."

"Have any idea what he was doing there?"

"I didn't ask Einstein, if that's what you mean. It wasn't my business."

"No, of course not. I only thought that Janousek might have said something to you."

Gottehrer snorted. "Janousek didn't have much to say to the likes of me. I might as well have been the maid."

"I take it there was no love lost—"

"I thought he was dangerous."

"Dangerous to—"

"—to the human race, actually."

"And Einstein in particular?"

This seemed a new idea. "I hadn't thought of it that way, but—now that I think about it, no."

"I see. And Einstein didn't say anything about Janousek."

"I already told you. He had other things on his mind. Look, what are you trying to get me to say? Einstein was a private man, entitled to die in his own time."

A strange way of putting it. "But we're talking about the way he lived, not the way he died," Harry said. I couldn't figure out where Harry was going. One minute interrogating, the next out for a stroll.

"Of course we are," Gottehrer said. "What else would we be talking about?"

His jittery eyes, his Brooklyn earnestness. A medium star was born if I could get him in front of a camera. Instead, I sat there, dithering, giving Harry a chance to play his hand—and lose the initiative.

"Tell me," Harry said, "what did you do while you were waiting to see Einstein?"

"Christ, I don't know, I must have paced, I bore witness. What was I supposed to do? See, my father died in the war. I wasn't there. For me, my father was never a dying man. One day a telegram came and he was dead. Fait accompli. But the day Einstein was dying, that day was vivid. Who knows if my own death is going to be so vivid?"

"I want to go back to something," Harry said abruptly.

"You said that Einstein thought he was close to a unified field theory that last day."

"That's what I said."

"Then what became of his final notes?"

"You haven't done your homework. They were found in his room after he died. They've all been published."

"One page on Israel was published, and one page of calculations," Harry said. "What if he left more?"

Gottehrer seemed startled. "Look: the newspapers said there was one page of each. The biographies say so. There are reproductions. If you come up to my place, I'll show you one."

· "Thanks, maybe later." There was some kind of illumination on Harry's face, as if he were standing before me in the office of *Eight Million Stories*, relishing deep knowledge. "I have another question, purely hypothetical. If Einstein really was on the verge of a unified field theory, isn't that something Janousek would have worried about?"

"I—I don't see what you're driving at."

"I'm not sure I'm driving at anything," Harry said.

I wasn't, either. I didn't grasp, or like, Harry's game anymore. Gottehrer had to have noticed that Harry was slinging his bait around every which way. I had to stifle a twinge of sympathy. Poor Gottehrer: Here's my new purse, why don't you slice it up, too? I wasn't any closer to understanding what Gottehrer was doing in my office. Maybe fishing around to find out what *we* knew. We were all fish fishing for fish. Not so funny. Whose show was this, anyway?

"Mr. Gottehrer," I said, "I'd like to take you downstairs and tape an interview."

Hard to tell who was more startled, Gottehrer or Harry. It was Harry who threw me the dubious look.

"Later," Gottehrer said. "Maybe. First, I want to know more about what you're doing."

"Fine, I'll go on," Harry said quickly. "I suppose Einstein talked to you about the atomic bomb."

"Sure. Quite a lot. What about the atomic bomb?"

"I'm interested in the question of chain reactions."

"What about them?"

"Chain reactions took Einstein by surprise, so I understand."

"You've lost me," Gottehrer said.

Harry stood bolt-upright and stabbed his finger in Gottehrer's direction. "O.K., look, $E = mc^2$ meant that you could get tremendous amounts of energy out of a tiny mass, because c is the speed of light, 186,000 miles per second, and if you square 186,000, you get a very large number."

"This is not news," Gottehrer said.

Harry surged on. "The point is that when Einstein set out $E = mc^2$ in 1905, he didn't think that you could start with uranium, say, and produce some neutrons which would shake loose more neutrons and so on and so on, until, bam, you reached the point of no return and got an atomic explosion, and suddenly there's nothing academic about 186,000 times 186,000."

Gottehrer said blandly, "The beginning of death." He looked like the beginning of death.

"What?"

"I see what you're getting at," came Gottehrer's rasp. "It wasn't till '39 that Szilard told him that they'd gotten a chain reaction. At Columbia. Einstein was astounded."

"He told you this."

Gottehrer nodded. "Right. I asked him. I was curious."

"Understandably. Now, suppose, for the sake of argument, that Einstein *had* anticipated a chain reaction in 1905. Would he have abandoned special relativity? Stuffed his manuscript into a drawer? Thrown it away?"

They stared at each other. Gottehrer blinked first. "I can't figure you out. One minute you're talking about Einstein in the hospital, and the next minute you want a thought experiment."

"Humor me."

I don't know why Gottehrer didn't pick himself up and walk out the door. He must have got a kick out of watching us fidget. We thought we were so smart, but we were the captive audience.

"He would have published," Gottehrer went on. "No question about it. He was convinced that science was God's map of the universe. I would say more a sort of psychoanalysis of the absolute Mind." He grinned. "Really what he was saying was that, in a funny way, the closer the human race gets to the mind of God, the more it can do without religion. Who needs faith if science can read God's mind? Einstein was a man of the turn of the century, you know. Knowledge is beauty, reason is mastery. The forces of light manage the forces of darkness. A beautiful vision. 1905 was a good year for this sort of thing. The best were full of conviction. They were new to the twentieth century."

The longer and weirder he went, the more annoyed I was getting. Whatever exactly he was talking about, he sounded like nothing I'd ever seen on television, and I was getting exactly zero percent of it on tape. Harry was taking his time poking around, pulling on loose ends, and Got-

tehrer was squandering all this spontaneous stuff. Sometimes you blow a take and you can never get a guy
pumping again.

Harry, lunge.

But Harry had sublime and deliberate confidence written all over his face. He'd pulled the fourth ace on the last
deal and wanted everybody to know it. "Suppose Einstein
was telling the truth that he was getting very damned close
to a unified field theory. *Very* damned close. And suppose
that's what was frightening."

"And why would that be?"

Harry sauntered to the door, turned around, folded his
arms, leaned against the wall, and looked down at Gottehrer with a prosecutorial glow that softened into something like pity. Gottehrer folded his own arms in imitation
defiance.

"You were saying before," Harry said, "that a unified
field theory would show how the universe was wired together."

"So you've been listening."

"You listen now. A unified field theory might be ex-
tremely dangerous, don't you think? There's never been a
physical discovery that hasn't been converted to weaponry
sooner or later."

"Yes. And?"

"Patience, Norman. Tell me: if the universe were all
wired together, couldn't it be unwired?"

"Explain."

"I think you know what. I mean."

Gottehrer said nothing.

"I'll spell it out. History's very clear: one minute there's theory, the next there's engineering. A formula lights a fuse. So somebody could say, Hmm, let's see, relativity is to chain reaction as unified field theory is to what? Interesting. Solve for x and you could blow up the world."

Gottehrer unfolded his arms and started picking at his thumb.

Harry went on making his points. The fingers of his right hand were a little stabbing wedge. "If there were a unified field theory, it just might be possible, in principle, to start a reaction that would destroy the universe. Or a big hunk of it. All the mass converts to all the energy, boom. Correct me if I'm wrong, but space would be gone and time would be gone. Afterward, there wouldn't be any afterward. All there would be is nothing, forever." There was an elegiacal look on Harry's face. "The universe, if it still existed, would be nostalgic for objects."

Harry waited. He knew he'd just unloaded his applause line.

"Interesting." Gottehrer was straining to sound noncommittal. "A remote possibility, I would think."

"Of course . . . In 1905, so was a chain reaction."

Gottehrer gouged his thumb with his fingernail. "Say, for the sake of argument, that this ultimate bomb was possible. What would be the point?" His sneer lacked conviction.

Harry made his wedge again. "The point, Norman, is to threaten! To lower the boom. Boom! Since 1945 the assumption has been that the bigger the bang, the bigger the clout. As you no doubt remember, there was lots of talk in the fifties and early sixties about ultimate weapons. A man named Herman Kahn liked what he called the doomsday machine. Influential fellow, Mr. Kahn. The idea was to sink this thing in a mine shaft and then announce: Take one dangerous step, mister, and I blow up the world."

"Some threat," Gottehrer protested.

"But it might just work. Your antagonist might just reason that anybody crazy enough to make such a threat, or even hint at it, might be crazy enough to carry it out. Maybe the chances of his carrying it out are only a hundred to one. Or a thousand to one, a million. Maybe the bomb doesn't even work . . . But what if there's a sliver of a chance it just might? Any odds at all might be persuasive enough. Then you could deter anything and—listen, you could also say to the other side, Do exactly what I say or I pull down the pillars. What chance would *you* take on blowing it all up? Personally, I'd take zero chance."

Electronic warbles of a far-off phone. Gottehrer refused to play.

"Suppose Hitler had gotten his hands on the universal bomb," Harry went on.

"Who would have believed him?"

"How much would you bet that Hitler was just bragging? Personally, I wouldn't want to see Jesus Christ in a position to take the gamble. Personally, I'd go a long way to keep the odds at zero. Wouldn't you?"

A vein rippled through Gottehrer's temple, but he sat like a big engine idling. "Clever idea. Very ingenious." He turned to me with his lacerated eyes. "Very good."

Up to this point, despite the purse and the phone call, Gottehrer had looked to me like a pathetic guy with a streak of malice. I could see him doing a lot of crazy and even vicious things out of some misguided sense of loyalty. Still, I couldn't see him as an assassin. Not of his prince.

But now there was the thinnest thread of a motive, and that was better than no thread at all. I vacillated. Maybe Harry was entitled to his tour de force after all. At least he was getting reactions. Still, at this rate, Gottehrer would go to the dark side of the moon to avoid the camera.

Gottehrer snapped: "Are you seriously trying to tell me that Einstein didn't die of natural causes?"

"I didn't say that," Harry said.

"No." Gottehrer inspected the corners of the room. He shifted around on the sofa, twisting himself into a scrawny sculpture. "Do you really want to know why I'm here?" he finally said. "Do you have any idea?"

"Why don't you enlighten us?" Harry said.

"This is almost funny. We're on the same side."

"Which side is that?"

He glanced from me to Harry, like a child trying to figure out which parent was going to beat him less. "What you said about theory and engineering. Absolutely right. Very very good. I've been thinking about this for years. Knowledge is power. Explain first, control later." His sentences buzzed like zaps from a high-power transmission line. "You study economic development in the desert, and the next thing you know, some Pentagon thug is reading your scholarly article and using it to justify blowing up power plants in Iraq. Right? That's Western science: If it's alive, dissect it. If it's opaque, see through it. If it moves, kill it. Everything begins with a formula and ends in a chain reaction." He had thought these words before, maybe spoken them. "No one should be trusted with a theory of everything. Especially not anyone who believes in the divinity of American power."

"You mean no one like Janousek," Harry said quietly.

"Janousek! Janousek is the wrong turn science took. Janousek is control, possession, death." The power line was broken, shooting sparks. He grinned too suddenly, like Jimmy Carter. "I'm still waiting to find out why you're so interested in the end of Einstein's life. Not the theory. I'm good at theory. I'd like some facts."

Nothing moved.

Harry's turn. "I suppose you have nothing better to do than come here to speculate."

Harry, I thought, get your sarcasm back on its leash.

"Speculating is my business." Gottehrer's laugh was strained. "Since you didn't ask, I'm in the service sector. I teach cram courses for college-admissions tests, a service for parents who want to speculate in their kids' futures. The hours are good. Rent control's good. The pay's good enough. I get to live in a leisure world and write poetry. Any more questions? Hearing none . . ." He laughed again, but this time it was more of a throttled moan. A ghastly sound. "You're the Harry Kramer who wrote *Fix*, aren't you?"

Harry with a straight face: "That was a long time ago."

"But you did write it."

"Oh yes."

"Congratulations. Strong prose. Fiction, the lie by which the truth is told. Picasso, more or less."

"Very—"

"—logical. I can see that. I know a clear mind. I'm the right guy to ask, but here's the thing, you don't go far enough. You don't really get it. I'm going to do you a favor, I'm going to save you the trouble of tripping around. Listen: if the unified field theory was dangerous in 1955, why should it be any less dangerous this minute?" He gave his words time to cool. "Tell me. No reason I can see. Can you?"

Harry shook his head slowly, No.

I wondered, did Gottehrer bray like this, wag his finger, talk in spurts back when Einstein adopted him?

I said, "You're saying that this theory would be so dangerous that you'd stop at nothing to keep it under wraps. Follow a man, threaten a woman, try to steal her purse—"

"What?" His eyes as wide as a lie.

"You heard me."

"You're out of your mind."

I kept him waiting. Then, mild as milk: "Fine, have it your way. But you did leave me messages every six and a half minutes and you did barge up to me pretty urgently this morning, so I think it's time you explained why."

Gottehrer bored into my eyes for three years. Then, with sadistic slowness: "You know what? I'm going to tell you. Rosenthal told me there was a writer who was interested in Einstein's last days. So I thought, Well, this is very peculiar, after all these years. Yesterday you went to see him"—he paused to let his knowledgeability sink in—"and after you left, Rosenthal told me that you had a special interest in the UFT. And that you, Miss Ross, were involved. Here's the point: You have resources. I knew Einstein. So why don't we—" He paused.

"Collaborate?" Harry finished the question for him. "You know, I didn't tell Rosenthal I was interested in Einstein's last days. What I said was 'last years.' "

"Rosenthal said 'last days.' "

"It doesn't matter," I said to nurse him down. "What kind of collaboration do you have in mind?"

"Find out, for example, if Einstein really left more notes."

I still couldn't see Gottehrer feeding Einstein a fistful of speed. But I could see him shuddering at the thought that if somebody got his hand on Einstein's field-theory notes, boom, the future belonged to the weapon to end all weapons and all futures.

Or suppose he didn't kill the man he loved. Suppose he found him dead. He could still have tucked away a page or two of Einstein's notes that no one would miss. I could see him burning the pages one at a time, holding them by their corners, flushing away the ashes.

"I've been wondering," Harry said, "why you went back to see Einstein the second time."

"I, ah . . . Who said there was a second time?"

"Did you go back for the notes?"

Gottehrer didn't wilt. "Who says I went back?"

"Sources," Harry said. Harry didn't deliver stupid lines very well.

" 'Sources,' " Gottehrer mimicked. "What is this, some comic-book version of *Fix*? *Fix* my fucking ass, I'm wasting my time."

Gottehrer jerked himself up on his feet, his right hand in his coat pocket. The lurker was going to kill us. Bang, bang, I clutch my head, Harry clutches his stomach like Lee Harvey Oswald, writhes, twists . . . Fade to black. But this time the camera's not rolling. Damn! Missed a great moment in television.

Gottehrer's voice ratcheted up, shriller. "Don't fuck with me!" His face was flushed, his half-opened fist came out of his pocket. That was his only weapon, and it was trembling. "Shit, I'm wasting—"

"Mr. Gottehrer—"

He squinted. Then a terrible twitch started. His whole right cheek seemed to collapse, dragging his eye down toward his mouth. The man was going to shake to pieces. But he just stood there, his coat flapping, his chest heaving, holding a fist that didn't know where to go.

Harry folded his arms, bunched them like a bundle of dynamite, and paced one step to his right, another to his left, leaving him where he had been but angrier. "Let me put it this way, Norman. I don't quite grasp what you were doing in Princeton. And I'm not alone. Your taking shelter in the bosom of Dr. Einstein was not universally welcome."

"Those people are nonentities," Gottehrer said, releasing his fist. "Resentful, petty—"

"They resented you, you mean."

"I was a walking scandal," Gottehrer said. The left end of his mouth wanted to grin. The right side wanted to break into a scream.

I fancied I saw a flash of pity in Harry's eyes. "All right, so it stands to reason somebody might, let's say, wish you ill. Look, help us. Who else knew that Einstein was on the brink of a unified field theory? Who else knew about those last notes at his bedside?"

"You tell me."

Harry was a statue of concentration. "Nurses."

Gottehrer nodded.

"Doctors."

"Sure."

"His stepdaughter."

Gottehrer nodded.

"His son."

"I heard."

"Otto Nathan."

"The economist. Yeah, I remember him."

"He's dead. Problem is, from our point of view, none of the above had any particular knowledge of physics. Then there's Franz Rosenthal. Then there's Janousek. Who else?"

"I get it. Janousek told you." Gottehrer's tone was cement.

"Neither confirm nor deny," I said.

"Right. Janousek has to have seen the notes. He doesn't miss a thing. Einstein might even have told him . . ." His eye was twitching again.

"I keep coming back to one fat fact," Harry said. "Einstein told you how close he was to a UFT. He told Otto Nathan. He may have told someone else, we don't know that. What we do know is that one person he certainly told is you."

Gottehrer's eyes could have pierced Janousek's fire-proof safe. "You don't know a thing," he said.

I gave him my irresistible smile. "Norman, I really want you to tell your story on camera. Just come down to makeup—or forget that, I'll get her down here—" I reached for the phone.

"And ask me about the missing notes, right? Fabulous technique. Fucking enough. You're wasting my time." I could hear the grating sound of *Pay attention, Margo . . . Forget Einstein or you're going to die,* going to die, going to die, who knows what evil lurks in the hearts of men. "Get—out —of—my—way."

Harry, stationary, showed all the emotion of an air conditioner.

Gottehrer took a step. "You're asking for it." I didn't

dare ask, for what? for fear I might find out. I watched my hand hover over the phone, as if it were an alien object, like Gottehrer. Freeze-frame.

Hold it there. One beat, two beats, three. Then Harry pulled the door open and said with a flourish, "Free country."

"Nobody's as stupid as intelligent people," Gottehrer rasped on his way out.

If I had had tongues, I would have spoken in them. Fortunately, my skirt had pockets I could jam my hands into. "Would you mind telling me what you were doing?"

"What do you mean?" Harry, lips tight, trying not to look pleased with himself, looked pleased with himself.

"You drove him out of here, Harry. You knew that Burke was reconsidering the piece and you made it impossible for me to get this guy in front of a camera."

We stared at each other, awkward, like survivors of an accident in which somebody else has just been killed but nobody knows exactly who.

"I was feeling my way. Thinking."

"With a bludgeon. What am I supposed to do, clap? We lost him, Harry."

"Maybe—well, what can I say? O.K., we lost him. So what? We don't have a thing on him, anyway."

"Blue coat."

"Sure. But it won't hold up in court."

"It's a good color on television. Somebody has to think television here."

My sarcasm stopped him. He went on defensively: "I was trying to feel out why Einstein picked this little puppy dog for philosophical discussion."

"Figure it out?"

"Gottehrer was advertising for a father. He still is. Someone to tell him to sit down and shut up."

"And Einstein needed this? Just to have somebody younger around? All the better if it's somebody a bit cracked?"

"To wrestle with. His agon, his son." He enjoyed restating my point in more elevated terms. "Somebody right there in the flesh who was just as wild on the surface as Einstein was under the skin. Somebody who could understand his terror."

"Namely?"

"That a unified field theory might be the beginning of the end of the world."

Wild ideas were spawning wilder ideas. I hated having to admit there was a bare chance that this one might be worth my brutalized nerves. "Tell me, Mr. Bad Cop, where you got this brilliant idea that a unified field theory could blow up the world."

"Something he said. My male intuition." He grinned but failed to light up the office.

"And now you're going to tell me why he went back to Einstein's room that night?"

"Either because (A) he just couldn't let go, or (B) he wanted to get the notes. He might not have been alone long enough the first time."

"I'm glad you didn't say (C) he wanted to make sure Einstein was dead," I said. "He's too blatant to be a killer, and too loyal. But he's a great character and a medium-good witness, and you blew him."

Harry was elsewhere. "*If* he took the notes—"

"What? You sounded convinced—"

"I'm not convinced that he didn't, mind you. Thought experiments."

"Here's an experiment of my own. Get out of here." Full stop. "I shouldn't have put it that way. But I need space, Harry."

"If that's the way you feel." He looked like a wounded, quizzical St. Bernard.

"I get crazy the day of a show. I should have warned you. Don't take it personally. Go home and change."

I gave him my apartment keys and told him I'd meet him there about an hour after the show.

Then I was alone for the first time in—what? Three days and two nights, suffused with strange affections, motives, reversals. And what I felt was relief.

I punched my code, THANE, into the computer and started to bat out my script: "Two decades ago, Billy Neill was the brightest, reddest star in the firm—" Delete. "Twenty years ago, Billy Neill was the go-for-broke, glad-to-be-bad boy of rock 'n'—" Fuck it, I couldn't find a voice if it fell on me. I went to the outer office, where Cyrilly passed me a pile of "While You Were Out" slips. Yolanda wanted to know if there was last-minute work to do. Bart proposed lunch. Elaine Barbanel, who was working on our *Lark* piece—this was the hot ticket on Broadway, a musical about romance among birdwatchers who meet on the annual bird count in Central Park—had second-row seats Thursday night, was I interested. Craven of the *Times* wanted a comment on CBS's new practice of spotting a celebrity interview at five minutes before every hour in prime time. Professor Kapp at Tufts wanted to know when the designer-drug story was going on the air. The Hungarian cultural attaché had a story idea. I called back Professor Kapp, a sweet man who had given me a solid interview about what he called America's periodic drug hysteria. For an academic, Dr. Kapp could sling a usable sound bite or two. I told him the piece was going on tonight but, alas, lacking his contribution, because my boss had proclaimed that we were not in the business of teaching history, quote unquote. The thud of Professor Kapp's disappointment was audible. I told him I owed him one. I called Elaine, begged off *Lark*, told her I was crashing a piece. She reeked of curiosity. If I told her about Einstein, the story would be all over the building in a minute and a half. "Can't talk about it, sweetie," I said. "Boss's orders."

I processed words. Humming nerves make a happy heart. ". . . Billy hit the bottom and learned how to feed there, like a catfish . . . In recent years, he's been sighted less often than Elvis . . ." Damn it, I wanted to write something without three dots in it. But had to switch over to a new file, DESIGNER, where I tapped out: "Once upon a time, in the innocent days of modern drugs . . ." Make that ". . . in the early days of the drug flood, petty drug dealers prided themselves on the purity of their product . . . But ideals faded and the mob moved in . . . There arrived marijuana laced with strychnine, LSD laced with amphetamines . . . Then . . . PAUSE . . . artificial heroin." Writing without a cigarette was like swimming without limbs. I sent that line to a new file, CIGS, for a piece on Japanese stop-smoking clinics.

Getting giddy. Click, click. "The law was precise about what it meant by illegal drugs . . . Heroin, for example, is a molecule with so many carbon atoms, so many hydrogen atoms, and so on, all in an exact configuration . . . Co-

caine was defined in the same way, and LSD, and the rest."
Remember to ask Burke if he got the graphic we'd talked
about. On a white background, a diagram of a molecule
with all blue atoms. Then change one atom to red. Same
structure, barely different drug, radically different effects.
If we were lucky, the diagram would be accurate and I'd be
spared a hundred huffy letters from chemists.

Back to composing: "The loophole was big enough to
drive a Brink's truck through . . . Change an atom and
heroin is no longer legally heroin . . . Now you can set up
a lab and, in three days, fabricate a fortune's worth of a
chemical which is almost exactly heroin, but not quite . . .
Technically, this mutation is no longer heroin . . . PAUSE.
It's legal . . . SIGNIFICANT PAUSE. The chemist shuts down
his operation after three days and makes off with his half a
million dollars. His designer drug has all the effects of
heroin, and one more—one shot can produce Parkinson's
disease . . . Irreversibly . . . And that's where our story
begins—in a hospital ward in Van Nuys, California. GO TO
WARD, SHOT OF TWITCHING TEEN."

Write your congressmen and -women, ladies and gents.
Hearings, angry parents, local news, laws, research grants,
sudden bureaucracies for treatment and law enforcement.
Nice. Professional pride is a whiff of pure oxygen.

But oxygen wears off. I came down. My office was full of
Harry's absence.

I picked up the phone and punched up Burke's extension. He picked up during the first ring and boomed:
"Burke." I told him I'd be right down with the designer-
drugs script. "Great, great," as if I'd said the sun was expected to set that night.

I was on my way out of my office when the phone trilled. I told Cyrilly, "I'm only here if the Holland Tunnel collapsed. Otherwise, I'm 'away from my desk.' "

"It's Harry Kramer," she said. I brightened rather too quickly. "Says it's urgent."

So my big bad cop was begging forgiveness already. Good thing for him I'd softened.

I skidded back into my office, picked up the phone.

"Are you sitting down?" His voice stripped bare.

"I am now. You have a way of sweeping a girl off her feet."

"I talked to Peter. We've got trouble. Taub's demanding his test results. Actively wondering why they're late."

"How long was it supposed to take?" I meant the chemical readout.

"I don't know." If there's anything Harry hated, it was not knowing. "It seems the National Science Foundation is about to pay a site visit."

"In English?"

"Coming to inspect the lab. They do that before renewing grants. Taub probably thinks that Einstein's brain will impress them, they can brag about it to Congress."

"So, if this sudden interest in the test results is innocent, I don't see the problem."

"It may or may not be innocent. Here's the point. Peter's been stringing Taub along about 'problems with the equipment,' but he's used up his excuses. He can't stall him past Friday."

"You're telling me that the day after tomorrow we lose the initiative. People start clamming up. And if Taub goes to the cops, end of exclusive, end of piece."

"Exactly."

"So what do we do?"

"That's what I'm asking you."

"I asked first."

"If you want the satisfaction of hearing me say I don't know, then here it is: I don't know."

I twirled the ends of my hair. The office seemed to tick. Everything in me wanted to go for broke. Throw Colin McShane for a loop, for the principle of the thing, for fun, play beat the clock again.

"I've got a crazy idea," I said. "We crash the piece."

"Crash . . ."

"Go for next Wednesday's show. So on Friday, if Taub calls the cops, or a press conference, all the better for us. 'Scientist Says Einstein Was Murdered,' the perfect *In Depth* promo. Let the competition descend on the cops. They'll just have heard about the murder themselves, so they'll stonewall. A few days later, what do you know, intrepid girl reporter identifies the murderer. Next question?"

I'm unstoppable when I speed-rap. Deadlines are my dope. "You're proposing, if I understand you correctly"— Harry slowed—"not only that we solve this murder that has been successfully hidden for forty years—"

"Whose bright idea was that?"

"Not to do it in one week, it wasn't."

"Well, I see you and raise you."

"Gilman's already given you the whole show this week."

"If we come up with a killer—how can he refuse? By the way, give me a better idea."

Of course, Burke wasn't going to yank his entire show, change promos, run ads for a murder exposé unless we had a murderer for him by, say, Monday noon.

"That settles it," Harry said, half mocking no one in particular.

My scheme was nothing but holes. We'd been digging for a grand total of two days. Scratching was more like it. We were still turning up motives and candidates. Gottehrer would duck the camera. Burke wouldn't take the chance. McShane wouldn't stand for it. Strike three.

"And tell Peter to keep trying to stall," I said.

Harry said admiringly, "I didn't realize you play high-stakes poker."

I told him there was a lot he didn't know about me. The chances were extraordinarily slight that I could pull off this high-wire stunt, but if I did, I'd be unendurably hot. Offers in the middle six figures. Renegotiate my deal with *In Depth,* run my own unit, turn into a five-hundred-pound gorilla, the Barbara Walters of serious journalism. Retire early, sail to Antigua with a lifelong supply of mystery novels. I unlaced my walking shoes, pulled open the file drawer in my desk, and slipped on the pumps I keep there. I needed all the leg I could get.

Burke's well-trained Tiffany inspected me as I clicked up to her desk. Ex officio, she owed me respect. Ex emotio, she hated me. Emotions swirled and dissolved in her face like an amoeboid projection in a light show from the old days.

Her romance novel was upside down next to her computer. She was wearing a whitened-pink lipstick, a pink velour top. Unfortunately for her color scheme, the cover of the novel was a lurid red.

"Is he in?"

"He was just trying to reach you."

I took this as a cue to march into the inner sanctum.

"How *are* you?" Burke looked up as if I were his long-lost ex-wife. I stopped short.

"About 'reconsidering'—" I started.

"First things first. Got some scripts for me?"

I passed over the page. He sat on the edge of his desk and made a show of looking for page 2. "I count one script."

"Is it two o'clock? My watch must have stopped."

After a stagy sigh, he proceeded to roam down the page. Burke didn't exactly read. There were rumors of learning disorders, tiny attention spans, coked-up synapses clogging his cortex.

"Great," he said, tossing the page on his desk. "Just lead with gas, O.K.?" Gas was the street name for the vapor that boils off from speed—the state of the art, so the papers were saying, in fabricating heaven.

"Gas isn't a designer drug. It's already illegal."

"Sure, but Joe Blow in Queens has heard all about gas. Throw in a hook for Joe Blow, the guy works hard for a living, do him a favor, will you?"

I could have used some gas. I was tempted to make up a new drug, smokable speed mixed with crack, or "croak." Put that out on the air and somebody'd cook it up. Instead, I took back the page and scribbled a new lead: "You've heard about gas, the methamphetamine vapor, more addictive and longer-lasting than crack." Strike "longer-lasting," that makes it sound terrific. ". . . more addictive than crack . . . But at least gas is illegal. What if there were something more dangerous, and as legal as chewing gum? . . . SIG. PAUSE. There is."

"Fantastic," Burke said. "Tiff, could you come in here?"

he shouted into his speaker-phone. Tiffany appeared in the doorway. Burke told her to see that my script got onto the TelePrompTer, then turned back to me: "Wait till you see the graphic. State of the art. You'll love it."

I settled down in his leather Breuer chair, crossed my legs, smoothed my blouse, and tried to show enthusiasm for a graphic that changes colors. I pulled down my skirt, taut. Nevertheless, Burke, gleaming with self-love, failed to run his eyes up and down my legs. My thick thighs, my peasant genes.

With chagrin and cheer, I finally felt Burke's glance touring down the length of my body.

"Watch this," Burke said. He bounced up and snapped a cassette into the VCR slot. There were clicks of mechanical efficiency. "By the way," he said, swiveling toward me, "you look fabulous."

"Thank you. Nice suspenders." He was wearing yellow suspenders with blue stars-and-stripes trim. Burke was right there on the cutting edge of eighties nostalgia.

Clicks, whirs, moans, colored bars. Then a deep hum, electronic resonance, the bars dissolving, the heroin mole-cule coming up, the atoms done as tiny blue circles, the letters H-E-R-O-I-N clicking in one at a time, in red, like amped-up typewriter keys. One of the blue atoms turns red. A-R-T-I-F-I-C-I-A-L. The whole image peels up, rotates to the right and away, a plane spun off into graphics hyper-space to die.

"What do you think?" Burke wanted to know.

"Fabulous, Burke."

"Bernie Gross is a fucking genius." Bernie had also de-signed the WE TAKE IN THE WORLD scoreboard. Burke was working his blue clay, waiting for me to chorus along. I didn't. His mind changed channels. "Heroin, I don't know. Sounds old-fashioned. In Queens they're worried about the crack house moving in next door, some crack baby growing up to blow Joe Blow's brains out for five bucks. I think we should switch to cocaine. The graphic, I mean."

I remembered not so many years ago when Burke's nose ran constantly. "The piece is about artificial heroin, not cocaine." My lips as tight as his smile.

"How right you are." He scribbled a note on a vellum strip imprinted with his name. Someone had told McShane that these were standard issue in Hollywood, and now they were standard issue at Con Comm.

When a man admits you're right, he's primed. "Now," I said, "as you were saying about reconsidering the Einstein story."

He shot me a long look. "Right. It's under active reconsideration."

"To what do we owe this dazzling development?"

"Above my department." He nodded toward the ceiling.

"Well, I have some bad news for upstairs. Our exclusive is about to run down the drain if we don't run after it."

"You've got my attention." He stopped working the clay.

I told him that Taub had regained his interest in Einstein's brain. I told him about Taub's Friday deadline. Burke was opaque. His eyes were smoked glass.

"What's the good news?" he wanted to know.

"I've got a head start. I've got characters, suspects. Shifty eyes, foreign accents. Witnesses, photogenic lies."

"I didn't hear you say you have a murderer," Burke said, with a little twist of his lips, but there was no smile in his eyes, only machinery.

"We're getting warm." I love off-white lies. I told him

about Gottehrer's two visits to Einstein's deathbed. I told him that we had witnesses who could place him there. I told him that one of the witnesses was Janousek.

"Oh? You've talked to this Gottehrer?" Burke didn't quite seem surprised.

I didn't act surprised that he didn't seem surprised. "Couldn't get him to *stop* talking. There is also a motive you wouldn't believe."

"I'm sure you'll be happy to tell me about it. How much time do we have?"

"Next week."

His go-getter eyes were green and not unattractive, catching the brash afternoon light. "Would you do me a favor?" he finally said.

"What?"

"Call the doctor. I'm hallucinating that Margo Ross is telling me to crash the murder of Albert Einstein the week after I've given her two pieces. She's got an undisclosed motive I quote wouldn't believe unquote and, by the way, no murderer. Jesus."

"Listen to me. The rest of the good news is that if Taub goes to the cops, that's not so bad, because I'll guarantee you that the news that Einstein was murdered is going to leak. By Monday we're on the front page of every tabloid in the country. We're on the evening news. By the time *60 Minutes* and *20/20* even think of cranking up, we're on the air. We're *America's Most Wanted* and *Unsolved Mysteries* rolled into one."

"The doctor will want to hear about the amazing motive," he said.

I delivered a short course on the unification hypothesis, the weapon to end all weapons.

"You're saying you want to crash a piece in front of sixty million eyeballs."

"A fifty share, Burke," I said, "or I buy you dinner at Happening."

Burke rolled his clay into a snake. He folded the snake in half, rolled out a new snake, then folded the new one in half. He studied the snake.

"We take on the world, Burke."

His expression had all the fire of a television screen with the volume off. "You don't have a murderer."

I felt the special helplessness that comes from making a lousy case for something you badly want. "I'll get one."

He came close to a sigh. "We're reconsidering, but we're not talking suicide."

He surveyed his whole canyon of power and glass—his by the sufferance of Colin McShane. He would wither without this niche in Manhattan airspace. "All right, suppose I commit to this lunatic scheme, seven days pass, and it's Wednesday afternoon and what do you know, we're sitting here with your antique brain like it's the Shroud of Turin or some goddamned thing, a wacko murder and no murderer. And I'm staring at dead air. And McShane is on the phone." He affected a singsong cockney accent: " 'You're fuckin' 'istory, Bhehhk.' And last but not least, you are staring at the shreds of your new contract." He smiled. "Candidly, Margo, I want to do the right thing as much as you. You're a wonderful correspondent and you're paid accordingly. *And* I'm paid to big-picture this business, I have responsibilities you don't. *And* I like flying this desk. I intend to keep flying this desk."

"This sounds like a no."

"Find me a murderer, then we'll talk. Meantime, don't you have work to do?"

The worst of it was, I felt sorry for him.

"Candidly, Burke," I said with a lilt, "thank you and fuck yourself." I smiled at him as sincerely as he deserved, and fled.

■

Einstein's shutters were black, his house bright white. Janousek's moon was bright white, his heart black. Burke's collar was excessively white. Take a note, Margo, for a doc in black and white.

But I wasn't taking notes, I was sitting in the makeup chair, churning, eyes closed, while Sally the makeup "girl," Sally of the overly tan skin and overly blond curls, made me over. Sally's assistant, the girl's girl, washed, blow-dried, and combed out my hair. Then Sally went to work salvaging my face. "Girl" was Sally's word, though she had long since passed to the wrong side of fifty. "Sweet blouse," she said. The network had paid for a color consultation; the result was my salmon-colored blouse and the floral-print scarf featuring blue and white—a logo of reliability. Sally swabbed off what was left of my morning face and put on my new one, resulting in hints of a high degree of experience, an engagé look. This broad is tough and knowing but hasn't surrendered her capacity to be shocked. Even my slightly sagging eyelids signified *character*. Or so I could convince myself. I anointed my lip with white undercoat and pale pink lipstick, put on my robin's-egg-blue blazer and strolled onto the set.

"Particular congratulations," Jesús the cameraman greeted me. Jesús wore dark shirts buttoned so high they pinched his neck. I sprayed smiles all over the place, received my personalized cup of metallic-tasting coffee from a gofer, let the sound man pin the mike on my collar, ran the wire up under the blazer, and three, two, one, taped nine or ten takes of the designer-drug intro.

Not smoothly. The first take, I slipped into a know-it-all *60 Minutes* tone—a Diane Sawyer imitation, haughty, jeering, weirdly jubilant. Catching myself bloating up, I overdid the singsong until I had Jesús cracking up. Start over: *Once upon a time, in the early days of the drug flood* . . . this time earnest and disgusted to have discovered the vile facts, rather than stuffed with glory at the fact that I, I, I had discovered them. I deepened my voice. Gazing into the lens, I thought of Harry, his care for words, his eye for flaws, his slow nod. Ten seconds . . . roll logo . . . roll music . . . four, three, two, one, red light, roll tape, the A.D. points, I smile, compose myself, and . . . we're . . . rolling, take four of the truth. Sounds quaint: "the truth," as if the truth were a buried treasure, waiting to be unearthed. The truth is a ghost, always slipping away. That's why journalism gives us a consolation: the story.

My story, my facts, seep into the world. Let Congress fulminate, ink flow, laws pass. Never mind that evil geniuses would find other ways to sell drugs.

And that's where our story begins—in a hospital ward in Van Nuys, California.

Sally came bounding up and said, "You were great." The A.D. said, "Great." Burke strolled in and said, "Very nice." This I took seriously. The hell with it, I *felt* great. Stones would weep with pleasure to be in my presence. In the studio, you can be blinded by your own reflected light.

■

"Tell me something," said Tony Carrera. "You think this Billy Neill move into Billy Null is part of the new nihilism?" Tony had read an article somewhere.

"Yeah, maybe so," I said. I tried to keep up, too.

We were sitting in Tony's office, the next corner down from Burke's, with a gaudier view. Tony's suit was a pinstriped, double-breasted charcoal job, his tie was peach, with a tight knot, and a peach-colored handkerchief swelled from his breast pocket. Our colors rhymed. I liked talking to Tony. He made me feel like a woman without making me feel dirty. Notwithstanding the way the pundits had chortled over his prior career as a model, Tony was smart, though you had to see under his patter to know it. He could pass as sophisticated—in the *GQ, Vanity Fair, Connoisseur* sense. For the network, he had one particularly endearing skill: a knack for timing his shiny sentences as if a stopwatch were built into his mind. Give him a fifty-five-second hole, he would deliver exactly fifty-five seconds of chat. Or he could go a minute and twelve, whatever, and land, boom, at the end, like Baryshnikov. He was also a master of career moves—from modeling to *In Depth,* with a Con Comm contract stretching into the next millennium.

"You think this is like cyberslash?" he asked. I looked blank. "You know, the new Japanese rock trend. Oo-ee."

"Probably. Don't you dare ask me that question on camera."

"Hey, what kind of a guy do you think I am? By the way, you read about these government bozos bombing the coca fields in Peru with pesticides and God knows what-all for the fourth year in a row? They cut down the supply while the demand stays sky-high, and what they get is a lot more entrepreneurs go into drug designing." I didn't doubt that Tony had firsthand experience with that sky-high demand. I had my own, thank you. But the glory days were gone forever, leaving us all high and dry on camera—puny consolation for the ecstasy we've lost.

"Sounds like a great piece," I said.

Tony went into singsong. "Well, I don't know-ow. Sounds mighty *com*-plicated. *Ab*-stract, you dig, for the bro' on the street. Where your *pic*-tures? We deal in show-and-tell-a-vision, sweetheart. We do not deal with hypotheticals or some kind of jive a-*nal*-ysis. You want to speculate, call Wall Street." He wasn't funny, but I laughed, anyway.

"You up for a little postgame chat about the demand side of drugs, one on one?" he asked.

"Sold."

I went back to my office, which was blessedly quiet—doors closed, halls empty. Cyrilly had gone home after the taping. I called the switchboard and told them to hold all calls. I opened my bottom right-hand desk drawer, took out a pair of earplugs and a sleep mask, and lay down on my couch. My mind was supercharged with Burke, Gottehrer, Harry, WE BLOW THE OPPOSITION OUT OF THE WATER, take another little piece of my heart. I counted backward from one hundred, and after I got to zero I started over. Before I hit zero again, my valves shut down.

Drug addicts, knitting needles . . . I woke up. The entire right side of my skull was pain. I wondered if I was having a stroke. I had no time for a stroke. Instead, I went to the ladies' room, irrigated my eyes, swallowed three Tylenols. Elaine popped in. Mouth-mouth. I told her I was swamped. She burst into sobs. She was sure her husband was having an affair. After I'd made reassuring noises, she asked what was going on with me. I told her Harry. Having heard my extended recent denunciations of Blond Bart, she was happy to hear that something potentially sensible was happening in my life. I wasn't making any grand claim that Harry was Mr. Right, I said, but in the age of fast tracks and viruses, Mr. Acceptable was fine for a while.

I went back to my office, accompanied by my headache and a lingering sense of dread. My ground note, my steady rumble, my horizon. Dread is what keeps me solid; otherwise, I would melt away.

I phoned Delaney, the cop who had held my hand that time when the breather was calling in the middle of the night, and asked him to find out anything about a Gottehrer, comma, Norman.

"What's he done?"

"I'm not sure," I said, "besides giving me the creeps."

"That's not against the law in New York State. I thought you were going to stay out of trouble." Delaney was a kid in his midtwenties who had the solicitous air of a little brother who feels tremendous relief that his big sister finally needs him.

"I want to check him out for a story."

"Well," Delaney said, "we certainly don't want anyone out walking around giving you the creeps."

I described Gottehrer as a poet who moonlights as a teacher of middle-class kids who are too dumb to get into college. Delaney had gone to John Jay College of Criminal Justice. He laughed and said he'd get to it first thing in the morning and give me a call.

A few minutes after eight, with a couple of hours still left to kill, I started returning calls, reaching more machines than people — just as well. I thought of calling Harry but let the thought wither and die. Telltale signs of dependency were breaking out all over me.

Dread is the horizon, and love? Love is a momentary eclipse. A particular human body with memorable eyebrows, chin, shoulders steps up and cancels out the essential fact and presence that silhouettes everything else: dread.

The pain in my head started to lift. I turned descriptions of Billy Neill around in my mind. I galloped through the *Times, Newsweek, The Wall Street Journal.* I paged through the ads in *Woman* and rejoiced that I'd saved my old vests, they were coming back. I studied the BEFORE and AFTER pictures in a plastic surgeon's ad for eyelid lifts . . . Too much. I slammed the magazine shut.

With an hour left before airtime, there was nothing to do but call home, punch in my code, and collect messages. First, there was the inevitable Blond Bart, prospecting again. Fast-forward for you, asshole. Yolanda said she was sure my show would be great.

The next voice, gruff and accented, stopped my breath.

"If this is the number of Miss Ross? Hello? This is Gustav Janousek. I am sorry to disturb you, but I have thought of something that might interest you concerning the mysterious Mr. Gottehrer. Since you are not at home, I shall try to reach you at your office, although you are no doubt preparing for your program. Well, in any event, this is not so urgent. Don't bother to call back tonight — I shall be busy with Mr. Gottehrer from eight o'clock on. I shall watch you later on television with interest, and look forward to discussing the matter with you in person tomorrow evening. Well, that's all. Good-bye. Janousek." The machine voice said, "Wednesday, 7:48 p.m."

I called the switchboard to see if Janousek had left a message. He had: that he'd called, nothing more.

I called back my machine and listened again. Maybe he'd been put off by the baritone growl on my message. There was a tension in his voice, no question about it. My watch said 8:18. By now, Gottehrer would be there with him.

I nibbled at cuticles. I pictured Janousek behind his fortress desk, moonlight bathing his study, a fidgety Norman Gottehrer contemplating the model missile. Finally I punched up Janousek's number and, remembering his odd system for answering the phone, let it ring twenty times. Could he have canceled his appointment with Gottehrer, decided to accompany his wife after all, and called from the theater?

Janousek, breathing hard, answered hello. I told him I had gotten his message.

"Good," he said, "but tomorrow would be more convenient to discuss this, do you understand?" He sounded annoyed.

"This is not a good time for you to talk?"

"Actually, it is not convenient, no."

"You have company, I take it."

"That is correct."

"Fine. I'm sorry to have bothered you. I just thought—"

"That's quite all right. We shall meet tomorrow." He hung up.

I went down to the seventh floor and Sally painted on my broadcast face.

There's sheer joy in a sleek show.

The *In Depth* lead-in is what we call a work of genius. The screen goes black and silent: there's a skitter of VDT keys: the "Going in Depth" theme rumbles, pulsates: fasten your seat belt, viewer, you're falling into a tunnel lined with instrument panels of light (variations on *2001, Star Wars,* video games): the synthesizer intones a soprano chant that sounds vaguely like *in depth, in depth:* rumbles intensify: photos of not-so-humble correspondents appear to the *p'ching p'ching* of a camera motor: and as the seconds tick down to zero hour, my mind starts to take leave of my body: "Going in Depth" stops dead with an unresolved chord: but I—have—the—forward—motion, I'm—*hot,* composing my face into an authoritative look: cameras swoop: the crew pad around in running shoes: I am the still center of the apparatus: and as I turn up the heat and bring my mind to a thin flame, as one crisp sentence thunks into place after another, as I leave zero hour behind for zero plus one—I die, I ascend to the plane of pure pleasure. I am the pure blue-white cone of light in the flame.

We're on the set, waiting for the Billy Neill piece to come to its musical climax. Tony crooks his finger at Jesús and asks, "Can you come in?" Jesús, perplexed, swoops closer. "No, on the knot," Tony says. He wants the camera to zoom in on the knot of his tie. Jesús obliges. Tony appraises his knot in the monitor and microscopically straightens it. They'll get a kick out of that in the control room.

The piece ends with the closing strum of "Absolute Zero Heart," the screen fades to black, the A.D.'s finger points, and Tony goes live. He's heard that Billy's style of yelling and thumping music is all the rage in Russia. *All the rage,* I say, *I like the way you put that. There's a lot of apocalypse in the air,* I say. One sentence thunks into place after another. *The third millennium's coming. Billy is right about the bomb, and there's also the greenhouse effect, the ozone layer, and so on. What you never heard of can kill you. If Chernobyl wasn't bad enough, the Mayak nuclear explosion last year gives the Russians plenty to be hysterical about. Billy's saying that extinction's got to be put to music.* Tony nods sagely. Without skipping a beat, he wants to know whether this career move of Billy's is cynical. *Why shouldn't somebody live the second half of his life under a different name?* I say. *Makes you think,* Tony says. Not for long, I think.

We'll take a break now, says Tony soberly into the lens. *When we return, a different kind of apocalypse.*

There's a beer commercial with a post-nuclear-war look: a postwar tribe gathers convivially to sip out of the can around the campfire in the blasted desert: salmon and gray are the featured colors: culminating in a mushroom cloud billowing up: a ribbon of words runs across the screen: WE BLOW THE COMPETITION OUT OF THE WATER. Segue to a sepia job, with jump cuts: boy meets girl: boy unzips an inch of zipper on girl's jeans: girl reciprocates: cut to a pink satin sheet, a female hand throwing it back: a breathy voice-over insinuates: TAKE OFF, IN THE JEANS YOU WANT TO TAKE OFF. How're we doing for time, Tony says off-air. Ten seconds over, the A.D. says. No problem, says Tony. We will have touchdown.

The designer-drugs piece runs smooth as an electric carving knife. A hospital ward: two teenagers uncontrollably shaking, faces obliterated by the digitizing process.

Hand-held authenticity. A man in a white coat says one of them, a first-timer, will never speak again. The shaky camera is there for the bust of Randall Bates, Ph.D., suburban chemist. The jail gate slams, with its echo amped. Cut to court, where a nice Jewish boy-lawyer says the only question at issue is whether the substance is illegal, because this is a nation of laws. Cut to Bates walking out of court. A cop glares.

Tony aside to me: Boil the motherfucker. Tear him apart.

The piece is not wrong, not at all. Dead right, as far as it goes, which is about six inches. *In Depth*, the lazy man's guide to the lower depths. Indignation washes over America. We never ask: Why do people want to shoot up with this shit?

Chat time. Tony wrinkles his handsome brow and wonders aloud why the authorities are taking their sweet time to respond to this menace. What do I think of the theory that dark-skinned victims get short shrift?

Not exactly the angle I was expecting. I feel as if Tony has knocked me into the water and it takes time to scope out which way is up before I can summon my strength and resolve to heave my arms against the water until—not quite too late—I break through the surface. The point is to keep swimming. On the one hand, on the other hand, yakkety-blah. I sound like a goddamned opinion machine. What I really want to say is that when the jail terms wind to an end, there's more net wickedness in the world than before, and fallen angels can kill you as they fall, and I don't understand the world, Tony, I swear I don't.

Whereupon Tony looks concerned and thanks me for my hard-hitting piece on this very important continuing story and says there are no easy answers but we'll keep our viewers informed. Fade-out with a two-shot of Margo and Tony, exemplary bearers of truth.

We'll be back in a minute with more from *In Depth*.

Go to commercial: the sound of a string quartet, suggesting a brokerage house or an upscale car.

I turn my stony face to Tony, who is fingering the knot of his tie as if he thinks it could still be tighter.

"You sandbagged me, Tony," I said. "I thought we agreed to go to the demand side of drugs."

"Thought about it," he says, "but I decided to do it this way, since it's not right to knock your own piece. You don't knock the hostess in her own living room."

He sees Burke walking up, hand behind his back. "You're a star, star," Burke says to me, and brings out a bouquet of white roses. I am as grateful as he deserves. He kisses the air between us.

"What about mine?" Tony says to him.

"You get yours later."

Sixty seconds, the A.D. says. I head to the corner of the studio, where stands a beat-up armchair bearing a sign: MARGO ROSS. A joke from the crew a few years ago.

"The switchboard is lit up like a forest of Christmas trees," Burke says, trailing after me. "A lady called claiming to be Billy Neill's long-lost love child. And, by the way, CALM demands equal time against your anti-nuclear propaganda." CALM is the Campaign Against Liberal Media. I savor a moment of vindication.

Collier Mack walks by, slightly glazed of eye, on his way to intro the final segment, which is about an architect who builds L.A. houses out of discarded Hollywood sets. This practice is said by *Angels* magazine to be chic, which instantly makes it chic. Collier's piece will make it très chic — that is, not chic at all.

Collier has looked at me funny ever since, during my first month at *In Depth*, he intimated that my prospects for upward mobility would depend on my "oral talents," as he delicately phrased it, and I told him only my mike would know for sure.

"I told the switchboard to feed you a half hour's worth of calls, hope that's all right," Burke tells me. The viewers get a charge out of the personal touch, the affiliates get a charge out of the viewers getting a charge. To tell the truth, I get off on the weirdness of vox pop.

"Ten seconds," the A.D. calls out. "Can we have quiet, please?"

Sally wipes my face clean. I go back to my office and take calls. A law professor in north Jersey thanks me for the drugs piece and wants to know, by the way, whether *In Depth* would be interested in a piece on his new approach to banning designer drugs, based on laws against distilling booze at home. A man with an ugly voice wants to know how I could get so worked up about designer drugs when I have just exalted Billy Neill, a well-known drug addict. I say I didn't think I was exalting him, exactly, and anyway, don't we Christians believe in redemption for sinners? An addict's mother wants to know where her son can receive treatment. My mother says she's proud of me but my hair is getting a little long. Twice there are long silences followed by "Is this Margo Ross? In person?" Piles of congratulations, one request for a date. Along the way, the rush wears off. Before I know it, an hour is up. I'm tired of other people's agendas. All I want is an actual person to talk to.

Damn, I'm good and muddled.

I am in so deep that no one can dredge me out, but I desperately want Harry, my mirror, my mentor, my lover, my last chance.

PART THREE

The most beautiful experience we can have is the mysterious.

ALBERT EINSTEIN

THURSDAY, OCTOBER 25

JUST AFTER MIDNIGHT, THE CAB DROPPED ME IN FRONT OF my building. Plastic bags of garbage were already slumped at the curb. From the crate on the sidewalk came snores. The moon looked iridescent, like mother-of-pearl. A chill wind gusted down the street.

Upstairs, Harry lay on the sofa watching a *Cagney and Lacey* rerun. Cagney was insisting she could damn well stop drinking any damn time she pleased. Her eyes looked puffy but her lids didn't droop. Harry's eyes were a bit glazed, his feet were up but his shoes were off. His socks were two slightly different browns. His entire ensemble was brown. He zapped the set off with the remote control and looked up with a little-boy smile: "You were marvelous."

Wasn't this what I wanted, a man who wasn't threatened by my renown, who rejoiced in my fleeting triumphs and yet understood how little they mattered? But in truth it was disconcerting to find a man waiting for me, even if he was trained to take off his shoes before putting his feet up on the sofa.

"Was I?"

"Fantastic. Especially, 'He hit the bottom and learned how to feed there, like a catfish.' And the 'We Blow the Competition' commercial. Sheer genius to slip that in after Billy Neill."

"You know perfectly well that was an accident, but I'm glad you enjoyed it. What about designer drugs?"

"Where'd you find the scumbag with his heartwarming tribute to entrepreneurship? I can't wait to see you do Gottehrer." When I didn't react, he asked, "What's wrong?"

"Oh, Tony Carrera blindsided me, that's all." I told him the story.

"If I'm your typical viewer," Harry said, scratching his chin, "no one had any idea. You looked effortless."

I knew he was right. TV words are fumes, they pass. But I needed to hear it from him. "The point is to keep talking," I said. "I've been doing it all my life. Move over, sweet thing." I kicked off my shoes and stretched out next to him, my head at his feet, his head at mine.

"Forward of you," he said.

"Harry, the way to a girl's heart is through her feet. Please." Two hands enfolding a foot produce spectacular comfort. Harry was good. His hands enveloped my arches and massaged as I described the nonevent of my conversation with Janousek. When I told him that Burke was blowing more cold than hot about crashing the Einstein show, the massage didn't stop. I closed my eyes and he worked on my toes, one at a time, then five together, stroking each foot from the ankle down. His fingers, bless them, took their time.

"Something else I'm good at?" he said. The line was like a virus passing back and forth in the household.

"I can think of another thing," I said.

■

The pips of the alarm pierced my sleep at 6:02, Eastern digital time, disrupting another dream. I couldn't imagine why I'd set the alarm for an hour best suited to Jersey commuters. In fact, I hadn't. The noise was the phone. I'd forgotten to pull the plug out of the jack. I groped for the receiver and dragged it down to the pillow.

"Have you heard?"

I groped through a fog, though I preferred the fog to the voice. "Who is this?"

"Burke. Rise and shine."

I shook my head like a wet dog. Harry groaned and stirred, a pitch-dark shape in a dark room, more a warm absence of light than a man.

"What the hell time is it?"

"Late. Turn on your radio."

"What are you talking about?"

"Your physicist is dead. Turn on your radio. I'll hold on."

Adrenaline spiked through my brain. I switched on the bed light, twisted the dial through a report on a Richard Gere retrospective, through commercials, traffic reports, and rap music, heard "—slovakian-born," tuned back and stopped at ". . . sudden end to the life of one of America's

best-known and at times most controversial physicists . . ."

Harry was sitting up, staring at me.

". . . in his Riverside Drive apartment, dead of a heart
attack . . ."

I covered the mouthpiece. "Harry, you hear—?" He
nodded.

". . . body was discovered by his wife. Gustav Janousek, dead at eighty-two. Now this." "This" was an ad for
pretorn Levi's. "We put in the holes, you put in the rest,"
said a sexy female voice.

Harry's face was crumpled, like a beach ball that's lost
air.

"Margo? You there?" Burke's voice boomed.

"I'm here."

"What do you know about this?"

"What?"

He shot the words out one at a time, BB-gun pellets:
"What—do—you—know?"

"The man's dead and I'm shocked. What do you mean,
what do I know?"

"You had the last interview. What did he say?"

From WINS, surges of electronic urgency thundered
down the scale. "You give us twenty-two minutes, we give
you the world."

"He talked about the Russians," I monotoned into the
phone. "And the nature of the universe."

"What else?"

Haze of sleep, enfold me. "He had a word or two to say
about Einstein. A physicist who died a long time ago,
Burke." Harry was shaking his head, *Stop.*

"For your information, Margo, we're very interested in the Einstein piece."

My mind raced. Janousek with his pointed face dead, the piece maybe alive. But to what end, since we were light-years from a murderer? Too much death crowding into my life, not enough fact. What had Janousek wanted to tell me?

If you find yourself asking the wrong question, my father once said, ask an easier one.

"Margo? You hear me? We want to talk about the Einstein piece."

"You want to talk about the Einstein piece."

"Sir Colin would like to have a word with you. He serves some very good coffee."

"When?"

"Now. By the way, the overnights were sensational. Calls came in till one in the morning. Craven says we've resurrected the good name of the television documentary. Sir Colin thinks your shit is angel's-food cake."

The kudos rolled off me. I'd done better work on less sexy subjects and the switchboard had stayed as dark as a Christmas tree in a power blackout.

I did wonder how Burke had heard so early that Janousek was dead. Was he usually awake at six giving WINS twenty-two minutes so that they could give him the world? By the time I thought to ask, he had clicked off.

A failure of heart. For Janousek, that seemed exactly right. The man had limited heart to begin with, to contemplate so casually the end of the world. The man thought with his spleen. He had mentioned two earlier heart attacks, one in

'68, the other—when? Had he said? But of course, at age eighty-two, a heart attack was no surprise.

"Strange, but I liked the old bastard." Harry's voice was lugubrious, deep in its morning pitch. "Or, crazy as this may sound, admired him. Listen to me. I'm going soft." He reached for his shirt, neatly hung around the back of my bedroom chair.

I went to the closet for my robe. Harry's eyes tracked me.

"O.K., 'liked' is too strong. But he awed me, in a way . . ." He trailed off, paced to the window and back toward the bed, and talked in that deliberate way of his, feeling around as if dowsing for water. "You know, those guys were giants. Janousek was a giant."

I knew what he meant, but I was too groggy to plunge into the thicket of my tangled feelings. The sound of his own voice seemed to encourage him, and he poked on: "Think about it. The Nazis, this avalanche, roaring down on them. Everything was at stake. They *so loved the world,* you know, sure, some twisted kind of love, but was it so unreasonable to think that the world had been placed in their hands to save?"

He sounded like a man trying out lines for a eulogy. Half of them made sense, but I wasn't sure which half.

Memory creaked: I had saved Janousek's message on my answering machine. I hit the rewind button. The squeaks from the voice of a dead man, rolled backward, sounded the same as the squeaks from a living man. When the squeaks broke off, I hit the playback button and that spectral, guttural voice was in the room:

If this is the number of Miss Ross? Hello? This is Gustav Janousek. I am sorry to disturb you, but I have thought of some-

thing that might interest you concerning the mysterious Mr. Gottehrer. Since you are not at home, I shall try to reach you at your office, although you are no doubt preparing for your program. Well, in any event, this is not so urgent. Don't bother to call back tonight—I shall be busy with Mr. Gottehrer from eight o'clock on. I shall watch you later on television with interest, and look forward to discussing the matter with you in person tomorrow evening. Well, that's all. Goodbye. Janousek.

Not so urgent. Mysterious Mr. Gottehrer. I went into the shower wondering if the plea I heard attached to Janousek's overly formal tone was something I was imagining. When I stuck my head out of the bathroom, Harry was sitting on the edge of the bed, socks on, shoes in front of him. He was staring. "A man calls you twice and tells you it's not so urgent. You call him back and he says it can wait. What couldn't he say in front of Gottehrer?"

I didn't know. So I worked on my face, which needed resurrection. There was a man in my apartment. I wanted to stroke him, I wanted to think with him, I wanted to roust him.

Harry poked his head into the bathroom. "Interesting, isn't it, the way when a man dies, he—loses his sting."

I appraised the mirror.

"You look gorgeous, by the way," Harry said. He ran a fingernail down the back of my neck.

I wanted to love him, I wanted to simplify my mood. "Advance to Go," I said, "but later. McShane's waiting."

I hustled to the closet and contemplated a gray-and-black diagonal-striped dress, but it was both too gaudy and not gaudy enough, so I hung it back in the closet and held a rust-colored scoop-necked knit against my body. The rust looked warm, stable, professional, opposed to death. Everything I was straining to be. "You're a good soul, Harry, but—"

"Come on."

"—aside from your terrific fingers down my spine, I don't like feeling touched. By Janousek."

I'd opened a vein. The words gushed out. "If you're like me, here's why you're touched. Think about the world as Janousek saw it. Hitler wasn't a cartoon but a flesh-and-blood man in power, with a killing machine, running Europe. The war is in doubt, and the ally on whom everything hangs is a real live Stalin. This is your one and only life. If you make the wrong move, the trapdoor opens, boom, you fall into hell. Maybe everyone you love or ever could love falls into hell. So what do you do? You do what you know how to do, which is physics. Total physics. Pull out the stops. You work up the secret of global power. If you can live with Stalin as your ally, why can't you live with atomic fire? And once you've lived with atomic fire, why not the threat of preventive war? Or the threat to blow up the world? Why the hell not? You never knew but that Hitler might be back."

I listened while slipping on the dress and adorning myself with large gold-button earrings and a thin gold chain, converting myself into the grateful minion of Sir Colin McShane. It isn't every day you're summoned to an audience with the commander in chief. If your heart isn't in it, your clothes have to be. "I don't care what the reasons were," I said. "Since when is anyone entitled to threaten to blow up the world?"

"Never, obviously. I'm only saying that the responsibility broke people. Once they built the bomb, anything was possible."

I stared at him.

"I'm trying to understand the man," he said. "Even a war criminal is entitled to that when he's dead. Or don't you think?"

His Buddhism looked forced. But I listened. His shoulders were stiff, his head out of line with his body. I sympathized.

"I know what you think," he went on. "You think it's a character flaw that I couldn't hate the guy."

"Speaks very well for your deep humanity," I said, and kissed him.

We sat in the back seat of a cab, separated from the turbaned Sikh driver by a smudged, scraped, gouged bulletproof plastic partition which he had left wide open. I felt like closing it. Amazingly, tears were backing up behind my eyes.

"Harry, I'm not as hard-assed as I sound. I felt something for the old bastard. Face it, we've both turned into liberal mush." After years of retraining, I'd learned to savor the humanity of ideologically despicable characters. Now here I was, choked up over a dead war criminal.

"Hatred is for the young, they have the energy," he said, and stroked my cheek.

The cab slid up Sixth Avenue, gulping six, seven blocks between lights. The air was the color of a dead elephant. The warm night had sucked vapor out of the ocean. Lightweight raincoats, furled umbrellas, men and women swinging their attaché cases.

At Twenty-third Street, a man staggered up to the cab, waving a dirty rag toward the windshield with his right hand, a Styrofoam cup with a crumpled rim in his left.

"Come here, brother," the driver said, and passed the man a quarter.

"Don't you have a dollar, man, a buck for a meal? Can't eat for a quarter."

The man was black, with lustrous black eyes. "Sister," he said to me, "help me."

I stared into his skull-filled face, wanting to help, refusing to be seduced. The feelings canceled out, I was paralyzed.

His face collapsed into a broken grin. "Come on," he said, in the singsong of a minstrel, "I'll . . . make . . . you . . . laugh."

Harry dragged out his wallet and passed me a dollar bill, which I passed through the window.

"Oh, sister," the black man said, his voice buoyant, "you gonna laugh when you think about me."

The light changed, the cab started up Broadway, and I said to the window, "I doubt it."

My mind was ticking along with the meter. I blew my nose, tried to make something serious of my face.

"Don't worry." Harry patted my hand. We were up to Forty-second Street before I was ready to talk business.

I began with a review of the obvious. "The trail to Einstein's murder passes through Janousek. We get onto the story—or, correction, you get onto the story." Harry shrugged. "Then what do you know, Janousek's dead. Don't you think this is a tiny bit fishy?"

"Um"—noncommittal. "The guy did have a bad heart, he was, what, eighty-two years old, he did not seem exactly easygoing—"

"Don't tell me Harry Kramer, author of *Fix*, all of a sudden believes in coincidence. I thought 'coincidence is another word for an undiscovered conspiracy.' " I fondled this old line of Harry's.

"Hell of a thing to confront a writer with his own line," he said.

"It's a great line. You don't think it's interesting that two great physicists die just after Norman Gottehrer pays them a visit?"

Harry looked past me, into the Avenue of the Americas, where energy was collecting. I cracked the window. A disconcertingly handsome midtown lawyer type jogged by in a T-shirt that read HARVARD CRIMSON. A woman in leather pants, all business, lugged a huge leather portfolio down the sidewalk. Harry's eyes had blanked out again, but now there were sacks, years, dragging his eyes down. The light turned green.

"You've been reading too many mysteries," Harry finally said. Which was not true, and he knew it. "Janousek was an old man with a bad heart. And Gottehrer's motive was?"

Ahead, traffic was bunching up. Two middle lanes were blocked. Water mains were always bursting, or streets caving in, or boilers exploding, asbestos showering all over town. I wondered what kind of disaster we were dealing with this morning. The driver eased into the right lane and inched ahead, stop-start. "What if Gottehrer killed him because he knew something that could trace him to the Einstein murder?" I said. "Suppose he agonized for years that this might happen. Just when he'd finally started to relax, Rosenthal told him you were nosing around. He didn't know what trail you were on, exactly. So he followed you. You led him to me. He tried lifting my purse to find out what I knew. He tried scaring me off. Just in case, he made his appointment with Janousek. The further along he went, the more desperate he got."

"He couldn't be sure what we knew."

"But if you're paranoid, which he is, what matters is that he couldn't be sure what we *didn't* know."

"And he killed Einstein because —?"

"That's your department, Harry."

Attitudes fast-forwarded through his eyes. He settled on a crease of his lips that could pass for a smile. "The guy *is* a walking volcano, isn't he."

The cab had finally pulled even with the cause of the tie-up: an open manhole where, mysteriously, no maintenance work was taking place. The manhole cover was missing. Two shopping carts had been placed in front of the hole and the adjacent lane. Traffic was creeping, drivers wanted a chance to see. The cab finally slipped to a stop in front of Big Glass, where the Senegalese were setting up scarf displays.

"Not conclusive," I said. "We're seeing Gottehrer on the edge forty years down the line. People suffer, their decorum wears down."

Harry, pensive, scrubbed his chin with his palm. "Let's get out," he said abruptly.

I didn't blame him for wanting to move the conversation outdoors. We slid out and started toward the building, but Harry took my arm and led me over to the stone monument, that stump of the old Con Comm Building. We leaned back against the cold stone.

He fucked me, slowly, with words, the beautiful in-and-out of logic. "The father thing is the hinge."

"Explain. I'm a girl."

"Look. Einstein was everything to him, Gottehrer told us that, right? O.K., suppose that Einstein failed him. The more he gave him, the more Gottehrer wanted. You can imagine how greedy he was for Einstein's time. And how annoyed Einstein was to be nagged. Norman's been led on, and now, lo and behold, he's spurned—and why?"

"I give up."

He accelerated. "How about this? Because his holy father is laying the theoretical basis for a death ray. Now, on top of that, Gottehrer is honest-to-goodness wacko. Einstein himself has become death, destroyer of worlds. The field theory has got to be stopped. All this explodes in Gottehrer's cramped little one-cylinder mind. He decides Einstein's a fanatic who's endangering the world with his goddamned field theory—all in the name of his belief in ninety-nine and forty-four one-hundredths percent pure science. By now, our Gottehrer is fuming. He goes to Einstein's hospital room and he sees, right there on the bed stand, those last notes on the field theory. When he goes back to the visiting room, he doesn't know what to do."

Harry twiddled his fingers as if warming up to play an invisible piano. "O.K., now enter Janousek. Gottehrer gives a sigh of relief. Here's the perfect foil, in the unlikely event anyone ever raises a question about the not-so-untimely death of a seventy-six-year-old sage already known to be suffering from an aneurysm. Janousek's known to hate Einstein. Or maybe his running into Janousek is gratuitous, Gottehrer's already made up his mind. That's a detail. The key is that all Gottehrer has to do is pass Einstein some speed pills—easy to get for a night owl who lives in the Village. Here, Herr Dr. Professor, take these pills, the nurse left them for you while you were napping. Einstein thanks his loyal, servile, intellectually ravenous devotee. A few hours later, the speed explodes and Einstein is dead of terrible bleeding, which was sadly expected, and poor Gottehrer is weeping for what he's lost. What do you think?"

"Jesus" was the whole of my contribution.

"So now, to go back to your thought," Harry resumed, "here's our paranoid Mr. Gottehrer hoping to enjoy a soft decline into his mellow years, having gotten away with murder, and forty years later these news hounds arrive. Could it be that they're wondering just what Janousek might have noticed at Princeton Hospital in April 1955?"

"Too melodramatic."

"Worse. The observers tipped the observed over the edge." He made a loose fist and banged his knee. "Einstein would have appreciated the joke."

I could see the panel discussions on ethics coming, the symposium in the *Columbia Journalism Review.* "Back up a minute. Why wasn't Gottehrer worried all these years about what Janousek knew?"

"He might have been, but not urgently, since nobody knew that Einstein had been murdered."

"So a week ago it became urgent." I was drawn back into the hunt now. "He made his appointment with Janousek to see what Janousek knew. When he found out we'd talked to him ourselves, he was scared shitless. Which would make us involuntary accessories-after-the-fact, if there were such a thing."

Silence washed through this conversation in waves. We stared at implications.

"I should have figured the bastard out," Harry said to the air, to the weathered stone, to no one. "I should have figured him out. He was sitting right there in front of us, ranting. I should have warned Janousek." He firmed up his right fist, pounded it into his palm, and muffled a shout of "Damn!" A man in a black leather coat, passing, shot an alarmed look in Harry's direction, then adjusted his look to streetwise bemusement and strode on.

"Let's go inside," I said.

Harry had gone inert. "Shouldn't I?"

"Harry, Harry, what did we know? We still don't know." I held his palm, but he seemed not to notice.

"What if Janousek smelled a rat," he said, "and called you to alert you about Gottehrer, and then got cold feet?"

"Why?"

"I don't know. Or Gottehrer calmed him down. Or—I don't know."

Hard to believe that Gottehrer, with his paranoid glow, could have calmed Janousek, who was not exactly a deeply trusting soul.

"Maybe Gottehrer had a gun at his head," Harry said. "Figuratively. Or not so figuratively."

I reminded him that Janousek had tried to reach me twice—once at home, once at the office.

"You're right." Harry filled his lungs with an invisible cigarette. "Wait a minute, here's a crazy idea—what if Gottehrer *wanted* him to leave this message?"

I needed cunning to proceed in this vein, but cunning wasn't my strong suit. The light in Harry's eyes repelled me. I couldn't find Harry, my friend, my lover. He was off on a moon by himself.

■

"I'm going to be honest with you, Margo—you don't
mind me calling you Margo, now, do you, Margo?" said
Colin McShane, not expecting an answer.

At the sound of the word "honest," I felt, and resisted,
the impulse to clutch my purse.

We were sitting on tender leather of a pale blond complexion. The sofas, at right angles to one another, took up
one corner of McShane's vast office. The massive desk in
the far corner was blanched oak. The deep wraparound
glass-steel canyon, all hard edges and rectangles, was like
Burke's, but twenty-four stories farther away from earth.

Harry and I sat on one sofa, McShane and Burke on the
other. McShane was a squat, barrel-chested, big-bellied
man with a squarish face, bulbous eyes, rough skin—yet he
exuded some sort of magnetism. Possibly his shaggy black
eyebrows did the trick. Or possibly he gave off, sublimi-
nally, the scent of his seven or seventeen billion dollars. He
was fifty-five or so and had never been near a health club—
Turkish baths looked more his speed. There was a big red
mole next to his right ear—a mark of plain humanity Rem-
brandt would have appreciated. Burke was wearing his
crimson bow tie, with matching suspenders.

The entire wall opposite the desk was taken up with a
map made of electronic-looking circuits. Twelve countries
were colored blue—here Con Comm held majority owner-
ship of national telecommunications systems. A hundred or
so red dots for up- and downlinks. Digital clocks recorded
Greenwich, Beijing, Tokyo, Los Angeles, and New York
time. The paintings on the remaining wall, in steel frames,
were hard-edged pastel auras taking the form of unspeci-
fied flowers.

Know your enemy, as Harry would say.

Harry and I were sipping coffee that had been delivered by McShane's secretary Melissa, who spoke a BBC English considerably classier than Sir Colin's.

"Not at all, Sir Colin," I said.

"Let's get right to the point, Margo, shall we? Cards on the table, yes?" His jaw was too close to mine, our knees almost intimate. He didn't pause for an answer. "Gustav Janousek was my friend. Ilse Janousek is my friend. My friends know I'm a man they can count on." He swallowed a cough deep in his chest. "Pardon me. Ilse rang me up at one o'clock this morning. Very upset, as you might expect. She came home from the theater about midnight, with her son, and her husband was slumped in his chair, dead. I want to know what you know about this."

"I know he had two previous heart attacks," I said.

"Yes, yes. He also had medicines, and the best medical care. And—shall we be candid?—he had enemies, didn't he? Like *The New York Times* and *The Washington Post* and the Democratic Party and"—significant pause—"Mr. Norman Gottehrer and"—he glanced toward Harry—"a handful of leftover revolutionaries here and there."

Harry, deadpan, massaged his chin. McShane, all eyebrows and teeth, grinned until another little cough erupted.

"Don't take what I say personally, Mr. Kramer," McShane went on. "I know all about your background—also yours, Margo, as a matter of fact—and if you want to know, I've got nothin' against it. Nothin' at all. To the contrary, I approve. You're clever, you have energy. You appreciate facts. So do I. You're curious to know how the world is put together. So am I. The difference is, your attitude is ideological and mine is scientific. You think you already understand how the capitalists operate. Whilst I am a real capitalist, not your papier-mâché sort. I study the situation and take action, which is always a bit of an experiment, isn't it? You study what you would call the system with an eye to its unalterable strength — a bit self-defeating for a revolutionary, I would think, but never mind. I study characters with an eye to their weakness. Then I alter some facts and watch what happens." He coughed again into his upraised fist.

So far Harry was unflappable, or at any rate unflapped. "And do you investigate all your prospective consultants?"

McShane's eyes gave nothing away. "Why, of course I do, Mr. Kramer! Do you think I could have put together my company without — how d'you say it? — doin' my homework?" He waved at the map on the wall, Con Comm's world. A stagy har-har-har came welling up out of his chest. "The difference between you and me, Mr. Kramer, is that I can afford to hire you." An alligator leer sprang up on his lips. "And I propose to do just that."

Harry's brow shot up. I slowly, steadily landed my coffee cup and saucer on the coffee table.

"I want you to investigate the death of Albert Einstein."

"Pardon me?" Harry said.

"I want you on my team, Mr. Kramer, what do you think of that? At — three thousand dollars per week, yes? Effective, shall we say, one week ago. I want exclusive rights to your research and I am prepared to guarantee you ten weeks' work, with an option to renew. What do you say to that?"

Across from McShane's shaggy eyebrows, Harry's were delicate, wary. The twitch of a blood vessel at his cheekbone was the only sign of surprise, or antagonism. After a moment he volleyed back: "I say I'm all ears." A puff of euphoria went off deep in my brain.

"*Very* good," McShane said. "You see how easy it is to traffic with the enemy. Now I want just one thing, which is that you tell me everything you know."

"I take it," Harry said, as if he chatted with Sir Colin every day of the week, "that you spoke with Janousek about our meeting with him."

"You take it correctly. There is honor among friends."

"And I'm curious, when did you last talk to your friend?"

"Yesterday."

"I gathered as much, but what time yesterday?"

"I don't exactly recall. Sometime in the afternoon. Time is short, Mr. Kramer. I'm going to be blunt. Do you know how he died?"

I wondered why, exactly, McShane thought time was short. He couldn't have known that Taub was about to discover the speed in Einstein's brain. Unless he had tapped my phone or bugged my office.

"Do *I* know how he died?"

"He's only been dead for a few hours," I threw in. "I'm waiting to hear from the police." I refrained from noting that what I was waiting to hear had nothing to do with Janousek. "Have *you* talked to the police?"

Burke glared at me.

For a diminutive man, McShane had a way of simulating height—pulling himself up in his seat. He also knew how to slip away from an unpleasant question. "Listen to me. Very closely. I want to know what happened to Gustav Janousek. It is very important that I know. We are an information organization, Margo. If we are any good, we ought to know quite a bit more, quite a bit sooner, than the police, don't you think? Especially since you are a super-reporter and you have a head start."

He hauled himself up and strode to his desk, whose surface didn't come far above his knees. I remembered having read in the *Times* or *Vanity Fair* that the desk had been built diminutive for the undernourished nobility of the sixteenth century, and then had been salvaged from the estate of a minor Italian noble who had gone down with the *Andrea Doria*. Fine, rococo stuff, full of serpentine curves, passed on down three centuries, said to contain secret compartments. Sir Colin had bought it at auction from a surviving daughter, an aging London model with an expensive drug habit. He was said to have spent $2.4 million, before repairs. The man wanted to make a point.

McShane barked: "I want to know what in the bloody hell Gustav said to you."

If I displeased McShane, he would happily fire me and leak to Page Six that I was a lesbian who'd been caught with an intern under my desk. But if he was prepared to give me the next edition of *In Depth* for Einstein, what did I have to lose? Meanwhile, there was airtime to gain.

Harry's eyes gave me no guidance.

A trill sounded. McShane grabbed a phone on the desk, said summarily, "Yes," listened and said softly, "Yes, Ilse. No, that's all right." After a pause: "Just now? Well, it's up to you, of course. My advice is to tell them to go to hell."

"Excuse me," McShane said when he had replaced the receiver. "Time's getting shorter, Margo."

I rearranged my legs, smoothed my dress over my thighs.

Burke cleared his throat and said, "This is a unique

window of opportunity." Which made him what, the stained glass?

McShane slouched back to his seat on the sofa. "Margo, I'm going to answer the question you haven't asked before you embarrass us both by asking it. The death of my friend has caused me to reevaluate this Einstein business. Obviously. Let's not fondle our grievances, shall we?" There was altogether too much twinkling under his eyebrows.

"We all believe in getting the story," Burke chipped in.

I turned to Harry and smiled. "Why don't you fill Mr. McShane in?"

Harry hesitated. Possibly he was arranging a summary statement, tidying up chronology. But once he started to narrate, he was elegant. All the essentials were there: Einstein's brain, Taub's lab, the speed, our search for motives, the politics, the unified field theory, the nurse, Rosenthal, Janousek, Gottehrer. When his speech clicked to an end, Harry sat back, exuding satisfaction.

McShane was enthralled. I don't know to this day how much of the theory he followed, but he didn't let his ignorance show. He made an appreciative noise and said, "I want this Gottehrer of yours, Margo."

"I'm sure the police do, too." The words were more confident than I was, but McShane couldn't tell.

He leaned forward and tapped my knee as if ringing a bell for service. "No, you misunderstand me, my dear. I want 'im on camera." He turned up the volume and tapped again. "I want 'im on *In Depth*. I want 'im before the police have 'im." Tap. "I want 'im before the competition has 'im. I want the bloody murderer for dinner. I want the real"— tap—"bleedin'"—tap—"thing." By the time he was done, his voice was a boom. Hard lines framed his mouth. "I want 'im yesterday, but I'll settle for next week, what d'you think of that?"

I cooked up a smile—thank you, Daddy, I remain, respectfully yours, a good girl, pretending not to notice your lousy temper.

"*Human Interest* is crawlin' all over Mrs. Janousek," McShane said. "The woman's just lost her husband and they're throwin' money at her for an exclusive."

You'd never stoop so low, I thought.

"Has she spoken to them?" Harry asked.

"Are you mad? But, from the sound of it, it's not long before they find out about this Gottehrer without her. Pay off the doorman, who knows. *Wanted* will be swarmin' 'round next, count on it. And *People This Week*. But you, my dear, are goin' to get to Gottehrer first. Find him. Wear a wire, take a Minicam, whatever you want. Wring a confession out of the little prick."

"Is that all?" I said.

"People will talk t'you, Margo. They trust you. Take me. I fancy talkin' t'you myself."

"They're more likely to talk to the police in their little rooms with their file cabinets and their heavy flashlights," I said.

McShane produced an infinitesimal smile. "Don't underestimate yourself, m'dear. People confess to you. Look at Billy Neill. They eat it up when you tell them to go now and sin no more. They respect you because you can't be bought. 'Come what may, we shall be back next week to absolve the general sin.' The police enforce the law but we enforce the police, yes? We give the people what they want. Give them a taste of 'appiness, absolution, righteousness, all wrapped up in one. Who more than us, right?"

He leaned forward, gleaming with assurance. "Tell you something, Margo. You think you're real One Worlders, don't you? 'Absolute Zero,' no nukes, yes, all very clever. But you didn't invent it, you know. I was a socialist too, ban the bomb and all that. I'm a bus conductor's lad, I know all about the struggle against the bosses. Might even be that I know a bit more than the two o' you about how to eat your way through a strike one hundred and two days long on tinned sardines. Could that be?"

He paused for effect. I tried to pretend McShane was scolding somebody else.

"One hundred and two winter days at that, runnin' short of coal. Can't touch a sardine to this day, and isn't it fortunate that I don't have to? But we're all adults, so let's stare the facts right in the eyeballs. You start out campaignin' for socialism and what you get is the KGB, the soddin' 'Ome Office and National 'Ealth and Inland Revenue and Scotland Yard and the rest of the faceless dwarves tellin' you what side o' your arse to wipe, if you don't mind my French. I've been called a lot of things, includin' trashy and brutal"—he chortled—"but no one has ever called me faceless."

No one demurred.

"So, tell me, what did Professor Janousek think about this unified field?"

"He thought it was garbage," I said.

"Mmn." McShane chewed on that. "You know what I think? You know what actually unifies the field?" He drew his forefinger out of the air and poked Harry's knee. "*Television* unifies the field. Con Comm unifies the world. Shows Mrs. O'Malley the likes of Mrs. O'Nalley halfway around the world. The telly's where they meet to eat. We make 'em learn to live with each other. And you know exactly what I mean, both of you, because you and me, we want the same thing."

Burke was rigid, having been left off the list of the saved, but McShane didn't notice.

"Oh yes we do!" he rumbled on. "We believe in the vast community of man. And woman, right. We *care.* I want to give my old dad a comedy to laugh at while he slogs around the 'ouse wheezing from emphysema. My dad laughs, the advertiser's happy, and because he's happy, I get to pay you a salary and you get to go inform the people in bleedin' depth. *And*: all of us wanderin' Jews, no slight intended, we all beat back the bureaucrats, the hacks and the geezers, the lamebrains, yes? We create. Care and create, C and C, Con and Comm. We're the bleedin' guerrillas. We forage among the people. And that's why they love us and feed us and vote for us, and that's why we don't take prisoners, and we don't care who knows it, do we?"

He grinned as if acknowledging prodigious applause. "You're the boss" was all I could say.

"In other words," Burke said crisply, "we're crashing your piece for next week." His smile was so tight he seemed to have had a face-lift.

McShane started up. Burke leaped. Starting a split second after McShane, he arrived on his feet first. "We want you to big-picture it," Burke said. "Background on Einstein and Janousek, Gottehrer, confession, the whole schmear. Go live at the end if you have to. I don't give a shit. Just tell me what you need and you've got it."

"I expect an ornament," McShane said.

Was I expected to curtsy? The audience was over. "We

start the promotion Sunday night," McShane said. "I would hate to promote 'The Murder of Albert Einstein' for three days and then at the last minute fail to deliver."

"So tell me what you need," Burke said.

◼

After everything that had gone down, damned if I was going to be outrun by Taub, the National Science Foundation, or the competition. Anyone can be right, in Burke's immortal words, but the point is to be fast.

So I was off and speeding, a blur of efficiency. From McShane, I collected the name and number of Janousek's doctor, who—raise your hand if you're surprised—happened to be his own, a Park Avenue type named Goldensohn. Goldensohn wasn't in yet, so I left a message with his service. I installed Harry with a yellow pad behind a desk in an office down the hall. I arranged for a camerawoman, Michelle. I sent a second camerawoman to Princeton to bring back establishing shots, B roll, wallpaper by the yard: the hospital, the Institute for Advanced Study, the white house on Mercer Street. I sent a researcher, a hulking Hunter graduate with two tiny rings in his right ear, to the Con Comm archive to check out footage of Einstein and Janousek. I sent an intern, a UCLA graduate wearing a thousand dollars' worth of clothes, to the public library for microfilm blowups of the '49 and '53 *Times* pieces on the UFT. She watched me reverently. For all she knew, this might be the breakthrough moment of her career.

Every time I looked in on Harry, he was scribbling away, not happy exactly, but looking at one with himself, fused with his pen and pad, the way a rider is supposed to be with his horse. Once, when I crossed to his side of the desk and put out my hand, he held it against his lips, kissed it, pressed it against his cheek. He held me around the hip and rested his head against my waist, and I squeezed him back.

"But today the struggle," he said, relinquishing my hip. He asked for an intern to check some facts. He wanted to know how he was going to write his text without knowing what pictures we had.

"Not to worry, leave the pictures to me." If I had learned anything at *In Depth*, it was how to pump up emotions out of zooms, close-ups, tracking shots, sinister music, achingly slow pans. A whiff of revelations, hints of imminent fact. Thicken the sub-text. The old dream of the unity of the universe was dead—worse, had given birth to a zombie laying waste to life itself . . . that sort of thing. The murder of Einstein as metaphor for the end of faith, innocence, pure knowledge, something. Segue to Janousek.

How poignant Einstein would look, all sweet reason and tender sad eyes, back to back with Gottehrer dancing his lunatic ballet.

I punched up Gottehrer's number, and stopped counting rings at eighteen. Seven-forty in the morning and already Gottehrer was up and roaming the city, sitting slack-jawed on the subway, or staring into a cup of coffee—

"We'll find him. Or he'll find us." Harry paused. A clear plastic shell had formed around his eyes. He crossed out a line with a slow, elaborate scratch of his pen. Not satisfied with a single delete line, he methodically blackened the entire line. For some reason I felt a touch of relief when Harry went all business again.

Back in my office, I made a list of what we had without Gottehrer:

> HPLC spikes & numbers
> stock footage Einstein, Janousek, & who else?
> wallpaper Princeton
> tearful widow?
> Goldensohn on autopsy if +?
> Rosenthal on E, J, unified field th
> nurse Parenti w/ eyewit report?
> Peter M
> Taub
> cops? (trouble)

Face it, a scramble. Basically, a history sketch with hints of menace. Lots of Margo Ross on camera pointing at diagrams. Covering holes with half-wistful, half-apprehensive electronic suspense moans, intimations, auras of mystery. Load atmosphere into TV and, presto, we're uptown.

I called Burke and told him to send me Bernie Gross, the graphics maven, along with the house musician, as soon as they came in. Forgive me: it was pure pleasure telling Burke Gilman what to do.

I tried convincing myself that people wanted to hear about unsolved crimes these days—liked to feel they'd been brought into the solution process. Participate. Dial 1-800-KILLERS.

Right. Face it: I had to hope Gottehrer would turn up, a fountain of facts, eager to spill. Such things were possible. Feints did work. Miracles happened. We hadn't expected it to be so easy to hook up with Gottehrer the first time either, and look what he had already given us, just because his friend Franz Rosenthal had told him in passing that one Harry Kramer was interested—

Roll that one back, Margo.

Whoever could connect Gottehrer to Princeton Hospital on April 17, 1955, was a suddenly valuable commodity. That made Rosenthal more than a friend—made him a potential witness. Unimpeachable, in fact.

Gottehrer could be in Princeton already. In a cab, or on Rosenthal's doorstep. *Good morning, Norman, let me take your overcoat . . . What a pleasant surprise. A little early for schnapps, is it not?*

And Angela Parenti with her memory for teenagers with large ears.

A third murder is farfetched.

That is no argument.

I call Rosenthal's number. My mind gallops ahead of my fingers. I get the number wrong. I try again.

Rosenthal neglects to ask why I am calling before eight in the morning. No, I have not woken him, he is capable of waking himself, thank you very much. I ask him, can we bring our camera down Sunday morning at, say, ten? Ten would be fine, Rosenthal says. And by the way, I ask, has he heard from Norman Gottehrer? No, not a word, but he doesn't expect to, and why, by the way, do I ask? I tell him I must speak with Gottehrer immediately about an interview. I beg him to call me if Gottehrer visits or calls. I beg him to call me first thing. You have already spoken with him? he asks. Yes, Professor, I've met with him. Interesting fellow, no? Very interesting, yes. And please don't wait should you hear from him, Professor Rosenthal. Urgent. Yes, yes.

Evidently Rosenthal gets through his day without the early-morning news. The name Gustav Janousek doesn't pass his lips. I decide, without knowing why, it is not my business to break his spell.

I tell Harry we'd better get a message to Angela Parenti. He calls the Princeton Home for the Aged and advises the woman on duty not to let anyone they don't recognize past the front office. They want to know what business it is of his. He says his associate Margo Ross will explain, passes me the phone. I tell the woman on duty this is an emergency that I'll describe in person, and she says, Oh yes, Margo, I understand, of course, don't worry about a thing, she looks forward to meeting me.

A few minutes after eight, Delaney calls to report. "Policewise," as he puts it, Norman Gottehrer has never made a name for himself. Specifically, one arrest for possession of marijuana in 1962: "Your man was a pioneer." One bust and one conviction: six months, suspended. Four other police encounters. In 1979, landlord attempts to evict him on the ground that he's violated his lease by subletting. Landlord tries to convince cops that Gottehrer's trespassing and committing disorderly conduct, but the cops don't buy it. In the end, landlord fails to prove subletting, and Gottehrer stays. He tries again in '81, '85, '88, to no avail. In '91, Gottehrer takes *him* to court. Case still pending. There is zero credit information. Zero information of any other kind. No record of marriage. No record of children.

"Your guy's got a clean nose," Delaney is saying. "Or he keeps it to himself. Unlike some animals I have met."

This is doing me no good, and the digital clock on the wall is rolling from 8:06 to 8:07, and if I am not careful, I am going to end up with a script without a star. But if I babble to Delaney, he can arrange to get very interested and scare off my hypothetical star. Of course, my star is hypothetical to the vanishing point, and even if he does me a favor and shows up in time, there is information I am going to need if I am to use him. This is information I am not supposed to have.

Why stop taking chances now?

Sir Colin's coffee is beginning to burn through my gastrointestinal tract.

"I need more, Frank," I say.

"Anything in particular?"

"Anything. Whether he's been, say, in the loony bin. Source of support. Bank accounts. Reputation on the job — he works for one of these exam prep-course schools. Whatever."

I can hear Delaney thinking, trying out bargains, discarding them. Finally: "I don't think you would casually ask me to overstretch the powers of law enforcement. Would you. Information is money, Margo; it takes some to get some. What's goin' on, this guy threaten to hurt you? You got phone problems again?"

"Not exactly."

"So what's the fuckin' guy done?"

"You're not going to believe this, Frank, but it has to do with physics." I lower my voice into the confidential range. Oh, the truth is a ragged fraction.

"Oh, yeah?" Delaney says. I realize that this is why cops play dumb: to get civilians to spill beans. The equivalent of what I do with my eyes.

"What about physics?" Delaney wants to know.

"We're doing a show."

"Yeah?"

"About Einstein. This guy knew Einstein. I'm trying to reconstruct their, you know, relationship."

"No kidding," Delaney says. He's not satisfied, exactly, but he doesn't know where to go with this dead fish I've dropped on his plate. So he leaves it there, stinking.

"I'd never ask you to do anything immoral," I say.

"What a relief. Tell you what. I'll ask around."

We are done with that and I ask Delaney what he has heard about the death of Gustav Janousek.

"Janousek, Janousek," he said. "Name rings a bell but I can't place it."

I place it for him. Delaney says he will poke around about this one, too.

"I owe you, Frank."

"Yes you do."

By now a hot iron is poking around the lining of my stomach. I toss down a Zantac, call Leon Taub, arrange to do him at his lab the next morning, Friday—before he has a chance to find out what Peter Minasian has found out about the brain of brains.

Delaney calls back. The precinct says that Janousek's widow is screaming bloody murder about foul play but offering zero evidence. No one sees any reason to order an autopsy just because of a hysterical widow. The guy was in his eighties, for Christ's sake, with two prior heart attacks. It's not my understanding that she is hysterical, I say. Delaney says he's just telling me what the precinct says. Anyway, she's entitled to an autopsy if she wants one and the doctor goes along.

As for Gottehrer, a little birdie is on the job, and I'll be the first to know.

Dr. Goldensohn calls back. There's every indication of myocardial infarction, he says with a practiced dolefulness. Heart attack. Nothing extraordinary, from a medical point of view. Did I know that Professor Janousek had two earlier incidents?

Yes, I've heard. Can he tell me whether he's planning an autopsy?

Much as Dr. Goldensohn would like to help me, this information is medically confidential.

The call I dread is the one I save for last. I work up a passable angle. My middle finger develops a life of its own and punches up the Janousek number.

The voice that answers is unfamiliar to me, a formal tenor without an accent. This must be Ilse's son, Thomas Fleischmann, minimum grief in his voice. "Who shall I say is calling?" he wants to know. I tell him.

After a moment, the widow comes to the phone. I apologize, in all sincerity, for intruding. How shocked and sorry I am to hear about the death of her husband.

As graceful without Gustav as she was with him, she lets my awkwardness pass without comment. "Miss Ross, I have prepared myself for this moment for twenty years, but let me tell you, there is nothing like it. Nothing." Her tone is impenetrable. She sounds subdued, or sedated. Or the power of will is holding her together. Yet there is a touch of intimacy, if I am not mistaken. She is speaking woman to woman.

And then I wonder: Does a wife prepare herself for her husband's death for twenty years? And then again, why drop such a remark into a reporter's lap, if it is anything other than innocent? Nuisance questions, burrs. What do I know about matters of lengthy love, if that is what lengthy marriage is?

As gingerly as I can manage, I tell the widow that Sir Colin McShane has asked me to go ahead with the *In Depth* story, only now the focus has changed, it is going to be about both Janousek and Einstein. Two great physicists arguing about science and power and the meaning of the twentieth century, that's my new tag. Not the whole truth, but a variety of truth.

She musters a stately "I see. You are telling me that your story will not be complete without the weeping widow. I suppose I should be grateful because you are not barking outside my door like the hounds of your competition."

"Mrs. Janousek, you should know that—"

"You are not like them. Of course not. You are a—a—a vulture with a human face. Even for Sir Colin McShane I will not allow the camera to violate me, do you hear?"

"Mrs. Janousek, I am not asking—"

"I am not waiting for you to ask. I am telling you. As a favor to Sir Colin I am not hanging up the phone."

"I'm very sorry," I say, idiotically.

She waits, I writhe. Finally, she drops her voice and says: "If you wish to help, tell me about that creature."

"Creature—"

"You know exactly who I mean. Excuse me a moment." She covers the receiver but I hear traces of muffled German in the background. Thomas sounds insistent. Ilse protests. She gets the last word, and the loudest. Then she is back on the phone, confiding: "The man was a ticking bomb. That horrible tic. I told Gustav he should not meet with this man. I should have stayed home and refused to let him in." I am not sure at whom she is angrier, herself or her late husband. Or her son for telling her to hang up on me?

I also wonder if I detect a shudder of pleasure that she proves to have been right all along about the ticking bomb, Mr. Gottehrer.

But she has given me my opening. I tell her my colleague and I spoke with Mr. Gottehrer. Before he saw her husband last night. We have noticed that Gottehrer is temperamental, yes. I do not tell her that he displayed his temper in this very office by ranting about how dreadful her dreadful husband was. By the way, does she remember Gottehrer from Princeton?

She hesitates. This may be the moment when she begins to resign herself to the fact that my piece is going to air with or without her. No, she has no firsthand memory of Gottehrer, though she remembers hearing about him in Princeton. Her former husband thought the man was a ridiculous poseur and had the eyes of a lunatic; in fact, she thinks she remembers that Martin Fleischmann advised Einstein to get rid of him. But about recent history she is emphatic: she advised Gustav not to see him. "He was unstoppable, Gustav. So—I did not stop him. He knew the man was crazy but he said that it didn't matter. Now he is dead." No sobs in her voice, just the blank fact.

So that makes three—Rosenthal, Janousek, and Fleischmann had all cautioned Einstein away from Gottehrer. And Ilse warned Janousek. With equally meager results.

Facts stream in but arrive dead.

"I understand that you don't want to be interviewed. But if you could speak to me off the record—"

"Miss Ross!"

"I am only trying to get at the truth, Mrs. Janousek."

That long-cultivated composure does not desert her. "Very well, you are only going to badger me. I must tell you that I am not convinced that my husband has died of natural causes. The autopsy will take place this afternoon."

A call to Elaine tells me what I need to know. Curtain time for *Crime and Punishment* is six. In order to get there on time, Ilse and her son would have to have left the Upper West Side no later than five-thirty. Ergo, they could not have laid eyes on Gottehrer. Yet she knows about his "horrible tic." Then she has preserved this memory from Princeton, forty years ago. But possibly she has a remarkable memory for detail—all the more impressive because she has never laid eyes on the creature, as she calls him.

Or she got to the theater late.

In any event, she or her informant must have come face to face with Gottehrer far along toward the end of his tether. Gottehrer probably doesn't produce his tic casually.

I picture the widow with her perfectly styled, perfectly silver pompadour. She gazes out over the Palisades. Thomas pads across the carpet bearing a cup of strong black tea. She finds it strange to be served. She contemplates a life in which no one commands her. She smooths the afghan over her lap and wonders what to do with Margo Ross now that I am a character in her story . . .

And suddenly my mind's kaleidoscope tilts, facts reshuffle, and through a different prism Ilse Janousek appears to me as the wife of a man renowned for sexual swashbuckling, a man who might well not have wholly abandoned his bachelor habits upon marriage, who into his eighties gave signs of still-ravenous appetite, running a practiced eye up and down my person. I see Ilse at work on her needlepoint, confiding in her devoted son, at home on one of the hundred evenings a year her great man of a husband has been out and around, lionized, bemedaled, inspecting newly arrived candidates for his unexpired charms . . . How might she have felt about that? A man of advanced age, with a heart condition, who might any day have the bad taste to humiliate her (unless the good Dr. Goldensohn could be brought in to fix matters) by dropping dead in flagrante?

Consider, too, the ferociously loyal Thomas Fleischmann, about whom I know nothing.

Consider now that it is Ilse who orders up the autopsy. So tender-minded reporter Margo Ross holds the widow's grief up for inspection and finds it wanting . . . Congratulations, Margo. I am tangled in webs I myself spin. I am beginning to wonder whether, having learned the habit of suspicion, I am ever going to break it.

I want to send Cyrilly for a pack of cigarettes, but she hasn't come in yet.

Outside Big Glass, the atmosphere—you couldn't exactly call it sky—was viscous, a pale murk. Fog choked up the canyon. Light from the opposite buildings barely filtered through. In the office next door, Harry scribbled away on his script notes. When my phone twittered, I ran back to my office to pick up the receiver and heard a long staticky nothing, like a windstorm through the galaxy, and then the rasp of Norman Gottehrer saying, "You know who this is. Are you alone?"

The windstorm was traffic noise.

"I've been trying to reach you," I said. I imagined his small, blinking eyes, the streak of wildness behind them.

"I said, are you alone?"

"I am absolutely alone."

I could hear him listening. "Who else is on this line?"

"Nobody."

"I'll talk to you but I'm not talking to Harry Kramer." He bit off chunks of words and spat them out.

"Fine."

I waited, but he wasn't going to help. There were faint honks, an air brake hissing. "Where are you?"

"Never mind. Just where I want to be."

There was something he wanted to say, I had to give him room. Leave him alone, pretend he's a garbage truck, grinding, filling the street with noise. That's all he wants to do, make noise. Wait him out.

I waited. A siren, muted, passed by. How long before Gottehrer's coins would run out?

"You're keeping me on the line, you're having this traced," he said.

"Norman, you're the one who called me, which I'm very glad of, believe me. I want to see you."

"How do I know you're not tracing this call?"

"You have my word."

"Your word! How quaint!"

Harshness I associated with a death threat. I tried sweeping the memory aside.

"Look, Norman—"

"I know what you think. Listen to me." His voice went down a third of an octave, as if he were concealing his words from an eavesdropper. "I'm not staying on, so listen.

He was alive when I left there. Hear me? He was alive, that's all you have to know."

"You're talking about—"

He sounded like metal chewing into metal. "You're a smart woman, don't play dumb with me! You know who I mean. Listen to me! People are going to know! Christ, are you listening?"

Imagine my eyes, Norman, talk to my eyes, my eyes are your friends. "I am. *Please* go on."

"You know what he said?"

Beat one, beat two, and— "No, what?"

"Am I wasting my time? He said that he killed Einstein."

"He said *what*?"

"Are you deaf? Pay attention. You hear me?"

Patience, my mother would say, is not a gift; it's an achievement. "All right, he said he killed Einstein. How?"

"He didn't say, Margo."

"All right, did he say why?"

"A profound question, Margo. You met him, you know who he was. Ranting about Einstein betraying his country. I'll tell you why. Einstein was love and Janousek was hate —isn't that reason enough?"

"I don't know." I just wanted to keep him talking.

"Look, Janousek was a killer from way back. Could it be more obvious? Didn't the Janousek effect amount to a death sentence? Chalk on the blackboard, vaporized bodies. Trillions for arms translates into how much infant mortality, how many dead babies?" I could see Gottehrer on camera, a tight shot, the rasping voice, Gottehrer stoking himself up, the camera zooming in on the rampage.

He went on: "You're in the investigation business, Margo, so the rest is up to you."

A mechanical voice broke in: "Please deposit fifty cents for the next three minutes."

"Give me your number, I'll call you back."

"That's it, I've said all I have to say. So—"

"Norman, *don't hang up*. Please. I want you to tell your story on *In Depth*. Just give me your number."

The rustle of traffic. Delivery honks. There are eight million side streets in the big city, Norman Gottehrer is standing on one of them.

If Janousek did kill Einstein, then Gottehrer has just announced a perfect motive for killing Janousek. Why would he do that?

"Hello?"

I heard one small bong, then another. Bastard had been standing there holding extra quarters the whole time.

"I want to see *you*, Margo, nobody else. No cops."

Engines ignited, we had lift-off. "I guarantee it, Norman, no cops. Thank you. But I have to bring a crew, you know, a camera."

"No cops, and no Kramer, he sounds like a cop."

Engines sputtered, acid poured into my stomach. Paranoia, his or mine or both, swirled in the air. "Norman, come on. Harry's worked with me from the beginning—"

"I said no, Margo, I'm not going to be pushed around, you hear me?"

"Sure, but—"

"I don't want any cross-examinations. No trick questions. No traps. I'm telling you, hear me?"

Cul-de-sac. "It's a deal. I'll do it without him."

He proposed noon. I countered with five o'clock, saying that I needed more time to prepare the physics, get my crew together. In truth, I also wanted to have the autopsy

results before I confronted him. We settled on four. Gottehrer gave me the Lower East Side address I already had
—but then people were always telling me things I already
knew.

I hated breaking the bad news to Harry that Gottehrer's
condition for the interview was that I do it solo. I told him
not to worry about me. He thought it over, looked solicitous, then said, right, he knew I could take care of myself.

We sat on the rug and Harry laid pages of notes around
us. For the hundredth time we reviewed the story to date:
current hypotheses, loose ends, forks in the trail, dead-end
scenarios. Questions about Ilse and Thomas. Why Gottehrer returned to Einstein's room. Why Janousek would
confess to Gottehrer. Nothing changed two big facts: one,
Gottehrer hovered around Einstein and Einstein died; two,
Gottehrer hovered around Janousek and Janousek died.
Two old sick great men, linked by the attentions of Norman
Gottehrer. Through the morning Harry and I sat, partners
in the unraveling of crime, reviewing scraps, working out
lines of questioning. Closure, first cousin of genius, was
coming. Certain doors would click shut behind us, forking
paths would be abandoned, and good riddance.

When Cyrilly showed up, hair perfectly moussed to give
her a just-tousled look, I sent her out for cinnamon-apple
tea for me and a double espresso for Harry, and tried out
questions. What did you have to say to Janousek to get
him to admit he killed Einstein? What were his exact
words? By the way, you knew Einstein was close to the
unified field theory, didn't you, Norman? Smile sweetly
and slip the question between his ribs: Did you go back to
Einstein's hospital room for his notes?

"See if you can get him going about the end of the world," Harry said. "Dramatize the universal bomb." A quick study, Harry, thinking television already.

I went to the phone to mollify Burke. When I came back, Harry's intern was just leaving. Harry was sorting through a sheaf of photocopies.

"Listen to this," he said. He was on his second double espresso. "I've got something terrific for you. Play up 1942."

"Sorry, I wasn't there."

Harry made his fingers into a little wedge and pushed fact at me. "In 1942, Teller computed that a hypothetical H-bomb, or even an A-bomb, might be hot enough to set fire to the atmosphere, or the oceans, and burn up the whole world. Right, that's what I said, burn up the world. Say goodbye to nitrogen, or the hydrogen in the sea, and turn the earth into an imitation sun. This will interest our friend Gottehrer, no? Anyway, atomic scientists seriously worried about this. As well they better have. Oppenheimer worried. Oppenheimer was no crank."

"You don't say, Harry."

He charged ahead with his lecture. "He freaked, actually. Enough to take a train all the way from California to northern Michigan to consult with"—he flicked through his pages—"Arthur Compton, who was on vacation." Anyone else, sitting cross-legged on the floor and lecturing away slightly bug-eyed, would have looked ridiculous, but not Harry.

I scribbled: *Get file footage Teller, Oppenheimer, Compton.*

"He took the *train*?"

"The hotshots were forbidden to fly. Army orders." A

knowing smile, pixie crow's-feet. "Anyway, they went down to the beach. Compton was horrified, he said it would be better to let Hitler take over the world than blow it up"—Harry consulted his page again—"or, 'draw the final curtain on humanity' was the way he put it. They agreed to make new computations."

I thought reenactments: Teller with his shaggy eyebrows, the gaunt and ethereal Oppenheimer, and this Compton, whom I imagined with a Victorian mustache to match his metaphor, staring over the beach, ashen, lugubrious, enough to coax a "Holy shit" out of Josephine Sixpak . . . But scratch reenactments, there wasn't going to be time to rehearse anything half decent.

"Turned out Teller was sloppy," Harry plunged on. "He'd gotten carried away and plugged in some numbers that were way too high. Fermi and Bethe recalculated and, what do you know, the heat of the explosion wouldn't be nearly enough to blow up the world. Everyone trusted them, so they stopped worrying and went ahead on the bomb."

"Trust. That's what we need today. Trust."

"But do you know? Even to the end of the war, there was a dispute about the risk. Bethe and Teller thought they had proved there was no chance of this runaway explosion, quote 'effectively zero,' unquote"—Harry made air quotes—"whatever that means. Others said the odds were three in a million—meaning three in a million that their calculations were off."

"If they were wrong, whoops, sorry about that."

"Exactly. All the way down into '45, younger physicists would show up once in a while and ask the big shots, Excuse me, sir, have you thought about the possibility that this contraption could burn up the atmosphere of the earth? *The point is, even after the scare they went ahead with the test. They thought this was a risk worth taking. The experiment's got to go on.* Now here's the clincher."

Tell the music people: amp up synthesizer menace, dark chord moans, hollow reverberations. "I get it, Harry. I sneak up on Gottehrer. He's getting worked up about how revolting it is that the physicists will take even the slightest chance of blowing up the world. My deep sympathetic eyes have never been deeper or more sympathetic."

He stroked my cheek down to the tip of my chin.

"Then you're home."

"And then he killed Janousek because—because of what, Harry, tell me, I'm running down."

He made that wedge with his fingers and drove his points home. "Because Janousek was going to pin the Einstein murder on him. Or he found out that Janousek had made off with the unified-field-theory notes. Or Janousek really did confess. Or, for all we know, Janousek looked at him cross-eyed."

I took his wedge of fingers in my mouth and looked at him cross-eyed.

Sometime in the late morning, Bernie Gross came by, in jeans and a black turtleneck that did not flatter his bulging gut, and I told him I needed the world's most impressive animation of the universe breaking apart. People were getting bored with garden-variety mushroom clouds, I said. Beer ads, for Christ's sake. We needed an image of absolute extinction. I said that I also wanted my characters' names punched out on the Chyron one letter at a time in an old-fashioned typewriter face. I wanted them sounding like machine-gun bursts ripping through the paper. And I wanted to dramatize connections. A had an office down the hall from B, years later here he is with C.

Bernie said he could cheat my stills together with the Scitex. If I liked, he could have me interviewing Sir Isaac Newton. Quick and dirty. I said that probably crossed the line.

Come afternoon, I switched to a pale turquoise dress that I kept on hand for emergencies—slightly scoop neck, tight bust. Gottehrer was more grotesque than frightening, but I couldn't help being frightened.

Michelle the photographer boosted my sense of security. She was muscular and lean, with high cheekbones, black and stunning—this woman did not look like a pushover, she could trundle the camera and lights around without help. As if it weren't hard enough to be a woman breaking into the cameramen's club, you needed upper-body strength, arms of steel, hours of training on Nautilus machines. McShane had broken the union and gone to the one-person crew still known anachronistically as the one-man band—at the same time he was the toast of the Urban League and NOW for affirmative action. I briefed Michelle about Gottehrer, warned her that he might jump out of the frame in the process of jumping out of his skin. No problem, she said. She'd done low-budget documentary after film school, she loved to do hand-held.

Just before four, Delaney called. There was no hospital record on Gottehrer. No other records anywhere. No credit cards, nothing. The man barely existed. I thanked

Delaney and told him I couldn't chat, I was on my way to a shoot.

"Too bad you're in a hurry," he said. "I thought you might want to know that the autopsy's done on Janousek."

"On second thought, I've got all the time in the world."

"There was digoxin in his blood. Better known as digitalis. The widow confirms that he had a prescription. He took it to slow down his heart, even it out."

"Are you saying overdose?"

"Can't rule it out, can't rule it in. Could be his regular dose showing up—he took his pills at night. The pathologist's sending out slides to find out how much was in him. We'll know in three, four days if we're lucky."

I counted five days to showtime. "What does an overdose do to you?"

"Could be vomiting, could be blurring of vision, low pulse, convulsions. It varies. Could be, uh, urination. Then arrhythmia, then death."

"And? Did he vomit?"

"Vomit, no."

"No?"

"But he did mess up his pants."

I let that one work its way around my brain. "What does Goldensohn say?"

"Goldensohn doesn't know. Assistant M.E. I talked to says he can't tell a thing till the pathologist reports back. Also says that digoxin is a drug with a narrow margin of safety. A few extra pills and goodbye, you're off to a better place."

"How many extra?"

"Depends."

"How long before it takes effect?"

"You could be a cop, you know? A couple of hours, give or take."

Gottehrer got to Janousek before seven. Ilse found him after midnight.

"If I was you, Frank, I'd look into the possibility that the widow, formerly wife, got to the theater late."

"Thanks. Now tell me about Gottehrer."

"I owe you, Frank, but I gotta run."

■

By the time Michelle and I got to Gottehrer's, my stomach was burning again, never mind two Zantacs and a container of low-fat yogurt. Michelle wanted to know more about this guy we were crawling through rush-hour traffic to interview. The adjectives that came to mind, I said, were distracted, paranoid, possibly dangerous. Sounds great, she said, I thought this was about physics. It is, I said. I didn't feel like elaborating. She reached into the right-hand breast pocket of her neatly pressed work shirt, pulled out a tiny canister of Mace and said, Well, I always go out on a shoot prepared.

Getting six blocks crosstown to Second Avenue took twenty minutes. Below Fourteenth Street, traffic finally thinned out. So did the houses. Toward the East River, clumps of brick apartment buildings, their windows sealed with concrete blocks, stood in cleared space like leftover teeth in ancient gums. Weedy vacant lots were strewn with discarded blankets and plastic bags. On one lot, half a block long, three kids played football near a charred auto chassis. The chassis along with the kids would be bulldozed once self-exalting billionaires put up high-rises for advertising executives possessed of a pioneer spirit—homesteading among the savages. HOMES NOT SHELTERS, AIDS WON'T WAIT, and LIVE FREE OR DIE were neatly painted in white. But most of the graffiti were squiggles in codes not meant to be easily decoded. There were outdated handbills for rock groups called BREAKAGE, END IT, NERVOUS SYSTEM, OVER & OUT. The lot next to Gottehrer's building was fenced off, turned into a display of trash art — oil barrels suspended in wire mesh, plus auto wheels painted yellow and a motorcycle painted white. Dead potted plants on the seats of abandoned kitchen chairs. An anarchist's circle-A in thin, gnarled, wrought iron à la Giacometti mounted high over the street. Someday one of the billionaire developers would send a crew to sweep down at dawn and remove the whole corner lot to the Whitney Museum, where it would stand for centuries as a domestic Elgin Marbles. The developer would be featured on *In Depth* as a farsighted preservationist.

The shoot started lucky, with a parking space smack in front of Gottehrer's building. No great achievement — only two other cars were parked on the block. One, across the street, was a Lincoln Versailles with a sheet of plywood covering the hole where the rear window had once been, and nothing covering a crater in the smashed windshield, as if a boulder had been dropped from the roof. The other, next to a yellow-on-black FALLOUT SHELTER sign, was a Buick, hood up. A man in jeans was leaning over the engine and four others, young, three brown, one black, wearing chinos, were standing around in quilted jackets. A rooster crowed from a backyard chicken coop somewhere. My voice-over wrote itself: . . . *we caught up with Gottehrer where he lives today in this rundown New York apartment building on the desolate Lower East Side, living on dreams and the memory*

*of the man who dreamed of packing all the forces in the universe
into a single formula . . .*

The young men next to the Buick appraised us with
opaque expressions. One had a birthmark as big as a fist on
the side of his face. From a second-floor window over the
fire escape, a black-haired young woman stuck out her
head. The wind ripped through the street from the river.
The guy under the Buick hood caught a scent and extri-
cated his head. Two little boys strolled by, and one burbled:
"Hey, look, the lady from TV!" "Too big for you to handle,
small stuff," said birthmark. "Hey," said the guy who had
been under the hood, "we wanna *get* into the *iss*ues in *dep'*,
you know what I mean?" High-fives and jubilation all
around. Burke would be pleased that the show had circulation, although the group demographics were not so desir-
able.

"You're younger than you look on TV," said the guy
who had been under the hood. Michelle snapped off a
don't-fuck-with-me smile. She unloaded equipment from
the back of the van, held the Minicam to her eye like a
sniperscope, got establishing shots. I didn't have to ask her
to zoom in on DOOM, sprayed on the freshly red-painted
brick with curlicues sprouting out of the arms of the M—
too obvious to pass up. She proceeded to circle the boys,
shooting an arty 360 which startled them, *will ya look at this
broad!*, gave them a chance to mug and preen.

The circle shot wouldn't survive into the piece but would
fit nicely into her tape of greatest outtakes.

Having made her point, Michelle hoisted her case of
lights and tripods. I took the camera.

A blond young man with a ponytail under a backward
baseball cap inscribed N.W.A. loped by, knees slightly

bent. "Whatchoo say?" said birthmark. "Not much," said ponytail without breaking stride, and slouched around the corner.

"You come to take our pictures?" birthmark said.

"Watch *In Depth* Wednesday night and find out."

"Whatchoo doin' after the show?"

"Going home to my 220-pound husband, who's a black belt in karate," I said.

"You have a nice day," he said.

"What do you call a female TV correspondent?" I said quietly to Michelle as we checked the buzzers. She was a step behind me with the equipment case, which even as a miracle of miniaturization must have weighed fifty pounds.

"I give up."

"Cunt."

Her laugh was throaty, but I think she was humoring me.

The name was neatly inscribed beneath his buzzer, N. GOTTEHRER, along with a note typed in caps, BELL BROKEN. Most of the name slots were empty. A crumpled beer can was wedged underneath the outer door, holding it open. The inner door, with plywood tacked up where a glass panel had once been, opened with a push. We sweated our way up narrow, ill-lit stairs, through a zone of hamburger grease, to the sixth floor.

Gottehrer's studio apartment was neater than I expected. In fact, I didn't see much to keep clean. There was one of those backless chairs you kneel on; a ladder-back wooden chair of fifties vintage; an ancient maroon armchair with a back-support pillow; a stand-up draftsman's desk; a mattress on the floor covered in a cheap Indian print. Next to the desk were file cabinets painted a streaky, too-bright blue. Under the desk were several slightly disheveled piles of magazines. The floor was bare wood but for two identical Indian rugs made of thin stripes of multicolored rags. On the wall over the mattress was a poster featuring Hindu figures with elephant faces and women with multiple sets of arms; behind his desk, a bookcase filled with the spines of dozens of looseleaf notebooks; next to that, a poster of Einstein featuring this quote: "The pursuit of knowledge for its own sake, an almost fanatical love of justice, and the desire for personal independence . . . these are the features of the Jewish tradition that make me thank my stars I belong to it."

The remaining wall space, floor to ceiling, was taken up by bricks and unstained, unpainted boards sagging under the weight of thousands of books. Sections stood out: the *Ramayana* and *Mahabharata,* three translations of the *Bhagavad Gita*; Heraclitus, Protagoras, Nietzsche, Heidegger; the Holocaust; poetry featuring Pound, Black Mountain, Ashbery, Robert Kelly; fiction featuring Henry Miller, Djuna Barnes, Céline, Hawkes; science featuring relativity, chaos and catastrophe theory; reflections—as Rosenthal had said—by aging physicists about the nature of nature; Einstein's letters and papers. There was a cheap stereo; hundreds of long-play records stacked—jazz, Bach, ragas; no CDs. One record sleeve was conspicuously leaning against the stack: Kraftwerk, *Radio-Activity,* the jacket depicting a radio speaker, bearing a yellow radioactivity-warning sticker.

Gottehrer was not a man to forgo theatrical opportunities.

On the desk, in a small metal dish, a cone of incense had

left a cone of ash and the tinge of sandalwood in the air. The window was sooty and the walls hadn't been painted in twenty years. But Gottehrer looked clean in a blue work shirt and black exercise pants, and he had shaved. His hair was pulled back tight into his little ponytail. He even attempted a hospitality smile, but it came off wolfish, his upper lip stuck to his tooth.

"Wow," said Michelle, "look at all these books." Great stuff for an all-around pan, do it afterward with the cutaways.

While she was lighting the room, setting up her little white umbrellas to diffuse the glow, Gottehrer went to the kitchen to make tea. I surveyed his desk, where a thick loose-leaf notebook had been left open. Coming back with black mugs of tea, he said stiffly, "Go ahead and look." The lines, neatly handwritten, were broken, staggered, uneven in length, interspersed with small photos and words in headline type cut from magazines. He had glued the clippings down two or three to the page—oil-soaked sea otters, Lee Iacocca, a smashed Nintendo game, the severed heads of wild horses, blurred pedestrians shot at low shutter speeds in urban rain; phrases like AIDS PLAGUE, CRIME WAVE, and WONDERFUL TIME IS ALL. I started reading: *end of all spirit is to begin, darker spirit*—here appeared a shot of the blackened sky over Kuwait after Saddam Hussein had torched the oil wells—*is the heart of light and / the search which is only the starting or end- / point of the bottom-of-all-granite mystery /* a photo of Rock Hudson set next to a head-shot of Doris Day so that they seemed to be grinning past one another like ex-spouses / *Come to me, fire, cleanse forest, release seeds, reveal the / motion of all energy tending toward / somewhere the black arms spinning from the galaxy helicopter*—a photo of a

galaxy whorl trailing arms of stars—*and yet it moves* . . .
Stop-and-start stuttering rhythm wasn't my thing, but I'd
seen worse. The next page went on in the same vein, the
cutouts including the death mask of William S. Paley and
an ad of a sleek black woman smoking a cigarette by a
waterfall, and the words NO ONE COULD BELIEVE. There was
rubber cement and a pair of long scissors on the desk next
to the manuscript. There were piles of magazines under his
desk—*People, American Photographer, Aviation Week, Pent-
house, Meat.*

So this is what Norman Gottehrer did when he wasn't
spooking correspondents or physicists, or boosting well-
heeled teens into the better colleges. "My way of keeping
track of first and last things," he said. "My book of the
dead." Unification poetry, I thought. Evidence, but of
what?

Michelle, lights and tripod set up, sat Gottehrer near his
file cabinet, on his backless chair, so that she could get
the Einstein poster into the frame, with the blue edge of the
cabinet for foreground. "Beautiful," I said, meaning the
looseleaf notebook.

"I have one hundred nineteen of them. I've been working on them since college."

"Are you going to publish them?"

"Absolutely not. They're my meditation-in-action. I have
no desire to drop them into the world, defenseless against
cheap and thoughtless interpretation, ridiculous cults, at
the risk of violating the *spirit* of the work and turning it into
a means to my own so-called success, or some academic's."
His anthracite eyes glittered and darted as he threw down
the word *spirit*.

For a guy who's lived in the dark, Harry will comment,

Gottehrer's certainly left a lot of his life's work lying around in the open.

Even later that night, watching the tapes in my office, Harry can't find fault with the way the interview started. I can't, either. To this day, I can't. Chatting about his notebooks put Gottehrer in charge. Even my own stomach started to cool. Gottehrer was a good interview, articulate; he spoke whole sentences, he didn't freeze, didn't sound guarded or prerecorded like Billy Neill. Even his looks were right. On tape his eyes looked smaller and more deep-set—funny what the camera does to a face—and a lot of iris showed underneath his pupils, so that he acquired an otherworldly glow which suited his wild bursts of speech, his sputtering laugh. In the early minutes you can see his eyes dart around and off to the side. But, maybe ten minutes into the first cassette, he settled down and got used to the hot lights, the mike and the pocket transmitter, the camera's unimpressed gaze. This was his fifteen minutes in the spotlight and he was going to occupy it in style.

So I sat in the ladder-back chair, Michelle hovering at my shoulder, and walked him through questions he'd already answered in my office. How he'd seen the *Times* article about Einstein's unification theory. How Einstein had answered his letter. Did he have the letter, I asked. He reached into his file cabinet, pulled out a thick file, slid from the back of it an envelope bearing a purple Jefferson-head 3-cent stamp, from which he extracted a yellowing sheet of plain paper he held just above his lap, the careful European script inching its way methodically across the page, which he read aloud: ". . . you will please forgive my ignorance of the pre-Socratic philosophers . . . It is true that reason is not God, just as the journey is not the destination, but the former is certainly our most reliable route to the latter . . . Thank you very much for writing to me, Yours, A. Einstein." I can still smell the page. Michelle zoomed in. I scribbled a note to Bernie Gross: Highlight R-E-A-S-O-N I-S N-O-T G-O-D.

I nodded as Gottehrer rattled on about the times he sipped tea with Einstein in his study, their long walks through Princeton, Einstein once losing his bearings somewhere down Nassau Street and having to ask directions home, and the old man's kindnesses—this was the subject that softened the outline of Gottehrer's face.

"So he was like a father to you," I said.

"Better."

Evidence of a murder? Two? None.

My own back was starting to ache. A man with a back bad enough to require one of those kneeling chairs would own this ladder-back monstrosity only to torture a visitor. Or for sentimental value—Gottehrer was not a man to let go of things.

His riff on the sweetness of life and times with Einstein rambled on. When Michelle said that she had about three minutes left on the first cassette, I told her to load the second one—I wanted pure uninterrupted Gottehrer from here on, no break to give him an easy opportunity to rein himself in. I gave him a medium-good segue. He paused, stared into space, thought for half a minute, then stared straight at the camera and took off into a great earnest looping rendition of Einstein's obsession: the search to show how all the forces in the universe were hooked together. He scooped sentences into paragraphs, curving up, curving down, nicely tailored. He was Einstein's born-again passion, with the missionary eyes of a dead man—though on tape you can see one moment of self-awareness, when Gottehrer stops and says, "You sure you want all of this?" and I say, "Absolutely," so he says matter-of-factly, "Good, nothing could be more important," in a tone of I-like-my-toast-dark, and runs through the theory.

I let him burn off most of another cassette about the unified field theory. For free, Gottehrer threw in his own riffs on the pre-Socratics, the unity of being and nonbeing, the convergence of Eastern and Western philosophical traditions on the idea that dualities like mind / body and appearance / reality are inseparable, so that all concepts (whatever Plato thought) depend on one another utterly as aspects or angles of the same field—he talked that way. I knew this stuff was an automatic outtake when I let Gottehrer ramble on, I just wanted him to feel happy proselytizing. I didn't bring up the question of whether a unified field theory might lead to a universal bomb, and Gottehrer didn't, either.

And so, when Michelle had tucked a fresh cassette into the camera, I spun him over to the subject of Einstein's colleagues at the Institute and how physicists felt about this unification business. "Dubious," Gottehrer said, "dubious," his spooky half grin coming back as he noted that, for example, Martin Fleischmann had called the unified field theory "Einstein's Fountain of Youth," and others had muttered about "theory run amok," "nostalgia for the clockwork universe," "confusion of religion and science." Even Einstein's friends had only humored him. Shameful! vicious! the unkindness and envy of grown men confronted with a deeper mind and a more powerful, more devout spirit . . .

Oh, I had him rocking and rolling, sounding like a semi-rational human being ready to be moved to the subject of Janousek. Harry, watching the tape, nods minutely at my impeccable timing.

A flicker of upset on Gottehrer's face, very noticeable in slow-mo. Then a brief stare, his small eyes going into retreat until he could wrestle his loathing down, package his words. Then recovery—everyone knew that Einstein and Janousek had their differences, he said, but Einstein was not the kind of man to be troubled by petty jealousies, he looked forward to ultimate vindication, he could wait. His God was in no hurry.

Go ahead, cut loose, say it, I thought—wake up the vast dispersed millions of American folks with the truth about Gustav Janousek, that he was a lousy, bitter bastard, a danger to the species, and we're better off with him dead. But Gottehrer was determined to play the good boy. Janousek did significant work, it was his understanding that the Janousek effect was important, Einstein respected his early work, et cetera. Cut.

I had one move left: "Must have been terrible for you, Einstein's aneurysm attack and the unexpected company at his bedside."

Stop tape, replay. Jiggle the scenario six different ways, permutations, combinations, play it out sideways. Flick through the mental thesaurus, find some other words—would that have made a difference? I certainly wanted to sound concerned. Damn, I did sound concerned, my eyes as wide as they get. But in the end I have to conclude: there was no way around the unavoidable subject.

He tensed—if you watch this sequence frame by frame,

you can see Gottehrer's head snap back, like John F. Kennedy's head in the Zapruder film. But Gottehrer didn't collapse like a sack of grain. He yanked himself upright. "Attack?"

"You know, his—" I couldn't think of another word— "illness."

"Let me ask you a personal question. Have you lost a parent?"

"As a matter of fact, I have."

"Then you ask how terrible—" He let the reproach sink in.

"I only meant—"

"I know, I know—yeah, it was absolutely a terrible day in my life. I never recovered." Harry stops tape, plays this sequence back, verifies that he said, "*I* never recovered."

"But when he sat up and felt better," I said, "his second day at the hospital, you must have been hopeful."

"Yeah, that was cheering news." In the tone of when-does-the-next-train-depart.

I waited for him to elaborate, but he stood pat. "I understand that he sent for his notes, he wanted to keep working."

"Yeah."

"A speech about Israel, calling for peace."

"Right."

I tried tickling him on this theme, but the Middle East didn't interest him more than a monosyllable's worth. So he evaded. What did evasion prove? The radiator across the room clunked. What did that prove?

"And he sent for his notes on the unification theory, too, I understand."

"Um-hmm."

"He thought he was close, then."

"He could smell it, sure."

I danced him away from the edge and said: "Let's talk about the last day Einstein was conscious. You saw Rosenthal at the hospital."

"Yes, I remember seeing Professor Rosenthal at the hospital. He was such a good friend of Einstein's, I'd have been surprised *not* to see him. The son came to visit, of course. Also Miss Dukas. Also Professor Nathan."

"Also Janousek," I said.

"Yeah, that was a surprise." His jaw tightened—noticeable on tape, though not in real time, not to me, and I was the one who was there.

"Your second visit," I said. "You know, I really don't understand why you went back to his room, so many hours later."

His jaw started working, he wanted to chew me and my bright lights and half-bright questions and millions of viewers to shreds. Tremors, subterranean energies surged behind his face. He made a heroic effort to tamp his furies back into place. Words leaked out. "Look, I tried to explain —I'll put it simply, O.K.? The man saved my life. Does that sound melodramatic? *I wanted to say goodbye to the man who saved my life.* That isn't illegal yet, is it?"

"Mr. Gottehrer, would you like me to stop, I don't want you to misinter—"

The dybbuk voice, harsh, unstuck, welled up from deep in his concave chest, but it no longer sounded like Einstein's passion reborn, more like some beast let loose in the room, snarling: "He was a force of love! A dead concept! Nobody knows—" He sputtered out.

Timing is everything. Motive is evidence. Get him to the

universal bomb, Margo. If not now, what was I waiting for? "Something I'd like you to clear up. You thought the unification theory was a great achievement."

"Monumental."

"But could also be dangerous."

Heat circulated. I felt suddenly dry. Gottehrer sent his tongue on an expedition around his lips. I watched, embarrassed. Finally: "Yes."

"Would you like a glass of water?" I asked.

"No"—in a dead voice.

"I wonder if you could talk about what was so—"

"Careful. Danger ahead. Men working. The whole twentieth century says theoretical physics is dangerous." The words burst out. He squeezed his lips together: end of discussion.

Harry stops tape, freezing the frame on Gottehrer's glare. "What I don't understand is, why didn't he just tell you to get out?"

"Because I was *the media*, Harry. His vehicle to glory."

"But this was his nightmare. You blurt about the danger of a universal bomb, and the next thing you know, somebody gets ideas."

"He must have been star-struck. The way he was looking at me. He couldn't get over the fact that I was his guest. He didn't want to throw me out of his house."

So I asked Gottehrer to talk about the bomb to end all bombs.

The tic started. The tape shows his right cheek jerking up toward his eye. And still he struggled to hold himself together. The effect on the screen is just short of funny. The weird thing is that his glare didn't let up.

"Turn off the camera."

My turn to stare.

"You heard me. Do I have to rip the plug out of the wall?"

I told Michelle to cut off the picture. She did. He didn't realize that his transmitter was still giving us sound.

"The idea of the bomb's no secret, Norman. You know about genies and bottles."

No comment.

"You can only help. Put the world on notice."

His eyes drilled into mine. "Christ, what won't you people do?" He jabbed his right index finger toward my face, then into the flesh of his own thigh, keeping the beat of his rap: "Help, right. The *doc*tor is the di*sea*se, for *Christ's sake*. The *more* we *know*, the *more stu*pid we *are. People* have *got* to under*stand*, we're on the *edge* of the *end*. It's the eighth *in*ning, folks, *sor*ry about that."

"Do you mind if I record now?"

"Record away! What the hell! This is only the *ul*timate bomb we're talking about, the world's gotten *used* to extermination! History's bad karma. Not that it matters, you're right. Once Einstein established that *mass*, see, could be converted to *en*ergy, it was just a matter of *time* before someone was going to convert a little mass into a lot of energy and produce an *a*tomic *bomb*. It was like discovering that *love* can be converted to *hate*, you know? Only a matter of time before someone was going to convert an *a*tom into a *bomb* for *blow*ing apart the *u*niverse. What happens when the wrong people get hold of the universal bomb?"

"Like Iraq, or China—"

"Nazis working for Pakistan, why not. Or North Korea, or Khomeini II, or whoever's running Russian R&D now. Who the hell knows who, sometime between here and eternity. Everybody will want one. Let me ask *you* a question. What if the *right* people get hold of it? Ever think of that? You think there aren't stables of physicists working on unification theory as we speak? Put all the monkeys to work on word processors, how long before some of them cook up this nifty U-bomb?"

"And you don't think that the changing world situation—"

The dumb question he'd been lying back expecting, proof that I was one of the gullible dodos who *didn't get the point.* He smirked. "Right, the Cold War's over. We were supposed to live happily ever after, right? Wrong. Who showed up at the party but Saddam Hussein! Surprise! You think we're not a target at this minute? Some peace. We're hostages. The danger hides out, it outwaits the thaws. *All* the thaws. *Al*ways."

"Beautiful." Harry, chin on heel of hand, peering at the tape. "He's playing with fifty-three, fifty-four cards, jokers wild, and they're all there on the screen."

"Amazed me." I feel a sick sort of triumph. I look from the frozen frame to Harry, who shakes his head. He knows that seeing is disbelieving.

"Bastard must have decided he had to warn the world," he says. "Damn the torpedoes, sound the alarm. He must have figured he'd be safe, he got on the record how much he loved Einstein. Maybe."

"You don't pity him enough," I say.

Gottehrer did punch through, no question about that. Sitting on my sofa with Harry, watching the tormented head of Norman Gottehrer shake and rattle, I know this is pay dirt. Cassettes full of ore. The huge whites of Gottehrer's eyes, all his neurosis right there on the surface. Beautiful in its way, like a creep demolishing himself in a cartoon, that's all, folks. Crescendo to break through the snooze. "The Murder of Albert Einstein," my Surprise Symphony.

But who was the Haydn here? What weird collaboration of Gottehrer, me, Yolanda, all of us composing in the dark?

Gottehrer sputtered on: "One Manhattan Project leads to another. Nobody wants to be last. Make the A-bomb to throw at Hitler, next thing you know, there's fifty thousand of them, and you're an inch from turning *Russia* into a smoking radioactive ruin. Death in life." When he ran out of steam, Michelle changed cassettes. So the tape doesn't show the sarcasm on his lips, which seemed to say: All right, Miss Margo Ross, if this is the best you can do, you might as well surrender gracefully.

"Rolling," Michelle said.

I leveled my look, ready, set, shoot. "I have to tell you that an autopsy's been performed on Dr. Janousek. He may not have died of natural causes."

He lowered his right foot to the floor and jumped up, clumsily shoving his chair back. "That's it. O.K., enough!" —waving his right arm. Then silence, his tic working. I eased myself up as if I had all the time in the world. Michelle unlocked the camera from the tripod, found him in the frame, focused, kept shooting. Gottehrer stood frozen behind his chair. "What do you mean, *accu*sing me—"

"I'm not—"

"You just thought I'd like to kno-ow," he said, singsong.

"I want your comment. You did see him just before he died—"

"*I* get it. He *told* you. You were *working* together. *You* think I'm out of my *mind*?"

"I want to be fair."

"*Yes*, of *course* you do, don't think I don't ap*pre*ciate your taking the *time*. I be*lieve* in the fairness doctrine, I'm a *true* believer. I can *tell* you don't be*lieve* me." The right side of his face twitched violently. He took a step back and banged into his file cabinet, narrowly missing the sharp corner of the extended drawer. He ricocheted away from the cabinet and lurched back toward the chair. Recovering his balance, he eased back against the cabinet—hands feeling behind him—noticed the protruding drawer, slammed it shut with his left hand, and pressing his right hand against the cabinet stood there, stock-still. Samson; or a cornered man who needed to know where the corner was.

Michelle, gripping the camera, braced herself. Gottehrer pivoted toward the lens. "Now that you mention it, there *is* something I want to say. I'm going to stand here and say it."

"Fine."

"If I were Janousek, I'd have had reason to stop being."

I held on to the back rung of the chair. No sudden movements. "Could you be specific?"

"Could I be specific, right. He said he killed Einstein."

"Said what?"

"The word was *killed*. I'll tell you something else."

I couldn't wait. "Some people might say that you had a strong motive to kill whoever killed Einstein."

"I'll tell you something else"—louder. "He was alive when I left him. I'll tell you something else."

"I'm listening."

"He was an evil, ugly, violent, unforgiving—"

There was a very loud knock on the door.

At this point, the tape lurches. Michelle was startled and shook the camera. And Gottehrer trembled. As I did. There was another rap on the doorjamb. On tape the sound is thin, but fills out as I turn, with the mike pinned to my dress, toward the door.

Pan away, then back to Gottehrer, inspecting me for signs of betrayal, but I shrug—you can see my shoulder enter the frame.

I hit the pause button on the remote. Great still: Gottehrer's trapped eyes, the overly blue file cabinet. I go into my kitchen, where I pour myself a glass of water and pop antacid pills. For Harry I bring over to the coffee table an ancient and barely sampled bottle of fancy Scotch, found in my father's bottom desk drawer after he died. For twenty years I've hoarded this bottle, sipping from it only a couple of times, best forgotten. I tell myself I'm keeping it for a suitably magnificent or desperate occasion—falling in love or approaching insanity.

Harry, with a trying-to-cheer-you-up smile, offers his glass for a clink. I sniff the thick brandy-like sweetness of the Scotch.

"You're not going to drink? With what you've been through?"

"Don't feel like it, Harry." Not wanting to say my stomach is burning. Harry moves his hand to my knee. He leans in toward the monitor. Play.

Another sharp rap on the door panel, and through the door a shout: "Police! Want to talk to you!" Delaney. Gottehrer shoots a glance to the floor at the foot of the door, where his long bar of a police lock is lying useless to keep out police or anyone else.

"Just want to talk, Mr. Gottehrer." The name comes out "Gotter."

Wild looks scramble around the room. "What about?"

"Just want to ask you some questions." Delaney is flat and authoritative.

Gleams of intelligence and panic creep into Gottehrer's eyes, but his voice is almost sheepish. "You have a warrant?"

"There's no need for a warrant, unless you have something to hide." Silence. No one moves. "I hope you don't have anything to hide, Mr. Gottehrer."

A long moment when everything suspends, Gottehrer is trying to pull together a mind to make up, but the tape shows that only six seconds pass while Gottehrer's eyes dart from the door to the desk to the camera, while I take a step toward the door, and his scowl settles on me and he says, "Fucking bitch, you set this up."

I wouldn't have thought he could move so fast. He charged. He was a deranged bull. All praise to Michelle, the camera stayed with him, more or less. My hands flew up to protect my face, and I stepped aside. He didn't slow down, but swerved past me as if I didn't matter after all, plunged to his desk, and grabbed the long scissors. For a fraction of a moment he looked down at the blades as if he couldn't believe what he was holding in his hand: a foot of shining, pointed steel. He held the scissors in his fist at the handle end and came back toward me. My hands flew up again. Michelle, gripping the camera with one hand, swiveled and poked it at his face with her free hand, but he ducked, in the process knocking over the ladder-back chair.

I thought he was on his way to the door behind my back, but having passed me, he turned, came up behind me, reached around my neck with his left arm, and grabbed my chin with the cup of his palm, as if I were drowning and he was going to save me. But with his right hand he reached around and touched the point of the scissors to my throat.

Michelle, who'd kept a photographer's distance to hold Gottehrer in the frame, swung the camera back and away from her body—she was about to bowl the dead weight at his head. He pulled the point of the scissors a fraction of an inch away from my throat and growled, "Don't."

Michelle froze.

"Put the camera down. Right now. Very carefully."

I had a sense of slow motion. Something was happening somewhere else to someone else. The scissors touched my throat. I swallowed. The cold steel was easily sharp enough to make its point. He pulled the scissors away from my neck—not very far away.

Michelle bent down very, very deliberately, keeping her eyes on Gottehrer, except for one flash when she looked to me for some kind of signal, but I was blank—I hadn't the faintest idea what to signal. She set the camera down at her feet and stood back up. The tape was rolling, picking up sound, but Gottehrer didn't know that. Casually, she touched the breast pocket, left unbuttoned, where she kept her Mace. Her breast might be enough camouflage, I thought, though Gottehrer seemed to have all the sexual juice of a brick. Gottehrer watched Michelle's hand move until it came to rest on her pocket.

Gottehrer jerked my chin back. The point of the scissors scraped my neck. "Drop your hand. *Now.*"

"Margo, you in there?" Delaney shouted through the door.

Michelle shot a glance at the door, then back to me.

"Margo?" Delaney again.

"Hold on," Gottehrer half whined, whether to Margo or me or the cops I don't know. The rough skin of his cheek scraped against my ear. "Tell him to go away."

Michelle yelled, "Don't—"

A huge bash at the door, the sound of a shoulder hurled against plywood, then again, and the sound of the lock starting to give.

"Heroes," Gottehrer said vaguely, more or less to himself. He mumbled something that sounded like "What's new?" More pressure against my chin as he jerked me back toward the desk, away from the door, letting the point of the scissors drop an inch or two from my neck. I went hip-hopping, skidding backward, everything I could do to keep my footing, as if staggering on ice, watching my feet slide out in front of me.

Then he stopped short—I don't understand why—and lost control and staggered back against a bookcase. I fell back on him, full-body, but still on my feet, with my throat somehow intact. I snapped my head back, hoping to smash his nose or his forehead, while with my right elbow I hit him as hard as possible in what I hoped would be his solar plexus. I missed his head and hit his ribs, which hurt me more than it hurt him, and gave me another reason to scream. He staggered back. I waited for the scissor point to gouge into my neck. But it didn't.

The jamb splintered, the door crashed open, and Delaney charged into the room, another plainclothesman just behind him, both with their guns drawn. With his left hand, Gottehrer shoved me toward them. I staggered into Delaney, who had to lower his gun. I heard a slight grunt behind me, swiveled, the grunt went guttural and turned into a long-drawn-out groan. The handle end of the long scissors was in Gottehrer's hand, and several inches of blade were in his abdomen.

Michelle missed the shove, but she got the groan and the thump as he hit the floor, the fetal coil of his legs, the blood seeping onto the Indian rug. She caught Delaney's astonishment, my wrecked face.

Fear is the horizon.

I barely made it to Gottehrer's kitchen sink before I threw up. Not until Michelle came after me, took my icy hand, and hugged me (the Mace canister digging into my back) did I stop shaking. A police photographer showed up a while later, and a doctor and a squad to clean up the mess. Delaney stomped around trying to sound official, but mostly he snarled. "Hey, I feel sick myself. Fuckin' fruitcake, all I was gonna do was question him, you know? Doorman on Riverside Drive saw him come outa the building, all agitated. What was this guy, some kind of fuckin' Japanese?" Right, Delaney, some kind of Japanese. You seen one Buddhist, you seen 'em all.

Delaney denied he'd followed me all the way down from Big Glass. But I hadn't been exactly hard to track down, had I now? "Give me some credit." Meaning that my office had told him. But why shouldn't they have? So, in the name of precaution and the strong arm of the law, I was almost dead, and Gottehrer more than almost. It hadn't been too hard to tip Norman Gottehrer over the edge.

Downstairs, there were two uniformed cops at the front door and two muddy-brown unmarked Plymouths half up on the sidewalk staring each other down. A man older than me, wearing a helmet painted with the Stars and Stripes, rumbled by on a motorcycle, spattering the air with a Bronx cheer. The fog was darkening and the man working on the Buick was wiping his hands on an oily cloth. Locals had gathered—teenagers talking Spanish, older women full of solemnity, giggling kids. I pulled my cape around me. "We gonna be on *Wanted*?" a ten-year-old wanted to know. Sir Colin would have cringed to know that the competition had that kind of following with the youth of tomorrow.

The steel points of the scissors were still at my throat. I kept falling, Gottehrer kept dying.

Michelle drove around the block. I got out at a bodega a block away and asked the proprietor whether he knew a certain customer, skinny white guy, early sixties, thinning white hair, shoulders hunched, in the habit of wearing a blue coat. "Sure thing, Mr. Gotter, a nice man," the proprietor said. "But a strange man." Strange, what do you mean strange? "You know, he talk to himself sometime." I didn't have the heart to hear more. I said I would come back, but I never did.

At Big Glass, I ran off a complete set of the Gottehrer cassettes for myself and left the originals in an office safe reserved for producers. In a pang of on-the-job loyalty I called Burke's office to check in, but no one picked up. Harry had left me a note saying he'd gone home and I should call as soon as I got back from the shoot. The door-jamb was still splintering, Gottehrer was still groaning, and I was ashamed to need Harry so much.

Michelle retrieved the company van and gave me a ride home. She had her all-in-a-day's-work breeziness back and I felt as though I'd been run over. "You sure you're all right?" she said. "Half right, anyway." There was a shop-ping cart full of bottles next to the steps in front of my building. The man who lived in the box was rummaging through the garbage can. An ecologically useful citizen of our time. We nodded at each other. When I unlocked the outside door, the murmur of the devout leaked from the synagogue door into the lobby, and the stairwell was full of the smell of boiled cabbage.

I called Harry. When he came, I was weeping. I wept for myself, who had barely avoided having a hole torn in my throat. I wept for Gottehrer, whom I'd driven into a cor-ner. I wept for Einstein. When I brought out the Gottehrer cassettes to see whether anything might have gone differ-ently, Harry understood.

I wouldn't have predicted that he would tend me so well. He didn't tell me to get a grip on myself. He cradled my head in his lap and sifted through my hair. When I was calmer, we watched the tapes. He convinced me that I would feel better in the morning. "Sweet liar," I said.

Gottehrer didn't feel better in the morning. He hung on for two days, then died. Nobody claimed the body.

I WOKE UP IN AN EMPTY BED WITH A FIST BASHING AT MY skull from the inside. I slogged into the living room, where Harry was scribbling on a yellow pad. I told him not to speak—there weren't enough hours between me and the memory at my throat. He sat me down and kneaded the knot in my shoulder.

After coffee, I called Burke's office number. The phone rang endlessly. But this was Friday. All over Manhattan, offices would be racing their clocks. Taub would be cracking his whip over Minasian about Einstein's glial cells, Burke would be cracking his on me if I wasn't careful. Would a fast-lane, blast-lane news director take a three-day weekend at a time like this for the sheer thrill of sharing a room at a country inn with his Tiffany? What would they talk about? Other country inns he has known, other country inns she would hope to know.

On the odd chance that I'd guessed wrong, I dialed Burke's home phone and he picked up on the first ring: "Burke." I described the afternoon at Gottehrer's. He listened. When I stopped, he was still listening. His silence took up a lot of space.

"What's wrong?"

"Wrong? What could be wrong? I've got a great severance package and McShane gave me until six to clear out my office." The words crisp but toneless. Someday there would be computer-generated patter and Burke Gilman would make a fortune at software.

"Very funny. Come on."

"Mr. McShane has opted to buy out my contract."

"Burke, cut it out. I just saw a man murder himself."

"That's nothing. I just saw a man dumped in the gutter."

"Stop. This is serious."

"I don't do serious. I don't do windows. I don't do anything. And by the way, no comment, no comment, no comment. And just between us, no comment."

"Burke, talk to me."

Nothing. Then: "On the deepest possible background. O.K.? You didn't get this from me. Or I'm coming after you."

"Of course."

Pause. "Creative differences."

"Pardon?"

"Mhmmm, mhmmm," came over the phone, an intense moan on its way to a whine.

"You're trying to say that you've got the golden gag in your mouth."

"Can neither confirm nor deny. Now here's a question for you. Did you ever wonder how much interference you'll run to protect your people? I hope to hell you don't have to find out. I really do."

I was about to ask to whom I would now report when I heard the unmistakable click of an incoming call on his call-waiting.

"Gotta go, Margo." He sounded relieved to get off.

I should have felt relieved to be rid of him. But during the course of the day, I shifted from astonished to paranoid. Après Burke Gilman, le déluge? Burke had spent years in training to be Secretary of Servility in some future yuppie government and had still ended up offending the boss. What hope was there for an ordinary dinner-party sweet-talker like me?

Go figure. McShane was inscrutable, a cunning Occidental. I would have thought *In Depth* had been bringing in big enough bucks. Harry suggested that Burke had been fucking Lady McShane on the piano while Sir Colin roamed the earth looking for acquisitions. I told him he was underestimating what men will do for their friends. "Burke was playing both ends against the middle, Harry. McShane thought we were going to skewer his friend and tried to kill the piece. But Burke got me Janousek's number. Then, lo and behold, Janousek's dead. When it's too late to save his friend's life, McShane smells a rat, so you and I are no longer Commie moles, right, to mix the species a bit. Turns out we're apostles of truth."

"Lions, lions of truth."

"Lions, fine. Has to be somebody's fault, see, that he missed the story and failed to stop the murder."

"Time to round up a scapegoat, a lamb, some other kind of woolly ruminant."

"Exactly. Burke is the sacrifice to the greater glory of Colin McShane's self-love. And the schmuck spent years walking on marbles to anticipate McShane's every whim."

"Power's its own argument," Harry said.

And then a door slammed in my mind. I was damned if I was going to put in more of my prime years walking on marbles, risking broken bones, anticipating the infinitely larger number of whims Sir Colin McShane had left in him. I was going to put in exactly six more days, count 'em, Friday, Saturday, Sunday, Monday, Tuesday, Wednesday, zero, and then, because there was no bottom to my loathing, because I had gathered facts as best I could and now two more men were dead, because I was sick at heart and mind with the suspicion that I was playing out an assigned role in a horror story scripted by Sir Colin McShane, because I didn't care if I was slated to be best supporting actress in his cast of thousands—for all these and a number of other good and sufficient reasons, in five days I was going to be a walking and talking, free, forty-plus ex-producer and ex-correspondent, I was going to cut loose, lift off, break out of the shallows of *In Depth.* That or go off my head with fury.

■

So I free-fell headlong toward the deadline.

Harry stayed at the office, fiddling with the script, while I mainlined TV speed, moving around town in the van with Michelle to tie up loose ends. Keep moving toward the horizon. Adrenaline, my dope, I'm going to miss the zero-to-sixty rush! Keep moving, Margo, you'll have time later to fall apart.

The images kept flashing back: Gottehrer's fist around his scissors, the blade in his abdomen, the astonishment on his face, the spreading puddle of blood.

Stop one was Leon Taub's lab in a former packing plant on a side street in Tribeca. The sign, LABORATORY FOR NEUROANATOMICAL AND HISTOLOGICAL STUDIES, was discreet. The lab had a high ceiling, fluorescent lighting, and no windows. Unusual place for a lab, I commented. Taub said that any lab studying animal tissue, living or dead, human or not, had to be high-security, located with animal righters in mind, for they did not do their homework scrupulously, and he did not want to lose any of his valuable brains.

Taub was a short man with an unpleasantly thin mustache and a high dome of forehead. It was Taub's D-day, but he seemed unperturbed—either Peter had succeeded in stalling him; or Taub, all science, was skilled at keeping his amazement under wraps; or he knew about the speed, but had his own reasons not to give me the story. I hadn't a clue. I tried chatting him up, but his idea of chat was to let loose a torrent of polysyllables about brains and brain research—neurotransmitters, dopamine, cortical gray matter, myelinated fibers, celloidin, blue stains, radioactive decay, and other matters I did not fathom and did not particularly care to. But I kept nodding, Michelle kept shooting, Taub kept talking with proprietary pride about glial-cell-to-neuron ratios that he was finding in various spots around the cranium of Einstein and other physicists as compared to artists, poets, architects, plain folks. "Our preliminary finding"—he cleared his throat—"our preliminary finding is that visual artists have relatively high glial-to-neuronal ratios and that Einstein is unusual among physicists in the high ratio of the glia located at least in the superior frontal and inferior parietal areas," et cetera. I kept nodding. Politeness counts. I wasn't going to use this stuff, anyway.

Like packaged tourists, we toured up and down the aisles, along the cluttered lab counters, sinks, shelves. I had expected gleaming steel, alphabetically organized chemical bottles, so I was surprised by the strewn paper towels, the hand-scrawled note reminding the staff to clean up the sink. Michelle shot B roll ambience by the yard, the better to decorate voice-overs: machines, beakers, bottles. Photogenically intricate devices, mostly in pale tans and off-whites. Amplifiers and preamps, connected by cables to the quietly humming machine called the HPLC system, for high-performance liquid chromatography—the kind that had produced the printout that Harry had passed to me at Happening a hundred years ago. There was a second machine with a strip-chart recorder, its two needles wiggling from opposite sides of the slowly unfurling graph paper, producing lovely peaks and valleys, traces of chemicals. Michelle didn't need to be told to get a lot of that one: it moved. We shot microscopes, scales, calculators, lamps, solution bottles, a Geiger counter, a large centrifuge, a small one. A homogenizer, a sort of electric mixer for tissue —Taub demonstrated the vibrating blades with a wicked-looking smile. Wire racks, bottles of chemicals. A fancy balance, measuring weights down to the milligrams. Little yellow radioactivity-warning labels everywhere. A padlocked refrigerator.

"And the brains?" I asked.

"Yes, of course." He took a step toward the refrigerator. I felt the thrill of a tomb robber, expecting to see a soft thing in a jar, the sole remain of A. Einstein, his lease on his organs expired. But Taub passed the refrigerator and walked to a closet, opened a wooden door, pointed at a stack of gray cardboard boxes. He picked up the top one and rested it on the floor. He opened it, took out a wooden box, removed the lid. Glass slides were positioned in vertical slots. He took out a slide on which was mounted a slice of flesh about an inch square. The surface was smooth. The convolutions were picturesque. The inner area, a sort of delta with indentations, was greenish. One border was gray. There was a visible dot. It looked not quite like an aerial map, not quite like a piece of coral.

"Einstein?"

A crisp smile. "No, Harlan McElwaine, a physical chemist. As a matter of fact, I'm expecting a report on Einstein later today."

I suppressed a sigh of relief. Why, I asked, was McElwaine greenish?

"The white matter ages," Taub said with a twinkle. "Like fat. You know, when you go to the meat market, you always look for the fat to be clean and white."

"I'm a vegetarian," I lied.

Michelle shot the slides from every conceivable angle: in the box, in Taub's hand. Taub smiled.

Norman Gottehrer's brain, Janousek's brain. The fat would be fresh, pristine.

"Would you like to see where the samples are prepared?" Taub asked with enthusiasm, and ushered us into a tiny room opening off the main lab. On a table stood a long steel contraption equipped with a blade. A guillotine for dead things, or, technically, a sliding microtome. Taub didn't have to be told we were looking for photogenic.

Michelle was drawn to the steel surface, a sort of tabletop where little geometric forms shone in the metal under the harsh fluorescent light. This is where neurons and glial cells of Albert Einstein had been sliced thin for the greater knowledge of humankind. The camera played over the steel surface. Taub preened over Einstein's glial cells as if he had spawned them himself.

In the main lab, around a table, six staff assistants were eating hamburgers off paper wrappings. There was a buzz of shop talk. From a big radio emanated a low volume of reggae music. There was a dart board in the corner of the room. Taub introduced his team. I shook hands all around. The man with the blotchy olive skin, the whitening hair, and the black mustache was Peter Minasian, and I don't think I would have recognized him without the name. He didn't wear his surplus decades well. Neither of us displayed a sign that we had any connection.

Uptown traffic, stop-and-go rush. When traffic clots, the ambulance turns up the siren. Gottehrer smashes against the bookcase. I smash against Gottehrer. The door splinters. The miracle of my intact throat. Gottehrer's ruptured abdomen, a groan as deep as ecstasy. The pleasures of running a red light.

Cut to Riverside Drive. Ilse Janousek was dignified in a tailored black suit. "I am barely holding together," she said, "thank you for asking." Resentment flickering at the bottom of her eyes. I've seen redder eyes in the mirror after two glasses of wine. Thomas Fleischmann, in his early fifties, sleek in a three-piece suit, hovered filially. His card said INVESTMENTS and listed a single-digit address on East Eighty-fourth Street. Close enough to the Metropolitan

Museum, he could stroll clients around the Temple of Karnak and invite them to think about art values and long-term real estate in one package.

Ilse required plenty of prompting. She shut down after every sentence or two. On the subject of Janousek's on-again off-again days with Einstein, she gave only one medium-good moment: a sour look as she said that people around the Institute had considered Gottehrer "a pest, or worse." Questions about Einstein got nowhere, so I jumped to the subject of her husband's last day. Her tight jaw was eloquent.

"My husband was not happy he had made an appointment with this nuisance."

"Nuisance—that was his word?"

"Yes."

"Did he say that Gottehrer had approached him before?"

"I assumed so. He did not say and I did not ask. I did suggest that he call and cancel the appointment."

"And what did he say to that?"

"He said he did not know how to reach him, and anyway it would be better to get the nuisance out of his hair."

I had the feeling that she thought her husband had been holding something back. But she denied it. The more she denied it, the more she left the impression that Gustav Janousek was not a man to be argued with, once he had made up his mind. So she had left for the theater at five-thirty with her son.

It didn't take more than half an hour to outstay our welcome, such as it was. Thomas looked relieved as he showed us out.

.   .   .

In the lobby, I stopped for a word with the doorman. He lifted his eyes from the TV to pay tribute to Michelle, and agreed it was a terrible thing about Professor Janousek. Did he remember anyone visiting the night of the professor's death? "Only one guy, you know. I told the officer from the police. Tall gentleman wearing a blue coat. I call up to the professor. The professor said send him up, then I send him up."

"And what time was that?"

"Well, before eight. A little before eight."

"How can you be sure?"

"Well, is my job."

"You check your watch?"

"Yes, sure."

"I have to say, I didn't notice you looking at your watch the other evening. Or today."

His eyes were very cool. "I don' want to get in trouble, you understand."

"What kind of trouble?"

"That microphone on?" He pointed to Michelle's camera with its attached mike.

"Absolutely not."

"I watch the television, you know, at seven-thirty, before my shift end."

I didn't have to ask which program. It had to be *Wanted*. At the moment, the screen was a dull gray-green. Apparently, he was immune to the blandishments of soaps, quiz shows, other miscellaneous thrills.

I assured him that I was not going to broadcast the fact that he watched TV on duty. I only wanted to know when the man with the blue coat left. "After eight, is all I can tell you."

Outside, Michelle wanted to know if I really noticed whether or not this guy looked at his watch. I assured her that even a seeker after the truth gets lucky once in a while.

Sunday morning, Michelle, Harry, and I drove down to Princeton. The sky was absurdly bright, the green of Rosenthal's lawn was blinding, his tea was already hot. I apologized for the early hour. "You are never too early for me, I am awake with the bats," he replied. It wasn't hard to get him to sail into stories about Einstein, the unified field theory, and Gottehrer. But, on the subject of Janousek, he led with *De mortuis nil nisi bonum,* which left him little to add. Still, we filled two cassettes with Einstein and Gottehrer stories and charm, which was enough, and when I had what I needed, I broke the news that Gottehrer was dead, a suicide. I didn't specify the circumstances and Rosenthal didn't ask. The color drained from his face. "I am an old man," he said. "It is not right that I should outlive him"—as if Gottehrer were still the adoring, promising young poet-philosopher who had wandered into Princeton forty years earlier with odd ideas and a light in his eye. Rosenthal's shoulders sank. He could not go on with the interview. I was just as glad. I was even gladder that he didn't chastise me for saving the news about Gottehrer until I had milked him for everything I needed.

The Princeton Home for the Aged, close by, was a sprawling low-rise brick building identified by a discreet white wood sign with Gothic letters at the edge of a lawn still vaster than Rosenthal's. The woman in charge offered a guest book for me to autograph and assured us that no other visitors, thin or otherwise, had come to visit Angela

Parenti. The words "murder investigation" extracted from her a promise of silence. She escorted us to a small private room painted a womblike pink, cooed that Mrs. Parenti was very excited about our visit, and left with a reminder that filming was not permitted in public quarters.

Einstein's surviving nurse was a small, stout lady with hair so silver it gleamed, and an amazingly sharp memory for her remote and momentarily glorious past. It took a bit of prompting, at first, before she remembered that Harry had been there to see her a week before; but then *of course* she remembered talking about Professor Einstein and the young man with the big ears who had sat up all night in the visiting room. But Angela Parenti required no prompting to talk about her most renowned patient. She sat in a floral dressing gown in her own fluorescently overlit visiting room, leafed through her diary, and reminisced about the routines of Professor Einstein's final day, his visitors, and his last, mysterious German words, of which the syllables she could recall sounded, she said, something like "conic compen." She thought German an ugly language, it didn't seem to go with Professor Einstein. No, she had no idea what had become of Einstein's notes. All the personal property should have gone to the next of kin, his step-daughter, what was her name, Margot—"Interesting that it's your name too." I didn't tell her we spelled it differently.

The rest was just as Harry had said. She remembered the chubby visitor, yes, and the tall one with the flat nose— this one had bossed her around, who did he think he was? No, she had never heard the name Janousek. Did she remember anything more about the young man with the big ears? "Oh, he was very intense and very—concerned.

He kept asking about the professor's condition. In fact, I had to call the orderly to make him leave, late at night. Of course, this was a long time ago."

She had rheumy eyes, and her voice cracked, but I was inclined to believe her, because there were also details that she admitted she didn't remember, like the orderly's name and description, though she thought he might have been Greek. Her diary added no information but looked photogenic on her lap. Her clippings were in perfect order. For B roll, I had her leaf through. I smiled through my cutaways. "Oh, I am so proud to meet you," Angela Parenti said, still glowing, as we left.

On the way back to New York, Harry said that "conic compen" might be *"kann nicht kampfen"*: cannot struggle.

Monday morning, Delaney called to say that the path report on Janousek was back. He had indeed died of a spectacular overdose of digoxin. Harry holed up at Big Glass to keep watch over Yolanda's shoulder while Michelle and I dashed up to Park Avenue to do Goldensohn on camera, professionally brisk and somber as he ticked off the grim facts. I checked some details with the good doctor, who was perkier once the camera was off. By now I would have been amazed if Janousek hadn't been poisoned.

When I got back to the office, there were two dozen long-stemmed roses on my desk, with a card that read, "Heroine," and an invitation, or summons, to an audience with Colin McShane. McShane had screened the Gottehrer cassettes—the safe combination was the last service supplied him by the departed Burke Gilman. "I'm no heroine," I told McShane. "The guy tripped, that's all, and he happened to fall the right way." "That's the *point*, luv," he

said. "Be good and ready when the other fellow trips, because he always does. By the way"—with a wink—"it
doesn't 'urt to rest your foot in the aisle as he strolls by,
does it."

McShane was eager, in fact desperate, to know what he
could do for me. I told him to send Michelle some flowers,
too. And to make sure Tony Carrera didn't upstage me
during the live segments. I will extract his teeth one by one
if he so much as steps on your shadow, said Sir Colin.

Free-fall wasn't fast enough. Harry and I went into the
high gears, two days' worth. I was barely a body on earth
anymore, I was a blur oscillating between my office and the
editing room. Harry was supercharged, drafting my intro
and outro, meditating on tentative edits, going back to his
drafts. He scribbled notes, I tore them up, I rewrote. I ate
yogurt and guzzled antacid. Yolanda said the rewrite was
wonderful and suggested a touch here, a touch there.
Freeze-frame on the blade at my throat. And again on
Gottehrer bleeding—hold, hold, hold, *there.* Over the top,
Harry thought. He was right, but wrong.

I barely slept. I barely had time for Harry, but he was
filled with his own manic cheer, leaning back in my chair,
feet on my desk, all motion even at rest, man in his element:
at work. I will always have in my mind these images to play
back, traces of days when I had no doubt what I was on:
deadline. Freeze-frame: Harry joyfully wolfing down tuna-
fish sandwiches. Freeze-frame: Harry barking out yeses
and noes on hard cuts and dissolves. Freeze-frame: Harry,
fist in the air, punches a *yes* when we see Bernie Gross's
graphic simulation of the universe after the U-bomb—the
electronic riff stopping dead in mid-bar, the screen going to

snow going to gray-blue going to blue-black going to ink-black and holding one second, two seconds, *agony*. Freeze-frame: I'm back-seat-driving the mix: smash-smash of the typewriter sound for the supers, electronic ripples and cascades, dead silence during the jittery sequence when Gottehrer holds the steel against my neck. *Beautiful.* I watch Gottehrer die twenty or thirty times until I can deadpan, *He's got me by the throat, Harry,* and we crack up. Harry is revved up to industrial pace. We're ripped together, rushing and crashing on the speed of all speeds, master and lifeline of all drugs.

■

"The Murder of Albert Einstein" ran a little ragged, a little confusing, a little short, but the raggedness seemed right. In spots it had the improvised look, the faux authenticity, of one of those old Spike Lee basketball-shoe commercials. True, for the first twenty minutes or so, we were stuck with a surfeit of facts, characters, and I was afraid that we'd lost Einstein, lost the unification theory, lost the tremor of Gottehrer's desperation, lost the big story. Einstein had become a sainted old smarty-pants, the kind you see in the college magazine ad for class rings. But Gottehrer's darkness brought the show to life. Fades to black were the perfect lead-in and -out for Bernie Gross's end-of-the-world cartoon. The steel points of Gottehrer's scissors at my throat gleamed. From there on, the show was torrential. There wasn't five seconds' letup. The electronic growls swept the piece past breaches in logic, missing facts, flimsy conclusions. Start a musical measure at the end of one scene and use it to bridge to the next, and presto! you have manufactured continuity, which is all anyone can ask.

Segue is power. Only connect. Continuity isn't born, it's

cut. God the Editor stitched together His continuity, too. Just look at the stop-and-go rhythm of Genesis, basting the world together, barely.

And then the A.D.'s fingers pointing at me for the outro, *quiet, please,* everyone on the set pivoting toward me because, whether they wished me well or ill, I was the face at the pulpit; the word. *Five, four, three, two, one* and the red light on the camera came on, meaning Go.

I went: "If this were a self-respecting mystery story, this is the moment when I'd round up all the suspects who couldn't wait for Albert Einstein to take his last breath. I'd make them squirm. First, I'd bark up a wrong tree or two. Possibly, I'd coax the murderer into a choice bit of self-incrimination. I'd dazzle you with brilliant deductions. Well, it's confession time, all right, time for me to confess. We don't know who killed Albert Einstein. We don't know who killed Gustav Janousek. We don't know, in fact, if before he died he said to Norman Gottehrer what Gottehrer said he said. All we know is who killed Gottehrer. It's a safe bet that they were all killed for what they knew. But we are not all-knowing on this side of the screen. No matter how authoritative we sound, don't believe us. We scrape together evidence, if we're lucky, and we offer it. We know a lot less than we pretend to." Pause. Wistful look into the lens. Slight toss of the head. Seconds register in the TelePrompTer. "I'm Margo Ross. I only ask questions." And out.

Tony Carrera should have been proud of me. I stretched my pauses, slowed, stopped with the precision of a sewing machine. Tony sat speechless. Colin McShane had made him swear to keep his mouth shut. In the two-shot, he tried to look rapt, a steadfast witness to truth. The light on the camera went off, and no sooner were the credits rolling than the crew broke into manic applause, like passengers in a 747 that's just touched down in heavy fog with a damaged landing gear. "Beautiful, Margo," said Sally, swabbing my makeup off. Never mind that the piece ended with two bodies and no murderers. For all anyone knew, Einstein was murdered by some ex-Nazi gas-station attendant, some former concentration-camp guard who'd been passed down the rat line by army counterintelligence in 1947 and bided his time in Princeton, New Jersey, awaiting a chance to slip speed into this old nemesis of the Third Reich, Einstein the Jew. *I only ask questions.* Necessity into virtue.

I waved Harry up onto the set and let him bask in glory.

The phones were already trilling like a field full of locusts, but there was no Burke Gilman to tell me to chat up the customers. Elaine Barbanel came up and said, "Guess what, McShane's appointed me acting exec prod for news." "That's wonderful, Elaine," I said, "but I still don't want to take calls." Even if I was princess for a day. A whiff of mild euphoria carried me through the gauntlet of congratulations and stayed with me as far as the elevator.

I went to my office for the last time. My memories should have been fonder, I kept thinking. I rummaged around for anything worth keeping and settled on photographs of my parents, GREETINGS FROM PAPUA NEW GUINEA, and four cassettes: the first girl chess champion in New York; pesticides secretly used on organic farms; the American arms merchant who had designed super-artillery for Iraq, Iran, and Syria; and the great Long Island oil spill, done without dialogue or voice-over, only elegiacal violins.

On second thought, I decided to keep a copy of designer drugs, too. I riffed through files. None of the stories in progress interested me. I slammed the file drawer shut and stuffed things in a backpack. In truth, I'd been quitting for a long time.

On impulse, I called Ilse Janousek to thank her. "For what?" she said. "For cooperating." "I did not watch your program. Please do not take this personally." Her voice full of regal grief. I told her I was getting too old to take anything personally. In case she thought of anything else she wanted to tell me, I left her my home number.

I punched a note to Sir Colin via electronic mail, thanked him for his vote of confidence, hoped he liked the piece, added that effective immediately I was sick at heart, stomach, and mind, and therefore I was taking all accumulated sick leave and I was walking, yes indeed, I was talking, yes indeed, I was hoping that I'd never come back to him and all his works.

"Very nice," said a voice in the doorway. I jumped. Delaney was standing there wearing a smirk. "I love to hear about a homicide on television. What is it, you got some Jersey cop workin' the Einstein case?"

"I protect my sources," I said, but he knew I was embarrassed.

"Seems to me I protected you not too long ago"—dropping himself onto my couch like a bomb. "Your sources do that?"

"Don't think I'm not grateful. Look—"

"You could have trusted me."

"No, I couldn't. Those were the terms on which the story was given to me." I waited for his face to soften, but it didn't. His eyes flashed around the room, taking in evidence. I said: "You started with one murder and now you have two, right? You ought to be grateful yourself."

"Thank you. If I hadn't barged into Gottehrer's, I might have had three, lucky me."

All the rage from the scene at Gottehrer's blew up inside me. "He wasn't going to kill me. He panicked. He panicked because you barged in to rescue me. If I'd wanted you there, I would have whistled. Now you've got the best-documented suicide in history."

"Oh, yeah?"

"Don't 'oh, yeah' me. Do me a favor. The next time you want to rescue me, ask my permission, O.K.?"

The corners of his mouth hitched up, but his level eyes were rivets. "Sure thing."

When I said I was quitting, he nodded and said nothing. When I said I was sick and tired of people yanking my chain, ditto.

"I go after Janousek, and Janousek dies," I threw in. "I go after Gottehrer and Gottehrer dies. You ought to be glad I don't go after you."

His gray eyes twinkled as stars do when low-flying clouds pass in front of them. "All right, I owe you. Now give me the rest," he said, and I did. I laid out the whole Einstein story from the time Harry had laid it out for me: Rosenthal, Janousek, Gottehrer, Janousek's message on my machine. Delaney took it all in. By the time I was done, he had kindness in his eyes, or some quality of ambivalence I could take as kindness.

Once he was gone, I sat behind my desk and stared into space. When the phone trilled, I felt like smashing the receiver against the wall. So much for telling Elaine I wouldn't take calls. "Yes," I said as brusquely as possible into the phone.

"Miss Ross, please," said a prim voice I couldn't place. "Who is this?"

"This is Leon Taub"—his annoyance barely suppressed. "I have to speak to you."

"How did you get through?"

"I explained who I was. You should have been more forthcoming with me, Miss Ross. You should have told me you were looking into this business of methamphetamine in Einstein's brain. This came as an absolute shock."

So Peter *had* stalled him. "All right, I should have. Now what?"

"I expect more of the media," he said to the last person on earth who would expect more of the media. "You have conducted an interview under false pretenses. Do you consider this ethical?"

I felt like screaming, You know what you can do with your ethics? You know what this piece has cost me? I felt scream-down-the-hallways crazy. I picked up a cassette of Billy Neill and hurled it against the wall. The plastic casing broke apart. Tape unspooled on the floor. The Mylar gleamed.

"Hello? Hello?" came the thin voice at the other end of the line.

"You're right, I'm wrong, O.K.? Mea culpa. What else do you want me to say?"

"I could have spared you a good deal of embarrassment."

"I don't have the time—"

"There is something I have to explain," he said, and cleared his throat.

■

"You did it," Harry kept saying, "you did it," kissing my hair, nuzzling into the tender zone in my neck. We were in a cab on the way to my place. I was not in a sexy mood, and pulled away.

"You know," I said, "about those extra glial cells Einstein is supposed to have had? I've got them, too. I keep seeing Gottehrer."

He petted my hair.

There was no horizon at all. I was out there in space.

"You think there's a sound equivalent?" I went on. "Voice patterns. A voice pops up in your memory. You hear the truth and it makes you free. I wonder if I'm developing this kind of talent in my old age."

"You have many talents." He got back to my hair.

"Look, I've got Janousek's voice knocking around in my skull," I said, "and the more I think about it, the more I think Gottehrer got him all wrong. I can hear Janousek telling him, 'Ja, sure, I killed Einstein.' That's Janousek jeering, Harry."

He waited, as if to say, That's all? and then breezed, "Pure sulfuric Mitteleuropa. I know. We're short one murderer."

He didn't know.

"Janousek wasn't the type to walk up to Einstein lying there in a hospital bed and pump him full of speed," I tripped ahead. "Simply couldn't. He was the long-distance-killer type."

"Some kill you with a six-gun, some with an equation."

"Exactly."

"Doesn't scan."

"Get serious, Harry."

"People have been telling me that all my life. That leaves Gottehrer, right? He had motive and opportunity, he had spleen, malice, a hair-trigger temper. Christ, he came within one cop of killing you."

"It doesn't compute, Harry," I said too sharply. "He didn't set out to kill me. That was spontaneous freak-out."

He gazed into my eyes, as if into a muddy fountain to see how many coins were lying there. "What's the matter?"

"I'm postpartum and unemployed. So where are we?" I wanted to know.

"Pardon me?" said the cab driver, who was Turkish.

"Didn't mean you," I said. In fact, we had been gliding down Fifth Avenue—past the Japanese and Italian boutiques with their one-man security stations out front, little gold-painted huts each just big enough for a single guard; past the Public Library, where sleeping men were curled between the paws of the lions; past bus shelters proclaiming the inevitable WE BLOW THE COMPETITION OUT OF THE WATER (the ubiquitous mushroom cloud) and GIVE TILL IT HURTS (a sulky model, manacle on her wrist, for the United Way); through the interzone of sub-Forty-second Street shops specializing in combinations of sex and electronic equipment; past low-rent office buildings where private cops stood watch in their own guard huts, Uzis cradled, just in case the youth gangs tried smashing in to convert the unused office space to squats.

In the low Twenties, traffic slowed and clogged. At Nineteenth Street, we waited through two red lights and two greens before I figured it out: the Halloween parade.

Living outside calendar time, I'd forgotten the date, and realized with a start that by crashing the Einstein show McShane had slipped it in before the November sweeps, thereby limiting his risk. Our driver joined the cacophony of horns, to no effect. A barricade was up at Fourteenth Street, an imperious cop was diverting traffic right and left.

I paid, Harry hoisted my backpack of cassettes and miscellany over his shoulder, and we moved down Fifth Avenue on foot. The uncanny fog was gone, but the air still stung my face. The sidewalk was thickening with revelers. A knot of skinheads shoved past us, Chinese, black, white —equal-opportunity thugs. I hugged my purse—Harry's gift.

At the intersection of Tenth Street, the horde was turning slowly down Fifth toward the eerily white arch in Washington Square. A black man in fluorescent whiteface, wearing a Keystone Kops uniform, stood in the middle of the street, waving them on. At the corner, a woman in a long dress carried a picket sign that was absolutely blank; closer up, long face and thick wrists marked her as a man. We turned down Tenth, against the parade's grain. Fun wasn't the fun it had been before AIDS, but the crowd was doing its best. Electronic synthesizer whistles sounded musical fragments that had been generated by computer chips —trills, trumpet blasts, fake fugues, faintly atonal riffs. There were rubber death's-head masks; Nixon and Reagan masks, for auld lang syne; King Kong, Darth Vader, Madonna costumes. Flashlights pointing up into the nostrils turned high-school kids and accountants into ghouls. A man holding the skull of some sort of animal in front of his face and a black cape over his eyes with his free hand came roaring up to me, and I jumped.

Slowly toward us, over the heads of the horde, came the traditional Day-Glo orange dragon, thirty sinuous feet long, winding to right and left, elevated by pairs of sticks. The men holding the sticks had drooping mustaches and dead looks. The dragon's huge and dignified papier-mâché head nuzzled onto the long balcony that stretched across several apartment buildings on the south side of the street. Residents on the balcony hacked away at the dragon with Styrofoam swords. From the east end of the balcony, an Elizabeth Taylor lookalike with a camcorder and strong lights was shooting the dragon joust; at the west end, a flat twenty-foot screen projected the ritual for the Sixth Avenue side of the parade.

"So he goes, what are you trying to do, kill me?" said a young man with a high-pitched voice.

"*Kill* you?" said his friend with a giggle. "I would have thought he'd be happy to blow you."

Four musclemen wearing breechcloths carried a sedan chair decorated in what looked at first like gold leaf but turned out to be peeling contact paper. A sign on the side read AMERICA = ANTICLIMAX. In the chair there reclined, according to her silver sash, Miss Trans-America, with balloon breasts and a fixed grin, clutching to her bosom the replica of a syringe, six feet long. A pennant flew from the stretcher bearing the words BORN TO DIE. A black man with a beard the shape of an inverted beehive walked behind the stretcher, flagellating himself with what looked like a Mylar cat-o'-nine-tails, emitting a stagy groan every other step.

A woman was yelling, "Hey! Stop!" Three teenagers in flight brushed past me. Nobody stopped them. "What happened?" Harry said to the woman. "I don't carry anything in my bag," she said, "but it's the principle, you know? Great Margo Ross mask, by the way." She was a skinny thing wearing a Billy Null T-shirt under a leather bomber jacket.

"You're not kidding," I said.

■

The man who lives in the crate outside my building was possibly at the parade. In any event, he wasn't to be seen.

Just inside my door, Harry helped me off with my coat. I kicked off my shoes and sought advice, or solace, from the Haitian sheet-metal man on my wall. With spikes cut in his mouth as teeth, the sculpture shrieked like a *Guernica* horse. His eyes were gashes, mocking me. He belonged on Tenth Street.

"Not now, Harry," I said.

He let go of my zipper.

I turned and faced him. "Trite as it sounds, I don't feel so terrific."

"You're entitled," he said with a gentleman's shrug.

"What I need this second is not to go to bed with you. Pour yourself some Scotch, O.K.? And give me a minute."

The answering machine was flashing. Maybe the widow Janousek had taken a break from her grief to call back. I didn't have the stamina for her, I felt too raw and muddled. In fact, I didn't want to be interrupted at all, so I turned the machine volume down to zero, then went into the bathroom, bathed my eyes, swallowed a prophylactic Zantac. When I came out, Harry was sitting in the far corner of the couch, watching me with calf eyes and a smile. There was an empty cobalt-blue shot glass in his hand. I poured him another Scotch and sat at the opposite end of the couch. He downed the second, daintily set the glass down on the coffee table, slid in my direction, and reached toward my hand, which happened to be in my lap. I eked out a smile in a minor key.

"You did it, kiddo," Harry said, "you really did it." He patted the seat cushion next to him, affectionately, as if it were a loyal dog. "To think that unified field theory is going to be a household phrase."

"Power of television," I said. "Just ask Sir Colin McShane."

"This may sound pious," he said, "but I had confidence in you from the moment we had that lunch. I always did, you know, even back in the old days."

"*We* did it, Harry," I said.

"Come," he said. He started lifting away from the sofa while tugging at my hand, wanting to take me along, but my hand did not want to be moved.

"I'm wiped."

He made a sad little-boy face, as if I'd refused to take him to the circus. I kept my smile, but my face felt wrong, as if I'd held a pose for a photo too long.

Harry offered his room-filling grin. "It's a well-known fact that fucking's the best way to oblivion."

"Oh, I'm well fucked, Harry. You fucked my brains out."

He gave me his slow nod. His face was radiant, brash as a conquistador's. "I'll take that as a compliment."

"You know what I mean, Harry." I got up.

"What do you mean, I know what you mean?"

The room was suddenly too quiet. I poured myself a glass of water. The refrigerator motor kicked on. I stood in the kitchen doorway, arms folded, contemplating Harry.

The phone rang once, twice. I let the machine take the call. Click, click—a hang-up. Machines all around, going about their business. I sipped my water. I folded my arms again. Harry plumped the pillow next to him, but I didn't move. His smile was full of anticipation. He had a small boy's readiness to be surprised by an act of love.

I said, "Mystery man."

"Yes, it's in my FBI file." His grin, flaring up, could have lit a scene. He swung his right foot up, let it alight on my coffee table before he thought better of his manners and settled the foot down on his left knee. The top of his sock was ragged. He pulled out a thread, balled it together, and tucked it into his breast pocket. "My driver's license says Harry Kramer, 6'2", 174, hard to know, harder to please."

He studied my eyes with the routine curiosity of an entomologist—which made me the insect. He ran the nail side of his pinkie over his right eyebrow. After a long time, he blinked. Gears meshed in his mind. "You're not exactly transparent yourself, you know." I let the volley go by and kept up my scrutiny. "Some of my best ex-friends have been known to say that I'm hard to know," he resumed. "But if I did jabber along nonstop, 'talking about my feelings,' as the saying goes, that wouldn't make me easy to know, would it?"

"Might help."

"Come on. Everyone gabbles about feelings. 'How do you feel about the laws of arithmetic?' 'I have negative feelings about the end of the world.' We're all living inside some ridiculous opera. Nobody thinks, everybody feels. If you're not careful, the next time you go down to the subway, the guy in the token booth is going to break into song telling you how he feels about his alcoholic parents, and by the way, since you didn't ask, here's the lowdown on his terrible childhood."

I wrapped my arms around my chest, my hands holding on to my upper arms, forming a carapace. "Cute and true," I said, "very cute, very true, and you know, Harry, very remote and beside the point, which is, I'm talking about you."

"Did I miss the part where you explained to me why I should 'want to be known'?" A flash of grin, like an after-image of lightning, went by.

Anxiety spread from my collarbone through my chest. I drained my glass of water. No sooner had I finished than my mouth was sandpaper again.

"No, I didn't think so." He ran his hand from his fore-head back over his skull. "All right. There's no mystery. Here's the story: Knowledge is power."

"Knowledge is power," I echoed, like a backup singer. I badly wanted to go to the refrigerator, bring out another bottle of water. I badly wanted to run out the door. I resisted all desires and tightened my folded arms as waves of stage fright passed through me. "As in: Whoever has the unified field theory gets the universal bomb."

"Exactly. Or: Whoever uncovers the scandal brings down the government. This is the reason why you became a famous journalist, right? To set off fact bombs."

"Correction. That's why I *was* a famous journalist."

"Stop it. The minute the word's out that you're on the market, your answering machine's going to light up with offers you can't refuse. Probably's lit up already just on the strength of 'The Murder of Albert Einstein.'"

"You were saying that knowledge is power," I said.

"Absolutely"—with a small knowing nod. "Can you doubt it? A journalist breaks down doors. That's a violent act. No getting around it. That's why doors are closed in the first place. The question is which doors, and in whose interest." He spread his smile the way a cardplayer spreads a winning hand.

"Let me ask you a question," I said. "If knowledge is power, what does that make gullibility?"

"Interesting question. Depends, I suppose."

"I think it's the prerequisite of power, Harry. The flip side of the other guy's power."

"Oh?"—with his right eyebrow cocked. "This is getting a bit abstract, don't you think?"

"All right, I'll make it concrete. Somebody once taught me the key question is always *Cui bono?*"

Harry described curlicues in the air with his open right hand, a Hollywood *yes, effendi* gesture.

"By those lights," he said, "McShane would have to be the killer. Wait till you see his ratings points."

"But, meanwhile, he's lost his friend Janousek."

"Don't sound like Barbara Walters," Harry snapped, "it doesn't become you. The McShanes of the world don't have friends. They collect 'associates.' Why are you looking at me that way? I'm not telling you anything you don't know."

"I'm listening, that's all."

He measured out words. "You know perfectly well that every move these guys make, every assignation, every dinner party, every name dropped and story spiked is a tactic, tic-tac-dough, you know, a move in the great game of merger and acquisition."

Despite myself, I felt a trace of the old awe, a shadow of

what I'd felt when Harry had walked into the office of
Eight Million Stories eight million years ago—awed by his
full crisp sentences, his air of speaking on the record for
some absolute surveillance which was the closest anyone
could possibly come to posterity.

"Can you doubt it?" he rolled on. "You know perfectly
well that people aren't stupid, they're misled. If they saw
clearly, they'd burn down the penthouses. So while his
'friends' in the ruling class are looting the world, bulldozing
the trees and shoving dark-skinned people into the gold
mines, the Colin McShanes are blowing smoke in the eyes
of people on four continents."

In my experience, hardly anyone wanted to burn down
the penthouses. Everyone wanted to move into them before
somebody else did. But, never mind, I wasn't in an arguing
mood.

"You must be right," I said. "If you ask me, they deserve
to die."

"What?"

"A thought experiment. You heard me."

His eyes were like steel bearings. "What are you talking
about?"

"Logic. You've convinced me. Exterminate all the
brutes!"

The refrigerator motor sighed off. The silence seemed to
whimper. Or it was my heart that was whimpering, begging for peace, solace, the end of days. My chest was tight
and burning, as if my blood had been drained and replaced
by acid, a scourge from within. I wanted to be persuaded, I
wanted to walk through the wall into an uninhabited universe.

I waited while none of this happened.

"Are you all right?" Harry wanted to know.

"Just fabulous."

"Margo, look, no one is going to forget what you did tonight. A landmark in the history of television."

I could hear the ping of the quotation marks. "Right. Reach out and diddle the millions. Look, Harry, what I did tonight was sheer bluff and insinuation with high production values touched up with a whiff of suspense to fill the void before bedtime. And you know it. Right?"

"I think"—delicately—"that the show is over and you're post-coital."

"A man's problem. Don't project."

His tongue came out to moisten his lips.

"I don't care how much Gottehrer feared the unified field theory," I said, "or how scary and nuts he was, I can't convince myself that he killed his beloved Einstein."

Harry measured out his words. "Don't overestimate reason the way Gottehrer did. Gottehrer wasn't a calculator. He was tight-wired and he snapped. We saw him do that. Twice. In spades. You, of all people—"

"Both times spontaneously."

"Look, Margo, we've been through this. He had opportunity—"

"I remember."

"—And I'll bet he didn't have to go any farther than his medicine cabinet for means. When he left for the hospital, he might not even have known he was going to kill anybody. Probably didn't, as the lawyers say, 'form the intention.' He might simply have put some speed in his pocket in case he needed to keep himself awake. And then he sat by

Einstein's bedside, he saw Einstein's last notes, he heard Einstein say how close he was to the theory to end all theories, he thought about the universe wired together, and the history of atomic energy flashed for the hundredth time through his mind, and suddenly there was motive, opportunity, everything at the flash point, and he said to Einstein, Let me give you a drink of water . . ."

"Nobody ever said you couldn't lay out a plot, Harry." Look at *Fix*: even reviewers who hated the book had cooed over the "tight," "elegant," "effortless intricacy" of the plotting, the way character *A* grazed character *B*, who goosed *C*, who in turn nudged *A*, who bumped into *D*, until *A* and *B* and *C* and *D* were bound together in a master web that (at first) none of them comprehended, until it turned out that *B* was actually calling the shots and *A* was on his payroll—this being a provisional revelation, it turning out, still later, that *B* only *thought* he was calling the shots, while actually *E*, the marginal mastermind hitherto noted only in passing, had contrived to set *B* in motion in the first place. Harry wrote as if each character were genuinely and irreducibly an extension, a shadow, a returning repressed of every other, so that, as you watched each plot line weave gorgeously around and into the next, you felt a tiny quiver of pleasure and said to yourself, *Of course!*

"You're cold," Harry said. He saw that my hands were clutching at my shoulders, my arms folded under my breasts, my shoulder blades hunched over.

"Do you need a sweater?"

"My cape, please, thank you."

He went to the closet, brought my cape, arranged it around my shoulders. I accepted this offering, inert. He exerted a slight pressure, trying to draw me toward the couch. "No," I shook him off, "I want to stand." He went back to the couch and peered at me as if I were a sick butterfly under quarantine for observation.

"You're sure you're all right?"

"I'm terrific. I just want a conclusion."

"You want a conclusion."

"I had a shrink once. Whenever he was at a loss for words, he repeated mine."

"Everyone's entitled to temporize."

I heard that as a refrain—*Everyone's entitled to temporize,* by, say, Cole Porter.

The phone trilled again, the answering machine clicked, whirred, and somebody's words started onto the tape.

"It goes like this, Harry," I said. "Once we're convinced that Gottehrer killed Einstein, we can think up a way he did it, right? A perfectly plausible chain of events."

"Plausible's not nothing," Harry said. "But you know what? I'd have preferred Janousek as a murderer. As it is, all we end up with is a dead lunatic. Not very satisfying. Maybe we should take another look at Janousek."

I watched him spin his filigree of words. I couldn't get any of my own out of my throat.

"Although, you know, let's face it, there is a sort of aesthetic—this is interesting—a kind of comedy of good ends and bad means in this scenario; namely, that the man who killed Janousek and came within a hair of killing Margo Ross killed Einstein for the good of the world. The world hangs by a thread."

Each of us waited for the other, as if for rescue from a collision that we could see coming a long way off.

"You don't like it." He shrugged. "Square one."

"No fault of yours, Harry," I said. "You did a spectacular job."

"Thank you."

"There's only one problem," I said.

"What's that?"

Fasten seat belt. Open mouth. "Celloidin."

Now, I am a collector of moments. Moments of truth if
possible, but moments in any case. I've stayed up all night
staring at film, looking for one glimpse into the actual
depths, one tear in the painted curtain that conceals the all-
too-real real world. I've won awards for moments. It
may not be too much to say that I live for them, just as the
local eyewitness news team lives for the tear leaking out
of the eye of the bereaved. I know the objections. I know
all about the pictorial fallacy. I know all the truth that
action doesn't reveal. I don't care—moments are what I
collect.

I have collected this moment. I will carry it always.

"Pardon?"

I repeated: "Celloidin."

He struggled to keep his face closed but couldn't suppress the tentative smile of a little boy about to be sent to
his room. The result was: "I give up."

"A sort of glue," I explained, "the stuff that you use to
keep an organ from falling apart. A liver, a kidney, whatever."

"Never heard of it."

"Or a chunk of brain."

He smiled a smile of supreme ingratiation.

"It's elementary equipment for neuroscientific research,
Harry. I'm surprised that you didn't know about celloidin."

"Well"—with a slow, deliberate spread of his empty hands—"you see, there are limits to my expertise."

"Evidently."

There was yearning in his hands. I could picture myself sitting in his lap, his hands around my waist—some kind of sweet custody that would cancel the world in a flash and start time again, and all the long mistakes and detours would turn out to be rehearsals, throat-clearings, nothing more.

But the time was a hard-and-fast 10:31 as registered by the answering machine. I walked over to the coffee table and poured myself a Scotch before he had a chance to pour it for me. I walked back to the counter and placed the glass there, next to the answering machine.

If I were Michelle, shooting this scene, I would start with an achingly slow pan from my face, down along the taut ropes described by the muscles of my neck, across the coffee table, and over to the quizzical and expectant Harry, craning upward, inspecting me. He folds his arms. The camera pans along the sofa while we wait for someone to break the silence.

But I had no camera, I was alone with my collaborator and lover Harry Kramer.

"Brains ooze," I said. "If you want to study brain cells, you don't use the original tissue just as it comes out of the skull. Are you with me?"

He was immobile. "Right alongside you."

"Say you want to see how many glial cells, as opposed to neurons, there are in one spot or another. You use a chunk that's been sealed in celloidin. You slice it. You stain the slices and you look at them under the microscope and you count cells."

He leaned back on a sofa pillow and looked up at me with a kind of wonder.

"Go back to the Einstein autopsy," I went on. My mouth was parchment. "The pathologist knew exactly what he was doing. He wanted to prepare the brain for future study. So, first, he fixed the brain in formaldehyde. Then he sectioned it up, cut up chunks from various regions, numbered them for identification, and sealed the chunks in celloidin. Anticipating that whenever a neuroscientist got around to examining a chunk, he could cut off a nicely preserved slice, stain it, and put it under the microscope. Are you with me?"

"Very impressed," he said gravely. "Have you been going to physiology school in your off-moments? No. I get it. You've talked to Minasian."

"Taub," I said. "Taub called."

"You were saying," he said after a silence.

"Celloidin keeps organs firm."

"I still don't see—"

"If you're going to test the brain for the presence of chemicals, Harry, you don't want it firm. You want to grind it up in a blender, reduce it to pulp. Then you take that pulp and test it for chemicals."

"I explained that to you, Margo. High-pressure liquid chromatography. The printout—"

"Taub wasn't checking Einstein's brain for chemicals, Harry. He was checking it for anatomical structure. Once an organ has been sealed in celloidin, it's useless for chemical tests. Therefore, useless for detecting speed."

He stared at me, away from me, through me. He picked up the blue shot glass and twirled it. He ran his finger around the inside. He held up his finger, inspected it. With the glass cupped in his hand, he heaved himself up from the sofa and, like a stoop-shouldered old man whose only child has just died, hauled himself over to the curtained window. "Jesus Christ" was all he said.

"Peter couldn't have found speed in Einstein's brain," I said. "Even if it was there."

He turned around. A hurricane of expressions blew through his face so fast I could not tell what they meant. His face was the debris of all those expressions. "Are you saying he made this up? The bastard made it all up?" His words sprayed around the room. "Why would he do that?"

"You're supposed to say, 'Are you sure?'"

"I value you too much, Margo, to ask you a question that answers itself." He sounded a little indignant, a lot depressed. "I know you wouldn't go to this trouble if you weren't sure. But why would the son of a bitch lie to me? I don't—"

"Tell me what else to think, Harry. I'm willing to think something else but you have to help."

He peered at me. But the doubt he was looking for, I had stifled.

"Talk to me," I said without hope.

With short, slow steps he started to pace. He stopped once, glanced at me, hesitated, paced. At the wall near the door, he turned. His lips were compressed between his teeth. My shot glass was in his hand as his hand became a fist which he raised to fling the glass somewhere, anywhere.

His fist came down. His lips opened. Then he took three quick steps and jammed the glass down on the counter next to the answering machine. He veered back toward the coffee table, heading for the phone.

"What are you—"

"I'm going to get hold of that bastard Peter—"

"Harry—"

"Don't Harry me. No—as a matter of fact, I'm going to find him—" He whirled and made for the front door. I got there first. My back and my hands and my will stood between him and the door.

"Get away, Margo, *I want out*"—the words climbing a scale of intensity. He planted one palm against the door inches from my head, then the other palm on the other side of my head. I didn't move. He might as well have been throwing knives with precision aim, with me the assistant-stooge. Only, I wasn't smiling. His breath came heavily. "Let me fucking out of here."

"Harry," I said, "what about Janousek?"

"What *about* him? You think Peter—"

"You did it, Harry. You killed him."

An ember of smile flared up on his lips. Then a laugh burst out. "Very good, I needed a laugh. Happy Halloween." He aimed a kiss at my mouth, but I turned my head to the side and he missed my lips.

"Don't jerk me around, Harry. I'm dizzy."

"Who's jerking whom?"

My knight of manners, Harry. My apostle of reasons.

"Cut the bullshit," I said.

He pushed himself up and backed off—one step, two. He cocked his head, appraised me, approached again. The half smile died on his lips. He stood inches away, glaring. Jolts of dread shot through me, and something thicker, more complicated: a kind of shame. The dread and the shame pooled together and in a sort of fusion reaction produced fury. There was a big bang of fury going off slow-mo in my mind against all the betrayals.

"I have the sickening feeling," he said, "that you're serious."

"So you finally got to strike a blow at the killer class. Payback. History is crime, right? Congratulations. You think I don't get it?"

"You're flipping out, Margo." He moved his mouth, but the embers didn't want to revive. "I'm going to find Peter. I'll get to the bottom —"

"This is the bottom, Harry. We've hit it. Boom. Crash."

Something cruel burned in his eyes, the cruelty of a small boy on a boring day. Or some kind of spent passion, an afterburn that wanted to scourge everything in a wrong world.

"So, let's see," he said with a leer. "How am I supposed to have bumped off Janousek? With my little bow and arrow?"

"The story's going, Harry. Gone. Say goodbye."

He took a step back and stood with his hands on his hips and his head cocked, and switched on his little-boy grin. My palms were flat behind me against the door. The feel of thick paint was a comfort.

"You knew that he had a heart condition," I said. "No secret about that. Maybe you toyed with the idea of scaring him to death, but that wouldn't have been easy. What were you going to do, stalk him when he went for a walk with his wife down Riverside Drive? I imagine that you couldn't figure out how to off this particular pig without sacrificing yourself, which wouldn't have been a fair trade. So you brooded. You wrote your unpublishable manuscripts and

unproduceable screenplays. You watched Janousek accu-
mulate honors and Presidents. You seethed. Détente came
and went, Janousek stayed. Nixon went, Reagan went, the
Cold War went, and the Big Bomber stayed, with his hot
line to the Oval Office. Am I getting warm?"

His smile came back—the smile of a man who lacked, in
the end, a sense of humor. "You're right about one thing,"
he said. "I'm patient. Don't stop now."

"I think the thought of Janousek on the loose ate at you,
just as the thought of Jan Masaryk's murderers ate at
Janousek—even after they fell from power. I think you
prided yourself on remembering when everyone else forgot. For you, there was one terrible truth that made your
life make sense: Janousek was a star among war criminals,
he had past, present, and future blood on his hands, and no
one was ever going to make him pay. All the war criminals
walking around unfazed; no one was ever going to make
any of them pay. And then I imagine you ran into Peter
Minasian one day. You drank some beer, reminisced,
agreed that the bad old days were better than the good new
days, you fumbled for something else to talk about, and
what do you know, you stumbled onto a final solution to
the Janousek problem. Make an example for all the white-
collar mass murderers. Peter told you about Taub's brain
research. Click! On with the light bulbs. You needed access. Access, props, and camouflage. Peter gave you props,
Einstein was camouflage, I was access. How'm I doing?"

"You missed your calling, Scheherazade. You should be
writing mid-range thrillers."

"Plot summary, that's all. You're the detail man, right?
There are details I don't understand. For example, Peter
owed you. I don't know why, exactly."

"What a shame."

"But I can guess: he was doing heavy drugs, which meant he needed money and he was vulnerable. All he had to do, for openers, was pass you a printout, right? from a brain that was swimming in methamphetamine—not hard to find in the midst of the drug wars. He didn't even have to know the reason, come to think of it. Then he'd have to avoid the press—not hard either, since Taub had his policies and his vanities. Elements clicked into place. The next thing, you traced Parenti, probably from hospital records, one thing you didn't lie about, and she gave you a possible suspect, Gottehrer. You figured that sooner or later Janousek would be brought into the investigation. You couldn't know for sure how you'd kill him, but you thought that once you got me involved, you could get in to see him, ingratiate yourself, and as for the exact means, the exact opportunity, well, that would take care of itself, right?"

His eyebrow was up. I seemed to amuse him.

"And then there was me. I was easy. I could be had."

Harry moistened his lips. "You know I think more of you than that."

"I could be had"—upping the volume—"but, if there was any doubt that you could talk me into the story, there was always fear. I had to be scared. First, you pretended you were being followed. You thought that would suck me in, right? And then there was the third thing you needed from Peter. He had to dress up in a blue coat and try to steal my purse. Or pretend to try. Same difference."

"And I suppose it came to me in a dream that Gottehrer wore a blue coat."

"Oh yes, this one stopped me, but there's an answer so obvious I could fall over it. Two answers: blind luck and naïveté. Both of them mine. *I* was the one who brought up the question of the color of the guy's coat. Rosenthal said blue, and you hit the jackpot. I convinced myself. Had Rosenthal said khaki, I would have had to talk myself into assuming that Gottehrer had another coat."

"You're outdoing yourself. You've taken your new genre to heart." He rubbed his cheek as if trying to erase a stain. "You're forgetting the threat on the phone."

"Right, how could I forget the famous 'Forget the Einstein story'? Peter's fourth contribution. I couldn't say no after a death threat, now, could I?"

He opened his mouth, then thought better of it.

"Don't bother faking it, Harry, don't even bother to try. So. Everything broke your way. I was a good little girl with my wide eyes, taking notes. Rosenthal played his part and steered me to Janousek. You wheedled and coaxed and jiggled him until he brought up Gottehrer, right? Oh, that must have felt good. How'm I doing?"

Harry's eyes played over my face like a spotlight on opening night. "You'll do all right at screenplays. Not a bad plot structure, but still flawed. Was I running Rosenthal, too? Tell me, how much did it cost me to bribe him?"

"Cut it out, Harry. If Rosenthal hadn't played, you would have pointed me at Gottehrer some other way. Still, it must have amazed you how things fell your way. When Gottehrer turned out to be a nut about unified field theory, you couldn't believe your luck, right? When he showed up at my office, you planted the idea that Einstein was murdered. You pointed him at Janousek, riled him up and set him loose. I watched you do it—in fact, I fronted for you—but I didn't get the point. Very clever—you got yourself a terrific suspect and you even fed him a motive for killing

Einstein: to stop the universal bomb. What I can't figure out is whether you suspected from the beginning that he was going to prove quite so perfect, or did you improvise as you went along? Close your mouth. I think you improvised. The same way you made up the story about Einstein's missing notes. You played me like a violin. Luck and gullibility, hell of a combination."

"I hope you're enjoying yourself."

"You'd better believe I'm enjoying myself. Tell me, did you have any more murders in mind for him before Mr. Gottehrer dropped out of the running in such an untimely and photogenic fashion?"

"Oh, my, the temperature's rising. Before you burst into flame would you remind me how I killed Janousek? I forget. By the way, if I'm so smart, why didn't I kill him with speed? Digoxin didn't do much for the serial-killer theory, did it?"

"You tell me. Maybe you thought, why take any chances at all if the old guy keeps a supply of poison in his medicine chest? Maybe no one would suspect murder at all, in which case at least he's dead, right? When we went to see Janousek, you paid a visit to the bathroom. You looked in the medicine chest and, lo and behold, elixir of death! A vial of digoxin. All you had to do was go back there on your own. It wasn't hard to find out what a lethal dose would be — your very good friend and employee Peter's a chemist, right? Or you looked it up at the library. What I want to know is: did you force the stuff down his throat, or pass it to him in the sherry?"

The metallic man on my wall was full of mockery and disgust.

Harry's face was frozen in its show of bemusement, but

something behind the crust was breaking down. His voice was frayed. "Crude, but passable. I'm waiting for the part where you reveal how I managed to kill the retired prince of darkness while lying on your couch"—he pointed—"watching Margo Ross presenting Billy Neill and designer drugs on *In Depth*. Or did I send a confederate to slip digoxin to Janousek that afternoon in time-release capsules? Or did I fax it to him? Get serious."

"I'm getting so serious, mister, your head's going to spin. You left my office and you came up here to this apartment, *my* apartment, with *my* key—"

"This is not news."

"No, the news is that you set my VCR to record *In Depth* at ten and you took off again. You went up to Riverside Drive and you waited around till you saw Gottehrer leave. Then you went to a pay phone and you called the old war criminal, told him you had some follow-up questions about Einstein, or Gottehrer, or Janousek's enormous contributions to world civilization, it doesn't matter what. And he told you to come ahead. Am I close?"

Harry said nothing, but his grin said he found me entertaining, or frightening, or both.

"I think I'm very damned close. I think you waited around outside Janousek's building till the doorman turned his back to watch his TV program, or went to pee or run the service elevator, whatever. Piece of cake—I've been getting past doormen for years, you can't get a story or commit a murder without it. Then you went upstairs and you sat Janousek down and asked your reverent questions, put him at his ease. And then, before he knew what was happening, you were telling him what kind of a bastard he was and you were a one-man Nuremberg court and there was no statute of limitations for crimes against humanity. You tried him, convicted him, watched him plead, and administered the sentence, right? Fed him the digoxin and sauntered out. Easy in, easy out. You got back here at ten-fifteen, ten-thirty—whatever—flicked on the switch and watched the rest of *In Depth*. As soon as it was over, you wound the tape back to the beginning and watched the part you hadn't already seen. Then you switched over to *Cagney and Lacey*. When I walked in, it was 'Hi, dear, did you have a nice day at the office?' "

"That wouldn't have been so clever of me, Margo." His voice dragged by a fraction of an inch per second. "What if the cops checked to see if Janousek had any other visitors?"

"Not so clever of you, you're damn right. This was your little gamble. If there was no autopsy—and there was no reason why there would have to be—Janousek's death would be passed off as a heart attack, and that was that. Or, in the unlikely event that the cops thought that Janousek might in fact have been murdered, Gottehrer would be the obvious suspect, right? Nobody had any reason to think of you, so nobody saw you."

Harry's head was tilted in an attitude of appraisal, as if he were thinking of buying a painting, but his tone was mocking. "For someone who's supposed to be such a careful plotter, I certainly was taking a lot of chances."

"But that's who you are, Harry. Hell-bent on seeing what you could get away with. The way you risked telling me Taub was going to find out about the speed on Friday, right, so we'd have to crash the piece. You calculated that by the time Friday rolled around, I'd have so much on my mind I wouldn't pay much attention to one little smelly rat, namely that Taub evidently hadn't gotten Peter to come clean about the hypothetical speed. And you were right. Then you gambled that I wouldn't insist on interviewing Peter, give him a chance to blurt out a contradiction. You knew what kind of a sucker had jumped into bed with you. Thursday morning you even let *me* talk *you* into the notion that Janousek had been murdered, knowing that I'd go after Gottehrer and light his fuse."

He nodded appreciatively. The actor inside the character he was playing peered out from beneath his act and looked for applause.

"Nobody ever said you weren't committed, Harry. You hated Janousek enough. The fifty-megaton man. I don't blame you for hating him." I didn't feel like thinking about what kind of accessory that made me.

"If you're right, there's a tape in your collection"—he waved toward the VCR—"with last week's *In Depth* on it."

"I never said you were stupid, Harry. You would have erased the tape."

He thought that over. "Then there'd be a blank tape, wouldn't there? Taken out of its box but blank." He waved toward the living room as if it were his. "Go ahead and look."

I couldn't move.

"Come on, Margo!" he said abruptly. "Let's go!" He clapped his hands, step right up! then charged into the living room toward the VCR and the shelf of videotapes.

I leaned against the door and heard myself breathing hard.

When he saw I wasn't coming along, he came back toward me. My voice, slow and deepened, didn't belong to me. "If you were clever enough to tape the show, Harry, you were clever enough to smuggle it out of here, drop it in a trash can in the course of the day, right? As I remember, you were wearing your sport jacket. Nice big inside pockets."

He had planted his feet in front of me. "Not that big." He shrugged. He ran his hand over his head, smoothing his hair, and recovered his cockeyed grin. Preening again, I thought—remaking himself, as he had remade himself after *Fix*, after the sixties, as he had all through his life lifted one Chinese box after another out of himself and taken a bow for his performance, expecting to be loved because he was, after all, the lovable darling sent to redeem the world, wasn't he?

"To paraphrase Gottehrer paraphrasing Picasso," he said, "plot is the lie by which the truth is known." He was standing not more than a foot in front of me.

I said, "I'm calling the cops, Harry," but I didn't move.

"Let me ask you a question. Is the world worse off without Janousek?"

I said nothing.

He must have thought he had me. "Is his widow worse off? Is anyone suffering? Life expectancy shortened? What?"

"Who appointed you divine executioner in charge of ethics?" I said.

"Go ahead, *call* the cops. You think I don't know which side you're on? You think I don't know why McShane trusts you, when push comes to shove?" His words gave him ideas. He jerked back his arm and tensed, as if to shove me out of his way. I flinched. Then we both froze.

He melted first, relaxed his fist, lowered his arm. "Poor

little rich girl, cook up your sound bites, collect your awards, pile up your moral dilemmas, and when you get worn out, you buy your way to St. Croix."

"I've quit my job," I said quietly, "in case you've forgotten."

"You've quit your job! Isn't that something! Choirs of angels will now be heard from. How much do you have squirreled away, five mil, ten?"

"Stop."

He jabbed at me with a didactic finger. "Too bad for the inconvenient Third World, later for gooks and spics and all those dirty dark-skinned peasants starving to death while you're living high. 'I'll get back to you.' It's all *so terrible,* sigh. Now somebody comes along and takes direct action, and oh! my! you're crawling with scruples. I'll tell you something, Margo. Gottehrer was right about the universal bomb. In principle, absolutely correct. It's just a matter of time. Some Janousek or other, give him years, decades, centuries, all the time in the world—which is what we're talking about—sooner or later he's going to figure out a way to light a match in one corner of the world and watch the fuse sputter all the way to the other end. Some Indian lunatics will hire him. Or Pakistan. Already there's a black market in old Russian H-bombs. You watch. The U-bomb is next. Gottehrer saw it, maybe he had the guts to let the truth drive him crazy, and everyone else is gutless crazy for going through the motions as if—"

"I'm right here, you don't have to yell."

He got louder. "The warning's out, Margo, thanks to tonight's show, which I"—he stabbed his chest with his index finger—"I'm responsible for, don't forget that when you're waving your holiness at me."

"Congratulations," I said. "I don't know whether Gottehrer had a point about the danger of unification theory or not, but has it occurred to you that the warning is now identified with a lunatic who committed hara-kiri in living color?"

"That's shortsighted, Margo. You watch. The idea's going to be discussed. Give it time. Janousek died to put the fear of God in all the smart bombers till kingdom come. I'll tell you something. Terror is all they respect. Before you get all sentimental about a person who would devise a bomb to deliver the force of fifty million tons of TNT . . . You can't reason with these people. Let them jump every time a car backfires. Otherwise, what, we lie down and wait for them to blow up the world?"

"You give two flying fucks about the end of the world. *You're* death, do you hear me? Playing God is death. *You* want to blow up the world. You're Janousek with a human face."

What I hated about him was: he had arguments.

"You believe this garbage, don't you," he said. "You do. They've got you, kiddo. You think the worst thing in the world is a lie. Churchill said, you know, that the truth was so precious she needed to be attended by a bodyguard of lies."

I slapped him hard, once, on the cheek, with the flat of my hand. But I was the one who felt shocked, as if I'd just stuck my finger in a live socket. Harry looked cool, he belonged to the age of heroes. Churchill, Einstein, Janousek, Kramer—the heroes had made a world that required heroes. Do what you have to do. Make a difference.

I suddenly understood why Harry hadn't published a

novel since *Fix. Fix* was, in the end, a diagram. The details were arrows: this way through the labyrinth. After *Fix*, his world had gone murky: he'd lost his fixed stars. Now he'd gotten them back. I was the fuel he burned.

He searched long and hard for some kind of forgiveness that I might have been tempted to give him if he had asked. But he didn't ask.

"I'm going to walk out of here," he said, "and you're going to step away from the door and make it easy for me."

I did. He walked.

I don't know how much time passed before I picked up the phone and punched up the emergency number Delaney had given me, which was patched through to the van parked in front of my house. "Got him," he said. "Perfect fidelity, you're a champ."

"You sure you got enough on tape?"

"I'm not a prosecutor, but I think, yeah."

I can't remember whether wearing the wireless transmitter had been Delaney's idea or mine—let's say that we'd agreed. While Harry and I had been slogging through the Halloween parade, Delaney had used passkeys to get into my apartment and, as a backup, bugged the phone. Two cops were waiting on the landing above my floor. I had made Delaney swear that no one would come unless I called out that I needed cops.

I didn't need cops. I needed a world which would not murder Albert Einstein where he slept.

Oh, Harry, my partner in crime, my original, my imperfect master, I have never ceased wanting to believe, and what broke in me was more than my heart.

There is no faith, and I must keep it.

"Go easy on him," I told Delaney. The grief and rage that filled my chest became a sentence I couldn't speak but couldn't shake either; namely, the question was always who, or what, you were going to betray.

ABOUT THE AUTHOR

ABOUT THE AUTHOR

T ODD GITLIN is professor of sociology at the University of California, Berkeley. He is author of the bestselling *The Sixties: Years of Hope, Days of Rage, The Whole World Is Watching,* and *Inside Prime Time,* as well as editor of *Watching Television.* His articles on politics and culture have appeared in *The New York Times, Harper's, The Nation, Mother Jones, The New Republic, Dissent, Tikkun,* and many other periodicals and newspapers.